INTENSE DEVICE

A Journey through Lust, Murder & the Fires of Hell

Simon Whitechapel

HEADPRESS critical vision

Critical Vision
an imprint of Headpress

A Critical Vision Book
First published in 1997
by Headpress

Headpress
40 Rossall Avenue
Radcliffe
Manchester
M26 1JD
Great Britain
Fax: +44 (0)161 796 1935

Front cover artwork: 'Happy Hunting Ground' © 1997 Dogger
Burning Headpress logo by Bill Babouris

British Library Cataloguing in Publication Data

Whitechapel, Simon
Intense Device : a journey through lust, murder & the fires of hell
1. English essays - 20th century
I. Title II. Kerekes, David
824.9'14

ISBN 0952328895

for Faustine

I would find grievous ways to have thee slain,
Intense Device, and superflux of pain.

"Anactoria", C.A. Swinburne

ACKNOWLEDGEMENTS

Big book, big evil. I'm not sure if this qualifies, but I've done my best. Unfortunately, not everyone who helped can be acknowledged here, because not everyone who helped knew what I was up to. I'd like to thank those who did: David Kerekes (no Dave, no book); Dave Slater; Dave Mitchell (for inspiration); Georgio Tskamorvili and Steve Philips (for contributions); Dean James (for help with "Ritual in Prague"); Pat Ayre; Rob Scott (to get his name into print); Cameron Milaš (for access to the Internet)... and others, not all of whom meant it. Thanks again: hope you enjoy the book.

Simon Whitechapel

CONTENTS

AFTERLIFE

A GUIDED TOUR OF THE FIRES OF HELL

"Hell", opined the late and, yes, great Bon Scott, "ain't a bad place to be". But that was, you know, just rock'n'roll bravado. If it exists, hell won't be just a bad place to be, it will be, by definition, the worst possible place to be. And it will last for ever.

But does it exist? Probably not, but who can be certain? Perhaps God is a sadistic lunatic and everyone goes to hell, in the end. That seems to me at least as likely as the possibility that heaven exists and everyone goes there in the end. However, heaven doesn't interest me very much: there seems little to choose between heaven and oblivion; between hell and oblivion, there seems everything to choose.

One of the reasons for this is, I suppose, that heaven is difficult to imagine. Christianity found it particularly difficult because heaven, after all, would be pleasurable, and Christianity has never liked pleasure, and has positively hated pleasure in its most intense form, that of sex. But even the Islamic heaven, which contains sex in the form of voluptuous young women with gazelle-like eyes and bodies made of sandalwood, doesn't seem so very attractive.[1] Can you imagine having sex for ever? Can you imagine having sex, with breaks for the most delicious foods and drinks, for ever? It's hard. Pleasures don't last for ever on earth: we get bored with them or they cease to be pleasurable. Presumably in heaven our minds and senses would change so that they could last for ever, but it's very difficult to imagine what this would be like.

Hell, on the other hand, is easy to imagine, because pain never gets boring and never ceases to be, well, painful. There are many forms of pleasure, available at many times, but many more forms of pain, potentially available at any time. The only way of escaping pain for good, it seems, is to die, but that is on the assumption that death is oblivion. If it isn't, and there is some form of consciousness after death, why can't pain carry on after death too? And if that consciousness lasts for ever, why can't pain last for ever too?

That question occurred to people long before Christianity, and was answered in the affirmative long before Christianity too. The ancient Greeks had an eternal afterlife, and it was a hell for some of those who were in it. In fact, no-one had much of a time in the Greek afterlife. During his journey home from the Trojan War as described in the **Odyssey**, the Greek hero Odysseus finds it necessary to consult the spirits of the dead. He lands on the coast of the underworld, sacrifices a sheep, and pours its blood into a trench. The spirits crowd to him to savour the blood's fragrance, and if so little can draw them so readily, what Odysseus subsequently learns from them about the afterlife can hardly seem surprising. The spirit of Achilles, for example, has this to say about the world he is now in:

> Speak not unfitting words about death, reknowned Odysseus.
> So I could be once more on the wholesome earth, I would rather
> Serve as a slave to a man who had neither fortune nor comforts
> Than be king of all the dead in the region of shadows.[2]

This region of shadows is Hades, the cold, sunless subterranean kingdom of the god Hades where, for most, there was no real pleasure, no real pain, for ever. This is a kind of hell, I suppose, but the Greeks also had a true hell, which was called Tartarus. Here the truly wicked were punished for their sins: Tantalus, for some crime or other involving food and drink, was eternally neck-deep in a pool of water that he could never drink and eternally shaded by a bough of delicious fruit that he could never pluck; Sisyphus, for trying to trick his way out of Hades, was set the task of rolling to the top of a hill a stone that always became just too much for him a finger's-breadth from the summit; Ixion, for trying to rape Zeus's wife Hera, was fixed to an eternally revolving wheel; forty-nine sisters called the Danaides, for murdering their husbands on their conjoint wedding night, eternally tried to fill sieves from a pool; and a Titan called Tityus, for trying to rape Leto, the mother of Apollo and Artemis, had vultures eternally feasting on his eternally renewed entrails.

Homer, Virgil and Ovid all wrote about these punishments, but they did not write about them in great detail. Homer — or some later interpolator, for there is some doubt about the authenticity of the following passages — describes Tityus's punishment like this:

> And I saw Tityus, son of splendid Gaea,
> Stretched on the earth: he stretched over nine acres;
> A vulture squatting on each side of him tore at his liver,
> Reaching into his very bowels: he could not keep them off with his hands.

He spends a little longer on Tantalus's and Sisyphus's:

> Tantalus too did I see, who suffered unspeakable torment,
> Standing upright in a pool, which rose till his chin was bedabbled:
> Yet he continued athirst, and never could reach to the water:
> For when he bent his head, in his passionate longing for drinking,
> All of it sank in the ground, through some supernatural Power,
> And, round his feet, the black earth showed, and left him unsated.
> And, over his head, tall trees were shedding their dainties around him,

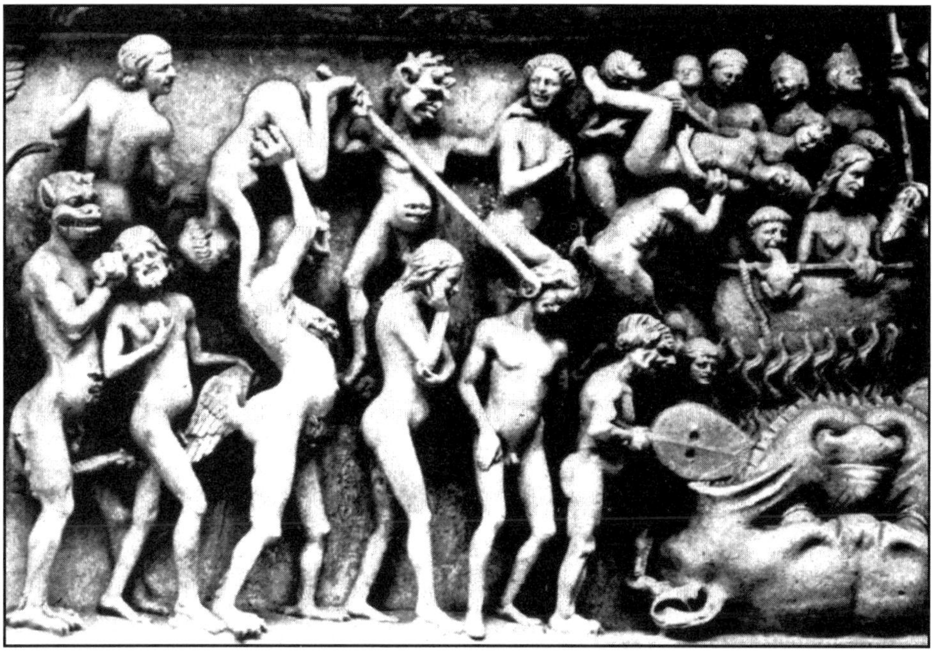

Pears and pomegranates were there, and others with glorious apples,
Fig trees with luscious fruit, and olives wide-spreading and leafy:
But when the ancient tried to pick one up and to eat it,
Then came a gust of wind, and whirled them away to the heavens.
Sisyphus … he too was suffering torment,
Pushing, with might and main, an enormous stone to a hill-top:
And when with hands and feet, by utmost strain, he had nearly
Toppled it over the edge, its ponderous weight overbore him,
And, without conscience or strain, it rolled to the plain that it came from.
Then he began once more to strain at the stone, till the sweat would
Stream from his limbs, and a cloud of steam rise up from his brow.[3]

But if these punishments are described at greater length than that of Tityus, they are, after all, much less gruesome. The descriptions of the three punishments in Virgil's **Aeneid** is almost the same,[4] and in Ovid's **Metamorphoses** they are whisked by at great speed:

Viscera praebebat Tityos lanianda novemque/ Lugeribus distentus erat; tibi, Tantale, null' deprenduntur aqu', qu'que inminet, effugit arbos;/ Aut petis aut urgues rediturum, Sisyphe saxum;/ Volvitur Ixion et se sequiturque fugitque,/ Molirique suis letum patruelibus ausae/ Adsiduae repetunt, quas perdant, Belides undas. Book IV, 457-463

Here Tityus offered his vitals to be torn, lying stretched out over nine broad acres. Thy lips can catch no water, Tantalus, and the tree that overhangs ever eludes thee. Thou, Sisyphus, dost either push or chase the rock that must always be rolling down the hill again. There whirls Ixion on his wheel, both following himself and fleeing, all in one; and the Belides, for daring to work destruction on their cousin-husbands, with unremitting toil seek again and again the waters, only to lose them.[5]

Tartarus is an undeniable hell, it would seem, but it is, except for Tityus, rather a mild one. The French writer Albert Camus (1913-60) even managed to see something positive in Sisyphus's fate:

La lutte elle-même vers les sommets suffit à remplir un coeur d'homme. Il faut imaginer Sisyphe heureux.

The battle to the top is in itself enough to satisfy the heart of man. One must imagine Sisyphus to be happy.[6]

And if Sisyphus, then perhaps the Danaides and Tantalus too. I would imagine that most people, though, like me, would not accept Camus's reasoning. Sisyphus is in hell, but not in the worst imaginable hell or the worst possible hell, which are not of course the same thing. Hell would be worse than we can imagine, but the people who came closest to imagining the worst were not the ancient Greeks, but the ancient and modern Christians.

The Christian hell was originally a tip. To the south-east of Jerusalem there was a valley that had been used in pagan times as a place of human sacrifice, principally, it seems, of children to the Canaanite god Moloch. It was called the "valley of the sons or son of Hinnom": in Hebrew גֵּיא בְנֵי־הִנֹּום (*gey' bᵉnêy-Hinnôm*), or, in contracted form, גֵּיא הִנֹּום (*gey' Hinnôm*). Ritually unclean to the Jews because of its past, it was used by them as a tip, and fires were kept burning there to dispose of rubbish and, later, of the corpses of executed criminals. As the originally vague Jewish concept of an afterlife developed, the valley came to be seen as the literal or metaphorical destination of all the wicked after their death, and its name passed into the Greek of the New Testament as Γεεννα (*Geenna*) and then, from the Greek via ecclesiastical Latin, into English as "Gehenna" (a synonymous Judaeo-Christian word for "hell", Tophet, had a similar journey from its beginnings as the name of a site — literally meaning a "place worthy of spitting" — in the Valley of Hinnom).

Gehenna, then, is one of the words translated as "hell" in the New Testament, but the original image of a rubbish-strewn, smoky, ritually unclean valley has already begun to be adapted for greater effect. The Gospel of Matthew warns "whosoever shall say, Thou fool" that he "shall be in danger of hell fire" (v 22), that is, the fire of Gehenna. By chapter xiii, the Gospel is describing the angels of the Son of man and their work gathering the wicked in order to

cast them into a furnace of fire: there shall be wailing and gnashing of teeth [xiii, 42]

This is stronger stuff. A little later, the Gospel of Mark draws on an image of hell already current in Judaic thinking from its appearance in the last verse of the book of Isaiah[7], but makes up in repetition what is lacking in originality. "If thy hand offend thee," says Jesus

> cut it off: it is better for thee to enter into life maimed, than having two hands to go into hell … Where the worm dieth not, and the fire is not quenched. [ix, 43-4]

Similar advice is offered for the foot and the eye — "cut it off", "pluck it out" — because it's better to be lame or half-blind than to go two-footed into hell

> Where the worm dieth not, and the fire is not quenched.

or two-eyed into hell

> Where the worm dieth not, and the fire is not quenched.

These images of hell are undeniably unpleasant, but they don't occur very often and aren't dwelt on at great length. Still, together with such ideas as that only very few of the human race will get to heaven (Matthew vii, 13-14), you might have supposed that they would suffice, particularly because there is no very strong image of heaven presented in the Gospels to set against them.

Needless to say, they did not suffice. The images of hell in the Gospels have been developed and added to literally *ad nauseam* throughout the entire history of Christianity. I say "literally" because it is in fact a literally nauseating, not to mention depressing, experience to read what some Christians believe their infinitely merciful, infinitely loving God gets up to in hell. The **Spiritual Exercises** of Saint Ignatius Loyola, the founder of the Jesuits, offer a typical example of traditional Christian beliefs on hell, and also of how modern Christianity, ashamed of its past, becomes positively Stalinist in its rewriting and suppression of parts of its founding texts.

First published in 1548, the **Spiritual Exercises** are a kind of hitchhiker's guide to the Christian universe, which the reader is invited to explore day by day in a series of meditations. Hell is one of the earliest destinations:

> Let us fancy we see hell, and imagine what is worst to behold — a horrible cavern, full of black flames, sulphur, devils, dragons, fire, swords, arrows, and innumerable damned, who roar in despair. Imagine the worst you can, then say: "All this is nothing if compared to hell."[8]

This, in a nineteenth-century Irish edition based on an Italian translation of the **Exercises**, is close or identical to Loyola's original words, but the Italian translator seems to have also taken upon himself the task of amplifying the saint's images and themes. Hence we go on to read:

> The sinner is a most vile worm. By sinning he crucified anew the King of kings — the redeemer

(Heb. xi., 6). If not in effect, at least with affection, he acted in a hostile manner against God. What punishment then shall be given him in hell, to repair the great outrage offered to God? Flames, swords, devils? All is little — all is nothing.

He who gave a mortal wound to William, Prince of Orange, was fastened on high by the extremities of his two thumbs, with a hundred pounds of lead attached to his toes. Then he was beaten with iron rods until he bled. Being loosened, very long needles were threaded, and passed through his nails and skin [sic]. The following day his hairs were plucked out one by one, and he was exposed to a slow fire. Finally, he was impaled; and, during his agony, the hand that inflicted the wound was burnt with plates of iron.

If such pain was adjudged to him who had presumed to wound a prince, what torments should be given in hell to him who outraged a crucified God?

This reference to the hated Protestant William of Orange (1650-1702), which could not have been made by St. Ignatius (1491-1556), may even be a further interpolation by the Irish translator intended to score political points for his Catholic readership. That this would present the reader with a logical *non sequitur* — indignation at William of Orange's cruelty couldn't of course imply indignation at the Catholic God's infinitely worse cruelty — can't be raised as an objection, because nobody who baulks at *non sequiturs* is likely to take Christianity seriously in the first place.

Similar gloating amplification of St. Ignatius's horrors occurs elsewhere. The Saint invites us to "Consider then, in particular, the pains of hell":

Imaginaberis:

1. *Te videre stagnus ignis ardentis et reproborum animas in eo tamquam pisces in oceano natantes. Ibi erit ardoris supplicium sine ullo lucis refrigerio.*
2. *Te audire planctus, gemitus, ululatus qui tartaream illam regionem pervadunt, necnon stridorem dentium, execrationes, blasphemias quas reprobi contra Christum ejusque sanctos continuo evomunt.*
3. *Te odorari sulphureas exhalationes, carcerum sordes, latrinarum immunditias, cadaverum foetorem atque putredinem.*
4. *Te gustare cibos amaros, venenosos, vomitum provacantes, et viscera discerpentes.*
5. *Te tangere inextinguibiles inferni flammas, in quibus reproborum animæ tanquam in igneis corporibus inclusæ perpetuo comburentur.*[9]

You will imagine:

1. Yourself seeing the lake of blazing fire and the souls of the damned in it like fish swimming in the ocean. Here there will be a punishment of fire without any relief of light.
2. Yourself hearing the shouts, groans, howls that fill that Tartarean region, not to mention the grinding of teeth, the curses, the blasphemies that the damned continually pour forth upon Christ and his saints.
3. Yourself smelling the sulphurous atmosphere, the foulness of prisons, the filthiness of latrines, the foetor and the rottenness of corpses.
4. Yourself tasting the bitter nourishment [of the damned], poisonous, provoking vomit, rending the viscera.

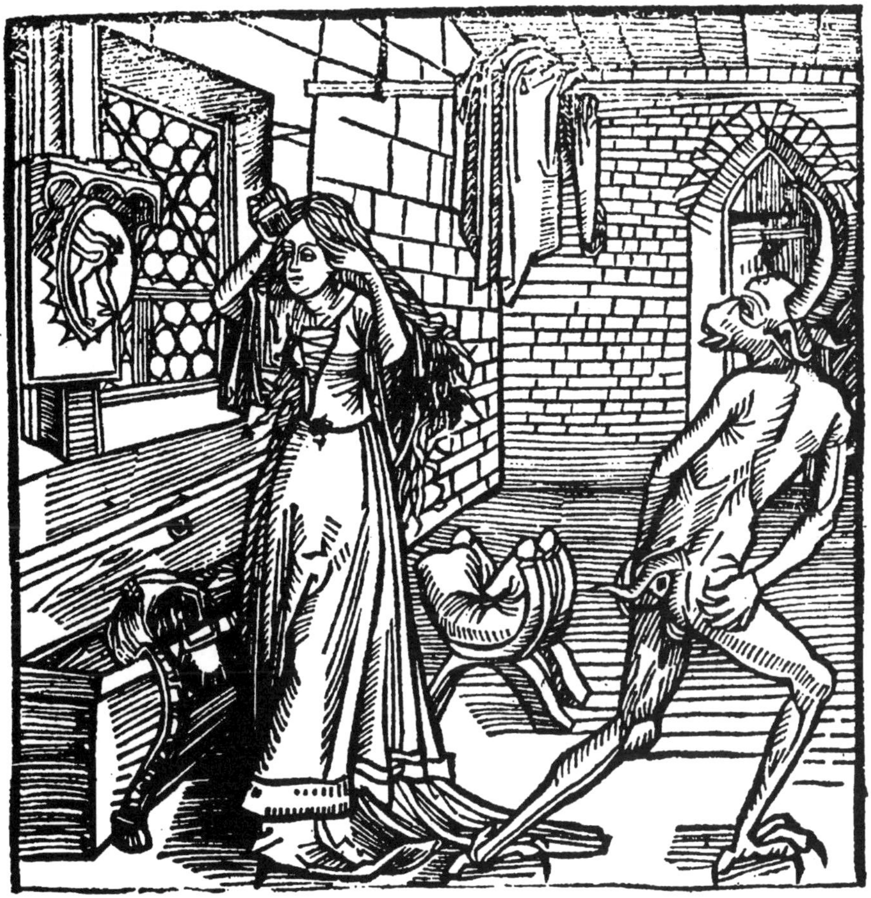

5. Yourself feeling the inextinguishable flames of hell, in which the souls of the damned burn as though sealed for ever in bodies of flame.

The original Latin has a concision and power that don't entirely survive translation into English, but survive well enough, and the sadistic ingenuity of a flame that tortures without light would be startling in any language. The Saint's *ipsissima verba* are insufficient for his translators, however. Number 3 of these mental exercises, for example, is amplified thus:

> The scent is tormented by the odour of sulphur, and by the noisomeness of all the sewers of the world, which crawl into that abyss, and by the bad odour of the damned, which is much worse than the most putrid dead bodies. One damned soul alone, says St. Bonaventura, if he came into the world, would suffice to infect the whole of it. What odour, then, will exhale from innumerable damned souls, united in one enclosure?

And if the remainder of the Saint's invitations to "imagine", and the remainder of his translators' detailed expansions of them, don't disgust you enough, well:

> Imagine what will never occur, namely, that God should send an angel to the damned with this embassy: "Listen, miserable and wretched creatures: God, moved with compassion for you, has resolved to take you out of the fire of hell. Do you know when? After each of you has formed with his tears a collection of water more vast than the ocean, and after there shall have passed as many millions of years as there are grains of sand in the sea, leaves on the trees, and atoms in the air." O God, what a terrible annunciation! How incomprehensible the number of years to pass to fulfil those conditions! If the damned received this announcement, they would abound in joy, and consider it all as nothing: for, as St. Augustine says, in Ps. lx,: "Omnis res, quæ finem habet, brevis est:" "Every thing that has an end is short."

But, the passage goes on to re-emphasize, this release from hell won't of course happen. God will not be moved with compassion for his miserable and wretched creatures, and they will be in hell for ever. And why? Perhaps for very little, by the standards of an other than psychopathic sense of justice:

> What then will be the agony and rage of a damned soul, remembering the slight cause, and short pleasures for which he finds himself in so horrible a hell?

And what, one might ask, will be the embarrassment and unease of Roman Catholics in a later century, when such full-blooded sentiments have come to be seen as reflecting a less than kindly light on the psychology of the Church and its senior management figures? That later century has arrived, and "liberal" Roman Catholics have adopted a typical device of totalitarianism: the suppression of historical fact. There are twelve-and-a-half pages devoted to "Infernus" in the nineteenth-century Latin edition of the **Spiritual Exercises** quoted from above; two years before Vatican Two began in 1962, a modern English translation has brought this down to a much more palatable page and a half. Bearing in mind first that Latin, because of its grammar and its orthography, usually manages to say as much as English in much less space, and second that the modern translation is in a prettified, wide-margined, imitation-gilt edition, one concludes rightly that many of the Saint's more sadistic details have gone AWOL:

> 66. First heading. To see in imagination those enormous fires, and the souls, as it were, with bodies of fire.
> 68. Third heading. To smell in imagination the fumes of sulphur and the stench of filth and corruption.
> 70. Fifth heading. To feel in imagination the heat of the flames that play on and burn the souls.[10]

After Vatican Two, one wonders how much more has had to go to order to spare the Church's blushes at Saint Loyola's unreconstructed, and unhypocritical, psychopathology. It is all rather as if a group calling itself the "Nazis" were to claim simultaneously that it stood in exactly the tradition that the use of the name would suggest and yet that it did not accept any of that

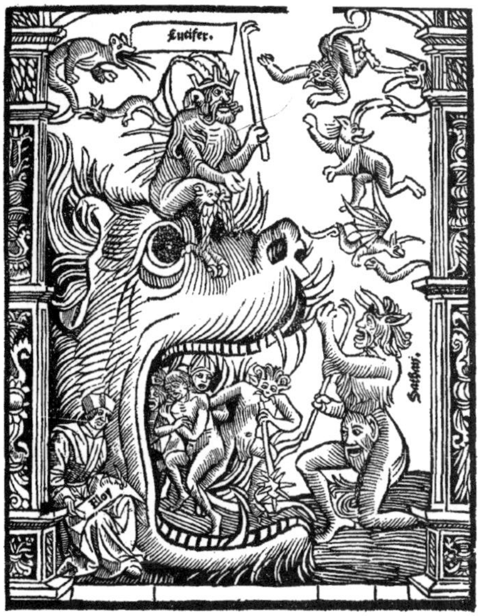

tradition as valid — indeed, that it repudiated the tradition in its entirety. Expressions of disgust or incredulity at the hypocrisy or intellectual dishonesty of the exactly equivalent case of liberal Christianity would be a waste of time, however, and would also miss the point, which is that Christianity is not a label for a coherent ideology or set of beliefs, but a brand-name. When the profits enjoyed by the shareholders of the company owning the brand-name are in the direct form of power and political influence, the company, to reclaim a metaphor, sings from one particular hymn-sheet. When they are in another form, another hymn-sheet is used. Almost always, though, the profits are partly in the form of money and influence, and that is why the hymn-sheet always refers to tradition and why the brand-name does not change.[11]

But this is not to say that hell is no longer believed in by large numbers of Christians, because, of course, it is. It would be easy to attack them by pointing out what I and many others would see as the true motives for their continued belief, but it's worthwhile taking a little time first to consider the possible existence of hell independently of the psychology of those who believe in it. Why beliefs are held does not necessarily say anything about the validity of those beliefs: someone who believes that the moon is made of rock because he dislikes cheese is just as right as someone who believes that the moon is made of rock because he has actually taken a giant leap for mankind onto it.

The question is, then, one of whether or not a belief in the existence of hell is intellectually respectable. I would say that it is not. None of the arguments adduced for the existence of hell in a long article in a 1912 **Catholic Encyclopaedia**,[12] for example, seems to me to be valid. The article claims that the "existence of hell is first of all proved from Holy Writ" and from the fact that "the [Church] Fathers, from the very earliest times, are unanimous in teaching that the wicked will be punished after death". If one is not a Christian and even, nowadays, if one is, these are not sufficient grounds for belief, and the **Encyclopaedia** itself admits that they are anyway not rational grounds:

> If we abstract from the eternity of its punishment, the existence of hell can be demonstrated even by the light of pure reason.

The argument goes like this. We can see that wickedness is not always punished in this life, so God, as the embodiment of perfect justice, must redress the balance in the hereafter. Annihilation of the souls of the wicked after their death would not be appropriate:

> due proportion between demerit and punishment would be rendered impossible by an indiscriminate annihilation of all the wicked

ergo there must be a hell. However, the hell the writer has in mind is one in which the wicked will be punished infinitely for their finite sins during life. This is an obvious *non sequitur*, too obvious for even the mind of a well-trained traditionalist Catholic to swallow up in double-think:

> The objection is made that there is no proportion between the brief moment of sin and an eternal punishment. But why not? We certainly admit a proportion between a momentary good deed and its eternal reward, not, it is true, a proportion of duration, but a proportion between the law and its appropriate sanction.

The sanction is appropriate because it is laid down by the law: a sanction sending the good to hell would be equally appropriate to a law that laid down such a sanction, and there would be an equally good proportion between the law and its appropriate sanction. Whoops. The writer of the article hurries on to say:

> Again, sin is an offence against the infinite authority of God, and the sinner is in some way aware of this, though but imperfectly.

In other words, because God has infinite authority, he is right to punish imperfect, or finite, beings infinitely. Using similar reasoning, mediæval Christians arraigned pigs and sparrows for crimes such as arson, theft and murder, and modern judges in the proudly Christian United States of America send mentally retarded adolescents to the gas chamber and electric chair.

The simple truth, it seems to me at least, is that the idea of an "infinitely good ... infinitely wise, just and holy God"[13] creating hell and despatching sinners there is a logical absurdity. If an individual is given a choice between heaven and hell and behaves in such a way as to go to hell, he is one or more of these things: irrational; mad; incapable of fully understanding the choice offered to him; or incapable of acting in accordance with his understanding. In none of these cases would it be just to send him to hell, and the concepts of hell and a god with the attributes just given are therefore irreconcilable.

And so, if you accept, as I hope you will have done, that a little over five hundred words from me have been sufficient to demolish any rational basis for a belief in hell, the question arises of why such a belief has lasted for so long and exercised such a powerful influence on Christian doctrine and practice. There are a number of ways of answering this question, but not all of them are complete.

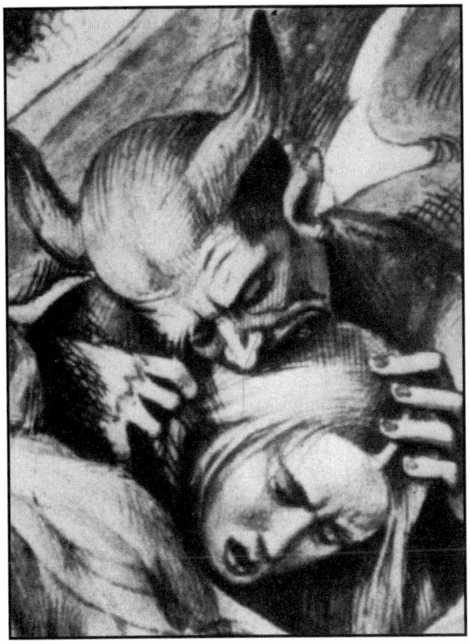
They are going to eat you. A demon gnawing on one of the damned in a fresco by Signorelli (detail).

It's undoubtedly true, for example, that descriptions of hell have been used as a form of sadistic pornography in the Christian churches. I wouldn't go quite as far as the feminist who claimed that a story in the **Gesta Romanorum** about a woman who was sent to hell was used as an *aide masturbatoire* by mediæval monks,[14] but sadism doesn't always have to be expressed sexually or consciously, and the gloating detail of many descriptions of hell in Christian texts would be difficult to explain in any other way.

On the other hand, you could perhaps say that if someone believed strongly in hell, it would be incumbent on him to do his very best to convince other people not only that it existed but that it was a very bad place to go to. That still raises the question of why so many rational, humane and decent people have subscribed to an irrational, inhumane and indecent concept like hell, because many undoubtedly have and still do. The short answer might simply be that hell works. By this, I mean that it is a very powerful way of manipulating people's behaviour to the advantage of the church. Many systems of morality are based on the instillation of fear: if you don't behave, the threat goes, you will be punished. Hell is the ultimate threat and the ultimate punishment, and although it is an absurd threat and an absurd punishment it nonetheless works because morality rarely has anything to do with logic or rationality. As I pointed out above, if you believe in heaven and hell and act so as to go to the latter, you are either irrational, mad, incapable of fully understanding the choice offered to you, or incapable of acting in accordance with your understanding. Or, as some people have destroyed their lives by believing, you have committed the unforgivable sin mentioned in the New Testament:

> Verily I say unto you, All sins shall be forgiven unto the sons of men, and blasphemies wherewith soever [sic] they shall blaspheme: But he that shall blaspheme against the Holy Ghost hath never forgiveness, but is danger of eternal damnation. [Mark iii, 29; cf. Matthew xxii, 31, Luke xxii, 10]

The cunning of this sin is that nobody is quite sure what it involves, and so nobody is quite sure how to avoid it. The creation of uncertainty, fear and guilt in this way is an excellent means of controlling people once they have accepted Christianity, and the threat of hell is an excellent way of getting people to accept

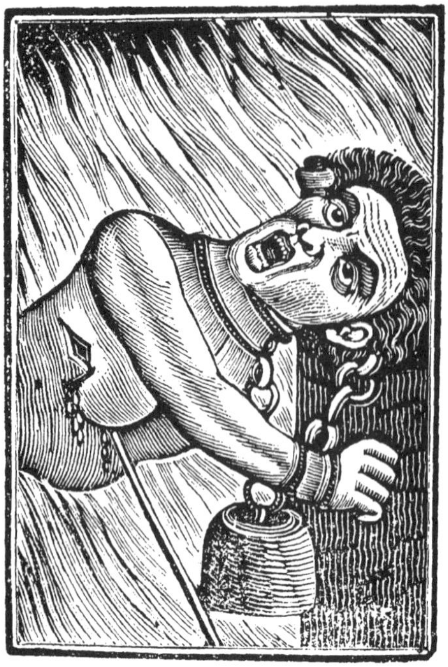

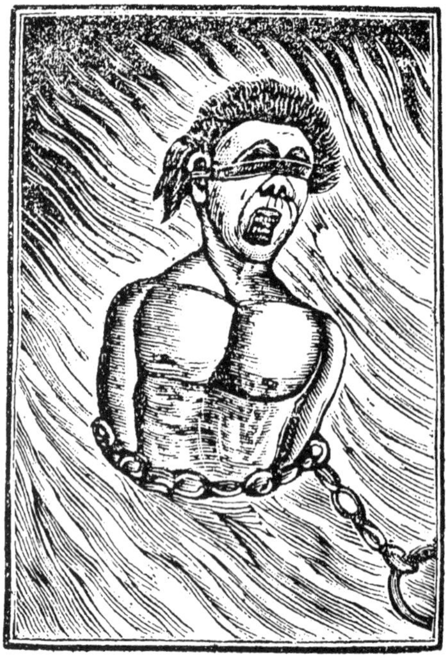

Christianity in the first place. In Darwinian terms, hell is simply the fittest way of getting bums onto pews, and that is why it became such an important part of Christian doctrine and why now, when it isn't used by the mainstream churches, they are all slowly dying.

But why should hell be such an effective recruiting aid? Again, a short answer might be: because it's frightening. The psychological effects of the overwhelming stress that can be caused by emotions like fear are very interesting. One of them is that the contents of the brain can undergo what might be called a reversal of polarity. All beliefs and patterns of behaviour can flip upside-down and become their opposites. Someone who hates cats before undergoing overwhelming stress may come to love them afterwards, or vice versa. Someone who is fiercely anti-censorship before undergoing overwhelming stress may be joining Mary Whitehouse's Viewers' And Listeners' Association afterwards, or vice versa. And someone who has spent all his time persecuting followers of a heretical new sect, may, after undergoing the overwhelming stress of a bad case of sunstroke, become the leading light of the sect afterwards.

That, at least, is one explanation of how the fanatically anti-Christian Saul become the fanatically pro-Christian St Paul. The psychologist who discusses St Paul's case in a book called **Battle for the Mind** is very careful to stress that his book "is not concerned with the truth or falsity of any particular religious or political belief",[15] but, whether he is being disingenuous or not, it's an unsettling experience to read in his book how what appear to be carefully reasoned and securely founded beliefs — such as one's own — may be nothing of the kind, and how they may be vulnerable to very crude and unsubtle forms of alteration.

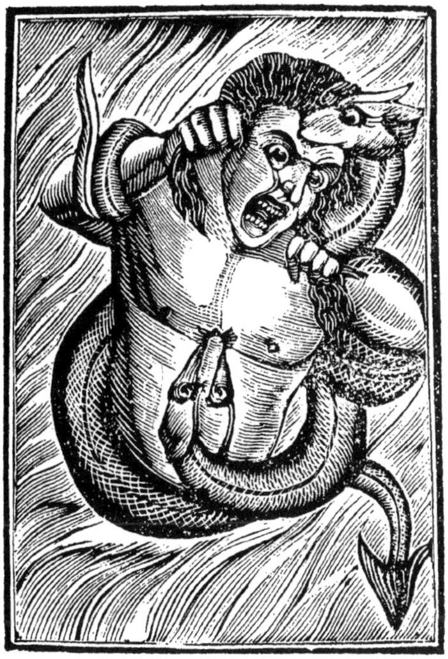

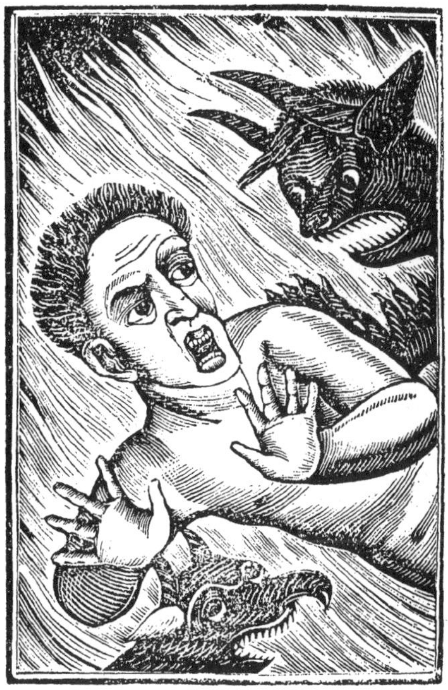

Hell comes into this book because it is a very good example of how brainwashing can work. Methodism, for example, was a spectacularly successful religious movement in its day, and its success was founded on hellfire preaching. Such was the eloquence and force of personality of men like John Wesley, the movement's founder, and so vivid and awe-inspiring were the visions of Hell they conjured for their revivalist audiences, that huge numbers of people experienced overwhelming fear and horror at the thought that they were on the road there. Their reason was suspended, their previous beliefs in a state of flux or complete collapse, and they become defenceless against a sudden change of tone in the sermons, which went to describe the joys of Heaven and the means of getting there instead. From trembling at the wrath of God, they wept with joy at His infinite mercy, and rushed to join the church.

Such emotion-inspired, irrational conversions were not necessarily permanent or long-lasting ones, but John Wesley was an acute psychologist and developed an effective system of after-scare service to ensure that converts stayed converted. Hell had its place here as it had its place in the original sermons. Whether the doctrine was true or not is irrelevant: it brought men and women into the church and kept them under control once they were there, as it has for centuries not only in the other Christian churches but also in Islam. Muhammad was just as acute a psychologist as John Wesley and Ignatius Loyola, and the Holy Koran contains descriptions of hell to rival anything produced by Christians:

In front of the sinner is Hell, and he is given for drink, boiling fetid water. In gulps will he sip it, but

> never will he be near swallowing it down his throat [*The Holy Koran*, Surah xiv, 16-17[16]]

> And thou wilt see the sinners that day bound together in fetters, their garments made of liquid pitch, and their faces covered with fire [ibid., 49-50]

In the Koran, moreover, unlike the Gospels, the concept of hell is fully developed and is presented with all the gruesome and sadistic details that had not appeared in Christianity until some time after the death of its founder. Muhammad made frequent reference to hell in his holy book, and left very little to the imagination:

> those who deny their Lord, for them will be cut out a garment of Fire: over their heads will be poured out boiling water. Within it will be scalded what is in their bodies, as well as their skins. In addition there will be maces of iron to punish them. Every time they wish to get away therefrom, from anguish, they will be forced back therein, and it will be said, "Taste ye the Penalty of Burning!" [Surah xxii, 20-22]

The reason for this is that Muhammad was born in about 570 AD, after Christian scholars and theologians had had centuries in which to brood over Jesus's references to hell and amplify them for the edification of the faithful, and although he rejected Christianity and claimed that it was a distortion of Jesus's true teaching, he was happy enough to accept the Christian refinements of Jesus's concept of hell, undoubtedly because he recognized their efficacy both for making converts and for controlling those converts afterwards. Nor was he content with what he said about hell in the Koran: the body of tradition known as the Hadith — personal sayings and deeds of Muhammad recorded from an initially oral tradition — contains further blood-curdling details of what awaits the unrepentant and unforgiven sinner. Not all of the Hadith can be accepted as trustworthy, but even if those parts of it appertaining to hell are sometimes invented or distorted, they certainly chime with the Koran in their sadism, ingenuity and ability to inspire fear in those susceptible to such absurdities:

> The mildest punishment that will be inflicted on a person in Hell is that he will be made to wear a pair of sandals made of fire which will be so hot as to set his brain boiling as if something was cooking in a pot on a stove ... The stinking pus that people will be made to drink in Hell is such that if a bucket of it was thrown into the world the whole world would be filled with its infernal stench.[17]

Islam, like Methodism and early Christianity, undoubtedly owes a great part of its great success to the stick-and-carrot approach of first threatening hell and then promising heaven. The fact that heaven is, as I pointed out at the very beginning, difficult or embarassing to describe isn't really important, because heaven exists mostly as a negative. Heaven isn't hell. What more do you need to know?

A GIRL'S SECOND-BEST FRIEND

DILDOES AND DILDOPHILES FROM ANCIENT GREECE TO THE PRESENT DAY

The evolution of the human race isn't yet a clear or even an uncontroversial matter, but it's generally believed that modern man, *Homo sapiens*, represents the tip of an evolutionary twig that descends via *Homo erectus* and *Homo habilis* to the branch we share with the great apes. *Sapiens* was named for his ability to reason; *erectus* for his ability to walk upright; and *habilis* for his ability to make tools. According to the **Guinness Book of Records**, the earliest habiline tools so far known are "abraded core-choppers" dating from approximately 2·7 million years BC and discovered by the French palaeontologist Hélène Roche in Hadar in Ethiopia.[1]

Prosaically enough, they, and "finger-held quartz slicers" of somewhere near the same age, would almost certainly have been used in the preparation of food. All work and no play makes Jack a dull boy, and Jill a dull girl, today; whether the same was true 2·7 million years ago is impossible to say, but it's pleasant, at least in the pages of a Critical Vision publication, to suppose that somewhere amongst the ancient tools filling the display cases and storage drawers of the world's museums there's a mislabelled specimen that represents the world's earliest surviving dildo.

On the other hand, the earliest dildos were probably made of something rather less forbidding — and durable — than stone, and before the invention of agriculture there may simply have been no time or incentive to create artificial substitutes for the penis when the plant kingdom offered so many natural ones — some of which, like cucumbers and bananas, are in use to the present day. Witness, for example, the adventures of the Sheffield model Fiona Wright with Sir Ralph Halpern during the 1980s:

> 'We had sex non-stop,' Ms Wright explained. 'We did it in front of the fire first, then as we were unpacking the shopping from Marks and Spencer he lifted me up on the kitchen unit. He got a banana and used it on me before unzipping it and scoffing it down at the crucial moment.'[2]

And even after the invention of agriculture, there is some reason to suppose that the ingenuity inspired by increased leisure, far from ignoring the old penis-substitutes, may actually have been lavished on them, at least in rural China.

In Brian Aldiss's erotic novel-cum-autobiography **A Soldier Erect** (1971), a Chinese prostitute in Malaysia excites the narrator with a description of how she and other women masturbated back home with gherkins of a peculiarly knobbly and warty kind. Did this represent a peculiarly Chinese synthesis of the erotic and the practical, a foodstuff bred over generations to a maximum of sexual utility, while losing none of its culinary value? Romantic feminists might even see in it an invaluable example of women's ability to subvert the patriarchial imposition of labour in field and kitchen: under the very noses of their menfolk, women shuttled Mendelian possibilities to create a dildo that satisfied both their vaginas and their stomachs. Less romantic and partisan feminists would see what is probably the truth, that the use of vegetables for sexual gratification, deliberately bred or otherwise, has more to do with poverty than with sexual politics: rich Chinese women, like rich women elsewhere, used artificial dildos.[3]

As women had for many centuries. The ancient Greek writer Herondas writes of how two women, Metro and Coritto, discuss a dildo lent by Coritto to another woman, Eubale, who has then lent it to someone else, in whose possession it has been seen by Metro, who has now come to the original owner to obtain details of where she might purchase a dildo for herself (the term used in the text is "baubon", which is probably related to the name of a Greek demi-goddess of lust called Baubo).[4] The manufacture of such dildos was undoubtedly a lucrative, if discreetly advertised, sideline of male artisans in ancient Greece, who seem to have made them mostly of leather. Forberg's **Manual of Classical Erotology** mentions that the term "tribad", generally used of lesbians, is

> also applied to those women who in default of a real mentula [penis], make use of their finger or of a leathern contrivance, which they introduce into their vulva, and so attain a fictitious enjoyment.[5]

The women of Miletus were particularly notorious for their use of these dildos, which were

> eight inches long and thick in proportion. Aristophanes tells us that the women of his

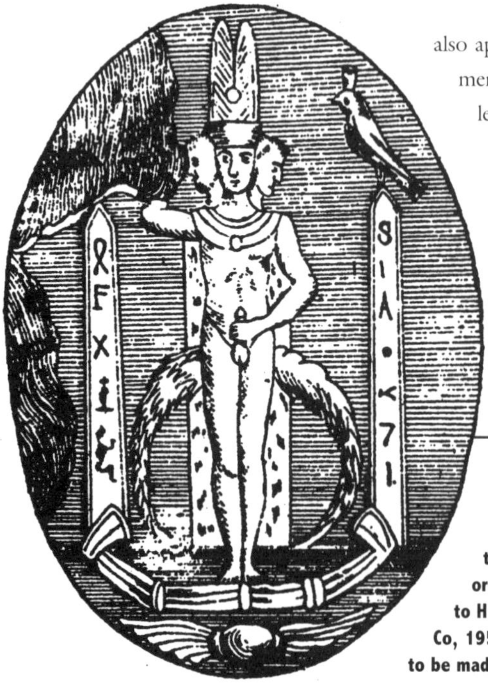

Left: Osiris. Legend has it that the Egyptian god was murdered by his brother, torn to pieces, and then cast to the four winds. Isis, the wife of Osiris, managed to track down all of the parts, with the exception of the sexual organ... this she substituted with a piece of wood. According to H. Cutner in *A Short History of Sex Worship* (pub: Watts & Co, 1950), Isis ordered 'special attention and solemn worship to be made to this part'.

> day habitually made use of such. And to this very day Italian, Spanish and Asiatic women honour this instrument with a place in their toilet apparatus; it is their most precious possession, and one very highly appreciated.[6]

In Greek times they were used by women both as a solitary and as a shared pleasure whose details are frequently pictured on ancient Greek vases:

> a naked hetaira [courtesan] with a thigh-band on her right leg [and a] leather olisbos [dildo], which she makes use of. The egg-shaped object, which the hetaira holds in her right hand, repeatedly occurs on vases of this period ... It is a flagon from which the hetaira drips oil on the phallus.[7]

Such phalluses were not used just by, or just on, women in the ancient world. The **Satyricon** of Petronius Arbiter has not survived complete to the present day, but does contain an interesting description of the sex therapy offered by a witch called Enothea to the narrator, a young man called Encolpius ("Encunted") who is suffering from impotence. After making him eat a concoction containing "a bean and some dead flies and the faeces of a hog", and then drink the "urine of a female goat", the witch

> drew out a leather object fashioned in the shape of an erect phallus, appended to which were metal testicles. Dipping this into a mixture of oil, small grains of pepper and the bruised seeds of nettles, she instructed me to undress.
>
> I did as she said, wondering what strange torment she had in store for me. My curiosity was soon satisfied.
>
> With unbelievable force, she jammed it up my anus; I cannot describe the pain, the fiery burning sensations that consumed me. Humping into the air, I let out a cry that I thought would shake the walls.[8]

This part of the treatment is a complete success; the story itself obviously raises the possibility that men in the ancient world used dildos on themselves or on other men in other than such special circumstances, although direct proof of this seems lacking. A passage from a slightly earlier period raises the possibility that Roman women, like working-class Chinese women, went directly to nature in default of a "real mentula". Suetonius, in his **Vita Augusti**, wrote of a story

> which I found in a book called *Theologumena*, by Asclepias of Mendes. Augustus's mother, Atia, with certain married women friends, once attended a solemn midnight service at the temple of Apollo, where she had her litter set down, and presently fell asleep as the others also did. Suddenly a serpent glided up, entered her, and then glided away again. On awakening, she purified herself, as if after intimacy with her husband.[9]

Forberg suggests that the snake had been used for sexual purposes by other women and penetrated Atia out of habit, which doesn't seem very likely: the story seems more likely to be connected with some sort of fertility rite involving a snake as a symbol of divinity. Suetonius goes on to say that

> An irremovable coloured mark in the shape of a serpent, which then appeared on her [Atia's] body, made her ashamed to visit the public baths any more; and the birth of Augustus nine months later suggested a divine paternity.[10]

The "irremovable coloured mark" sounds like a tattoo or brand received after initiation into an erotic cult, membership of which would probably have had to be concealed in the puritanical Rome of that period, and indeed later: in 8 AD Augustus himself would banish the poet Ovid for composing lewd verses.

On the other hand, snakes might seem an unsatisfactory choice as penis-substitute: they are very muscular and very difficult to keep still, and putting one into even a willing vagina might seem a difficult and even dangerous task. Perhaps so, but perhaps female snake-fanciers were familiar with the ancient techniques by which magicians and members of ancient ophiolatrous ("snake-worshipping") sects were able to persuade snakes into perfect rigidity:

> And Moses and Aaron went in unto Pharaoh, and they did so as the LORD had commanded: and Aaron cast down his rod before Pharaoh, and before his servants, and it became a serpent. [Exodus vii, 10]

As, very likely, it had been a serpent before it became a rod and was carried into Pharaoh's presence. **Peake's Commentary on the Bible** says of this part of Exodus:

> Serpent-charming still persists in Egypt, and experts can stiffen serpents by hypnotic devices into rods.[11]

In this state, perhaps a snake will tolerate insertion into the vagina; its struggles to get free once *in situ* may be very pleasurable, and the risk of its being able to open its mouth wide enough to bite its exploitrix might seem worth taking unless it were a particularly small or poisonous snake in a large vagina. Then again, perhaps the sensation of a very small snake in a vagina (or rectum) with its jaw tied shut can equal or surpass that of a gerbil *ibidem*: the possibility is, strictly speaking, however, beyond the scope of this article, because gerbils and very small snakes do not meet the definition of dildos as an inanimate and generally artificial penis-

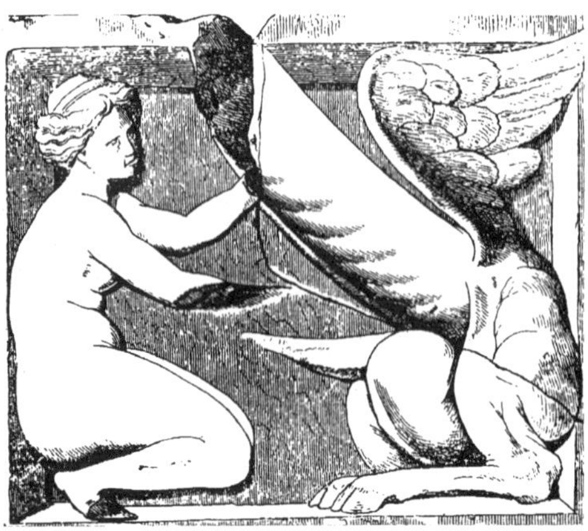

substitute.

Which definition has been used as a natural explanation for the confessions of supernatural congress with the Devil that were made by accused women during the Witch Crazes. Testimony from one woman accused of witchcraft in sixteenth century Normandy described how the devil

> had a black *membre viril* [male member] very stiff, and so thick that the witness experienced considerable pain when he copulated with her, because the said *membre* was hard as flint [*dur comme un caillou*] and extremely cold ... [12]

In testimony from another trial, after the *osculum nefandum*, the "unspeakable kiss" bestowed upon the Devil's anus, women were penetrated by him and found that "his genitals were hard and scaly, his seed 'cold as ice'".[13] These, and other descriptions, make it seem likely that a dildo of stone or metal was being used; presumably the "Devil" was a man in disguise whose human anus could plausibly pass for diabolical but whose human penis couldn't.

Another form of dildo may also have been involved in whatever actually lay behind the Church's accusations of traffic with the infernal powers. Witches are traditionally represented, especially for children, as flying on broomsticks. The theory that witches "flew" because the ingredients of their potions — "a thick stew of boiled children, preferably unbaptized ... juice of water parsnip, aconite, cinquefoil, deadly nightshade and soot"[14] — induced a form of delirium is probably the truth, but perhaps only part of it. It does not explain why broomsticks and nocturnal flight should be so closely associated, for example, while the fact that orgasm can give some women the sensation that they are flying does: it has been suggested that broomsticks symbolize the erect, orgasm-inducing penis rising from pubic hair. And yet perhaps broomsticks also symbolize simply broomsticks: they must have offered many women, especially the ageing women living alone who were so often accused of witchcraft, a highly convenient and discrete substitute for the penis. Allen Ginsberg, the homosexual American "beat" poet, once found the same in a hotel in Poland.[15]

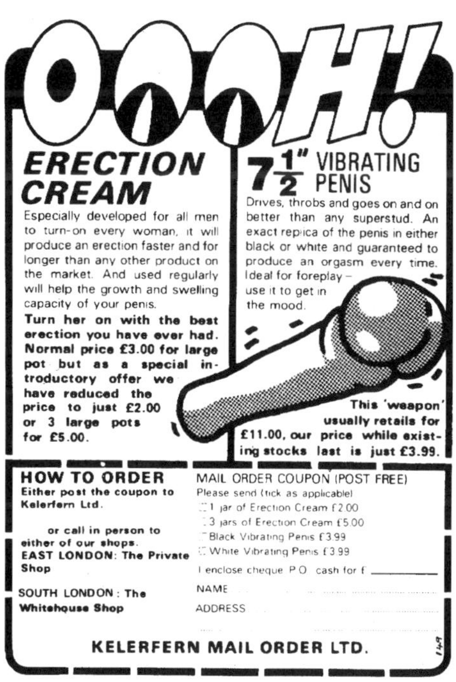

But whether they were such *objets trouvés* as broomsticks, gherkins and snakes, or were designed and made for the specific role of penis-substitute, dildos were, until the twentieth century, ringing the changes on a limited range of blunt, elongated shapes. The women of Miletus resorted to "the cobblers of the little city"[16], and millennia later, in the nineteenth-century **Tale of a Dildoe** (sic), female nature and the means to realize it seem to have changed very little:

> The scene is in New York. Three young American ladies resolve to procure a dildoe for their mutual gratification, and the purchase is effected by one of them through her milliner.[17]

The Twentieth Century provided not only new materials for the dildo — rubbers and plastics — but also the greatest advance in its technology since its invention however many thousands or millions of years before. Dildos could now become semi-autonomous, for with electricity came the "small electrically operated device for producing sexual stimulation"[18] that is best known as the vibrator.

Formerly dildos had moved because they were moved; now they could move themselves. It was at this point that they ceased to be simply a substitute for the penis, whether in intention, for heterosexual women and homosexual men, or in effect, for lesbians, and became a separate category of sexual device, affording sensations like none ever experienced before. Some types of vibrator, in fact, such as vibrating discs that strap into place over the clitoris, are designed purely for clitoral stimulation; vibrators still shaped like the traditional penis-substituting dildo may have, for some women in some circumstances, reduced the penis to the role of an unsatisfactory vibrator-substitute (the vildo?). In the novel on which the Michael Douglas-Kathleen Turner film **War of the Roses** was based, Barbara Rose begins to see the world differently after she initiates the divorce of her husband Oliver:

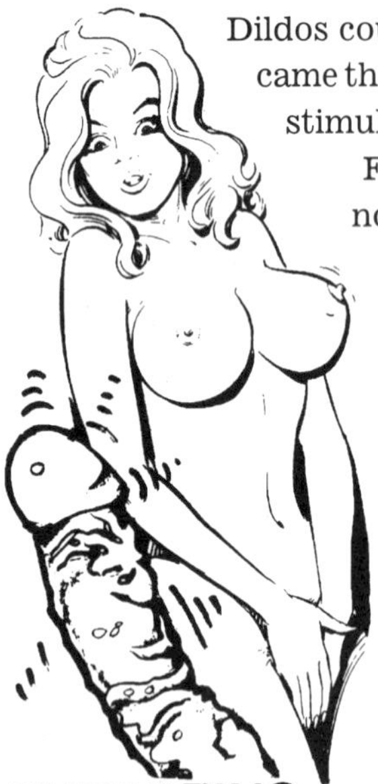

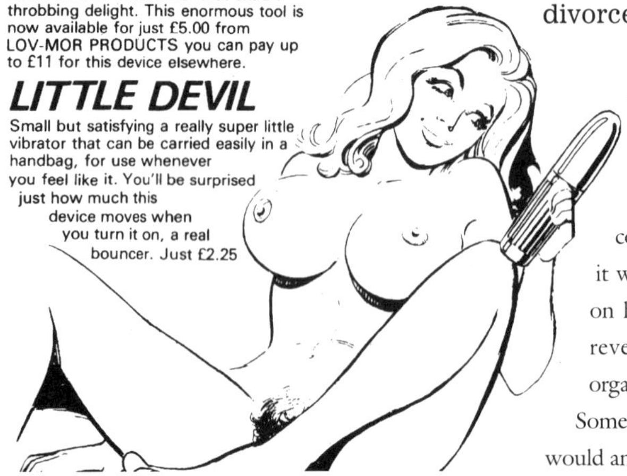

> As if to celebrate her newly perceived freedom, she bought herself a vibrator. It had a penis shape and wide ridges like corduroy along its shaft. The idea of it was almost as delicious as its effect on her private parts, which proved a revelation of pleasure as waves of orgasmic crescendos invaded her senses. Sometime in the middle of the day, she would announce to herself, Time for happy

hour, and would go up to her room and proceed to use her cock toy, as she called it. It was better than Oliver had ever been.

'You beautiful little technological miracle,' she would whisper to it when it had done particularly yeoman service. Who needs them?[19]

For other women, under other circumstances, the non-electric common or garden dildo may be preferable precisely because of what it substitutes for and resembles — and this may be so even for lesbians. In Cynthia Astuto's and Pat Califia's discussion of dildos in the "So You Wanna Be A Sadist...?" chapter of **The Lesbian S&M Safety Manual**,[20] we are advised to:

Also bear in mind that some women object to using a dildo that looks like a penis or is worn in a harness. Of course, there are also some women who don't see the point in using an object that is not clearly phallic.

Nuns, for example. In 1660 there was a sensational criminal case in France in which novices at one nunnery accused their superiors of sexual crimes against them. The standard of proof, however, seems well up to that of the twentieth century's Ritual Satanic Abuse panics, but the accusations almost certainly reflected something of what went on in the cloisters:

[A] sister had a vision of Barbara Buvée [the mother superior], who appeared to her holding in one hand a stolen sacred host on which reposed "la partie honteuse" [the shameful part] of a man, and in the other an artificial phallus made of linen with which "she committed on herself impure acts".[21]

Nuns wanted to use objects that looked like phalluses because what they really wanted were real phalluses, but even for women who don't really want the real thing, there are some roles for which the more subtle vibrating dildo is unsuited. Defloration, for example. Even phallophobic lesbians will have need of a penis-substitute if, still in possession of a hymen, they are anxious to avail themselves and their lovers of greater access to their vaginas, and many heterosexual women must have lost their "virginity" in the same way as Kitty, a servant who was one of the conquests immortalized by the satyromaniac "Walter" in his **A Secret Life**. Urged to reveal how she can be *virgo* but *non intacta*, she describes sleeping with, and "frigging" ("masturbating"), a fellow servant who

One night ... produced something like a man's thing, and put it up herself, saying it gave her more pleasure than frigging. Another night, when Kitty was made over-randy by talking, and feeling each other [sic], she let the woman put it up her. It was up her before she was aware of it almost, and did not hurt her much. She spent [i.e. achieved orgasm], it gave her pleasure, but she was bleeding, and she cried. "It was a dildo", said I. Kitty had never heard the word, the cook called it a sham-cock.[22]

Sham-cocks are not necessarily so sham. They can pass as the real thing, sometimes for a lifetime.[23] And sometimes not, as in the case of:

> Mary Hamilton, alias Charles Hamilton, alias George Hamilton, alias William Hamilton ... Her last 'bride' appeared in court and testified that having married Charles ... they had lived together for three months, she unsuspecting that her partner was anything other than male. Later, however, 'she became mistrustful and, comparing certain circumstances with her neighbours Mr and Mrs Goody, realised that her spouse had engaged in vile and deceitful practices'.[24]

Nowadays women are generally not so innocent before marriage, but they are certainly still susceptible to the shock-effect of the carefully deployed dildo. In some cultures the naked vulva has been regarded as uniquely terrifying — the mythical snake-haired gorgon's head, for example, may be a symbol of it — but more often the role of unique object of terror has been taken by the erect penis. "Panic" is etymologically the terror inspired by the enormous phallus of the god Pan. Women are able to borrow this effect by use of a strap-on dildo:

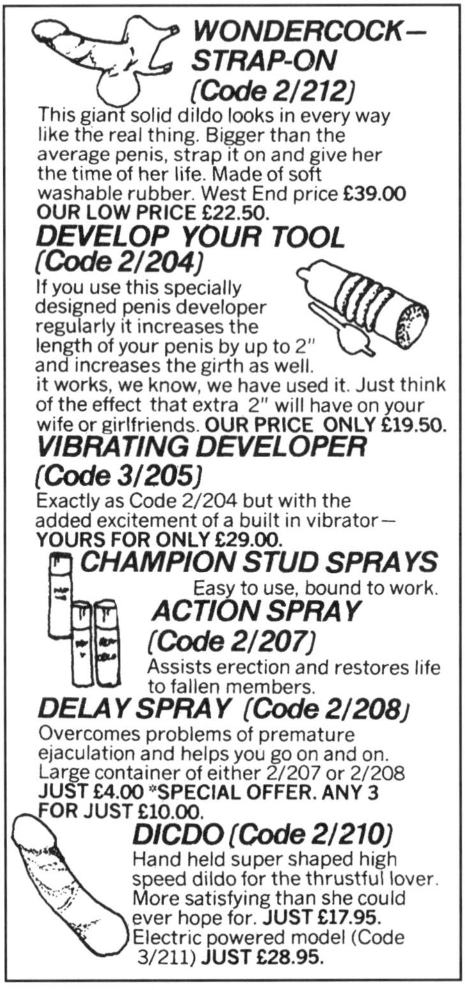

> Love should be an art, but sex is an act of basic theatre. Sex is crude, which doesn't mean that it isn't delightful, but we should not seek to pretend that it is anything but a grand, physical gesture. So, when I have a girl ready and willing, I always withdraw, telling her to undress. Then I put on one of my dildoes and return to confront my little victim. The look of shock on their faces is magnificent. Often they want to cry off, but I always assert myself, and eventually they are begging me to use my manly priapus upon them.[25]

This idea of sex as theatre affords me a rather contrived *segue* into the life of the sexual theatricist *par excellence*, the Marquis de Sade — and yet the role of dildos in de Sade's life was fundamentally physical. He used them not for affect, but for effect, that is, as aids to enhanced pleasure in the continual round of masturbation with which he warded off boredom and despair during his prison sentences. In letters to his wife

Renée-Pélagie that are quoted in Lever's **Marquis de Sade: A Biography**, he gave detailed instructions about the dimensions and construction of the *étuis* ("cases") and *flacons* ("flasks") he wanted to be commissioned from "carpenters in the faubourg Saint-Antoine".[26] Unfortunately Renée-Pélagie found that "the workmen take me for a madwoman when I speak to them of cases of that size", and the case she eventually sent to de Sade was "smaller than the one you want." Of a later case mentioned by Renée-Pélagie in a letter to her husband, Sade noted in the margin, "And the whole thing up the arse, quite comfortably, unfortunately too comfortably."[27]

These embarrassing commissions — the workmen, receiving "her orders with knowing smiles" according to Lever, very likely thought she was undertaking them on her own behalf — were surely a small but significant part of what brought Renée-Pélagie to request a separation from her husband in 1790; henceforth, de Sade's dildos would have to be improvised by de Sade himself. And successfully: in 1803, incarcerated again after his release during the Revolution, de Sade was transferred from the prison of Sainte-Pélagie to Bicêtre, and a police search of his hurriedly vacated cell

> turned up an enormous instrument that he had fabricated with wax and used on himself, for the instrument retained traces of its guilty insertion.[28]

Guilty? It's difficult to imagine that the marquis would have felt so. Anything nature urges us to is, by definition, natural, and in this case, he, or the characters of his satires, at least, may have been right. Human beings are not the only mammals to employ substitutes for the penis on themselves and on each other. We came in on the speculation that dildos are millions of years old. Let's go out on the probability that they are far older:

> The female porcupine (*Erethizon dorsatum*) is only on heat for four hours of the year. Although she feels sexual urges some months earlier and begins pressing sticks against her vulva, all of her sexual activity is crammed into that brief period.[29]

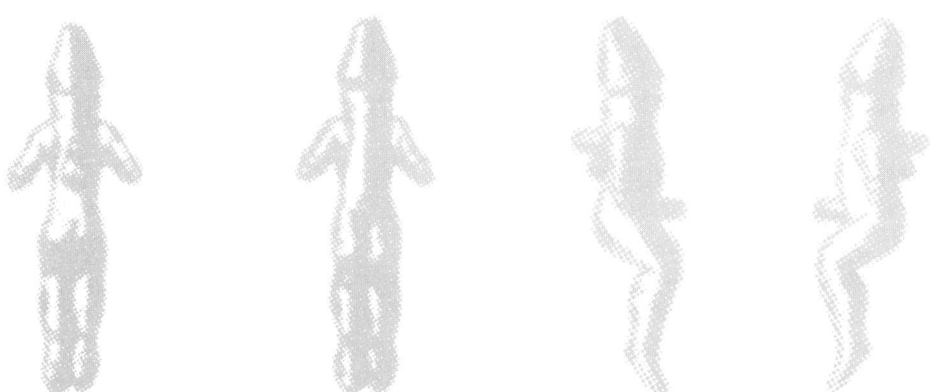

THE REVENGE OF CELLULOSE

FROM MOVING IMAGE TO PRINTED PAGE (AND BACK AGAIN)

I'm not particularly interested in moving pictures, and if I never see another film or television programme I won't be complaining. And yet I do greatly enjoy something that would never have existed without TV and the cinema. That something is the novelization.

"Novelization" is an odd and, some would say, ugly word. I'm not so sure myself: I find it hard to see the harm in a new word that describes a new thing. A novelization is a book that's based on a film or TV script. They didn't exist a hundred years ago; they do now, and if we're going to call them something, novelization doesn't seem the worst possible choice. And, as I've said, I greatly enjoy them. In a not very serious and not very obsessive fashion, I've started to collect them. In fact, I reserve a special space for them on my bookshelves.

To find its way into that space, a book has to be a true novelization. I've bought books thinking that they were books-based-on-films and subsequently discovered that they were in fact books-later-turned-into-films, and although I now prize one or two of them, they don't get shelved next to **Another Stir of Porridge** or **Are You Being Served? The Book of the Film**. And the funny thing is that there seems to be a rule of thumb in operation with books that get turned into films. If a book has been turned into a film, but the film is more famous than the book, the book isn't usually very good, as a book. **Picnic at Hanging Rock**, for example. **M*A*S*H**. **Midnight Express**. Novelizations, on the other, are usually good, as books, and are often better than the films or TV programmes to which they owe their existence. **Bonnie & Clyde** is the only novelization I've bought that I haven't thought worth making part of my collection. The only one, in fact, that I've never finished reading. It's undoubtedly not going to stay alone, but for now it forms the sole glaring exception to my other rule of thumb: books based on film or TV scripts are usually good.[1] Often very good. Here, then, is my guided tour to the Novelization, and to why I think it possesses the peculiar charm it does.

Counting my collection for the purposes of this article, I find I have thirty or so of the Real Thing, and three or four pseudo-novelizations. Pseudo-novelizations are books based on characters and situations from film and TV,

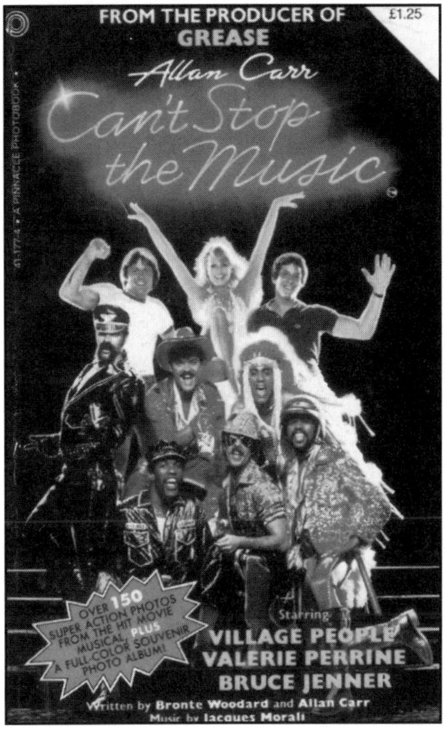

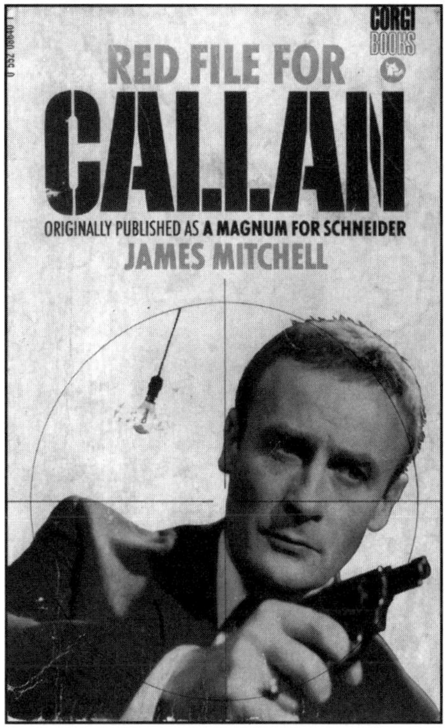

though not on actual films or programmes. Alan Dean Foster's **Splinter of the Mind's Eye** is a pure pseudo-novelization. Drawing inspiration from the **Star Wars** film cycle but not based on a real film, it's enjoyable enough as piece of adolescent space-opera and even has some weird atmosphere to it, but it's enjoyable mostly as an ordinary SF novel would be. James Mitchell's **Red File For Callan** is another pseudo-novelization. Based on the secret agent character Callan created by Mitchell and played on TV by Edward Woodward, it's again enjoyable, and even more than that, but it was written as a novel, and could easily stand alone as such without any support from a famous and well-made and acted TV series. Nonetheless, although it is not the Real Thing, I'm going to be returning to it to illustrate one of the points I raise about the Novelization pure and simple.

I'll start making those points now. The first, which is so obvious that whether I like making it or not it has to be made, is that novelizations are enjoyable because a lot of the work has already been done for you. Books contain words. Words have meanings. They refer to objects, people, expressions, colours, sounds, tones of voice, and so on. In most books, you have to put life into those meanings yourself. You have to imagine what a character looks like, how he moves, what his voice sounds like, and so on. In a novelization, you don't. Reading **James Bond & Moonraker**, I can picture and hear what's going on very easily because it's simply a question of remembering what happened in the film, not of imagining it for myself.

And yes, that does mean what it says. I don't collect novelizations simply for the sake of it. I have to have seen what they're based on before I buy them. I wouldn't bother otherwise. I like reading books that re-create the easy-on-the-brain visuals of TV and cinema, because at the same time they do things that TV and cinema can't do, or at least can't do very well or very often. Like characterization. Like motivation. Like psychological subtlety. Like offering you a chance to know what's going on inside someone's head as well as on his face. Take the Callan TV series and the pseudo-novelization **Red File For Callan**. In both series and book, the relationship between Callan and a middle-aged criminal called Lonely is very important. It's a funny relationship — funny ha-ha and funny peculiar — but there's a moment in the book where something is revealed about it that startles you, and that would be very hard to convey as well or as fully on the TV screen.

Callan has been kidnapped by a Greek master-criminal as a result of Lonely's carelessness. He has had to kill a man called Arthur to escape. He then goes to visit Lonely and, on the orders of his chief, demonstrates what will happen to Lonely if he's careless again by striking him "just below the sternum":

> Lonely fell to his knees, retching with an agony beyond bearing.
>
> 'I'm sorry,' said Callan. 'I really am sorry. But they said I had to, old son. Just so as you wouldn't forget what happened to Arthur.'
>
> He left then, and Lonely stayed on his knees, waiting for the pain to become bearable. When it did, he collapsed into a chair. Suddenly he realized that he had always hated Mr Callan. But it made no difference. No difference at all. Mr Callan was still the strong one.[2]

This has something of the impact of the last line of Orwell's **Nineteen Eighty-four**, but the difficulties of re-creating this impact on the TV screen are obvious. Lonely could grimace at Callan's departing back, but then his face would already be occupied in conveying his agony. If the pain wasn't so bad, and he did have facial space for a grimace, the viewer isn't likely to understand what the grimace truly means. In fact, if the pain isn't so bad, they're likely to be right in interpreting it as expressing anger or annoyance, rather than hatred. No, Lonely has to be badly hurt in order to realize his true feelings for Callan. The book can deal fully with both his physical and his mental reactions; the TV screen would have to express both through the former, and would lose a great deal by doing so. Chalk one up to the pseudo-novelization.

Chalk one up to the novelization, because you come across this sort of thing constantly in the genre. The film and TV screen is a very impatient thing. It has to be filled constantly, it has to change constantly, and it has to use pictures or the spoken word, and for all these reasons it doesn't have the time or the flexibility for asides and additions that are quickly and easily supplied on the printed page. This time take Martin Noble's novelization of the film **Bullshot**, which is a farce-cum-satire on Bulldog Drummond and other superman characters from the 1930s. The book is better than the film, I think, and part of

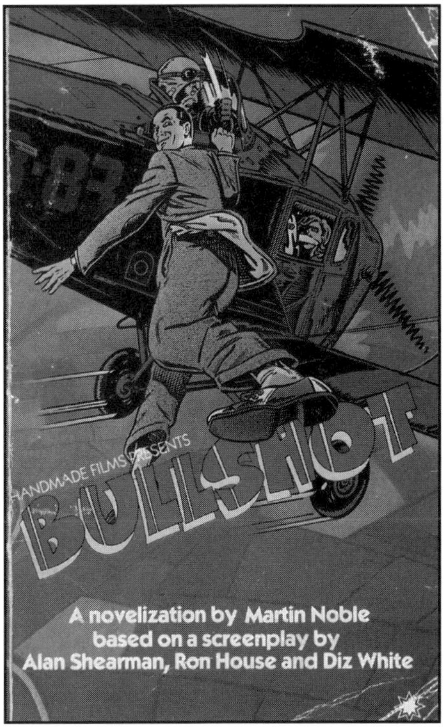

what helps it to be are the asides. The hero is called Bullshot Crummond and at one point in both book and film he is shown visiting the Royal Society of Scientific Discoverers. In the book Crummond is able to muse on the offerings he has himself made there:

> his underwater shooting umbrella had not only established itself as a technical classic of subaquatic engineering but had also made a decent contribution towards the safety of the human race in fishing up the abominable Scandinavian midget out of his icy hiding hole deep below the murky waters of the Skaggerak.[3]

How on earth would you put this onto celluloid? A flashback? Well, not really. It isn't important enough, for a start, and this sort of aside occurs throughout the book. If the underwater shooting umbrella and the Scandinavian Midget get a flashback, what about the Bolivian Hermaphrodite, the Arabian Lunatic, and the Mongolian Mangler? The film would have more flashbacks than action to flashback from. The thing is that although individually these asides aren't important and so the film can safely ignore each of them, as a whole they are important and the film loses something by not being able to incorporate them.

Technically speaking, though, it could be done. In some cases, however, the book can do things that the film or TV programme can't. Alan B'Stard MP, the "New Statesman", visits an S&M brothel in both book and TV series. A prostitute starts to beat him with a cane:

> 'You silly trollop!' I grabbed her arm and took the cane away from her. 'I'm not a masochist. I'm a sadist! I pay to beat you!'
>
> 'I'm sorry.' The silly bitch began to cry. 'I'm new here.'

So far, so funny, but the TV series can't go on to complete the joke. It doesn't have the time, and it doesn't have the balls. They've been cut off by the TV watchdogs — this is British TV, after all. The book carries on regardless:

> I took Chantelle in my arms to soothe away her tears. I tickled her gently to make her laugh, and when she was her cheerful self again, I gave her a good thrashing.[4]

This sort of thing doesn't only work with humour, of course. It can increase the impact of what happened on the screen in all manner of ways. For example, in **Return of the Jedi** there's an action scene in which Han Solo and Luke Skywalker battle their way out of the intergalactic villain Salacious Crumb's desert HQ. Buried in the sand outside there's a giant creature down whose metre-wide maw various extras are sent screaming. Horrible enough in the film, I suppose, but the book adds the detail that the creature's digestive processes take centuries to work, and that its food is kept alive throughout that time.

Well, actually, it's a bit too silly a detail to be very horrible, but it illustrates the point. Salacious Crumb himself illustrates another point, because his name is an example of a kind of humour that TV and film aren't very good at conveying. I'm not sure if his name is mentioned at all in the film; you can't avoid it in the book.[5] And even when film and TV are good at conveying something, they are often matched and bettered by the novelization. Dialogue is a very important part of film and TV in all kinds of ways. Again, I'll choose humour, illustrating the point this time from the **Porridge** TV and book series. On TV, Fletch (played by Ronnie Barker) is the central character, and his laconic wit is at the heart of why the series is so good. On TV, though, his wit has to be conveyed through dialogue; in the books, "written" by "him" in the first person, you get the wit not only in his dialogue but also in the descriptions and scene-setting. On TV, Ronnie Barker's acting ability, inevitably, isn't always matched by the acting ability of the supporting players; in the books, this doesn't matter, because the other characters and what they do are all re-created by Fletch's narration. There's an evenness of excellence to the book: your memory of occasionally less than excellent performances on TV is set against the fact that this memory being prompted by a witty and skilful narrator. What made the TV series so good — Ronnie Barker's performance — survives into the books because it's what you see and hear as you read; what marred the TV series — some of the supporting performances — is no longer important. Reading the **Porridge** books in some ways is better than watching the series, though the books wouldn't be as good if you hadn't watched the series first. A perfect example of what makes some novelizations so enjoyable.

But, of course, there are some things that film and TV are better at doing than books. The first obvious example that comes to mind is from **Bullshot**. (It's probably pointless to say this, but I'd advise you to skip the following section if you've never seen the film and you don't want to spoil a great moment for yourself when you do). Bullshot Crummond is rowing in the Henley regatta, where he has an lunch appointment with Miss Rosemary Fenton to discuss the kidnapping of her brilliant scientist father by the evil Black Baron of Blitzberg. Miss Fenton is watching the races:

> Suddenly a shout went up and the crowd turned their attention to the river. Between the boaters and parasols she could make out a rowing eight moving downstream. Their oars dipped and turned in the brilliant, sparkling water as, through a shiny megaphone, their cox urged them on.

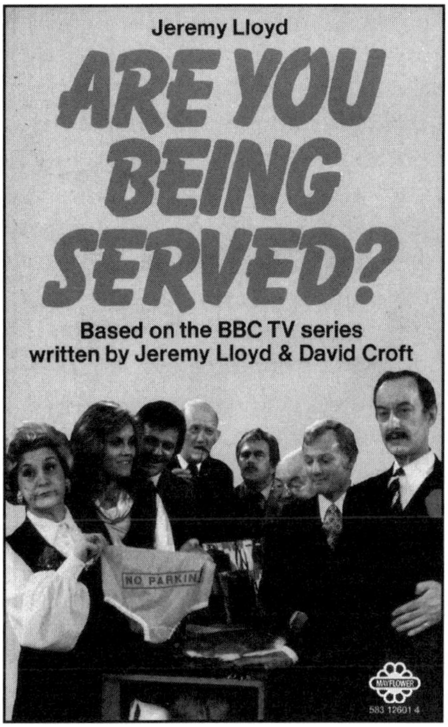

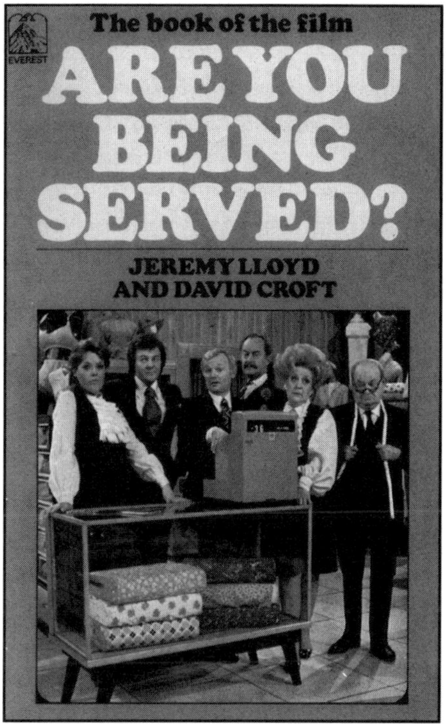

Then another boat came into view. To Rosemary's amazement, and that of the crowd, who began to buzz with excitement, she saw only one man rowing.[6]

That man being Bullshot Crummond, who has lost the rest of his crew to influenza and who goes on to win the race with ease over an utterly exhausted full eight-man crew in the other boat. The scene is startlingly funny in the film, much less so in the book, particularly, I would imagine, if you've never seen the film. Visual puns and jokes don't always transfer well to the printed page.

Neither do aural ones. The TV series **A Very Peculiar Practice**, for example, had a running gag based on the occasional mysterious and fleeting appearance of a pair of nuns who carried a ghetto-blaster playing Iron Maiden: visual and aural puns that don't transfer well to the printed page. In the **New Statesman** novelization, there's a visual pun that doesn't transfer at all. That is to say, there isn't. In the series, part of the joke of Alan B'Stard's sexual selfishness and inadequacy is that his wife Sarah is having a lesbian affair with his parliamentary agent Beatrice behind his back. In other words, he doesn't know about it and so the first person novelization can't mention it. In the series, we can have the joke of Sarah and Beatrice in bed together while Sarah talks to Alan on the phone; in the book, the closest we can get is:

I sat there thinking about Beatrice, who doubtless fancied me as much as I fancied her. Pity she wouldn't mix business with pleasure. I recalled yesterday at dinner at Sir Roland's when I'd squeezed

Beatrice's thigh under the table and encountered Sarah's hand entwined in hers on her lap. Ah well, at least it was nice to see old school friends still so close.[7]

I suppose you could say that the book is more subtle, but the point about Alan B'Stard and the TV series he stars in is that neither is subtle. Then again, subtlety is perhaps the word that best describes what often makes novelizations better than what they're novelizations of. Characters and situations are more detailed, more rounded, less three-dimensional. Characterization and motivation are fuller, worked at longer and more effectively, and come off better. Things that are opaque or liable to misinterpretation on screen are transparent and easy to understand on the page. A lot of what's good on screen survives onto the page, and sometimes gets better, or we're given more of it.

Which is ignoring all the other advantages books possess over moving pictures. And perhaps I'm wrong about the need to have seen a film before you read the book of the film. Perhaps it's better if you haven't seen what a novelization is based on. Certainly I've never seen the TV programme behind one of my favourite novelizations, Richard Carpenter's **Catweazle**. And I don't really want to, because I suspect that it's never going to be as good as the book. How good a book is depends on how good the author is. How good a film or TV programme is depends to a large extent on how much money is spent on it. But at least if I do ever see **Catweazle** the series, it won't matter that much if it spoils **Catweazle** the book. I mean, the book couldn't have existed without the series, and that will do a lot to remove the sense of annoyance I'm sure a lot of us have felt on seeing a favourite book translated to the screen.

Because the problem is that a good book is rarely bettered by the film made from it. The problem is that images, even — or especially — clumsy and ugly ones, are much stronger than words. I've recently re-read **Lord of the Rings** without seeing any of the images planted in my brain by a film version that I last watched ten years or more ago. It's taken a long time for me to be able to do that. I'm not sure whether the film was any good, but its visual techniques were interesting and innovative ones, and some of its images were very powerful. The problem is that they weren't my images — they weren't what I had made for myself out of J.R.R. Tolkien's words. There are only three ways to avoid books being ruined by films like this. One is not to see the films. The second is to see only films that aren't very faithful to the books — the James Bond series is a good example. The third is to read books that wouldn't have existed in the first place without the films. In other words, novelizations are the revenge of cellulose on celluloid. Can you think of a better one?

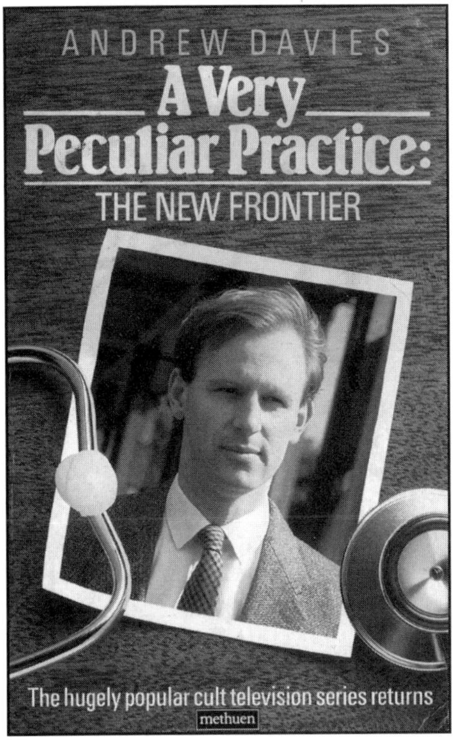

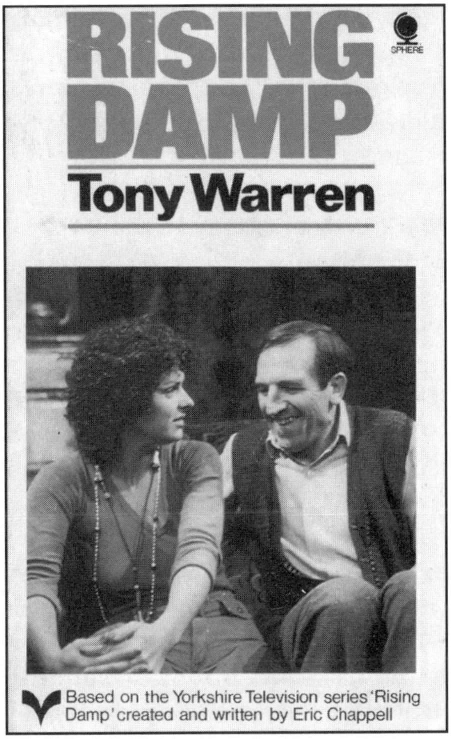

A Brief Look at a Few More

Alien/Aliens

Alan Dean Foster

J.G. Ballard has famously expressed his regret that he never took up the offer to novelize the first film in this SF series, and although Foster does his usual competent job with it instead, what can one do but concur with J.G.B.? The novelization of *Aliens*, the sequel, is an obnoxious piece of work, but could hardly have been otherwise given the obnoxious and cretinously violent film.

Bullshot

Martin Noble

My favourite novelization, although I no longer enjoy it as much as I used to do and I see more and more clearly how Martin Noble gets bored with everything in the last dozen or so pages. Still, as an example of how the printed page wins eight times out of ten over the silver screen, the book really is hard to beat — as is the film for examples of the two times out of ten that the silver screen wins over the printed page.

Are You Being Served?

Jeremy Lloyd & David Croft

Not a great programme all in all, but then again there were so many series of it that you could hardly expect it to be. Still, like the *Carry On* films — only a little less so — you knew exactly what you were going to get from *Are You Being Served?* and, despite yourself, you liked it. Well, I did anyway. And what did you get? Good old repressed British smut that ran the gamut all the way from the "A" of Mrs Slocombe's pussy to the "B" of John Inman's camp. But the jokes don't transfer particularly well to print, and, worse, neither do the characters. Worth reading all the same.

Are You Being Served? The Book of the Film
Jeremy Lloyd & David Croft
The 'seventies were, by all accounts, the heyday of split beaver and dildo insertion in British porn mags, with *Whitehouse* and the like setting up a kind of cultural rip-tide that sucked British TV into hitherto unknown regions of coarseness and filth. The explanation, I suppose, was that writers had stopped being scared of talking about sex and hadn't started being scared about offending minorities; the result was programmes like *On the Buses* and *Are You Being Served?*. *A.Y.B.S.? The Film*, as you'd expect from something intended for cinema release, was even worse. I remember being genuinely startled by this when I saw it on TV: expecting the long-range-sniping-with-occasional-brief-sallies of *Carry On*'s strategy of bad taste, what I got was a head-long Charge of the Shite Brigade against my aesthetic cannon. This film is so coarse that if it were sandpaper, you'd be able to use it to take the rough edges off the Himalayas. If you want to see more artistic mileage made out of excrement and the lower bodily functions than you ever imagined possible, read de Sade's *120 Days of Sodom*. If you can't read *120 Days of Sodom*, watch *Are You Being Served? The Film*. If you can't watch the film, read this book, although it is, alas, a very poor third.

Catweazle
Richard Carpenter
This would be my favourite novelization if I could regard it as such, but I can't, because I never saw the TV programme it's based on: my family moved back to the UK from overseas while *Catweazle* the series was still working its way through the two-year gap between a series being screened here and being screened there. Although I first read it when I was very young, I still love the book: what I lose from being a cynical and twisted adult I partly get back from being able to see things such as how book and series were actually some pretty clever propaganda for the Magickal Arts. How many budding Aleister Crowleys first took up the athame under *Catweazle*'s influence, I wonder?

Dr Strangelove, or How I Learned to Stop Worrying & Love the Bomb
Peter George
Good film, readable enough book, but why does all the political and moral point-making have to be so bleeding bloody obvious? Forget the nuclear arsenal for a moment: what about the very blunt and very heavy instrument book-and-film use against their viewers and readers?

Dirty Harry
Philip Rock
Not as good as the film and, most annoyingly, doesn't contain the "Listen punk, this is a .375 Magnum..." speech. Or whatever calibre it is.

Minder
Leon Griffiths
Minder[sic]

Anthony Masters

Minder: Back Again

Anthony Masters

Leon Griffiths created the series, which I never fully enjoyed until Dennis Waterman left, but wrote the poorest of these three novelizations of it. He seemed to be trying to make some sort of point about the complexities and hypocrisies of the British class system, and didn't do it very well — and you really do have to do that sort of thing well. Anthony Masters, on the other hand, concentrates on making the most of Arthur Daley, who is definitely one of the great fictional characters in British popular culture over the past hundred years. As with other greats like Frank Richards' Billy Bunter and George MacDonald Fraser's Flashman, the joke is to create an amoral personality for someone and then get him to act in it: George Cole was about as good as they come in supplying the personality on screen, Anthony Masters about as good as they come in re-capturing it for the printed page.

Raiders of the Lost Ark

Campbell Black

Indiana Jones & the Temple of Doom

James Kahn

Indiana Jones & the Last Crusade

Rob McGregor

I don't want to get too pretentious about this...but you can't always get what you want and the truth is that, with the partial exception of the first in the series, these are the sort of film that is much less interesting as entertainment than it is as sociological commentary — I thought the attitude towards Hinduism and the Exotic East displayed in *Indiana Jones & The Temple of Doom* was very dodgy indeed, for example. And so the novelizations are less interesting as entertainment than they are as a means of somewhat more leisurely reviewing the psychological and political workings of the films. They also possess the great advantage of not directly exposing you to the "acting" of Mr Harrison Ford.

The Black Hole

Alan Dean Foster

This was a Disney film, and I don't actually find the fact that Fred West liked Disney films a good argument for the absurdity of the "films influence madmen" school of censorship: there's something deeply sick about the Disney empire and its products. I can't really remember properly what this particular one of them was like but it certainly had the same plot as the book, which means that it was very likely much less sick than it was strange. I might almost go so far as to say "haunting": crazed scientific geniuses are so clichéd it's become a cliché to say that they are, but the c.s.g. here, alone but for his robots in a space station orbiting a black hole, is a memorable one, as is his sadistic robot lieutenant-in-chief, Maximillian. And not only does one of the heroes die, but the rest of the heroes don't live happily ever after: at the end of the book, they're inside a black hole undergoing something most peculiar. In other words, there are some interesting and original ideas in, admittedly, a flawed book and somewhat more flawed film, and I can't really think what Disney were doing getting involved with it all.

The Rise & Fall of Reginald Perrin
David Nobs
I used to like this book a lot, which I read a long time before I ever saw any of the bad series, and actually thought it was rather profound as well as being very funny. I'm really not so sure nowadays.

Rising Damp
Tony Warren
Leonard Rossiter was wrong for the role of Reginald Perrin, but perfect for the role of the miserly, scheming landlord Rigsby in *Rising Damp*. The novelization is good more because it reminds you of the characters and the way they delivered their lines than in its own right, but Tony Warren — the homosexual ex-alcoholic creator of Granada Television's long-running Northern soap-opera *Coronation Street* — is also pretty successful at creating all the background detail that you know must be there but films and TV programmes never get around to or never can get around to. Interior monologues, the dim and distant pasts of main characters, the personality and background of minor characters, that sort of thing.

Terminator 2: Judgment Day
Randall Frakes
One of those films that make you wonder whether there isn't something in all the recurring bilge about the moral disintegration of Western civilization after all. "The Amoral Thug As Super-Hero" just about sums it up, and although I hate having to concern myself with the lo-IQ adolescents who cheer this sort of thing at the cinema and then go home and play the tie-in computer-game on their Nintendos, what else can you do? We have to share the same planet, after all. The book is valuable exactly so far as it confirms the repulsive message of the film, and absolutely no further. Part of the additional material it carries is the fact that the heroine trained with the Nicaraguan Contras as part of her "Prepare for the Apocalypse" programme. What more needs to be said about the implicit political message *Terminator 2* and other films like it are conveying?

The New Statesman
Anna Morgan
Good series that was driven through great snowdrifts of careless plotting and obvious humour by the sheer energy of Rik Mayall's lead performance and the sheer variety of ways the scriptwriters found for him to express Alan B'Stard's amorality. Like the novelization of *Rising Damp*, this book is good both at capturing what made the TV programme enjoyable and at creating new material to go with it, and it might well make you laugh even if you've never seen the series.

Can't Stop the Music
Bronte Woodard & Allan Carr
Photo-novelization of the film, and listen, you don't even want me to *hint* what it's like. They'll be making possession of this sort of thing a serious criminal offence before very long. If they don't, they bloody well ought to.

ENDGAME

MASS PSYCHOLOGY, ASTROPHYSICS AND RAGNARÖK

And when he had opened the seventh seal, there was silence in heaven about the space of half an hour.

Which is, in some ways, the most powerful sentence in the Book of Revelation. What happens after the silence, in the remainder of chapter eight and beginning of chapter nine, might seem to fit very well with the crazed and disturbing imagery elsewhere, yet if you come to these verses fresh from a book called **The Cosmic Winter**, they seem disturbing not in their psychoticism but in their possible realism.[1]

Cosmic Winter suggests that the earth is periodically subject to bombardment by giant fragments of cometary debris:

> If [one] struck the ocean it would generate within seconds a cavity in the ocean water and underlying bed about 40 kilometres wide. ... A column of water, steam, rocks and dust many kilometres high would be hurled into the air, and waves about five kilometres high would rise around the impact site. [pg. 220]

> *And the second angel sounded, and as it were a great mountain burning with fire was cast into the sea ... And the third part of the creatures which were in the sea, and had life, died ...* [Revelation viii, 8-9]

> In the event of a land impact ... the huge fireball would be too energetic to be contained by the atmosphere. Laden with dust, it would rise upwards at several kilometres per second ... Within minutes it would soar to an altitude of several hundred kilometres, in the high stratosphere ... Closer to the ground, the intense heat of impact would generate fires over a wide area. ... Plumes of smoke would rise up to 10 kilometres (7 miles) into the atmosphere. [pg. 261-2]

> *And the fifth angel sounded, and I saw a star fall from heaven unto earth: and to him was given the key of the bottomless pit. And he opened the bottomless pit and there arose a smoke out of the pit, as the smoke of a great furnace; and the sun and the air were darkened by reason of the smoke of the air.* [ix, 1-2]

One of the sources of evidence used by **Cosmic Winter** to argue its thesis is such Biblical imagery, which it claims is not mythical or symbolic but descriptive of real events in the relatively near past. Some of the things described in the Book of Revelation do indeed seem stranger than fiction:

> And the first angel sounded, and there followed hail and fire mingled with blood, and they were cast upon the earth.

The association of hail and fire does not seem an obvious one either in this verse or in what has long been presumed to be its inspiration, the fifth plague of Egypt described in Exodus ix, 24:

> And there was hail, and fire mingled with the hail, very grievous.

However, the size and speed of descent of a large meteorite can easily mean that its interior is still frozen from the extreme cold of outer space on impact, in complete contrast to its blazing exterior; **Cosmic Winter** remarks of these two verses:

> The freezing hail is interesting in view of the icy nature of comets. Meteorites are known to have frozen the ground around them on impact.

And this seems a better explanation for the Bible's choice of words — "fire mingled with the hail" — than the more traditional "desolating thunderstorm with hail" mentioned in the discussion of the verse from Exodus in **Peake's Commentary on the Bible**.[2]

In Revelation, moreover, the chronology seems strikingly realistic, matching very well with **Cosmic Winter** 's description of "storms" of cometary debris that periodically cross the earth's orbit. During one of these storms there would come first a swarm of icy meteorites, terrifyingly intense but not annihilating, followed sooner or later by the truly giant fragments: first the "hail and fire mingled with blood", followed sooner or later by the "great mountain burning with fire" and the

> great star from heaven, burning as it were a lamp, [falling] upon the third part of the waters [viii, 10]

It's strange in fact how Revelation's apparent synthesis of older images achieves this realism: the hail and fire come from Exodus, in which there is no mention of falling stars, and the falling stars from Daniel and Isaiah, in which there is no mention of hail and fire.[3]

A passage in Revelation that doesn't draw on an older part of the Bible seems to make the realistic picture of celestial bombardment complete. We are told of the "great star from heaven, burning as it were a lamp" that "the name of the star is called Wormwood" (viii, 11), and of the waters on which it fell that they "became as wormwood: and many men died of the waters, because they were

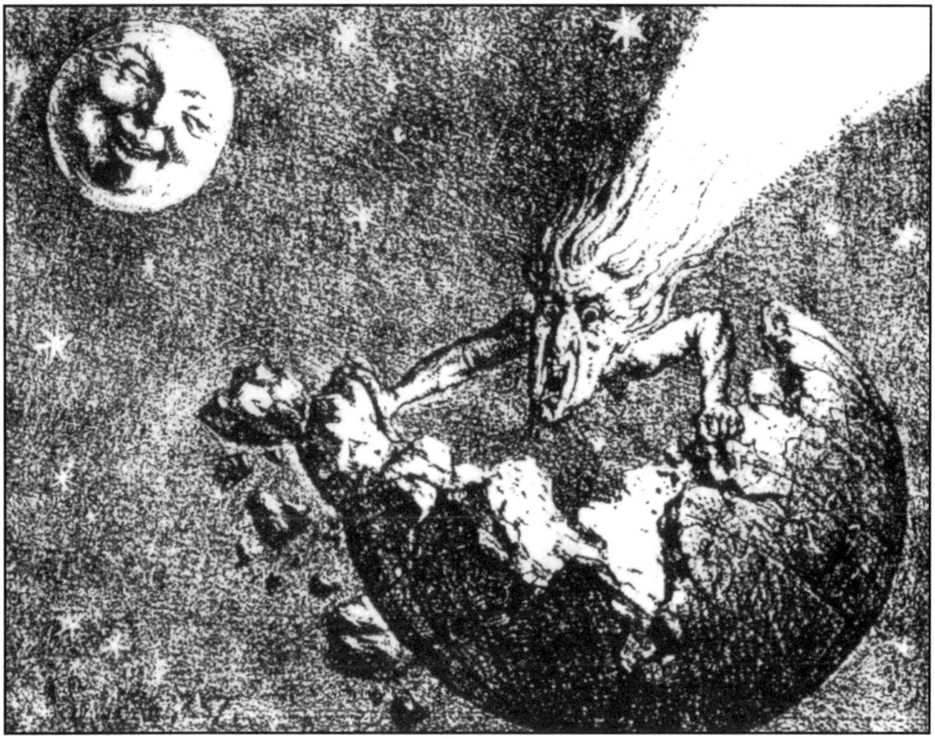

made bitter". This isn't paralleled earlier in the Bible, but it may nonetheless represent another strand of the folk-memories of celestial bombardment. **Cosmic Winter** comments of the "water poisoned by the fireball" that its "possible interpretation" is

> open to conjecture but widespread in myth, e.g. Python [an enormous fiery serpent slain by Apollo in Greek myth] has a "noxious interior". [pg. 195]

However, elsewhere in the book a possible explanation is provided in the fact that some meteorites show over-abundances of metals like tin, iridium, caesium, nickel, antimony and silver:[4] perhaps Revelation's "many men" have died of heavy metal poisoning. Or from the "cyanides and other poisons" mentioned as cometary constituents in Michael Allaby's and James Lovelock's **The Great Extinction**, which explores a similar cosmo-cataclysmic theme.[5]

Or perhaps, of course, as is no doubt suggested somewhere in the pages of Erich von Däniken or his imitators, they have died of radiation poisoning after the crash-landing of a nuclear-powered spacecraft. The truth is that such use of ancient texts out of their full context — and their full context is inevitably, by the passage of time, very difficult to reconstruct — cannot be a very certain foundation on which to base modern scientific theories. Perhaps these verses of the Book of Revelation, and the older verses they borrow from or are influenced by, are symbolic or allegorical. The star is called "Wormwood" and kills many men not because it is a cometary fragment literally poisonous with cyanides or a nuclear-powered spaceship, but because in the Old Testament:

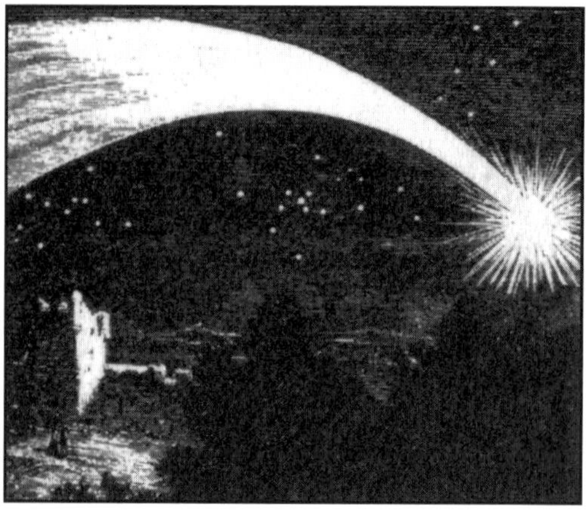

> the term is always used metaphorically to denote the bitterness of injustice or the fruits of idolatry or Divine chastisement.[6]

But it remains true that one of the best descriptions of the way late twentieth-century science suggests our world might end is provided in words written nearly two thousand years ago. Do not doubt, by the way, that the end of the world is precisely what it will be as far as the human race is concerned if the earth is hit again by a giant meteor or swarm of meteors as it has been many times in the past. The so-called Tunguska event of 1906, an enormous explosion in a remote region of Siberia, is believed to have been caused by a meteor that could easily have accounted for the entire population of Belgium had it fallen on Brussels, and has been weighed in on seismographic evidence as having an impact energy of 25 megatonnes, or the equivalent of 25 million tonnes of the explosive TNT. It seems very likely that the moon, with "an effective target area ... a twentieth that of the earth", was hit on the evening of June 25th, 1178, by a meteor with an impact energy of 100,000 megatonnes. Landing on the earth, such a meteor would probably

> cause prompt destruction of life over continental dimensions [and probably] have even more disastrous effects through a global climatic catastrophe.[7]

Probability would become certainty if such a meteor came with a similarly sized companion or two, and civilization might still be wrecked for many centuries by a cosmic handbagging on a much smaller scale. Particularly if, as is perfectly possible, we are able to see what's coming to us. Comets are by no means the only boy-racers in the solar system: certain asteroids have orbits that take regularly them back and forth across the earth's path:

> An asteroid in the Taurid orbit ... coming out of the night sky would be visible in binoculars for about six hours before impact. By the time it was a naked-eye object it would be at most half an hour from collision.[8]

Binoculars are not of course the only or the most powerful astronomical instruments that will be available, and so it seems likely that we may have days or even weeks to contemplate a fate that at the very best it would be only "marginally within the capacity of present-day technology to divert".[9] One small asteroid, detected with plenty of time to spare, might be warded off with suitably adapted nuclear missiles; if it were not small, or not detected with time to spare, or not alone, we would face something unlike anything else faced by the human race in its history. Billions of people would know for certain when they and the rest of their world were going to end: a cheap computer program using basic equations from Newtonian physics would be more than sufficient to supply a place, day and hour, perhaps even a minute, of impact.

I don't believe that we would wait quietly and I don't believe that any of the well-known fictions based on the possibility to date have been realistic about this fact. H.G. Wells' short story "The Star", for example, presents a world menaced by the "one vast mass of incandescence" that results from a collision between Neptune and a rogue planet from the interstellar wastes. The mass falls sunwards and a mathematician predicts that it will pass very near the earth with cataclysmic results. After a period of scepticism, it becomes obvious from the sky that he is right, but Wells does not examine the consequences for the human race of this universal knowledge, and quickly passes over the five days of relative calm we have to absorb it to examine the climatic and seismic horrors that overtake us afterwards.

Wells, however, was writing before the Second World War for an Anglo-Saxon audience, and could hardly have depicted truths about human nature that he was surely very well aware of. What about writers enjoying the greater artistic freedoms of the decades after the war? The science-fiction writer Arthur C. Clarke has written about the threat of giant meteors in at least two of his novels. **Rendezvous With Rama** (1973) opens like this:

> Sooner or later it was bound to happen ... At 09.46 GMT on the morning of 11th September, in the exceptionally beautiful summer of 2077, most of the inhabitants of Europe saw a dazzling fireball appear in the eastern sky. Within seconds it was brighter than the sun, and as it moved across the heavens — at first in utter silence — it left behind it a churning column of dust and smoke.
>
> Somewhere above Austria it began to disintegrate, producing a series of concussions so violent that more than a million people had their hearing permanently damaged. They were the lucky ones.
>
> Moving at fifty kilometres a second, a thousand tons of rock and metal impacted on the plains of northern Italy, destroying in a few flaming moments the labour of centuries. The cities of Padua and Venice were wiped from the face of the earth; and the glories of Venice sank forever beneath the sea as the waters of the Adriatic came thundering landwards after the hammerblow from space.[10]

But there was no warning of this disaster, and no warning means no interesting questions about societal breakdown. In **The Hammer of God** (1993), on the other hand, Clarke writes about the discovery of an earth-bound asteroid called Kali, and the race against time to knock it off course. He faces the question of the effects of this on mass psychology, but the novel (really a glorified short story) is set almost entirely away from the earth and references to these effects are glancing. Two members of the crew of *Goliath*, the spaceship attempting to deflect Kali, discuss their mission like this:

> "Let's hope all this doomsday talk is a waste of breath. And unless we can make them believe that Earth is going to be saved, a lot of people down there are going to go crazy."
>
> "They already have, Bob. Did you see the suicide statistics in the last quarterly report? They've fallen off now, but think of the panics, the rioting, that could happen in the next few months. Earth could be wrecked, even if Kali sails harmlessly past."[11]

The "doomsday talk" is coming from an extremist sect of Chrislam, a hybrid of Christianity and Islam Clarke imagines emerging from the encounter between the two religions during the 1990 Gulf War. Founded, in a tongue-in-cheek Clarkean twist, by one Ruby Goldenberg (a.k.a Fatima Magdalene), a female addition to the long line of Jewish charlatans who have poisoned the world with their ideologies[12], Chrislam is the first "Religion of the Byte", and has given birth by the time of Kali to an extremist sect called the "Reborn", who welcome the impending catastrophe as part of God's plan and go so far as to sabotage the first efforts to avert it. Apart from this sabotage, and the other opportunities the sect affords for some characteristic digs from Clarke at religion, not very much is made of the Reborn, and there's no suggestion that they have any competition from any rival sects or cults or that they or their rivals have any hand in events when Kali is split in two by a dud nuclear missile and:

> All that the SPACEGUARD computers could now guarantee was that Kali 2 [one of the two fragments] would not make a direct impact on any major landmass. That was some reassurance, but not enough to prevent mass panics, thousands of suicides, and partial breakdowns of law and order. Only the swift assumption of dictatorial powers by the World Council prevented worse disasters.[13]

Clarke is a lot more interesting, and a lot kinkier, than his reputation as a great science-fiction author might lead the uninitiated to suppose, but he hasn't delivered the goods here. Let's carry the search on a little further. Between these two Clarke novels, and distinctly inferior to both, was the 1979 film **Meteor**, which posed the question: "Is this the way the world will end?" My chief — no, my *only*— memory of the film from a viewing on TV is of a cameo appearance by Isaac Asimov; fortunately enough, **Meteor** the Movie spawned the much more easily digestible and trackdownable **Meteor** the Novelization.[14]

The story is pretty typical 'seventies disaster-movie schlock, its credibility and scientific literacy summed up in chapter one (and scene one or thereabouts of the movie, I presume) when a telescope observer spots a comet en route for the asteroid belt and instantly has a feeling that something bad is going down.[15]

Sure enough the comet hits an asteroid, which calves a giant meteor, which trundles off towards the earth sending a swarm of baby meteors on ahead of it to provide the movie with its disaster scenes before East and West unite to blast Big Mummy off collision course and into deep space.

But however implausible the disaster's genesis in the movie and book, they are both examining a perfectly plausible situation. A very large piece of rock is on its way to the earth, preceded by many large pieces of rock. We know this well in advance. We may be able to divert the single very large piece of rock; we can do nothing about the many large ones. How do we react?

From **Meteor** the answer appears to be: we don't. At least, we don't react very strongly. As in **The Hammer of God**, there is suggestion of religious stirrings, but they are presented very briefly in the book and perhaps not at all in the movie. The meteor has been detected, its course plotted, and now:

> the fear of its arrival would spread by radio and telegraph, even by drums. Cults would rise to claim it as their own. It would become the anti-Christ, on its way to destroy the world.[16]

But that is all we hear of the cults. Even after there have been direct and devastating hits from some of the smaller preceding meteors, there is what I'd call a completely unrealistic calm. More meteors are on their way to a landfall in Italy; a crowd gathers in St Peter's Square in Rome and is addressed by the Pope, who tells it to pray to God and "ask for His infinite mercy". After which:

> The Pope made the sign of the cross and blessed them, and then was gone. The people below crossed themselves and reluctantly, like children being dismissed by an all-knowing father, began to disperse.[17]

And as the meteors come in, that, apart from the stray Ballardian touch of people who listen to radio commentaries making them "in a curious way ... spectators, not participants", is it. Even the relief that follows the meteors' burning up in the atmosphere without reaching the ground is "quiet, subdued". Anywhere in the world such behaviour seems very unlikely; in a Latin country like Italy, it seems impossible.

The book, at least, acknowledges this fact. After another devastating impact in the Swiss Alps:

> Strangely enough, the public, all over the world, did not panic — a phenomenon that the World Psychological Institute found of prime interest. Basically, it seemed, people were unwilling to believe that it could happen to them.[18]

Not very likely, it seems to me — but I am, of course, asking for something that it's not reasonable to expect. **Meteor** is a disaster movie, an example of a superficial genre in a superficial medium. Disaster movies are interested in the destruction not of human beings but of human artefacts — cities, for preference.

Their interest in human beings and their psychology is narrow and must be related to this larger theme. In **Meteor**, the meteoric annihilation of Zaisan in Siberia, the meteor-triggered avalanche that obliterates Zukstein in the Austrian Alps, the meteor-generated tsunami that swallows Hong Kong are *hors d'oeuvres* before the final feast of the destruction of New York:

> The Empire State building trembled and fell.[19]

The spice for all this is provided by the social and political struggles of the very small group of people behind the attempt to divert the chief meteor; the violence of the conflicts that would surely take place in society at large would be feast and spice all in themselves, and not only extremely rich ones but also, in narrower settings, familiar from other genres of film — war, western, slasher and so on. It seems easily possible that the universal panic following any news of an incoming giant meteor would quickly destroy any chance of diverting the meteor in the way suggested in this book, and so the two or so hours of the film version of **Meteor** have to assume that there is no such panic. The book, a transplanting of this cinematic assumption into a slower, more thoughtful medium, has to acknowledge its shortcomings but cannot discard it. The makers of **Meteor** spent millions of dollars to create a more or less accurate picture of what giant meteors will do to our world when they land on it, but ignored what giant meteors may do to us before they even get here. The world may end before it ends, but no fiction of destruction from the heavens has adequately faced this possibility. We have to look elsewhere. We have, in fact, to look at history.

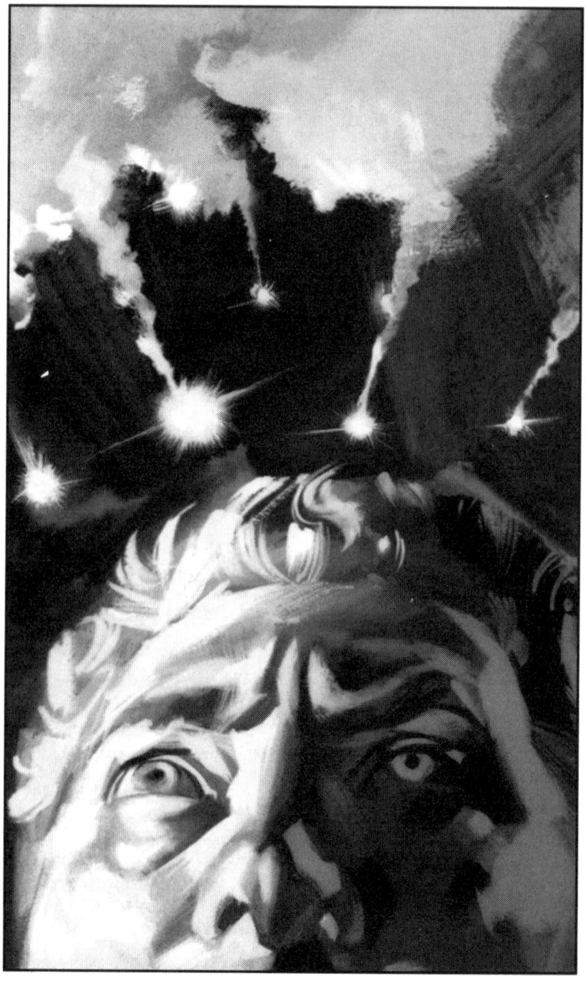

And there are certainly

examples to be found there of what seems to be precisely the situation being examined in this article. There have been "meteor" panics before: Patrick Moore describes three in **The Guinness Book of Astronomy**.[20] In 1719, for example, the exceptional brightness of the planet Mars at perihelic opposition convinced many that it was a blood-red comet en route for the earth;[21] in 1773 a paper by the French astronomer J.J. de Lalande was misinterpreted as predicting that a cometary impact was imminent; and there was a similar comet scare in 1832, again in France.

However, something noted by Moore of one of these scares demonstrates clearly that they are not good precedents for what might happen today. During the 1773 scare, the French clergy sold seats in heaven for high prices. Many people might have believed that the world was going to end, but they also believed very strongly that there would be another world to come, and that the way they behaved as it approached would determine what section of the next world they occupied. The Last Days were here, but they were being overseen by a God who cared very much about good and bad behaviour, not by a Mother Nature who was entirely indifferent to both.

In another way these scares are not good precedents for what might happen today. They were not universal, and even if they had been, there was no electronic web covering the earth to carry news of violent reaction in one corner of it instantly to all other corners, where the example could be taken up and acted on. There are, nonetheless, many historical examples of the kind of behaviour possible, or likely, before a giant meteor strike that has been predicted in advance. Some are more or less generic tales of sex, slaughter and sybaritism, very well exemplified in the following passages from the history of the Second World War. The first is from **Into that Darkness**, Gitta Sereny's biography of Franz Stangl, the commandant of the Treblinka extermination camp. Stangl is describing his first experience of the camp:

> "Treblinka that day was the most awful thing I saw during all of the Third Reich" — he buried his face in his hands — "it was Dante's Inferno," he said through his fingers. "It was Dante come to life. When I entered the camp and got out of the car on the square [the *Sortierungsplatz*] I stepped knee-deep into money; I didn't know which way to turn, where to go. I waded in notes, currency, precious stones, jewellery, clothes. The smell was indescribable; the hundreds, no the thousands of bodies everywhere, decomposing, putrefying. Across the square, in the woods, just a few hundred yards away on the other side of the barbed-wire fence and all around the perimeter of the camp, there were tents and open fires with groups of Ukrainian guards and girls — whores, I found out later, from all over the countryside — weaving drunk, dancing, singing, playing music..." [22]

The second comes from **The Last Battle**, Cornelius Ryan's history of the battle for Berlin in 1945:

> The nuns at Haus Dahlem were now working steadily around the clock. They had been overwhelmed by refugees, and by Russian bestiality. One Russian, attempting to rape the home's Ukrainian

cook, Lena, was so infuriated when Mother Superior Cunegundes intervened that he pulled out his pistol and fired at her. Fortunately, he was too drunk to shoot straight. Other soldiers entered the maternity wards and, despite all the nuns could do, repeatedly raped pregnant women and those who had recently given birth. 'Their screaming,' related one nun, 'went on day and night.' In the neighbourhood, Mother Superior Cunegundes said, rape victims included women of seventy and little girls of ten and twelve.[23]

The Second World War also realized some of the less obvious possibilities of a complete breakdown of law and order across entire cities and countries. Lynn H. Nicholas's **The Rape of Europa**, a study of the fate of Europe's art treasures during the war, has such a good story to tell, at least during the invasions and bombings, that the author's dull and sometimes solecistic prose can't quite spoil it, and this story contains surreal flashes worthy of J.G. Ballard at his best. After the Allied capture of Naples in 1943:

Troops soon were to be seen driving about the city in jeeps decorated with hundreds of fabulously coloured stuffed toucans, parrots, eagles, and even ostriches from the zoological collection [of the university].[24]

The Last Battle reveals that something similar happened in "in Babelsberg near Potsdam" in 1945:

Next to the warehouses were the big UFA film studios. Alexander Korab, a foreign student in Berlin, watched as hundreds of intoxicated soldiers who had broken into the costume department appeared in the streets wearing 'all sorts of fantastic costumes, from Spanish doublets with white ruff collars to Napoleonic uniforms and hats, to crinoline skirts. They began to dance in the streets to the accompaniment of accordions, and they fired their guns in the air — all while the battle was still raging.'[25]

Such conditions are one of the very few times at which anyone is likely to be able to indulge again the sartorial appetites of someone like the Roman emperor Heliogabalus. The more carnal appetites of someone like the Marquis de Sade could be indulged at the same time, of course, but I would think they were not fully satisfied even during the most lawless periods of the Second World War. Men were aware that their time for pleasure was limited, and that sooner or later more or less normal societies would reappear in the countries and cities in which they were fighting. The most extreme Sadean delights will be possible only when there seems no prospect of such reappearance, as before a giant meteor strike, or as when a nation has deliberately set out to destroy its old order. The latter happened during the Chinese Cultural Revolution in the 1960s, and much was apparent at the time of the consequences in murder and torture. Much more has come out since. Witness, for example:

[A] trove of secret Communist Party documents attesting to large-scale cannibalism during the

Cultural Revolution in the Guangxi region of southern China. ... [They] suggest that at least 137 people, and probably hundreds more, were eaten in the towns and villages of Guangxi Province in the late 1960s. In most cases, many people shared a corpse, so the cannibals may have numbered in the thousands. ...

The cannibalism took place in public, often organized by Communist Party officials, and people indulged communally ... At some high schools, students butchered and roasted their teachers and principals in the school courtyard and feasted on the meat ... Government-run cafetarias are said to have displayed corpses dangling on meat hooks and to have served human flesh to government employees.[26]

... The following comes from a single page in the account about the Cultural Revolution in Guizhou Province.

A mass meeting for dictatorship was held at Shangsi Junior High School, and twelve people, including cadres, were publicly killed. The livers were ripped out of some of the bodies and taken back to the cafeteria of the county government. ... Bodies were humiliated and destroyed, so that while the killing was awful, what came next was even worse. Three women ... were beaten to death, sticks were poked into their vaginas and their corpses were left naked by the roadside.

In Pubei County's Beitong Commune, ten hoodlums from the Boxue Work team tied up Liu Zhengjian and carried him to the hillside with his seventeen-year-old daughter. They beat him to death and then gang-raped his daughter. Then they beat the daughter to death with clubs and ripped out her liver and cut off her breasts and vagina. ... In the fighting in Qinzhou County, a broadcaster from a minor faction, Lu Jiezhen, was captured and stabbed to death. The assailants pulled off her pants, and forced a huge firecracker into her vagina. They lit it and exploded it.

Some of those involved in the cannibalism in Guangxi received minor punishments after the Cultural Revolution ended. ... A female deputy head of Wuxuan County, who liked to eat the genitals of men, was dismissed from her post and expelled from the party. She moved away from the county, and her whereabouts are not known.[27]

The conditions of the Cultural Revolution — huge numbers of people believing that their world is coming to an end and that the old authority will never be able to punish them because it will no longer exist — are precisely those that will apply before a giant meteor strike predicted in advance. What is already known of the Cultural Revolution, and further and perhaps even more gruesome details are still waiting to be revealed, may be a very good guide to what will happen during this period.

It is a disturbing prospect, but also one that raises an interesting question. Is there any possibility of making an aesthetic ethics of this kind of behaviour: that is, of arguing that rape and slaughter before and after a giant meteor strike could be morally negligible or neutral or even acceptable as artistic or existential acts? For the devout Maoist or Sadean the answer will, of course, be yes, but could someone who previously rejected Mao and de Sade find it acceptable under such conditions? After the meteor has struck, for example, hundreds of millions of people will be expiring in agony in many different ways; hundreds of

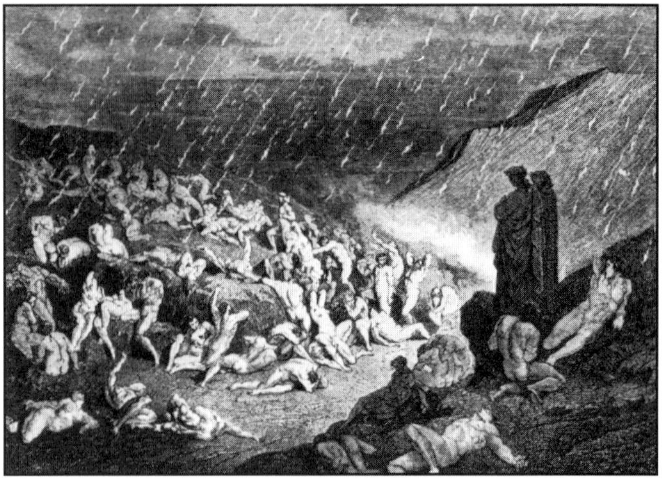

millions will be already dead: the pain added by one individual's acts of sadism and murder, however extreme, could only be an infinitesimal addition to the sum of human misery at the time, and so, if you think it's going to feel good, why not do it?

Curiously, one could find support for such an argument in the work of probably the most famous Christian apologist this century. In his book **The Problem of Pain**, C.S. Lewis sometimes reaches inspired heights of sophistry and special pleading, and is never higher or more inspired than in his argument against the notion of the "unimaginable sum of human misery":

> Suppose that I have a toothache of intensity x : and suppose that you, who are seated beside me, also begin to have a toothache of intensity x. You may, if you choose, say that the total amount of pain in the room is now $2x$. But you must remember that no-one is suffering $2x$: search all time and all space and you will not find that composite pain in anyone's consciousness. There is no such thing as a sum of suffering, for no-one ever suffers it. When we have reached the maximum that a single person can suffer, we have, no doubt, reached something very horrible, but we have reached all the suffering there can ever be in the universe. The addition of a million fellow sufferers adds no more pain.[28]

This passage deserves far lengthier consideration than I can give it here, but I could begin by saying that the argument it presents is an unsustainable one, based partly on rhetoric — note the deliberate bathos of "toothache" — and partly on faulty and incomplete analysis. In the phrase "sum of human misery", the term "sum" does have a meaning, though it is not, as Lewis tries to pretend, that the electro-chemical impulses creating the subjective impression of pain in individuals can be added together to arrive at a grand total in the way that, say, the electricity used by individuals to make cups of tea after a Cup Final can be.

We have an instinctive feeling that, individual pain and all other things being equal, it is worse for ten people to suffer than for one, and worse for a hundred to suffer than for ten, and for a thousand to suffer than for a hundred, and so on. That instinct has a rational basis, although it's difficult at first to understand what it is. Here's an attempt: when we feel that it is worse for a larger number to suffer than for a smaller, it's because we assume that pain is a bad thing that should be stopped, whether it is by our own or another's efforts, or by the efforts of those suffering the pain, or, in the final analysis, by death. Generally speaking, the pain of a hundred people is harder to stop than that of ten, so the pain of a hundred people is a worse thing. That is the meaning, or part of the meaning, of "the sum of human misery": "sum" refers to the difficulty of stopping the pain, or the likelihood of the pain's being stopped or stopping, or the length of time needed for this.

Happily therefore, Lewis's argument is as nugatory as it is revolting in its implications — it could easily be adapted for a Sadean manifesto, for example. A sum of human misery exists, and so someone who raped, tortured and murdered under the circumstances here being examined would have to accept that he was adding to it. If he did not accept that pain was a bad thing in others as it would be in himself, the argument would end there, but is it possible to accept this and still argue for the moral negligibility of adding a very small amount to what would be a very large sum of suffering?

Suppose someone has an existentialist desire to commit hitherto impossible crimes just before or after a giant meteor strike. He rapes and murders a dozen women and children. Hundreds of millions of women and children have died or are dying in more painful ways; he has added far less than a thousandth of one percent to that number: was he only very slightly wrong, or very slightly less than right, to surrender to his existential impulse under these very special circumstances?

On the undeveloped "sum of human misery" argument presented previously, I think the answer might be yes. The difficulty or likelihood of stopping the pain being suffered would only be very slightly affected by his hypothetical actions. Statistically speaking, they would be far below the threshold of noise. Note, however, that I said "undeveloped". As I've suggested, Lewis's argument against the concept of a sum of human misery has several faults. Another is the use he makes of the term "universe":

> When we have reached the maximum that a single person can suffer, we have, no doubt, reached something very horrible, but we have reached all the suffering there can ever be in the universe.

The universe cannot contain a cumulative sum of suffering because pain is contained in individual consciousnesses that are separate from each other. But what does "universe" mean? I would say that the implicit meaning of the term here is "that which is contained in the consciousness of an individual". C.S. Lewis, for example, did not suffer my pain or your pain or anybody else's pain, and so no pain was added to the "universe" beyond what was already there, which was, because Lewis was a single person, no more than "the maximum that a single person can suffer". But on the definition of universe just suggested, there are as many universes as there are individuals, as least as long as these individuals are conscious. The sum of human suffering can also mean the sum of universes affected by pain.

Examine the hypothetical situation again using this developed argument. Previously we concluded that adding a tiny fraction of a percent to the sum of human suffering might be only very slightly unacceptable. What are a dozen agonies and deaths out of many millions? On the developed argument, a great deal, perhaps infinitely much. To torture one person is to fill an entire universe with pain. To murder one person is to annihilate an entire universe. From one point of view, a dozen raped and murdered women and children are almost unnoticeable; from another, they are a dozen entire universes overturned and annihilated.

The thought would make it even better for some people, of course. For some of those who would not need a philosophical foundation to their refusal to indulge in the widest possibilities of meteor-born apocalypse, there may still be ample opportunity for the most monstrous crimes. Monstrous from the religious and puritanical secular point of view, that is, but the truth is that, unless their objects are killed to order, cannibalism and necrophilia are victimless crimes. In the aftermath of a giant meteor strike, it would be quite unnecessary to kill anyone to indulge in either. **Cosmic Winter** speaks of how, after a hypothetical meteor strike on central Belgium:

> Flying glass ... is the greatest hazard. Shopping precincts and office complexes within 50 kilometres find themselves swept without warning by lethal blizzards of flying glass. Indeed, shards of glass account for most of the loss of life in these areas.[29]

As in some vast Sadean butcher's shop, every conceivable cut of human meat would be made available by the law of averages and the vastness of the numbers killed. Additional ingredients for the feast will be on hand for free in wrecked supermarkets and specialist food shops, and in many cases the main course will be ready-cooked. Perhaps over-cooked:

> Immense destruction is caused by fire as well as blast. Serious flash burns from the thermal pulse of the fireball are sustained over an area of several thousand square kilometres, and virtually all exposed individuals within about 50 kilometres of ground zero [the point of direct impact] receive third degree burns.[30]

Which are also known as "charred skin". Necrophiles preferring undamaged goods will have a harder time of it here, at least, but those prepared to experiment with the many new orifices available may be commensurately rewarded. A living woman, or dead and undamaged one, offers three full sexual orifices and perhaps three or four partial ones; a woman killed by razor-sharp shards of glass may be almost literally all cunt. Necrophiliac homosexuals and paedophiles will find the penetrative possibilities of their objects of interest similarly multiplied.

But to enjoy these possibilities will, of course, require a great deal of luck. There is little use to be made of a decapitated and dismembered corpse by a cannibal or necrophile if he has been decapitated and dismembered himself: freedom from serious injury and shock will be a *sine qua non* of the deviant epicure determined to apply himself in truly dedicated fashion to the new freedoms of the immediately post-apocalyptic world. A great deal more luck will be required to stay healthy during the weeks, months and years that follow.

Much was once made of the threat of the so-called "Nuclear Winter". This, it was plausibly enough argued, would be brought about by the sun-obscuring smoke and dust thrown into the atmosphere by nuclear war. One study of the phenomenon based its projections, which included the possible annihilation of the human race, on a nuclear war involving the exchange of 6,000 megatonnes' worth of nuclear weapons.[31] Nuclear explosions and meteor strikes do not raise dust and cause fires in precisely the same way, but even if we assume that meteor strikes are much less liable to generate smoke and dust, 6,000 megatonnes of explosive energy are dwarfed by, for example, the 100,000 megatonnes of the meteor strike on the moon previously mentioned.

And yet, while the plunging of temperatures over much of the earth's surface to far below zero will probably mean the end of the party for the rapist and murderer, for the cannibal and necrophile it will be as though the climate has become a giant collaborator. Or will it? Well, on the whole, no, probably not. Cannibalism will almost certainly have been adopted by very many more of the survivors of the meteor before very long. It will not be a question of deviant pleasure, but of survival: there will simply be no other way of avoiding starvation. Those brief hours or days just before and after the meteor has struck will very likely be all the time the world's surviving deviants have to snatch vice from the jaws of universal defeat. Very shortly, they, and everyone else who has survived, will be too busy keeping alive to concern themselves with satisfying their genitals or their palates.

And that is on the not necessarily certain assumption that there will be survivors of a meteor strike. Megatonnages far larger than 100,000 are possible, and all life on earth, from human beings to the humblest virus, could even be wiped out by a near miss. A large enough meteor not entering the earth's atmosphere more or less vertically may

> move through about 8,000 kilometres of air, and at a speed of 20 kilometres per second this will take it almost 7 minutes, rather than the 7.5 seconds it would take were its approach vertical. As it moves through the air, friction caused by air molecules will cause it to heat and to lose energy, and the missile may disintegrate. The release of so much energy into the air would devastate the atmosphere, heating it strongly, causing chemical reactions within it, and releasing substances into the air. It is difficult to see how any living thing could [survive] an air burst of this kind.[32]

Though such complete destruction would, of course, be far, far better than that certain people should enjoy themselves amid the wreck of all human civilization. Wouldn't it?

GOLDEN LAUGHTER

THE HIDDEN MEANING BEHIND AN IMPERIAL PERVERT'S IGNOMINOUS DEATH

Earthly representatives of the sun-god tended not to die peacefully in bed. The Syro-Roman emperor Heliogabalus, hacked to death in a latrine, dragged around a circus, thrust into a sewer, pulled out again, and thrown finally into the river Tiber, might be taken as a paradigm of this truth. And yet there is no word from his ancient biographers that his death was very likely a ritual one, a king-slaying of the type so exhaustively examined in Frazer's **Golden Bough**. Perhaps it went without saying. Perhaps it was said, but was removed from the texts by their later Christian editors and epitomizers. One of those ancient biographers, the mysterious Ælius Lampridius who wrote during the reign of the militantly Christian Constantine the Great (c. 274-337), would have been well aware of this possible censorship, and may have sought to get around it by, in his own words, "using veiled language".[1]

For there does seem to be a lot more to the life and death of Heliogabalus than has generally been acknowledged. Patterns there link him not only to many strange aspects of paganism but also to Judaism and Christianity, with which in fact the religion of Heliogabalus has far more in common than has seemed comfortable for conventional history to recognize. He was the first monotheistic emperor, the first to set at the heart of Roman religion the *Sol Invictus*, or "Unconquered Sun", with which Constantine's Jesus Christ was later so easily identified. One must be aware, however, that historical patterns can sometimes arise out of nothing more than coincidence, particularly when they are based on linguistic or symbolic similarities like those to be examined in this article: Patrick Moore characterized this department of the conspiracy school of history very well when he wrote of the man who identified Moses with Middlebury by the simple expedient of deleting the "-oses" and adding the "-iddlebury".[2]

But one of the first interesting coincidences in Heliogabalus's recorded life may have a solidly scientific, indeed astronomical, basis. 218 AD, the year of Heliogabalus's proclamation and accession as Emperor, was also one of the years of Halley's comet. The comet was certainly seen and recorded by the ancient Chinese in that year,[3] and seems likely to have been a comet referred to in Dio Cassius's **Roman History** as one of the omens of doom for Macrinus, Heliogabalus's predecessor on the imperial throne:

> For a very distinct eclipse of the sun occurred just before that time and the comet was seen for a considerable time; also another star, whose tail extended from east to west for several nights, caused us terrible alarm.[4]

The "other star" also sounds like a comet, and which of the two was Halley's might seem uncertain. However, Dio's initial reference not to "a comet" but "the comet" — ὁ ἀστηρ ὁ κομητης, "the hairy star" — is interesting. Dio wrote in Greek, and Greek, unlike Latin, makes a distinction between definite and indefinite nouns; the wording here seems to suggest that the comet was recognised as distinctive in some way. Halley's comet is distinctive to us, of course, because it was the first to be recognised as periodic and the first to have its next date of return calculated. Ancient astronomers were capable of recognising celestial patterns extending over much longer periods than that of the orbit of Halley's comet, which is about 76 years long: is there any possibility that Dio's use of the definite article, apparently present in all manuscripts, is an indication that comets had been recognised as periodic phenomena many centuries before Edmund Halley and the flowering of Newtonian physics in the eighteenth century?

Yes, it seems, but how large a possiblity is impossible to say. The more generally recognized link of the two comets with Heliogabalus and his struggle for the imperial succession is made explicit in Dio, however. Comets were omens of doom, particularly for the head of state, and the comets would have lifted the morale of Heliogabalus's supporters just as they lowered that of Macrinus's. Emperor Macrinus, the sky would have been clearly indicating, is not going to be emperor very much longer. And the sky was, after all, the centre of Heliogabalus's cult, not only because his god Elah-Gabal was a sun-god but also because Elah-Gabal took the form on earth of something that had fallen from the sky: a black, conical meteorite.

Representations of this cult-object on coins issued during Heliogabalus's reign show something between perhaps two and three metres high and with a rounded appearance, similar to that of a giant *glans penis*, that was undoubtedly produced by the part melting and re-shaping of the meteorite by atmospheric friction during its fall. Meteors and meteorites would, then, have been of special interest to Elah-Gabal's cult — Heliogabalus would make attempts when established in Rome to marry the lithophallus, or stone-phallus, of Elah-Gabal to the lithophallus of Rome's patron goddess Vesta — and the actual date of Heliogabalus's proclamation as emperor on 18th May, 218, may have been intended to coincide with what are today known as the η Aquarids, a meteor shower occurring annually in May with a radiant, or apparent point of origin to an observer on earth, in the constellation of Aquarius, the Water-Bearer.

This meteor shower has several possible links with Heliogabalus. First of all, it may have been the means by which Elah-Gabal dispatched his lithophallus to earth. Second, its radiant is in a constellation that is named for Ganymedes, the beautiful Phrygian youth snatched up to Olympus by Zeus to serve as both his cup-bearer and, as the Etruscan corruption of "Ganymede" taken into Latin as *catamitus* shows, passive sexual partner: Heliogabalus's frenzied devotion to such practices is perhaps the most notorious feature of his reign. Third, the η Aquarids, like many other meteor showers, are now known to represent debris deposited across the earth's orbit by a comet near perihelion. In this case, the debris is that of Halley's comet.

If this association between meteor shower and comet was known to the priests of Elah-Gabal's cult, 218 AD, the year of Halley's comet sixth historically recorded return, and May, the month of the meteor shower associated with Halley's comet, would have been a particularly auspicious time for an attempt at the imperial throne. Perhaps the entire thing, from Macrinus's assassination of the emperor Caracalla *en route* to the moon-goddess's shrine at Carrhae to Macrinus's own brief reign and ignominious death at Heliogabalus's hands, was a giant stage-managed ritual. And perhaps Moses came from Middlebury.

But Elah-Gabal was associated with more than meteorites. He was a sun-god, and to the ancient pagans the sun-god was a celestial charioteer, riding a chariot drawn by fiery horses daily across the sky from east to west. The significance of chariots in Heliogabalus's life is certain. As he was to sex, food, and practical jokes, he was addicted to them. After his accession, the Elah-Gabal lithophallus was displayed to the people of Rome each midsummer's day like this:

> A six-horse chariot carried the divinity, the horses huge and flawlessly white, with expensive gold fittings and rich ornaments. No-one held the reins and no-one rode in the chariot; the vehicle was escorted as if the god himself were the charioteer.[5]

White horses were especially sacred to the sun-god, and the number six may have represented the days of the week additional to the *dies solis* or "day of the sun" that was taken up as the Christian holy day under the influence of the sun-cult in its Mithraic form.[6] Several of Heliogabalus's "associates in lewdness"[7] were charioteers, and Hierocles, perhaps the most important of these, may have been introduced to Heliogabalus in a deliberate solar ritual. Dio describes how:

> in a certain race Hierocles fell out of his chariot just opposite Sardanapalus [i.e. Heliogabalus], losing his helmet in his fall, and, being still beardless and adorned with a crown of yellow hair, he attracted the attention of the emperor and was immediately rushed to the palace; and there by his nocturnal feats he captivated Sardanapalus more than ever and became exceedingly powerful.[8]

According to Robert Graves in **The Greek Myths**, pre-arranged chariot crashes were a highly significant part of the solar cult, used to bring about the death of the king or a ritual substitute as a symbolic earthly counterpart of the sun's "death" during autumn and winter: Graves cites the myths of Glaucus, Hippolytus, Laius, Oenomaus, Abderus and Hector, amongst others.[9] Whether or not Heliogabalus was aware of the ritual in Hierocles' case, or whether there was a ritual at all, the significance of a chariot crash amidst which a head of golden hair suddenly flashes forth would have been obvious to a worshipper of the sun-god. The more usual outcome of the chariot-crash ritual, in which the king was caught up in the wreckage and dragged to death by horses sometimes deliberately maddened with drugs, may appear at the end of Heliogabalus's reign in the "veiled language" of Lampridius:

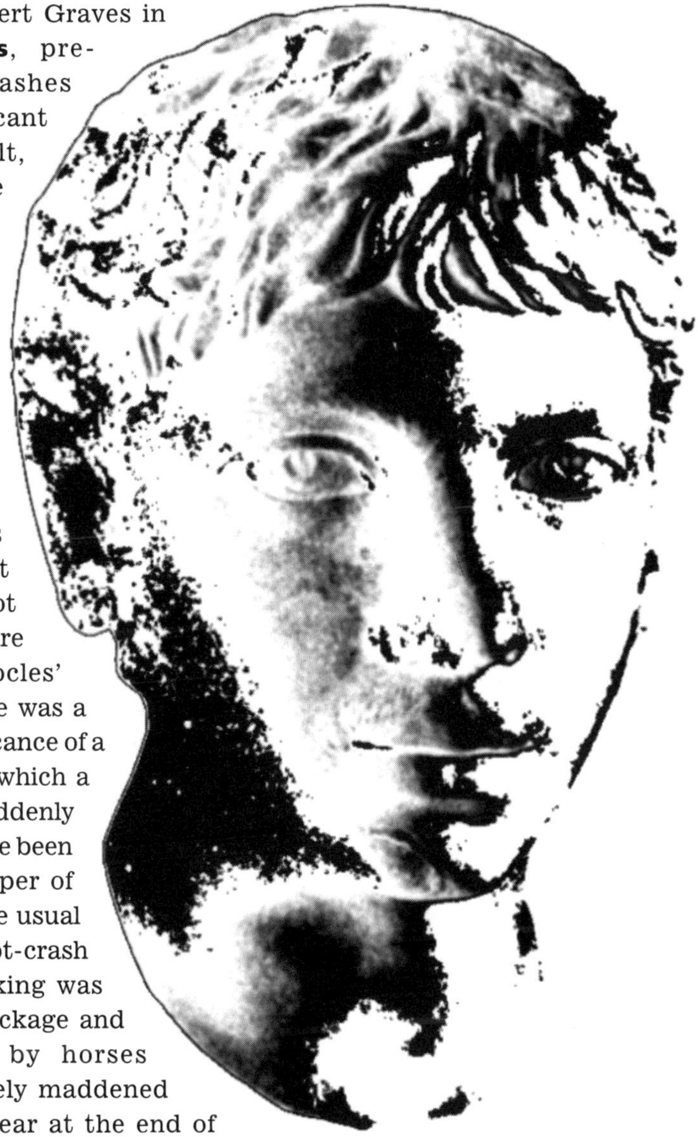
Heliogabalus. God star

> His [Heliogabalus's] body was also dragged around the track of the circus before it was hurled into the Tiber.[10]

The circus, of course, was the site of the chariot races, and it would seem likely that a body could be most easily and dramatically dragged around its track with the aid of a chariot. The hurling of the body into the Tiber that then took place is reminiscent of the chariot-crash myth of Phæthon, a son of Helios who persuaded his father to allow him to take charge of the sun-chariot for a day. Losing control of the chariot's horses and the chariot's course, Phæthon threatened the earth alternately with conflagration and refrigeration until Zeus knocked him dead into the river Po with a thunderbolt.

In its ritual acting out on earth, this myth would presumably take something like the form of Heliogabalus's death, at least as this is hinted at by Lampridius and Dio, the latter of whom says that Heliogabalus's decapitated corpse was "dragged all over the city" before being "thrown into the river".[11] The likely involvement of a chariot is less directly stated here, but is surely still to be inferred. Dragging a body on foot must be a slow, tiring and unsatisfactory business: dragging one to and fro on the end of a rope attached to a chariot would not.

Although a previous imperial assassination might seem *prima facie* to undermine this reasoning. The gluttonous and profligate Emperor Vitellius (AD 14-69), to whom Lampridius directly compares Heliogabalus more than once,[12] was also killed ignominiously and thrown into the Tiber, having been dragged there by his murderers on foot. They are said, however, to have dragged him to the river directly, and not to have taken any special care to ensure his corpse stayed in the river: it was later retrieved and buried by his wife. According to Lampridius, Heliogabalus's corpse was weighted beforehand "to prevent it floating, so it might never be buried",[13] and though Vitellius *post mortem* was reviled nearly as thoroughly as Heliogabalus would be, he was not re-christened with any new names to mark the manner of his death. Heliogabalus, of course, was: "After his death he was called Tiberinus and Tractatitius [the Dragged One]."[14]

Tiberinus was the name of a mythical king of Alba, mentioned by Livy and Ovid, whose drowning in the river Albula gave it the new name of Tiber. Albula is a clearly Latin name; Tiber is said to be Etruscan. Much of Roman religion was Etruscan in origin, and it would seem that this myth records an ancient practice of human sacrifice to the god of the river Tiber. It is echoed in a story of how the Syrian river Orontes, which flowed past Heliogabalus's natal city Emesa, was originally called the Typhon and took its new name from the first man "who built a bridge over it".[15] The dedication of important buildings has been associated with human sacrifice for a very long time, and bridges are more important buildings than most. Was the death of Phæthon or King Tiberinus, or the deaths of both, being re-enacted explicitly in Heliogabalus's consignment to the Tiber? Perhaps, but these similarities to mythic sacrifice are by no means the strongest pieces of evidence for the hidden presence of ritual in Heliogabalus's death.

Less direct, but stronger, for example, might seem to be the fact that Heliogabalus did his very best to provoke the assassination, and had done so almost from his first arrival in Rome. As Lampridius records, the new emperor, simply by virtue of being new, found a great deal of goodwill waiting for him in the city. Macrinus's standing was very poor during most of his reign. He had, for a start, been of lowly, foreign origin: Dio surely reflects the snobbery and racial prejudice of the time when he remarks that the emperor

> was ... the son of most obscure parents, so that he was very appropriately likened to the ass that was led up to the palace by the spirit ...[and] being a Moor, he was naturally timorous[16]

and the peace treaty Macrinus concluded with the Persians in 218 was on terms both ignominious and expensive to the empire. Heliogabalus, on the other hand, was young, handsome, aristocratic, and an illegitimate son of Caracalla of, by then, happy memory. Or so his propaganda claimed, with a great deal of assistance from the reputation of his mother Julia Soaemias Bassiana: one of Heliogabalus's Roman names, Varius, is said by Lampridius to have been

> given to him by his school-fellows because he appears to have been conceived by the seed of "various" men, as happens with a whore.[17]

He also adopted and exploited the associations of the name Antoninus, and had so thoroughly discredited it by the end of his reign that it was, like that of John in the British royal family, never used again by the head of state. Lampridius apologizes at length, perhaps ironically, for referring to him by that name in the **Vita Heliogabali**, and Dio makes a great point of using it only in the form Ψευδαντονινος, *Pseudantoninos* or "False-Antoninus".

Such a successful stripping of the lustre the name had taken from the reigns of the emperors Marcus and Pius required a great deal of effort; in fact, it would seem, a great deal of calculated effort. Religiously speaking, one can say that the Romans were narrow-minded only about narrow-mindedness: Christians were persecuted not because of their theological ideas, which were after all not particularly unusual, but because of their exclusivity and refusal to participate in the imperial cult. The high priest of Elah-Gabal, which was to the Roman mind merely another name for the "Jupiter or the Sun",[18] offended not because he introduced a new god to the city but because he assumed that he could interfere with the gods and goddesses already there. The worship of Vesta, with that of Jupiter Capitolinus, formed the heart of Roman religion, and Heliogabalus's attempts to seize her cult objects, which were defeated according to Lampridius by some Houdini-like misdirection

> He also tried to carry away the sacred inner shrine, and seized an earthenware one which the Chief Vestal Virgin had shown him as if it were the real one, as if to deceive him.[19]

got his residence in the city off to a very inauspicious start. If it was imagined that Heliogabalus had got the worst in first, the disillusion brought by news of his impending marriage to a Vestal Virgin must have been swift. And he is unlikely to have been able to offer the excuse that he was overwhelmed by the attractiveness of the young woman in question: from coins minted to celebrate the marriage, Julia Aquilia Severa seems to have been plain, at best. One coin suggests that she had a small moustache.[20] Heliogabalus had committed sacrilege without seeming to treat it seriously, and the impression that he was mocking Rome's religious sensibilities must have been strengthened when he divorced, married someone else, divorced again, and re-married Aquilia Severa.

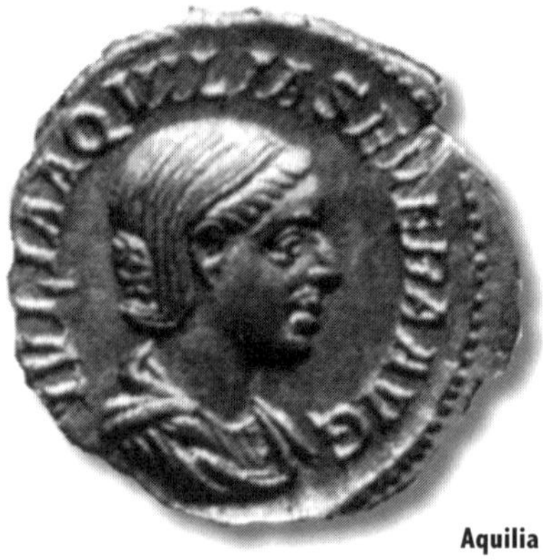

Aquilia

But then Macrinus had accused him of being mad (ἐμπληκτον εἰναι λεγων[21]). Whether or not the fantastic details of Heliogabalus's practical jokes set out by Lampridius have any truth, the accusation doesn't seem an unwarranted one. On the basis of the suggestively shaped parasols shading the Elah-Gabal lithophallus on some of Heliogabalus's coins, one could even speculate that he had over-indulged in magic mushrooms, which may have been part of secret ritual in the cult. Then again, he was a very heavy drinker, and he was, as Macrinus also pointed out, a very young man[22]. Perhaps he was permanently or semi-permamently drunk, either with the surreal oenophile recipes — wine flavoured with mastic, pennyroyal and ground-up pine-cones — "first invented by him"[23] or with the opportunities for excess his position afforded him. As Lampridius remarks: "Indeed, for him, life was nothing but a search for pleasures."[24]

But in fact the question of whether Heliogabalus himself knew what he was doing is unimportant. His grandmother and aunt certainly did, and even if they were unable to control his excesses, someone seems to have been directing the unerring steps of the dance in which Heliogabalus came down firmly and heavily on the toes of more and more of Rome's great and good. Perhaps that someone was Heliogabalus himself; perhaps not. The result was the same in either case.

Heliogabalus and Christian Chronology

And after what would seem to have been his deliberately provoked assassination, the legend of Heliogabalus began, perhaps even to the extent of adding a new word to the Greek language. Dio has a liking for giving nicknames to the emperors he disapproves of, and Heliogabalus appears not only as "Pseudantoninos" but also as "Sardanapallos" (Σαρδαναπαλλος), which was the name of

> the 40th and last king of Assyria, celebrated for his luxury and voluptuousness. ... His tomb was seen at Anchiale, ... where an inscription commemorated his effeminacy, and informed the reader, that during life he had luxuriously enjoyed himself in drinking and eating, and in every kind of voluptuousness; an epitaph, as Aristotle observes, more becoming a brute than a king.[25]

The parallels with Heliogabalus, to which should be added the fact that Sardanapallus also died violently, in his case by fire, are obvious and probably worthy of more exploration than they are going to receive here. An obscene modification of the name of this Assyrian king may have been a contribution made by Heliogabalus to Greek: the lexicographer Hesychius, working in the late fourth century, records an adjective σαρδαναφαλλος (*sardanaphallos)*, meaning "exciting laughter, ridiculous".[26] This may be a pun on "Sardanapallos" and "phallus": Heliogabalus seems a good candidate to have inspired the marriage of the two words.

Another link with the Assyrian king may still be extant, for the Greek form of Sardanapallus also appears on one of the many statues of Bacchus that have come down to us from antiquity:

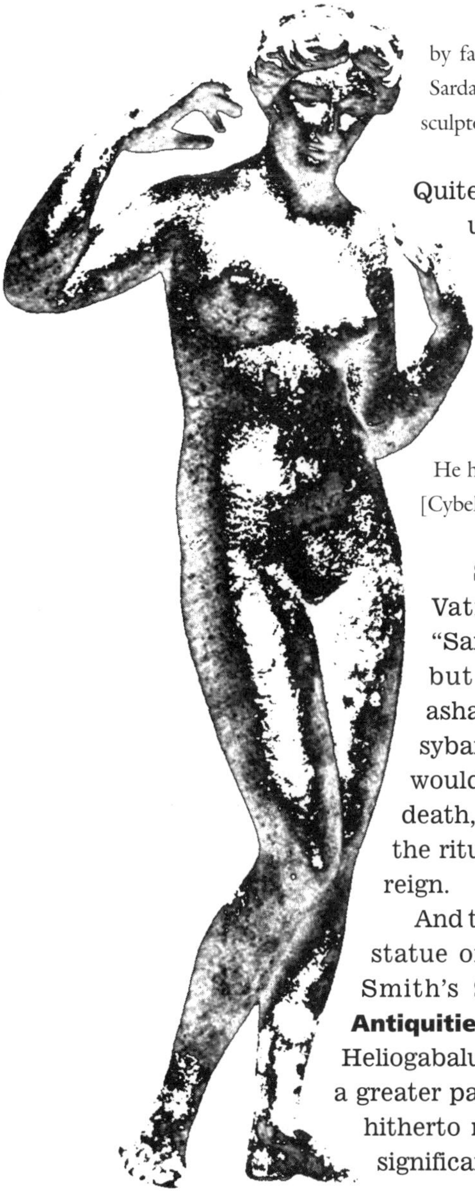

> by far the finest is that found in the Vatican, with the name Sardanapallos inscribed, which is supposed to be the name of the sculptor.[27]

Quite why this should be supposed is not clear. Dio's use of this substitute name for Heliogabalus undoubtedly reflects contemporary usage, because Dio was a contemporary of Heliogabalus, and Heliogabalus himself included Bacchus among the several deities he impersonated at chariot play:

> He harnessed lions too, calling himself the Mother of the Gods [Cybele], and tigers, calling himself Liber [Bacchus].[28]

So might this finest of statues of Bacchus in the Vatican be a representation of Heliogabalus? "Sardanapallos" is used as an abusive title by Dio, but Heliogabalus would not have been at all ashamed to be identified with the ancient Assyrian sybarite; perhaps the identification, implying as it would that Heliogabalus too would meet a violent death, was an important part of the preparation for the ritual king-slaying that would end Heliogabalus's reign.

And the Vatican preserves not only an oddly inscribed statue of Bacchus, but also, in the words of William Smith's **Shorter Dictionary of Greek & Roman Antiquities**, an "ancient chariot" of the kind with which Heliogabalus is so closely associated.[29] If Heliogabalus plays a greater part in the history of Christianity than has been hitherto recognized, these items may be of far greater significance than they appear. In themselves, they are, of course, no more than faintly suggestive. The Vatican preserves a great deal of pagan Rome's past because the Vatican is in Rome; Heliogabalus reigned and died there because Rome was the capital of the Roman empire and he was the emperor. Naturally enough, when the secular figure of the emperor was transmuted into the sacred figure of the pope, Rome was chosen as the seat of his temporal power. Much more than Jerusalem, Rome is the heart of the Roman Catholic church, and the church has directed history from there for many centuries. In one sense, the whole of history has been influenced by the work of a Roman Catholic monk who lived in Rome in the sixth century.

By that I mean that history is about dates, years in which things happened. In any given culture the numbering of these years is an arbitrary convention, generally taking as a starting point some important event in the past. Pagan Rome's years were dated A.U.C.: *Ab Urbe Condita*, "from the founding of the city"; the Greeks used the date of the first Olympic games, or Olympiad. I am not a Christian, but if I want to tell you when these events took place I would say that they took place in 753 and 776 BC, respectively: 753 years and 776 years before the birth of Christ. But Jesus Christ was himself born, it's generally agreed, in at least 4 BC. Christ was born "Before Christ" because the most influential man to calculate the year of Christ's birth got his sums wrong.

There is something odd about this. The man was called Dionysius Exiguus (c.490-c. 556), and he was the abbot of a monastery in Rome, a fine Greek and Latin scholar, and recognized as "one of the most learned men of his time"[30]. The work in which he determined the form Christianity chronology would eventually take is called variously the **Liber de Paschate** ("Book of Easter") and the **Cyclis Paschalis** ("Easter Cycle"). In it he stated that Christ was born, under the Roman system, in 754 AUC. However:

> That date, as we shall see, cannot be correct and is further from the truth than the dates assigned by the early fathers St Irenæus and Tertullian.[31]

The most important thing to note initially about the birth of Christ is that it took place during the reign of Herod the Great, the year of whose death therefore fixes the upper limit for the calculations. Herod was an important figure, and the year of his death is recorded by the historian Josephus in his **Jewish History** relative to the reign of the emperor Augustus. When Dionysius came to calculate the year of Christ's birth using Josephus's dates, something went wrong:

> Unfortunately, however, he omitted the four years during which Augustus had reigned under his own name of Octavian and this seriously upset his reckoning.[32]

This hardly seems like the work of "one of the most learned men of his time", and Dionysius should have been very familiar with such changes of name because at least half of his own name represented one. His surname "Exiguus" means "the Little", and was "adopted probably in self-deprecation and not because he was small in stature".[33]

Dionysius Exiguus, in other words, means "the little Dionysus": the forename is a variant of the name of the Greek god of wine whose Roman equivalent was Bacchus. "The little Dionysus" would also have been a good name for Heliogabalus, who once

> invited the common people to drink and he himself drank so much that it was thought, on seeing what he alone had drunk, that he had been drinking from a swimming pool.[34]

And if you look up the title Dio gave to Heliogabalus, *Pseudantoninos* or "false Antoninus", in a Greek dictionary, you'll find that it comes directly after a title of Dionysus, that of Ψευδανηρ/*Pseudaner* or "false man", given to the god because of his effeminacy[35]. Perhaps Dio used *Pseudantoninos* deliberately for the echo of the god's title it carries; in either case, Heliogabalus was a little Dionysus for more than his drinking:

> [Heliogabalus] ... sprang up with rhythmic movements, then, when Aurelius addressed him with the usual salutation, "My Lord Emperor, Hail!" he bent his neck so as to assume a ravishing feminine pose, and turning his eyes upon him with a melting gaze, answered without any hesitation, "Call me not Lord, for I am a Lady."[36]

The links between Dionysius Exiguus and Heliogabalus may not all be as tenuous as this, however. Dionysius was described by his fellow-scholar and friend Cassiodorus (c.490-c.580) as a Scythian.[37] This was almost as exotic a nationality then as it would be now: Scythians, the inhabitants of a vast and diffuse region comprising parts of present-day Turkey, Poland, Hungary and Russia, were almost a synonym for "barbarians" in ancient times, as the single appearance of the word in the Bible reflects:

> neither Greek nor Jew, circumcision nor uncircumcision, Barbarian, Scythian, bond nor free. [Colossians iii, 11]

The emergence of a highly learned Christian scholar, bilingual in Greek and Latin, from the wilds of Scythia seems unlikely, but not impossible. Nor is it impossible that Cassiodorus's SCYTHUS, or "Scythian", represents a *lapsus calami* for SYRUS, or "Syrian". When spoken, "Scythian" and "Syrian" are differentiated by only a single consonant in English just as they were in much of the Latin used at the time of Cassiodorus.

That is speculation, but Dionysius is also linked directly to Syria by one of his most famous works of scholarship: the translation from Greek into Latin of "the history of the discovery of the head of St John the Baptist", which took place in Syria. And not only in Syria, but in Emesa, Heliogabalus's natal city and the cult centre of Elah-Gabal. Elah-Gabal's temple in Emesa was converted into a church of St John in celebration of the discovery,[38] which would have been documented in Syriac, the native language of the region, as well as in Greek. Perhaps Dionysius's translation was from Syriac, his real mother tongue, and perhaps Cassiodorus's misleading use of "Scythian" was deliberate rather than accidental.

The obvious question to arise would then be that of why it was necessary to conceal the fact that Dionysius Exiguus was Syrian. The answer would be that this would have linked him rather too obviously to Heliogabalus, and made the possible significance of Dionysius's faulty chronology rather too apparent. The possible significance of Dionysius's chronology is that under it Heliogabalus died in 222, a year whose form makes it easy enough to remember in Arabic numbers. When it is translated into Hebrew letters, however, it may become significant for far more than its mnemonic convenience.

Chariots of Fire

The ancient Hebrews, like the ancient Greeks, used letters of their alphabet for numbers (see table below[39]).

Every letter is used, and so every Hebrew word can be read in two ways: as a word and as a number. 222 is written in Hebrew as רכב, or RKB: "R" stands for 200, "K" for 20 and "B" for 2. Although every Hebrew word can be read as a number, not every Hebrew number can be read as a word: it should be fairly easy to understand why if you imagine that we used letters of our alphabet for numbers in the same way. RKB, however, can be read both as a number and as a word, and the word is a highly significant one. Under the chronology of Dionysius Exiguus, the emperor Heliogabalus, high-priest of the divine solar charioteer Elah-Gabal, died in a year whose Hebrew form means "chariot" — רֶכֶב, or ReKeB.[40]

And the iconography of the chariot is perhaps even more important in Judaism than it was in worship of the pagan sun-god. This is certainly true, at least, in Jewish mysticism. The fact that every Hebrew word can be read as a number is of enormous significance in the Jewish mystical system known as the Qabbala, particularly because it can be used to "uncover" parallels between words that are not otherwise obviously linked: the numerical value of a group of consonants remains constant while its meaning changes, sometimes considerably. רכב/RKB, for example, are the root consonants of the Hebrew word for "chariot"; כבר/KBR are the root consonants of the Hebrew name for a river in Mesopotamia.[41] The meanings are completely different but the numerical value of these two words is identical, because they are permutations of the same consonants. To the Qabbalist, the fact that RKB and KBR are numerically identical is surely very significant in the context of the first and tenth chapters of the book of Ezekiel, which describe the visions had by the prophet of a heavenly chariot by the river Chebar in Mesopotamia. If one inserts the Hebrew vowels (which don't affect the numerical value), "chariot" is רֶכֶב/ReKeB, and "Chebar" is כְּבַר/KeBaR.

"Chebar", indeed, may be an invented word, a mystical disguising of the word for chariot, because its exact location in Mesopotamia has never been satisfactorily determined and Ezekiel never explicitly refers to his vision as a chariot. His description of his vision, which is now at the heart of Jewish mysticism, begins like this:

> The word of the LORD came expressly unto Ezekiel the priest, the sun of Buzi, in the land of the Chaldeans by the river Chebar; and the hand of the LORD was there upon him. And I looked, and behold, a whirlwind came out of the north, a great cloud, and a fire infolding itself, and a brightness was about it, and out of the midst thereof as the colour of amber, out of the midst of the fire.[i, 3-4]

This chariot of "fire", accompanied by a whirlwind, is immediately suggestive

Hebrew Letter	Phonetic Value	Name	Numeric Value
א	'	'aleph	1
ב	b	beth	2
ג	g	gimel	3
ד	d	daleth	4
ה	h	he	5
ו	w	waw	6
ז	z	zayin	7
ח	ḥ	ḥeth (pharyngeal)	8
ט	ṭ	ṭeth (pharyngeal)	10
י	y	yodh	9
כ	k	kaph	20
ל	l	lamedh	30
מ	m	mim	40
נ	n	nun	50
ס	ṣ	ṣamekh (pharyngeal)	60
ע	'	'ayin	70
פ	p	pe	80
צ	ç	çade	90
ק	q	qoph	100
ר	r	reš	200
ש	š	šin	300
ת	t	taw	400

of the chariot of the sun-god, and such a chariot with whirlwind is found elsewhere in the Bible:

> And it came to pass, as they still went on, and talked, that, behold, *there appeared* a chariot of fire, and horses of fire, and parted them both asunder; and Elijah went up by a whirlwind into heaven. [II Kings ii, 11]

And, in directly pagan form, in a description of the prophet Josiah's ideological cleansing of Judah:

> And he took away the horses that the kings of Judah had given to the sun, at the entering in of the house of the LORD, by the chamber of Nathan-melech the chamberlain, which was in the suburbs, and burned the chariots of the sun with fire. [II Kings xxiii, 11]

This verse clearly demonstrates that apostate Jews followed the solar cult in the form familiar in Heliogabalus's day, and in the remainder of his vision Ezekiel himself seems to reflect the pagan iconography by which the chariots of different pagan deities were drawn by different animals:

> Also out of the midst [of the fire] came the likeness of four living creatures. And this was their appearance; they had the likeness of a man. And every one had four faces, and every one had four wings. ... As for the likeness of their faces, they four had the face of a man, and the face of a lion, on the right side: and they four had the face of an ox on the left side; they four also had the face of an eagle. [i, 5-10]

Ezekiel's vision is developed many times elsewhere in the later mystical sections of the Old Testament, and although for some reason he never explicitly calls the fiery vehicle a chariot, the site of the vision at Chebar/ KeBaR and his frequent reference in chapter 10 to "cherubim" — the Hebrew root is KRB — must have meant that the consonants RKB and their numerical value were seen as having some special significance by the Qabbalistic interpreters of the text.

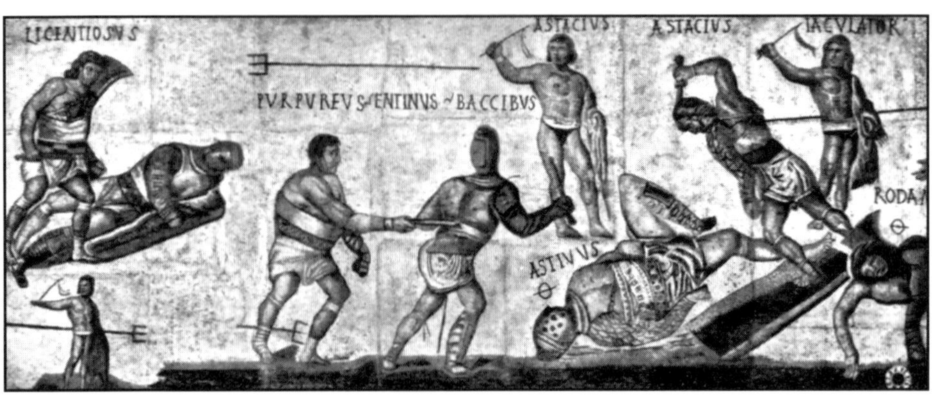

Amongst whom Dionysius Exiguus, "one of the most learned men of his time", may later have been numbered. The missing four years of his calculations of Christ's birth may have been not inexplicable carelessness, but a deliberate means of ensuring that the year of Heliogabalus's death encoded the emperor's significance for some hidden tradition in the history of Christianity — a hidden tradition that may be hinted at in another odd passage in Lampridius, which reads:

> He would often shut his friends in halting-places for the night with old hags from Ethiopia and compel them to stay there until morning, saying that the most beautiful women were kept in these places. He did this same thing with boys too — for then, before the time of Philip, that is, such a thing was lawful.[42]

Were old Ethiopian women proverbially hideous in Heliogabalus's day? If not, use of the word "Ethiopia" in fair proximity to the name "Philip" may be as close as Lampridius dared go in hinting at another odd passage in ancient literature, this time in chapter 8 of the Acts of the Apostles in the New Testament:

> 26. And the angel of the Lord spake unto Philip, saying, Arise, and go toward the south unto the way that goeth down from Jerusalem unto Gaza, which is desert.
> 27. And he arose and went: and, behold, a man of Ethiopia, an eunuch of great authority under Candace queen of the Ethiopians, who had the charge of all her treasure, and had come to Jerusalem for to worship.
> 28. And was returning, and sitting in his chariot read Esaias [Isaiah] the prophet.
> 29. And the Spirit said unto Philip, Go near, and join thyself to this chariot.
> 30. And Philip ran thither to *him*, and heard him read the prophet Esaias, and said, Understandest thou what thou readest?
> 31. And he said, How can I, except some man should guide me? And he desired Philip that he would come up and sit with him.
> 32. And the place of the scripture which he read was this, He was led as a lamb to the slaughter; and like a lamb dumb before his shearer, so opened he not his mouth:
> 33. In his humiliation his judgment was taken away: and who shall declare his generation? for his life is taken from the earth.
> 34. And the eunuch answered Philip, and said, I pray thee, of whom speaketh the prophet this? of himself, or of some other man?
> 35. Then Philip opened his mouth, and began at the same scripture, and preached unto him Jesus.
> 36. And as they went on *their* way, they came unto a certain water: and the eunuch said, See, *here is* water; what doth hinder me to be baptized?
> 37. And Philip said, If thou believest with all thine heart, thou mayest. And he answered and said, I believe that Jesus Christ is the Son of God.
> 38. And he commanded the chariot to stand still: and they went down both into the water, both Philip and the eunuch; and he baptized him.
> 39. And when they were come up out of the water, the Spirit of the Lord caught away Philip, that the eunuch saw him no more: and he went on his way rejoicing.

> 40. But Philip was found at Azotus: and passing through he preached in all the cities, until he came to Caesarea.

Some of the things that are interesting about this story can be seen only in the original languages underlying the English text; one can be seen in any language, including English. This is the way it doesn't seem to fit very comfortably with what comes before and after it. The first part of chapter 8 of Acts carries on naturally from the story of St. Stephen's martyrdom in chapter 7:

> And Saul [the later St Paul] was consenting to his death. And at that time there was a great persecution against the church at Jerusalem ... Therefore they that were scattered abroad went every where [sic] preaching the word. Then Philip went down to the city of Samaria, and preached Christ unto them.

Philip casts out evil spirits in Christ's name and attracts the attention of Simon Magus, the figure who is so important in the gnostic tradition and who here invents the sin of "simony" when he offers money to Philip and other apostles for the power to cast out evil spirits as they do. Simon is rebuked for this, and sees the error of his ways:

> Then answered Simon, and said, Pray ye to the Lord for me, that none of these things which ye have spoken come upon me. And they, when they had testified and preached the word of the Lord, returned to Jerusalem, and preached the gospel in many villages of the Samaritans.

Straight after this:

> And the angel of the Lord spake unto Philip, saying, Arise, and go toward the south unto the way that goeth down from Jerusalem unto Gaza, which is desert.

The story of Philip and the eunuch fills the rest of chapter 8, and chapter 9 carries on with the story of Saul:

> And Saul, yet breathing out threatenings and slaughter against the disciples of the Lord, went unto the high priest.

It's obvious that chapters 8 and 9 of Acts

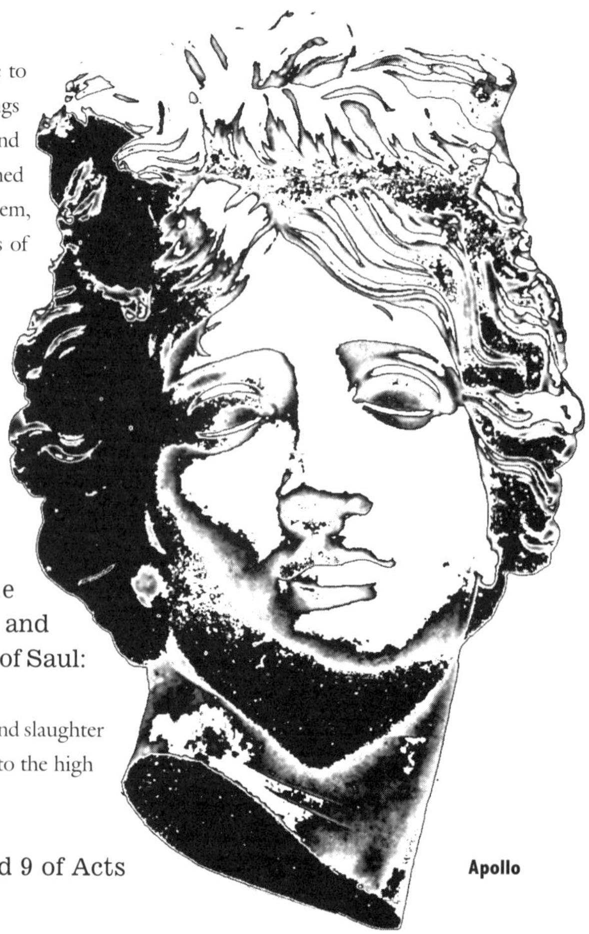
Apollo

would flow much better if the story of Philip and the eunuch were removed. The odd abruptness of its appearance and the odd elements of the story itself troubled Christians many centuries ago, because one of them added a verse to the text to make it seem more orthodox. Verse 37, which reads

> And Philip said, If thou believest with all thine heart, thou mayest. And he answered and said, I believe that Jesus Christ is the Son of God.

isn't found in early manuscripts of the New Testament. As that long-ago refiner of the story recognized, something puzzling is going on here.

Castration for Christ

Clues to what it may be can be found when you look at the original linguistic context of the earliest versions of Acts. One possible interpretation of the story which can be found this way, and which I haven't seen mentioned in any commentary on Acts, is that it represents an encounter with the sun-god. Look at the name of one of the figures involved. The name of the Ethiopian queen Candace would remind Latin speakers of the verb *candere*, "to shine", and Greek speakers of the verb γαναω *(ganao)*, with the same meaning.[43]

Candace was a title of the queen of an island-state called Meroë on the upper reaches of the Nile:

> The king was deified as child of the sun-god and regarded as too holy for secular functions; these were discharged for him by his mother, who bore the dynastic title of *Candace*.[emphasis not mine][44]

The term "eunuch", εὐνυχος, applied to this queen's representative in Acts isn't necessarily to be taken literally: sometimes it simply means an important official or "chamberlain", as in the verse of II Kings already mentioned, which runs:

> And he took away the horses that the kings of Judah had given to the sun, at the entering in of the house of the LORD, by the chamber of Nathan-melech the chamberlain, which was in the suburbs, and burned the chariots of the sun with fire. [xxiii 11]

The Hebrew word translated is סָרִיס/*saariis,* literally meaning a "castrated one" or "eunuch", but here doubtless more correctly translated as "chamberlain". Nonetheless, this verse from II Kings supports the idea that there is some Biblical connexion between the title of "eunuch", whether or not it is literally meant, and the worship of the sun-god.

And what of the nationality of the eunuch in Acts? He's described as an Ethiopian. This has no special significance in English, but in Greek the word Ethiopian, Ἀ'ιθιοψ *(Aithiops)*, literally means "burnt face", from the verb ἀ'ιθω (*aithó)*, meaning "to burn", and the noun ὤψ (*óps)*, meaning "face" or "eye". Aithiops is also nearly identical to the Greek adjective αἴθοψ (*aithops)*, which literally means "burning-faced" or "burning-eyed", but is usually translated into English as "fiery" or "keen". The sun-god, or a representative of the sun-god, might easily be described in this way, and the time of the encounter between Philip and the eunuch may also be significant.

In the original text the words κατα μεσημβριαν (*kata mesémbrian)* have two possible meanings. One, used in the Authorized Version, is "toward the south"; the other is "at midday". Μεσημβρια literally means "middle-day", when the sun is highest in the sky. Its additional meaning comes about because the nearer the equator you go in the northern hemisphere, that is, the further south, the higher the sun rises in the sky by midday. In the context of chapter 8, "south" seems the more logical translation because noon in the Middle East, for obvious reasons, "is not suitable for a long journey".[45] It is highly suitable, however, for an encounter with the sun-god in his chariot.[46]

And the word for chariot used here may also be significant. In Greek it's ἅρμα (*harma)*

> the common word for 'chariot' in Homer, [which] occurs in the LXX [the Septuagint, an ancient Judaeo-Greek translation of the Old Testament] usually for *rekeb*.[47]

In the Syriac translation of Acts, the word used for *harma* comes from the Syriac word ܪܟܒ/RaKeB, almost identical to the Hebrew רֶכֶב/ReKeB, and possessing the same numerical value. A *harma*/ RaKeB was usually a small war-chariot, similar to the one used by the sun-god, but the text indicates that the eunuch is sitting in something more like a carriage than a chariot, as modern translations sometimes recognize. He is, for example, reading from Isaiah as he sits in his chariot. In Greek, the word used for "read" is ἀναγιγνωσκω (*anagignóskó*), which means "to read aloud to others";[48] in Syriac, the word used is ܩܪܐ (*qara)*, which means "to read aloud to an audience", as opposed to ܗܓܐ (*haga)*, which means "to read aloud to oneself". The audience, presumably, is the driver. Finally, when the eunuch and Philip came to the water, the eunuch "commanded" the chariot to stop. Again the presence of a driver is implicit.

The baptism in this water too may be significant, because it is reminiscent of the myth of Phæthon, at the end of which Phæthon is plunged into the river Po. If the eunuch is a "burnt face" rather than a "burning face", this may be because, like Phæthon, he is only a proxy for the sun-god, not the sun-god himself. In the myth, the sun-god's proxy leaves the chariot and enters water; in chapter 8 of Acts, so does the Ethiopian eunuch:

> And he commanded the chariot to stand still: and they went down both into the water, both Philip and the eunuch; and he baptized him.

And when you look elsewhere for links between the Ethiopian eunuch and

Phæthon, they are easy to find. According to the main mythological sources, Phæthon was the son of Helios by Clymene, who was the wife of Merops, king of a people who became the Ethiopians, "the burnt faces", after the too-close approach of the sun-chariot under Phæthon's control, or lack of it. As already mentioned, the eunuch came from the island-state of Meroë, which was then in what the ancients called Ethiopia. Is the Phæthon myth, then, based on a king-slaying ritual in Meroë in which the king's son or a ritual substitute was cast into the Nile? Merops and Meroë are suggestively alike, and other sacrifices to the Nile are known in history, including, it is said, that of the beautiful youth Antinoüs, catamite of the emperor Hadrian, whose death one influential Byzantine chronology would later date to 122 AD, exactly a hundred years before Heliogabalus's possible sacrifice to the Tiber in 222.[49]

These echoes of the Acts story in pagan myth and history are tantalizing. They may include the name of Philip, which, like the nationality of the eunuch, may be a sort of Greek pun, because it literally means "fond-of-horses", another good description of the charioteer sun-god. Puns certainly seem to be used elsewhere in the story. The road Philip is commanded to seek, for example, leads from Jerusalem to Gaza. The eunuch is in charge of the Ethiopian queen's treasure. In Greek, Gaza is the same as it is in English, and "treasure" is γαζα — *gaza*.[50]

What might be called the "*gaz-*" syllable also crops up in the original language of the Old Testament prophet quoted by the eunuch. The prophet is Isaiah, and although his words are quoted by the eunuch in the Greek of an ancient Jewish version of the Old Testament called the Septuagint, they were originally written in Hebrew. In the Authorized Version's translation from the Hebrew, they read like this:

> He was oppressed, and he was afflicted, yet he opened not his mouth: he is brought as a lamb to the slaughterer, and as a sheep to the shearers is dumb, so he openeth not his mouth.He was taken from prison and from judgment: and who shall declare his generation? for he was cut off out of the land of the living: for the transgression of my people was he stricken. [liii, 7-8]

As can be seen by comparing these verses with their equivalent in Acts quoted above (32-3), the meaning of the Hebrew and Greek differs quite a lot. This may be significant, or may not (although it is generally true that quotations from the Septuagint in the New Testament differ in meaning from the original Hebrew).

Of the two interesting *gaz-* words in the Hebrew, for example, only one is translated directly and with reasonable accuracy into Greek. The first of these words is גֹזְזֶיהָ (*goz^{e}zêâ*) "her shearers", from the root גָּזַז (*gaazaz*) "to shear". The second is נִגְזַר (*nigazar*), "he was cut off [from the land of the living]", from the related root גָּזַר (*gaazar*), "to cut off". In Greek the first is translated as κειρων (*keirón*), "the one shearing": singular, not plural as in the Hebrew; and the second as αἰρεται (*airetai*), "[his life] is taken [from the earth]", from the verb αἰρω (*airó*), "to lift up, take away".

The Hebrew text would nonetheless have been regarded as the more sacred, and the mother-tongue speaker of the Semitic language Aramaic who wrote Acts, believed to have been St Luke, would probably have been familiar with it (although many Jews at the time used only the Septuagint, the Greek version of the Old Testament already mentioned). The *gaz-* syllable, then, occurs twice in the Greek text and twice in the Hebrew original of the Old Testament verses quoted in Greek. What is its significance?

There are two possibilities, neither of them necessarily excluding the other. The first is that there is some link being suggested with the Nazirites, an ancient Jewish sect whose adherents took vows, sometimes for life, never to drink wine, cut their hair, or be defiled by contact with a dead body. It is possible that "Nazarene", the term used of Christ in the Gospels, is actually a variant form of "Nazarite", but the most famous openly acknowledged adherent of the sect in the Bible is Samson. Although not entirely an orthodox Nazirite — he certainly came into contact with many dead bodies — Samson has several interesting links with the Acts story. His name, שִׁמְשׁוֹן *(Šimšôn)* in the original, means "sun-like", and comes from the Hebrew word שֶׁמֶשׁ *(šemeš)*, meaning "sun". His hair was bound or braided into "seven locks", which can easily be taken as symbolic of the seven days of the week ruled over by the sun. And then there is the way in which he is captured by the Philistines: by cutting or shearing:

> And she [Delilah] made him sleep upon her knees [בִּרְכֶּיהָ *birekeyaah*]; and she called for a man, and she caused him to shave off [תְּגַלַּח *t'gallaih*] the seven locks of his head; and she began to afflict him [vb. חָלַל *haalal*], and his strength went from him. [Judges xvi, 19]

Samson is then captured by the Philistines and brought to "grind in the prison house" in the city of Gaza after having his eyes put out. Candace, the sun-regent of Meroë, is described by Pliny the Elder as having only one eye. By accident, or by design? The Greek sun-hero Orion, blinded in both eyes like Samson after he raped a woman called Merope, restored his sight by travelling to the east and turning his face towards the sun-chariot as it rose at dawn.[51] Again there are tantalizing echoes of pagan ritual and myth in the supposedly monotheistic Bible.

This association with shaving and blindness is the first possible significance of the *gaz-* syllable. The second is that the words containing it in Isaiah are associated with castration. The man met on the road to Gaza who is in charge of the queen's *gaza*, or treasure, is a eunuch, a castrated man. The Hebrew verbs *gaazaz* and *gaazar* are both connected with cutting and removal, and although neither is used to mean "castrate" in the Old Testament, they form part of a pattern of meaning in chapter liii of Isaiah that might be taken to be advocating a form of ritual castration in honour of God. Verses 5 and 10, for example, read:

> But he was wounded for our transgressions, he was bruised for our iniquities ... Yet it pleased God to bruise him ...

The verbs are חָלַל *haalal*, "to be pierced, wounded" and דָּכָא *daakha'*, "to break into pieces, bruise". "Wound" might be taken as a euphemism for "castrate", particularly because "bruise" is certainly a euphemism in Hebrew for "castrate by crushing the testicles". In the first verse of Deuteronomy xxiii, for example, we read:

> He that is wounded in the stones, or hath his privy member cut off, shall not enter into the congregation of the LORD.

Here "wounded in the stones" is a translation of the Hebrew פְּצוּעַ־דַּכָּה *p^e tsûwa'-dakaah*, "wounded by crushing". Castrated men were not to enter the congregation of the Lord because

> such mutilations were required in Syrian and other religions, and for that reason disqualify for Yahweh's church.[52]

But it may be precisely because castration is unlawful, and thus repugnant in the eyes of God's people, that the prophet Isaiah is suggesting it. The description in Isaiah liii, later taken by Christians to be a prophecy of Christ, is that of a man undergoing deliberate humiliation for "the transgression of my people". And even if Isaiah did not mean "shearing" and "cutting off" to be references to ritual castration, these words may have been taken as such at a later date, when castration was seen as a holy act. In Matthew's gospel Jesus is recorded as speaking thus:

> All men cannot receive this saying, save they to whom it is given. For there are some eunuchs, which were so born from their mother's womb; and there are some eunuchs, which were made eunuchs of men: and there be eunuchs, which have made themselves eunuchs for the kingdom of heaven's sake. He that is able to receive it, let him receive it. [xix, 11-12]

This is one of the most cryptic of the many cryptic utterances made by Christ in the Gospels, and it has caused no little embarrassment to Christians down the centuries. Almost all commentators are agreed that his words are not to be taken literally but are rather an injunction to chastity:

> *eunuchs*, here denotes chastity of single life [53] ... We must probably interpret [these words as] praise of celibacy — there is no need to take the word "eunuchs" literally ... [54]

But if that is what Jesus meant, why did he use he use such extreme language and why did he use phrases like "eunuchs, which were made eunuchs of men", that is "by men"? Chastity is a matter of personal choice, or lack of it; being a eunuch generally isn't. Whatever is really meant here, there have been Christians who have taken these words in the easiest sense it is possible to take them in, that is, in their literal sense. The most famous of these was the theologian Origen, who, at about the age of 18,

> performed a strange act of self-mutilation, in obedience to what he regarded as the recommendation of Christ.[55]

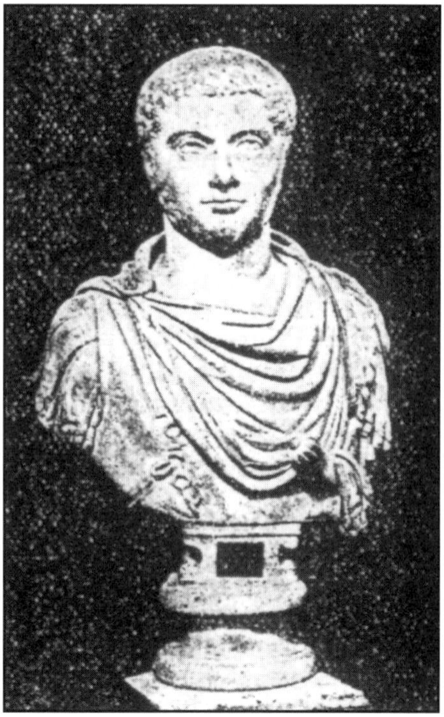
Heliogabalus

For further comment on this odd element of Christ's sexual teaching, as so often in the obscurer corners of sexology, there is no better person to turn to than Sir Richard Burton. In a note on the "Terminal Essay" to his **Arabian Nights**, Burton wrote:

> The texts justifying or enjoining castration [in the New Testament] are Matt. *xviii*. 8-9; Mark *ix*. 43-47; Luke *xxiii*. 29 and Col. *iii*. 5. St. Paul preached (1 Corin. *vii*. 29) that a man should live with his wife as if he had none. The Abelian heretics of Africa abstained from women because Abel died virginal. Origen mutilated himself after interpreting too vigorously Matth. *xix*. 12, and was duly excommunicated. But his disciple, the Arab Valerius founded (A.D. 250) the castrated sect called Valerians who, persecuted and dispersed by the Emperors Constantine and Justinian, became the spiritual fathers of the modern *Skopzis*. These eunuchs first appeared in Russia at the end of the xith century, when two Greeks, John and Jephrem, were metropolitans of Kiew [sic]: the former was brought thither in A.D. 1089 by Princess Anna Wassewolodowna and is called by the chronicles *Nawj* or the Corpse. But in the early part of the last century (1715-1733) a sect arose in the circle of Uglitseh and in Moscow, at first called *Clisti* or flagellants which developed into the modern *Skopzi*. For this extensive subject see *De Stein Zeitschrift für Ethn*. Berlin, 1875 and Mantegazza, chapt. vi.

Castration was an abhorrent act in mainstream Christianity because mainstream Christianity, although it hated the sexual pleasure that can accompany the creation of new adherents for the church, was firmly in the philoprogenitive Judaic tradition founded on this command in the 28th verse of Genesis:

> Be fruitful, and multiply, and replenish the earth

In paganism, however, castration was a fully accepted part of the worship of goddesses like Cybele, whose priests, the Galli, used to castrate themselves as part of their initiation into the goddess's worship. The emotions roused by the Galli's public castration ceremonies were so overwhelming, indeed, that male spectators who had had no intention of participating would sometimes come forward and perform an auto-castration that would be bitterly regretted by them when they had returned to their senses. Witness this description of the worship of a Cybele-like goddess in Syria:

> At the beginning of spring, when multitudes thronged to the sanctuary ... the flutes played, the drums beat, and the eunuch priests slashed themselves with knives, the religious excitement spread like a wave among the crowd of onlookers, and many a one did that which he little thought to do when he came as a holiday spectator to the festival. For man after man, his veins throbbing with the music, his eyes fascinated by the sight of streaming blood, flung his garments from him, leapt forth with a shout, and seizing one of the swords that stood ready for the purpose, castrated himself on the spot.[Lucian, *De Dea Syrica* ("Concerning the Syrian Goddess")][56]

Heliogabalus participated directly in Cybele's rites, but was apparently too fond of the pleasure his penis brought him to go all the way:

> Moreover he tossed up his head among the castrated devotees and tied up his genitals and did everything that the eunuch-priests were accustomed to do.[57]

Except, that is, what turned them into eunuch-priests in the first place:

> He had planned, indeed, to cut off his genitals altogether, but that desire was prompted solely by his effeminacy; the circumcision which he actually carried out was part of the priestly requirements of Elagabalus [i.e., the god Elah-Gabal], and he accordingly mutilated many of his companions in like manner.[58]

There is nonetheless a definite castration-and-eunuch motif in Heliogabalus's story, and it's interesting to note an indirect link with the castration tradition in Christianity in the visit, recorded by the church historian Eusebius, that the self-castrated Origen made to Heliogabalus's aunt Mammæa in Rome in the early part of the third century. A much more important eunuch in Heliogabalus's life, however, was his tutor Gannys, whose generalship helped his pupil to the imperial throne and whose name may be part of the links between Heliogabalus and the story of Philip and the eunuch.

First to note here is that there are obvious parallels between Heliogabalus and his co-regent mother Soaemias, and the king and mother of the Ethiopian sun-cult at Meroë. Second, the Ethiopian eunuch was in charge of the treasure of Candace, and Gannys's name may be derived from a Semitic word meaning "treasure". In Hebrew, for example, one word for "treasure" is גֶּנֶז (*genez),* which is related to the verb כָּנַס (*kaanas),* "to collect together". In ancient Greek the letter ζ, transliterated into English as "z", actually stood for the sound /zd/. A pure English or Semitic "z" occurring in final position in a word would have sounded more like "s" to a Greek ear, and so Gannys may represent a Greek transliteration of a Syriac original pronounced something like *genez* and meaning something like "treasurer".

Applying this kind of linguistic reasoning can in fact bind together more of the elements of myth and Biblical story already examined, and the fact that there may very well be no direct historical connexions between any of them is, in a sense, of little importance. Unreal connexions that are believed to exist influence behaviour just as effectively as connexions that actually do exist, and for a religious believer there is no clear distinction between unreal and real, coincidentally linguistic and demonstrably historical connexions anyway: language is as much under the control of God as history, and divine messages are as apt to come from the one as from the other.

Bearing this in mind, then, let's re-examine the verse from II Kings already presented as providing evidence of a link between eunuchs and worship of the sun-god. That link is transparent in any language that possesses these two concepts; a further link with the concept of treasure or the guardianship of treasure has to be sought in the ancient Greek of the Septuagint. In English, the verse in question runs thus:

> And he took away the horses that the kings of Judah had given to the sun, at the entering in of the house of the Lord, by the chamber of Nathan-Melech the chamberlain [*saaris*, literally meaning "eunuch"], which was in the suburbs, and burned the chariots of the sun with fire. [xxiii, 11]

"Chamber" translates the Hebrew לָשַׁךְ/*laašak*, meaning in general "a chamber" and in particular one attached to the side of a temple: one modern English translation, the Good News Bible, takes the word to mean the room in which Nathan-Melech lived and renders it as "living quarters". In the Septuagint, however, the word is given as γαζοφυλακιον *(gazophylakion)*, which means "treasury", from *gaza*, "treasure", and *phylakion*, "chamber". What is important here is not which translation is the most accurate, but which translation most closely reflects the religious preoccupations and beliefs of the ancient inhabitants of the Middle East. Obviously this will be the translation in the Septuagint, which was made around 135 BC by Jews to whom, equally obviously, there was something significant about treasure, eunuchs and worship of the sun-god. Indeed, another Hebrew word for the side-chamber of a temple, גִּזְרָה *(gizᵉraah)*, also seems to form part of the network of meaning around eunuchs, castration and treasure in Hebrew that is woven around the phonetic element *gaz-*.

We can now take this network and use it to trap more meaning in the story of Philip and the eunuch. The eunuch was the treasurer of queen Candace at Meroë, capital of the identically named

> island, so-called, and almost an island in reality, formed by the rivers Astapus (*Blue Nile*) and Astaboras (*Atbarah*), and the portion of the Nile between their mouths.[59]

From a map — or, without a map, from an overlooking piece of high ground — Meroë might be said to occupy a "groin" of land between the thighs formed by the rivers Astapus and Astaboras and the torso formed by the river Nile. In the light of the eunuch/castration motif of the Acts story, this possible topographical symbolism becomes highly significant when one looks for phonetic equivalents of "Meroë" in Biblical Hebrew, for amongst the closest is the verb מָרַח (*maarah)*, meaning "to crush, bruise", and by extension, like *daakha'*, "to crush the testicles", as in the verse in Leviticus xxi, 20 describing those to be excluded from the congregation of the Lord:

> Or a crookbackt, or a dwarf, or that hath a blemish in his eye, or be scurvy, or scabbed, or hath his stones broken [אָשֶׁךְ מְרוֹחַ (*'aašek m^erôah*)]

Finally, the site of Meroë falls in the ancient Æthiopian and modern Sudanese province of Gezira: yet another appearance of the *gaz-* element that has already been demonstrated to have close links with the name of Gannys, the eunuch-tutor of Heliogabalus, fanatical worshipper of the divine solar charioteer Elah-Gebal.

To whom it is now surely good time to turn our attention. What of the sun-god in the form Heliogabalus actually worshipped him? What does Elah-Gabal actually mean? The first element is pretty unambiguously a Semitic title for God, ܐܠܗ (*'elaah)*, meaning "the adored one". The second element may be related to a Hebrew verb meaning "to be powerful", or, as generally suggested, to the Syriac ܓܒܠ (*gabal)*, meaning "to form", rendering the full title "the Forming God", which is, in Gibbon's words, a "proper, and even happy epithet for the Sun".[60]

Possibly so, but I would suggest that the second element also carried the echo, at least, of the Hebrew גְּבַל (*gebal)* and the Arabic جَبَل (*jebel)*, both meaning "mountain". Elah-Gabal was the god of Emesa or Homs, and

> In truth the setting is apt for such a cult, because the acropolis of Homs, a rocky outcrop from the plain, stands up in the light of day like the gnomon on a sundial.[61]

That the "Gabal" of Elah-Gabal was interpreted in this way is a good way of explaining the enthusiasm with which Heliogabalus pursued the cult of Cybele in Rome, for Cybele was not only a mountain-goddess but was actually named after a mountain, Mount Cybelus in Phrygia.[62]

To someone like Heliogabalus, who was probably a native speaker of Syriac, her name could naturally have seemed like a variant of "Gabal". In ancient times Cybele's name was pronounced "Kybele"; the consonants /k/ and /g/ are articulated in an almost identical way and sometimes alternate in the Semitic languages. As pointed out above, the words *genez* and *kaanas* are related in Hebrew, and the name of one of Heliogabalus's "associates in lewdness" is given as "Gordius" by Dio and "Cordius" by Lampridius, very likely reflecting a contemporary confusion of the two forms.

Whether the names Cybele and Gabal were in fact related etymologically is

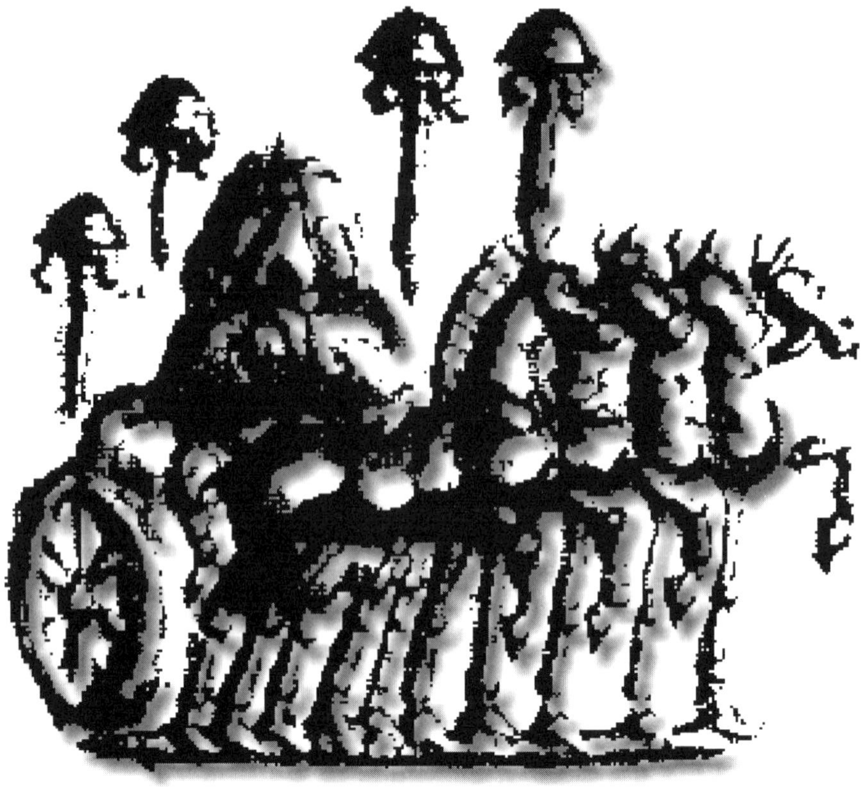

unimportant: if Heliogabalus believed they were and acted on that belief, it would have made no difference that he was mistaken, and this kind of consonant and vowel shuffling is an important part of the mystical Qabbalistic tradition in which the chariot, ReKeB, is so significant. Interestingly, ReKeB and Cybele/Gabal could be regarded as equivalents using Qabbalistic reasoning. As Japanese and Chinese speakers of English sometimes demonstrate, the consonants /l/ and /r/ are closely related, and they sometimes alternate in the Semitic languages, or at least appear to do so, which is the more important thing from the point of view of Qabbalists. The verb גָּזַל (*gaazal)*, for example, which means "to strip off", is cognate with גָּזַר (*gaazar)*, "to cut off", and, with another alternation of /k/ and /g/, the verb כָּבַר (*kaabar)*, "to be powerful", is cognate with גָּבַל (*gaabal)*, "to twist" and hence, "to form".

But could Qabbalistic reasoning, which is Jewish in origin, have been used by the devotees of a pagan god like Elah-Gabal? For two main reasons, the answer is yes. First, Judaism and paganism, like Christianity and paganism, are not as distinct as Jews, and Christians, would like to be supposed: pagan elements in both the Old and the New Testaments have already been examined several times in this article. Second, Heliogabalus was, like any good Roman emperor, a religious universalist, though with the difference that he asked that all other religions be subordinate to that of Elah-Gabal, rather than that Elah-Gabal be simply *primus inter pares*. As Lampridius remarks in the "reliable"

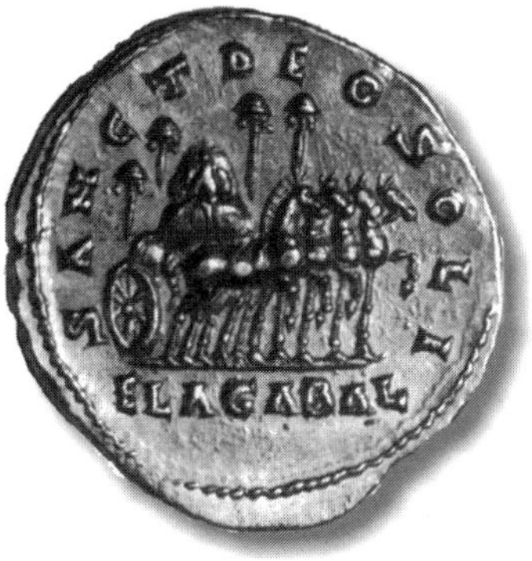

section of the **Vita**:

> He [Heliogabalus] used to say, furthermore, that the religion of the Jews and Samaritans ought to be transferred [to the temple of Elah-Gabal], so that the priesthood of [the god] might include the mysteries of every cult.[63]

And this priesthood contained what to modern ears are distinctly Jewish elements. Heliogabalus was circumcized as "part of the priestly requirements" of Elah-Gabal, and Dio also mentions his "abstaining from swine's flesh, on the ground that his devotion would thereby be purer"[64]. According to Lampridius, in one of those fantastical parts of the **Vita** that may be examples of his "veiled language", Heliogabalus sometimes "served ostriches at banquets, saying that the Jews had been commanded to eat them"[65].

Although one can prove nothing from an absence, it's worth remembering that Lampridius wrote after the triumph of Christianity and that every line of the pagan Dio and Herodian has come to us through centuries of Christian copyists and editors. Any too embarassing details of Heliogabalus's religious activities could easily have been omitted or re-written, and the books of Dio's history that deal with Heliogabalus, like many others in the history, have survived as such only in epitomes, or abridgments, carried out by two Byzantine monks called Xiphilinus of Trapezus and Johannes Zonaras in, respectively, the tenth and twelfth centuries. The epitomes may be reliable but they are also, by definition, incomplete. If we turn to Lampridius's **Vita** we find that a modern classical scholar called T.D. Barnes has

> demonstrated that chapters 1-18 derive from a reliable source, which he identifies with Marius Maximus. The remainder is fiction.[66]

Reading the **Vita** in the light of this remark, one can easily note the sudden change of tone and wording, and although the latter half of the **Vita** has been easily the most influential of all texts in shaping the tradition of Heliogabalus as the crazed, epicene pursuer of pleasure at all costs, one's ultimate feeling may be one of frustration that so much nonsense, however entertaining, has survived in place of so much historical truth, however uninspiring, as Lampridius sniggers his way through the salacious details of a portrait of Heliogabalus that distorts much more than it reveals.

Or does he? Does it? Perhaps not. It may be in Lampridius, who wrote in full knowledge of the censorship he would suffer if he were too explicit, that some or all of the truth about Heliogabalus's relationship with Judaism and Christianity lies. Lampridius is cloyingly sycophantic towards the dedicatee of his history, the emperor Constantine, who was christened "the Great" because his campaigning and slaughtering was carried out on behalf of the previously neglected Christian religion:

> But enough about that name [Antoninus], although he polluted that hallowed name of the Antonines, which you, Most Sacred Constantine, so revere that you have made Marcus and Pius golden examples for yourself, as though they were your own ancestors, adopting the virtues of the men of old which accord with your character and are pleasing and dear to you.[67]

But is this sycophancy, or mockery? And when Lampridius speaks of Heliogabalus's having driven "a chariot drawn by four elephants on the Vatican [hill], destroying the tombs which were in the way"[68] is this, as one modern translator of the **Vita** suggests, a "sly anti-Christian joke"? If so, what of the claim that Heliogabalus:

> never dined for less than hundred thousand sesterces, that is thirty pounds of silver [ch. 24][69]

Thirty pounds of silver? For a meal? One doesn't have to be a Christian to be reminded of another, somewhat smaller sum and another, somewhat less sumptuous meal. If Lampridius is taking concealed jabs at Christianity here, he may be concealing other things in other places. The **Vita** plunges after the relative sobriety of the first eighteen chapters into an orgy of surreal sybaritic detail. Heliogabalus offers as prizes in his lotteries

> ten bears, ten dormice, ten lettuces or ten pounds of gold. [ch. 21] [70]

He feeds

> the country folk in the inland regions with murenas' and pikes' milk [ch. 22] [71]

organizes competitions for

> his slaves, even asking them to bring him a thousand pounds of spiders' webs [ch. 26] [72]

and amuses himself by

> inviting eight bald men to dinner, or again, eight one-eyed men or eight men with gout, eight deaf men, eight dark men, eight tall men or eight fat men. [ch. 29][73]

If these are jokes, they are rather obscure ones; if they are not, rather being veiled parts of a serious, hidden message, Lampridius may one day supply what Goethe, echoing, surely, every historian who has ever lived, pleaded for on his death-bed. The plea is nowhere more appropriate than for the strange rise and fall of the high-priest of the Emesan sun-cult. *Mehr licht!* More light!

LORD OF THE RINGPIECE

A STICKY-FINGERED APPRECIATION OF THE MARQUIS DE SADE

Buggery can be a messy fucking business. Particularly if you follow the Marquis de Sade's recipe for success:

> 'Tis an essential condition for the receiver to be bursting with the urge to shit, so that the end of the bugger's cock can drive deep into his faeces, depositing therein all the more softly and warmly the fuck that irritates it and sets it ablaze.[1]

This passion for buggery in both its passive and its active forms is one of the exegetic conundrums that confront a prospective biographer of de Sade as of few if any other writers. What precisely was he? Bisexual? Homosexual? Omnisexual? And what does his work mean? Does it have a message? No message? Or several messages, some of them contradictory? A great deal has been written in an attempt to answer these questions, but because most biography — perhaps all — is really a disguised way of writing about the biographer, the value of the work has tended to rest on how well the biographer's prejudices and tastes chime with what is actually present in their subject's work.

Perhaps that is why the best two pieces I have ever read on de Sade, Camille Paglia's in her book **Sexual Personae**[2] and David Mitchell's in his forthcoming study of the Manchester publishers Savoy,[3] have been incidental to their writers' pursuit of a more important theme. Undazzled by a too direct and lengthy contemplation of the Marquis's *oeuvre*, Paglia and Mitchell seem to have been able to make out the *chiaroscuro* of his character and motives more clearly, and so have talked far more sense about him, and at much reduced length. De Sade, they conclude, was a satirist, and his work is for Paglia a Dionysiac *reductio ad absurdum* of Rousseau's philosophy of Nature, for Mitchell a manic expression of his utter hatred for the powerful of his day.

Lengthier works dedicated purely or primarily to de Sade seem far less valuable — although I cannot claim to have sampled very many of them. De Sade is interesting not because what he says is uniquely complex or subtle or intellectually stimulating, but because he says it so loudly and so forcefully. His work is an unsurpassable extreme, a peak of pornographic depravity that fascinates and attracts the reader simply because it is there, an abyss of depraved pornography to which we are drawn almost against our wills, and into which we cannot gaze without being gazed into ourselves.

But then we sometimes see there only what we want to see. Donald Thomas's biography,[4] for example, although admirable for its concision, manages to claim de Sade is hostile or indifferent to homosexuality in face of the enormous amount of ink de Sade expended advocating active and passive buggery, the enormous amount of energy de Sade expended acquiring or fashioning anal dildos whilst in prison, and the enormous amount of semen de Sade expended using those dildos when he was in prison and buggering or being buggered when he was not. Presumably Donald Thomas himself is not bisexually inclined; that de Sade undoubtedly was therefore does not interest him. Biography is a disguised form of talking about the biographer.

Something similar is true of Swinburne's reaction to de Sade. Simultaneously an anarchist and an idolater, Swinburne upheld the Marquis as "the acme and apostle of perfection, without as he says having read a word of his work"[5]. When he came to do so his immediate reaction was to roar with laughter — that is, laughter at de Sade, rather than, as seems to me should certainly be the case, with him. And yet despite this reaction, Swinburne never freed himself of de Sade's influence: uniquely amongst writers, de Sade seems able to inspire devotion in and exercise influence over those who entirely misunderstand or misinterpret his central messages. This may be because his central messages seem impossibly — perversely — simple, or because they are not particularly original or inspiring ones. Power corrupts, and the powerful are hypocrites. Many others have said it, but no-one else has said it so loudly or forcefully. There is the dilemma: the form of the message is too easily detached from the content: the soft meat falls completely off the unappetizing bones: de Sade's work is the product of a mental pressure-cooker. Subject a highly sexed, highly intelligent and highly self-indulgent eighteenth-century Frenchman to the frustrations of several grotesquely unjust and lengthy prison sentences, and he will either go mad or become the

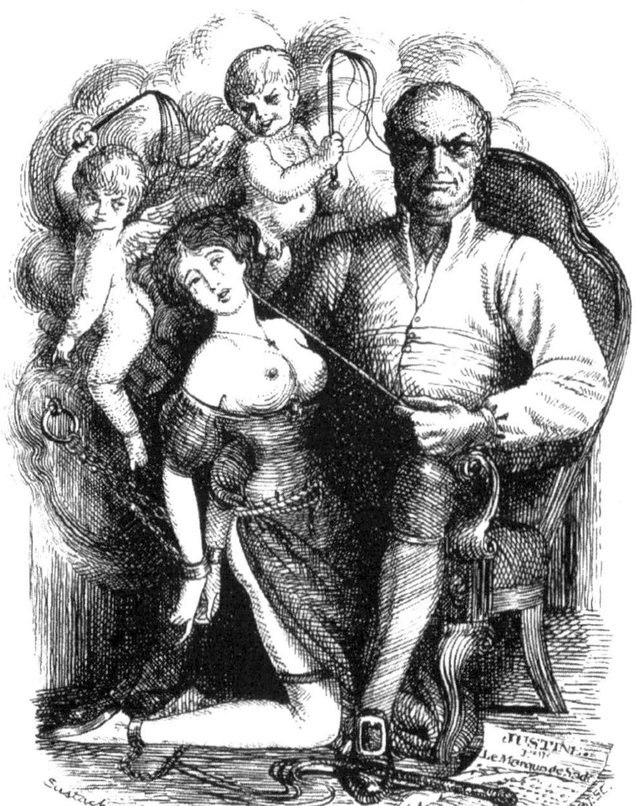

The Marquis de Sade

author of **Juliette** and **120 Days of Sodom**. The interesting question about de Sade is not whether he was wholly sane — he wasn't — but how he was not wholly insane. His books are fuelled by an overwhelming rage and hatred that would otherwise have gone to destroying his reason and perhaps his will to live. They are not entirely rational or reasoned, and so it's hardly surprising that they are not entirely consistent either. He had more than one reason for writing them, and, as I suggested above, they contain more than one message. Some of these messages are contradictory. All of them are to be found in **Juliette**, the innocent-sounding book that is, with **120 Days of Sodom**, the most notorious and extreme of his works.

Juliette is a sequel to **Justine**, and like many sequels it isn't as good as the original. **Justine** had shown de Sade that there was a market for extreme pornography; **Justine** had been criticized for its gleeful portrayal of woman as victim of suffering: **Juliette** bears both things in mind and sets out, at great length, first to be more extreme in its pornography and second to create a gleeful portrayal of woman as inflictor of suffering. It succeeds in its first ambition, not wholly in its second. The French surrealist Apollonaire characterized it as the proto-feminist left hook to which **Justine** was the right-hand feint:

> Justine is woman as she has been hitherto, enslaved, miserable and less than human; her opposite, Juliette[,] represents the woman whose advent [de Sade] anticipated, a figure of whom minds have as yet no conception, who is arising out of mankind, who shall have wings, and who shall renew the world.[6]

Robert del Quiaro's 1994 biography of de Sade[7] devotes some time to a discussion of why Apollonaire is wrong in this claim, and in this judgement on de Sade's work, as in very few if any others, I believe del Quiaro is right. However, he hardly needs to look very hard to find evidence to support his case, for Juliette is not the unchained, authentically autonomous woman of any ordinary conception of female liberation. This passage, in which the evil judge Saint-Fond bemoans the state of Juliette's anus, is a good guide to her relationship with the male libertines in the book:

> "O God!" he cried, all dismayed, "it's spotlessly clean! ... I like them unwiped, beshat...I like them perfectly foul — but this one is scrubbed, fresh as new-driven snow. Well, we shall have to resort to another; here you are, Juliette, behold mine — it is the way I wanted yours to be, you'll find shit in there aplenty. Kneel facing it, adore it, consider the honour I accord you in permitting you to do my arse the homage the entire nation, nay, the entire world aspires to render it — oh, how many people would be overcome with joy could they but exchange places with you! If the very gods were to descend into our midst it would be to vie for this favour. Suck, lick; drive deep your tongue; seize your chance, my child, this is not the moment for backwardness."[8]

And one would not have to know anything about where de Sade was when he wrote this, or about who had put him there, to suspect that it is also a good guide to his attitude to the judiciary. Any naïve interpretation of **Juliette**, under which it is simply a justification of and guided tour to extreme sexual depravity, would have to ignore such passages, as well as several in which the utterly selfish and amoral libertines have innocent men and women packed off to prison on rigged or invented evidence. At one point Juliette laments not being able to have a young woman unjustly hanged; the male libertine Noirceuil replies:

> "I must remind you that such pleasures are over and done with in fifteen or twenty minutes. I recommend that we somewhat prolong the wretch's sufferings; what say we make them extend over the rest of her life? It's a simple matter. I'll have her confined to a dungeon in Bicêtre; how old is she? Twenty? She could rot half a century in prison."[9]

It's impossible to believe that de Sade intended his readers to make no comparison with his own situation when he wrote such passages. Then again, might not the naïve interpretation arrive at the same conclusion as the more sophisticated? Is de Sade lacerating judges, priests, popes and kings not out of hatred and contempt, but out of jealousy?

> [T]he throne is to everybody's taste, and 'tis not the throne they detest but him who is seated on it.[10]

In part, the answer is yes. De Sade is jealous of what the powerful are able to do because part of him is attracted to it. The sex scenes in **Juliette** are masturbation fantasies and, in fantasy, de Sade is able to contemplate such things as the demolition of a young girl's anus by an over-sized penis with delight.

The fantasized power to do this is attractive, but this does not prevent him simultaneously detesting those who have the real power to do it. Moral indignation is jealousy with a halo: Sadean satire is jealousy with a hard-on. In other words, **Juliette** is ambivalent, although one might ask how much of the sex in it was composed to please its author and how much to entice readers into sampling the less immediately palatable philosophy and anti-moralizing that accompany it.

More disturbingly, one might also ask how much of it was based on personal experience. There is fart-fetishism in **Juliette**;[11] de Sade is known to have been a fart-fetishist. There is sexual torture and murder in **Juliette**; are we entitled to an *ergo* and a conclusion about de Sade's extra-curricular activities? Many people have thought so, and two of the very few truly disturbing passages in **Juliette** do in fact provide hints that they may not be entirely mistaken.

Truly disturbing passages in **Juliette** are few because it is not a realistic book. One wouldn't have to know that de Sade also wrote plays to be reminded constantly of stage-sets, fake blood and dialogue designed to be spoken aloud before a drunken audience to achieve its full effect:

> "The thing to do," said I, "is to cut her belly open, one horizontal slash, one vertical, I'll go into her

entrails with a hot iron, I'll cauterize her heart and viscera, she will die, but very gradually."

"Heavenly child," my father sighed, "little angel..."[12]

It's seldom that de Sade makes interesting use of purely literary effects. There is something both comic and sinister in his use of italics in dialogue from a libertine who has raked the interior of Juliette's vagina with "talon-like fingernails":

"*Lubin*," he then murmured to his valet, exhibiting his bloodied fingers, "*my dear Lubin, I triumph. Cunt-skin*."[13]

And something uncharacteristically erotic in his use of hyphens in dialogue from an Italian libertine who is "embuggering" a beautiful young Frenchwoman — with her consent, but to the surprise of Juliette:

"Pray do not interrupt anything on my account, Signor," I hastened to say to him, "simply remember that she is not the one you have contracted for."

"And I am dreadfully sorry about it," the rake replied, his words punctuated by gasps of pleasure, "I am dreadfully — sorry — for her arse — the most beautiful arse in creation, the — tightest fitting — oh, with this there are — wonders to be achieved ..."[14]

Descriptions of action, on the other hand, are generally lifeless. Vaginas and anuses split asunder, blood gushes, brains splatter, breasts are pincered to shreds, testicles crushed, but none of it is very realistic or vivid. Except very, very occasionally. A beautiful teenage girl is placed into "a drum, the inner surface of which was studded with steel spikes".[15] The drum is set spinning:

Very soon the ascending volume and tone of the victim's screams give us report of her pain. Violent you may be certain it was; judge thereof by this detail: the blood was coming off her like one of those fine rains blown almost to mist by a strong wind[16].

This detail, delicate, precise and naturalistic, is horrific not simply because of its clarity and novelty, but also because it doesn't sound like invention. De Sade, it seems to suggest, is not imagining here, but remembering.

Another unsettling chink through which reality seems to be showing is found in the reaction of another young girl to the news that she is to have "a rinse of boiling oil" injected into her rectum:

But then a very comical thing occurred: panic-stricken at the thought of the clyster intended for her, the girl let loose everything her bowels contained, flooding shit all over the floor.[17]

Once more in the midst of mannered, absurd, mostly unvisualizable sexual atrocity, there is a vivid, naturalistic touch that genuinely disturbs. People do lose control of their bowels under the influence of extreme terror or fright, but one doesn't usually know this or bring it readily to mind unless one has experienced it in oneself or in others.

De Sade, of course, did not always lead a sheltered life under the careful supervision of the state. He had been a soldier and had experienced battle, and although the fact that he was decorated for his bravery might suggest he never himself lost his bottle in this way,[18] he must have seen others do so. Why then should a description of the phenomenon in a young girl threatened with torture seem disturbing? It suggests imagination based on experience, not remembrance. Perhaps, but I find it disturbing here because the generic victim in **Juliette** is overwhelmingly passive and stereotyped in her responses to her oppressors. She never makes any attempt to escape, she never fights back, she very often weeps and wails and pleads for mercy, always in vain; only once does she bemerd herself from fright. This is highly unusual in the context of the fiction, highly likely in reality. That is why this passage is disturbing.

But whether or not there is evidence of autobiography in the worst sex tableaux of **Juliette**, as there certainly is in, say, the journeys made by various characters to Italy and Holland, is in some ways irrelevant to a consideration of what de Sade intended to say in the book. De Sade was a satirist, but also a human being: that he was a hypocrite or unable to control his worst impulses would not negate the aims of his satire. And there is evidence from other sources that he was in contact with men who actually enacted some of the horrors of **Juliette** or **120 Days**:

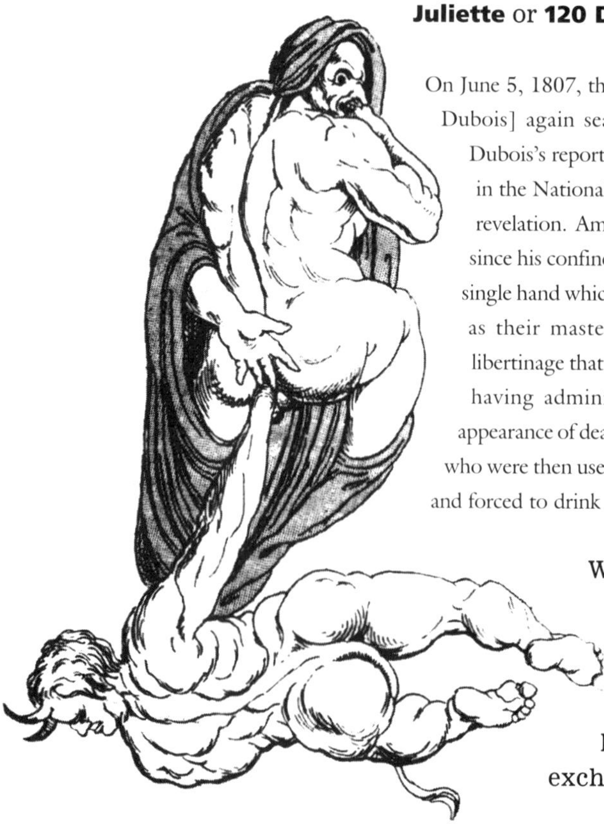

> On June 5, 1807, the police [headed by an officer called Dubois] again searched Sade's cell [at Charenton]. Dubois's report, which was discovered only recently in the National Archives, also yields an astonishing revelation. Among letters received by the marquis since his confinement, "there are several written by a single hand which prove he has disciples as horrifying as their master. The writer describes scenes of libertinage that have recently occurred and boasts of having administered poisons that produced an appearance of death lasting for several hours in women who were then used in every possible manner, tortured, and forced to drink three enormous bottles of blood".[19]

Whether de Sade went beyond exchanging letters with such disciples is presently impossible to say, and may remain so for ever; whether he even got so far as exchanging letters might also be asked. Police reports, then just as now, are not necessarily truthful. Assume, though, that the report is accurate, that the letters spoke of things that had actually happened and that de Sade, on the outside, collaborated with the libertine or libertines responsible for them. Assume that he and they went far beyond them.

What of it? Such things certainly went on at the time, sometimes in public with the blessing of the state, as with executions for high treason. De Sade lived in cruel times. The recipe given above for producing **Juliette** and **120 Days** is carefully worded: it is not just a case of any man and any unjust prison sentence. De Sade was an eighteenth-century Frenchman, and we must understand eighteenth-century France if we wish to understand him. Many have not made the effort to do so: unsurprisingly, because such an effort is very easy to forgo for a writer, particularly one relatively close in time like de Sade. When we look at a painting of contemporary life from the eighteenth century, it is impossible to avoid being aware that it is from the eighteenth century: the clothes, the hair-styles, the furniture, the buildings, perhaps even the facial expressions and poses are all clearly of their age, not of ours. We do not so easily fall into the trap of judging the picture's content out of the context provided by its form.

A de Sade text, on the other hand, although also a product of the eighteenth century, is not so obviously and permanently stamped with its date of origin. We are almost certainly reading it in a modern edition printed with a modern typeface on modern paper. We rapidly become used to the mildly archaic style of de Sade's writing, and such a style is anyway flattened or partly removed by translation if, as is overwhelmingly the case in English-speaking countries, we aren't reading in the original. De Sade is describing a world that is different from our own in many ways: there was no electricity, houses were cold, dark and draughty, city streets filthy and malodorous, to name only a few of the most important. These things were, however, perfectly obvious parts of life to eighteenth-century men and women, and good writing does not spend much time stating the obvious. An eighteenth-century reader knew what an eighteenth-century road looked like: that is why an eighteenth-century writer didn't find it necessary to describe one in detail. When de Sade writes:

> We escort her to the gate and out upon the highroad.[20]

there is a huge amount that he leaves unsaid. How are "we" dressed? How is the woman being escorted dressed? What does the gate look like? The highroad? A twentieth-century reader has to make a conscious, out-of-the-ordinary effort to picture a scene that for an eighteenth-century reader was conjured up automatically. Translate de Sade's words faithfully to the cinema or television screen, however, and there is no way of avoiding the eighteenth-century context, and it is also far harder to avoid the possible answers this context provides to moral questions about the scene.

And the scene does raise moral questions: it was not chosen at random. It describes Juliette and a libertine associate throwing their inevitable young female victim out onto the streets to live or die by begging. They have previously swindled her out of a fortune, raped her vaginally and anally, cut out her eyes, chopped off her hands, torn out her tongue, blown off one of her breasts with a firecracker and made her deaf by driving a knife-point into each of her ears. For some twentieth-century readers these horrors may take place in a kind of cultural vacuum: they seem gratuitous, grossly misogynistic, and clear evidence of de Sade's wickedness and delight in cruelty against women. We can understand what it means — what it *denotes* — for a man to bugger a young woman and ejaculate as her anus tightens under the agony of having an eye sliced out. These things are cultural universals, more or less independent of time and space: pain, sex, cruelty, human anatomy. But we don't necessarily understand what the action *connotes*, because we may forget that these cultural universals have a non-universal context. They take place in eighteenth-century France, they are being inflicted on a young woman who is to be cast out as a beggar. The words don't remind us strongly of this context; pictures inevitably would. That is why de Sade as a writer is much more liable to be misinterpreted than de Sade as the basis of a film or television play. Reading de Sade, we don't necessarily ask ourselves how many beggars there were at the time, how they came to be beggars and what physical condition many of them were in. Seeing de Sade, we well might, and we might decide that the young girl's fate is not or not simply an example of extreme pornography reflecting a warped delight in female pain, but an example of extreme black humour and satire, reflecting disgust at injustice and compassion for its victims.

But if this scene is presented as evidence of de Sade's compassion, the obvious rejoinder is that he has a funny way of showing it. True enough. De Sade was too full of rage to find subtlety of expression or water-colour portraiture attractive. He was rotting in prison without good justification because society was organized in such a way that his enemies didn't need any good justification to have him put there. Society and those who organized and ran it for their own ends — bankers, clerics, judges, aristocrats — were therefore to be assailed to the utmost with the only means de Sade had at his disposal. His enemies pretended that they were motivated by good, that God Almighty Himself smiled upon them and sanctified their power through the Christian religion. Very well, he would portray them and their religion in the starkest, foulest terms. He would invert their loudly proclaimed morality entirely and shriek constant manic justifications of all the crimes and horrors that the powerful pretended to abhor, punished with the utmost severity in others — and secretly indulged in themselves all the time.

That is why he wrote what he wrote — in part. As has already been pointed out, de Sade was ambivalent in his attitudes towards his themes. He exaggerated for satiric effect, but also for erotic, and this was for his own benefit at least as much as for the sake of sales. De Sade, like any writer — or any human being — was subject not only to cultural pressures, but also to physiological ones. He

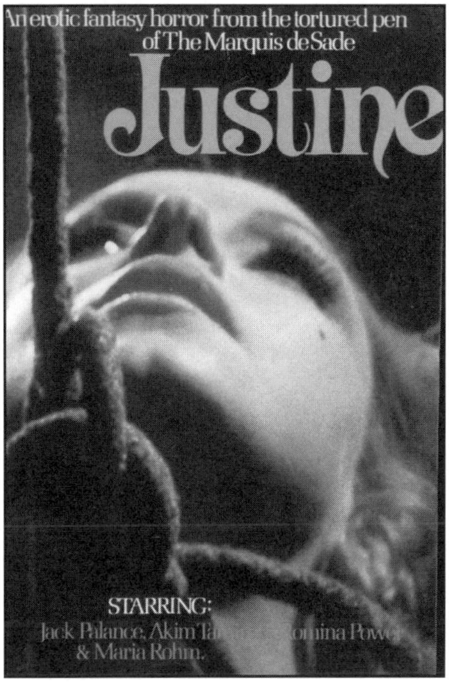

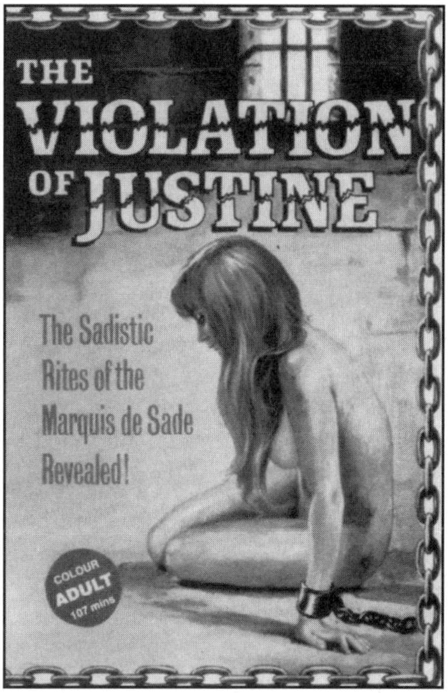

had difficulties with ejaculation, needing a greater than usual mental stimulus to achieve it while he was masturbating. Images of sex on their own was not enough: they had been to be amplified, embellished, supercharged with images of pain, degradation and filth. As Anthony Burgess puts it:

> The creator of these visions [in *120 Days of Sodom*] was evidently in a state of sexual frustration so intense that no imagined stimulus could procure a discharge. At the same time he was clear-headed enough to recognise, with a clarity never before known, a truth that not even Mrs Whitehouse may deny — that sex and cruelty have much to do with each other.[21]

Here is another way in which taking his work out of context leads to misinterpretation. De Sade did find the infliction of pain sexually arousing: there can be no doubt of this from proven incidents in his life. However, he did not necessarily find the most extreme forms of the infliction of pain sexually arousing, other, that is, than as fantasies. It was impossible for him to behave wickedly in a prison cell — to flout the despised morality of those who put him there — and so he had to behave wickedly in imagination. There, where there are no real consequences, no real victims, and no real policemen, the only limits are those one imposes on oneself. De Sade imposed fewer than anyone else who has ever lived.

It's clear, then, that another part of why he wrote was to help himself achieve sexual satisfaction during his prison sentences. A common but curiously old-fashioned way of disparaging a piece of writing that contains sex is to call it a

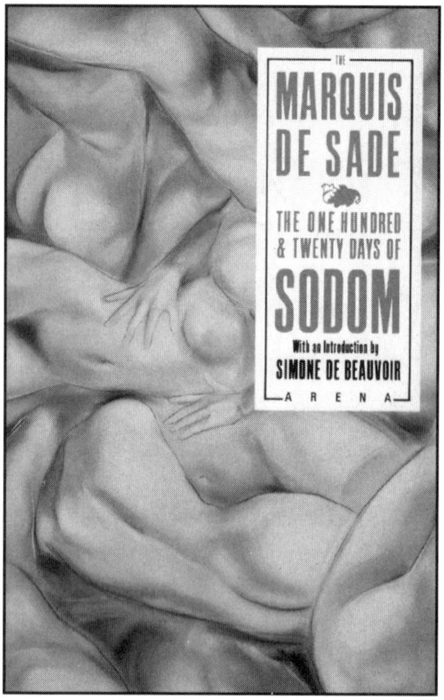

masturbation fantasy. De Sade's books are masturbation fantasies — amongst other things — but anyone who imagines that this is a way of dismissing them has to face the fact that de Sade would have been the first to admit it. De Sade, astonishing or unbelievable as it may seem to some people, did have virtues, and one of the most prominent of these was his honesty. Another was his sense of humour. The two are often combined in his writing. De Sade not only wanted to be wicked in his writing, he also, like any writer, wanted to be read. He wanted to be read so urgently that, as many will have discovered, it becomes difficult to read him. Most of his novels contain lengthy, obsessive stretches of philosophy and anti-moralizing. They get repeated. They get boring. They get easy to skip. Do you think de Sade didn't know this?

> During this learned dissertation, Madame de Noirceuil and the two Ganymedes had fallen asleep.[22]

But knowing that he got carried away too much and too often, and laughing at himself for it, didn't stop him doing it because, as he also realized, he wasn't able to control himself. De Sade — and this is another obstacle to many people's understanding of him — was a highly intelligent man, but don't suppose that this meant his behaviour or his work sets a consistently valuable example to follow. De Sade was highly intelligent; what he did and wrote often wasn't. David Mitchell points this out in a surprising way in his study of de Sade:

> His *stupid* inability to keep his activities quiet led him to spend most of his life in jail.[23]

Stupid? De Sade? The divine Marquis, freest spirit who ever lived? Well, yes. And again, he must have realized it himself, and it must have been another heaping of fuel on the fire that heated the mental pressure-cooker that cooked the ever-revolting, ever-enticing fare served up in **Justine**, **Juliette** and **120 Days of Sodom**. In his work, de Sade is not only anxious to attack his enemies, not only anxious to provide himself with literary *aides masturbatoires*, but also anxious to prove, all the evidence of his unnecessary and self-inflicted prison sentences to the contrary, that he is an intelligent man: an intellectual.

Here is yet another part of why he wrote, and another part of the context in which he wrote. De Sade, because he is the reddest in tooth and claw of the writers of his day by far, has survived very well to the present. Readers in the eighteenth century came to his work familiar with the literary background against which it was composed; more and more of his present-day readers don't. You can't understand de Sade the writer without knowing something of de Sade the reader. This is a truism, but one that is often overlooked, never more damagingly than in de Sade's case. De Sade wrote about sex and violence; Voltaire, Rousseau and the *Encyclopédistes* wrote about life, liberty, and the pursuit of happiness. It's easy to guess who has the larger potential audience nowadays, and easy to see why de Sade will only become more liable to be misinterpreted and misunderstood as time goes by. People tend to miss the point of satire when they don't know the target. People tend not to realize it is satire at all.

If you know, for example, that Rousseau celebrated the innate goodness of man and the joys that will flow from our wholehearted embrace of the impulses given to us by Nature, you understand what Camille Paglia means when she says that de Sade's work is a satire on Rousseau, or you will have already worked it out for yourself. Rousseau's noble savage is noble precisely because he is a savage, at one with Nature, guided by Her in all he does, uncorrupted by the deadening, unnatural influence of civilization. De Sade's ignoble savages are ignoble for precisely the same reasons. Rousseau asks us to look to other times and other races beyond reach of the dead hand of contemporary civilization for examples of how life can truly be lived to its fullest. De Sade does so, and produces catalogues of atrocity, one of which I would unhesitatingly call one of the two or three most disturbing parts of **Juliette**. Literary analysis of

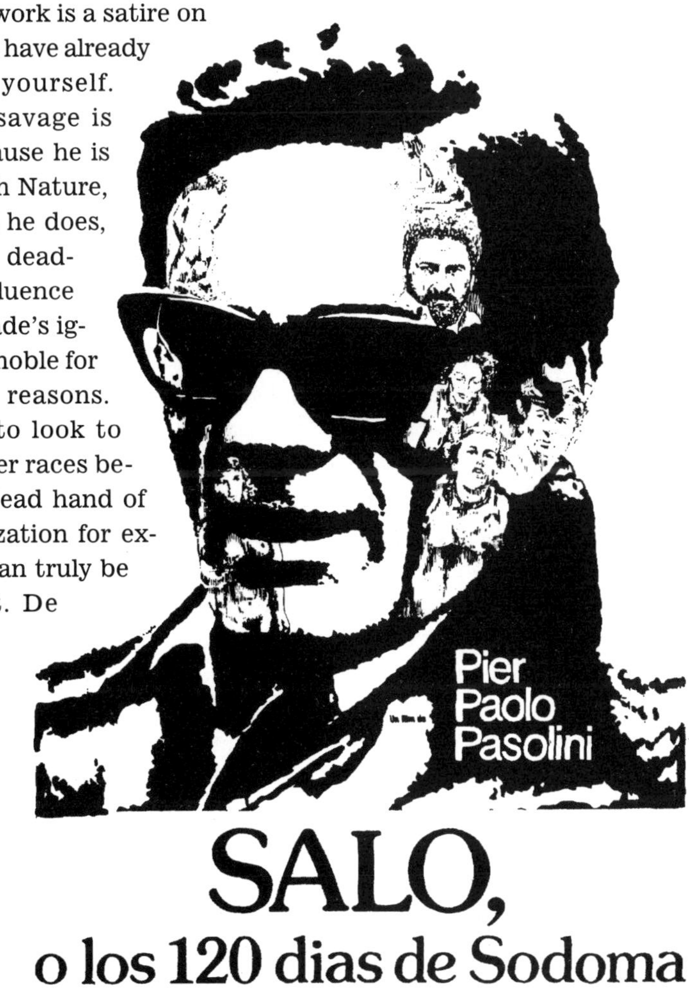

one or another unusually vivid touch in the book may suggest that de Sade actually indulged in horrific sex-crime, or may not. The section in which one of his characters justifies murder using Rousseau's recommended technique doesn't suggest what might have happened, it describes what actually did:

> The Irish used to crush their victims beneath weights. The Norwegians would stave in their skulls.... The Gauls broke their backs.... The Celts drove a sabre through their breastbones.... The Cimbrians disembowelled them or else roasted them in furnaces.[24] [de Sade's ellipses]

And so on, and on, and on, and for once de Sade's repetitiveness doesn't have a soporific or dulling effect:

> Historians tell us that in Mexico, the patient's four limbs would be held by four priests, the high priest would open him from throat to navel, tear out his still-throbbing heart and smear gore over the idol; at other times the patient would be drawn forward and back over a keen-edged stone until it sawed into his belly and his entrails spilled out ... Into the urethral channel the Americans insert a twig covered in little thorns, which they twirl in one direction, then in the other, spinning it between their palms and keeping at it for a considerable length of time, to the considerable distress of the victim ... the fierce Cossacks of Ousk and those parts tie the patient to the tail of a horse, which is ridden at a gallop over rough terrain ... the Persians used ... to grind between millstones ... Nowadays in the harems, the fashionable torture for women in whom some fault has been found is to cut multiple incisions in all their fleshlier parts, and then to pour molten lead into each of the wounds, one by one, drop by drop; to impale by way of the matrix, or to make a pincushion of the patient, using not pins, however, but sulphur-dipped splines which are lit and fuelled by the victim's own fat ... The Romans occasionally hung by the virile privities from a tree ... At other times the victim was strapped to the rim of a great wheel, which would be spun very swiftly for a while, then suddenly made to turn in the opposite direction, which loosened the victim inwardly and often caused him to vomit his very bowels. [ellipses mine][25]

Follow your natural impulses, consult the handbook of ethnology and history, as Rousseau so strongly recommends, and this is where you, with the anti-heroes and anti-heroines of **Juliette**, will be led. And yet de Sade has a similar message for those who repudiate Rousseau and his celebration of the irrational and impulsive, for Voltaire and the other high priests of Reason are targets of Sadean satire too. Juliette embraces vice because it is the rational thing to do, and her memoirs are full of carefully reasoned arguments for murder, for theft, for taking pleasure in the pain of others, for infanticide, for abortion, for genocide and for any other crime you care to mention or imagine:

> If from immolating three million human beings you stand to gain no livelier pleasure than that to be had from eating a good dinner, slender though this pleasure may appear in the light of its price, you ought to treat yourself to it without an instant's hesitation; for if you sacrifice that good dinner, the necessary result is a privation for you, whereas no privation results from the disappearance of the three million insignificant creatures you must do away with to obtain the dinner, because

> between it and you there exists a relationship, however, tenuous, whereas none exists between you and the three million victims.[26]

The argument is continued, and then amplified in a footnote

> wherefrom it is plain to see that were the choice even between a gumdrop and the entire universe, any wavering would be equally illogical and inexcusable. This argument serves to demonstrate the immense advantages of vice over virtue.[27]

And, although it is very likely tongue-in-cheek, it is also quite irrefutable (on the assumption the villain has another universe to go to, of course). Imagine trying to persuade a Sadean villain who wishes to sacrifice the universe for the sake of a gumdrop that he, or she, should not do so. Appeals to religion would be useless: Sadean villains do not believe in God or in a future reward or punishment and anyway, an appeal to religion has no true moral force: behave well or you will be punished is not a moral argument, and someone who accepts it is not behaving morally, only in rational self-interest. No other argument could conceivably succeed. If the impulse to pleasure is there and one possesses the power to indulge it and will not suffer from doing so, it is perfectly rational to surrender to it. As guides to moral behaviour, Rousseau's Nature and Voltaire's Reason are equally useless, and de Sade's work displays the *reductio ad absurdum* of them both.

It is de Sade's satire on rationalism, however, that is the truly frightening and threatening one. Very, very few people have ever argued openly for treachery and the selfish exploitation of others. Machiavelli was one — and de Sade explicitly acknowledges his example in **Juliette**[28] — but Machiavelli has a limited audience. Not everyone wants to succeed in politics; not everyone has the chance to. Far more people want to enjoy themselves, and far more people have the chance to. De Sade's villains demonstrate ways to achieve supreme pleasure, not supreme power, and that is why de Sade seems so threatening. That is why so many people believe he should be banned. That is why so many people blame him for inspiring criminals like Ian Brady and Myra Hindley. He is the *ne plus ultra* of pornography, the *ultima Thule* of moral philosophy, the *e pluribus unum* of the corrupting power of the written word. De Sade, in a much misused word, is dangerous.

IT'S HUMAN FINGERS!

JACK CHICK'S CRUSADERS AND THE CHRISTIAN COMIC PHENOMENON

Crusaders Comics Pack, Plus King of Kings and The Big Betrayal

Jack Chick

Eighteen Jack Chick Comic Books!! Two butch Born-Again do-gooders fight evil in the name of Jesus Christ! Includes titles like "Exorcists", "The Broken Cross", "Chaos", "Operation Bucharest", "Scar Face", and "Primal Man?" Plus two 64-page comic epics.

0593 (*PB/Illus*) $21.95[1]

Well, there were lots of things I liked the sound of in the Amok **Fourth Dispatch** catalogue, but few more than the Christian comics given write-ups like that. They really did look like heaps of fun. But, what with all that bother over currency conversion and postage, and my congenital meanness, I passed. And you know what? *Less than five years later, I picked up the entire set of Crusaders comics for 20p in a charity shop!* God rewarding me for my thrifty Protestant work ethic or what?

Except I don't have a Protestant work ethic, thrifty or otherwise. And it wasn't quite the entire set either. In fact, I'm rather glad it wasn't, because the binge I had with the ones I did get left me feeling decidedly odd. All those bright colours and relentlessly emoting faces. All that one-syllable propagandizing and heavy repetition. And that stark black-and-white page on the back inside cover of every issue, with the blunt question, "DO YOU ACCEPT JESUS CHRIST AS YOUR OWN PERSONAL SAVIOR?" and those two little boxes, one marked "YES", and one marked "NO". God alone knows what would have happened if I'd been able to read a couple more of the series. Ticked the "NO" box and spoiled my collection with a pathetic and very obvious joke, more than likely.

But these comics are undoubtedly extremely dangerous things to put into the wrong hands. The hands of the very stupid or the emotionally vulnerable, for example. If you're both, I couldn't hold out much hope for you should one of these slim, 32-page mind-warpers come athwart your existence at some critical moment. And it would almost certainly be one, because — no wonder I started to feel funny — these comics aren't designed to be read in batches. No, like an anti-personnel mine, each is designed to sit around on its own and wait for an unsuspecting passer-by, and in America, apparently, solitary copies intended for operation along those lines are pretty much ubiquitous:

> There is probably not an adult in the United States who has not encountered a Chick tract at some time in his life. They turn up in phone booths, taxis, laundromats, bus stops, tucked away in library books and magazines.[2]

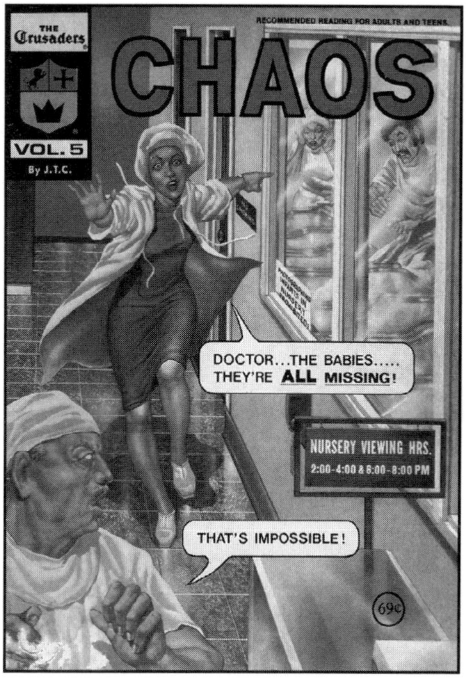

I'd never heard of them before I read the Amok catalogue, and never came across any in the flesh until that fateful moment beneath a pile of **Hello!** magazines in my favourite charity shop. David Kerekes, who is irresistibly drawn towards Christian bookshops during the full moon, has since told me that they are sometimes available here for around 15p a subsidized throw, but they are undoubtedly an all-American phenomenon, and all the more fascinating to someone living in post-Christian Europe for that.

And yes, fascinating is the word: they are much more than simply a good laugh. If you want to understand how fundamentalist American Christians think and what they believe, this is the sort of material you should be looking at. And no, it wouldn't be a purely academic exercise either, because you have to understand fundamentalist American Christians to understand American politics and, like it or not, American politics influence everyone on earth. This route to a better appreciation of America's role in the world was the one taken by what seems to have been a very rare serious look at the Jack Chick phenomenon in issue 145 of **The Comics Journal**. In fact, the article proves that Jack's brand of theology hasn't just informed American foreign policy, but has actually collaborated with it: amongst the material in Spanish churned out for use south of the border have been morality tales in which the downside to anti-capitalist rebellion is portrayed in very stark terms indeed. Yes, troops from your American-backed neo-Nazi government might come to your village, set fire to it and kill everyone in sight, but whatever you do, don't turn to Communism in response. Because there is no worthwhile response as long as sinful "men head up governments", and anyway, if you join the Communists, you'll go to Hell.[3]

But, good though it is on this aspect of the comics and tracts, the article

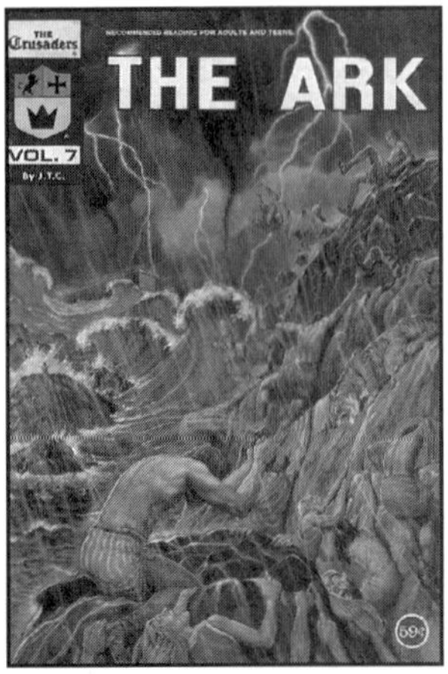

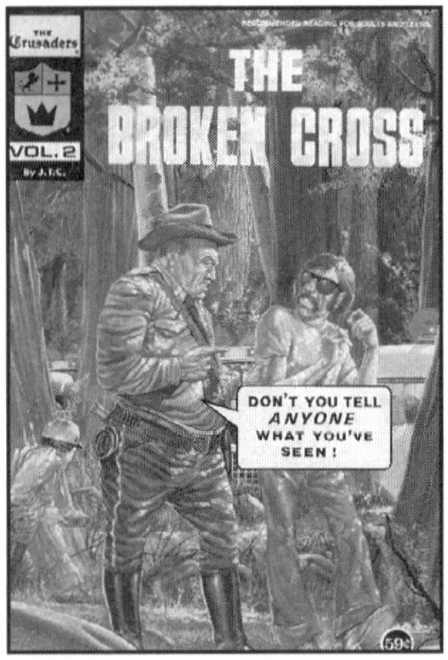

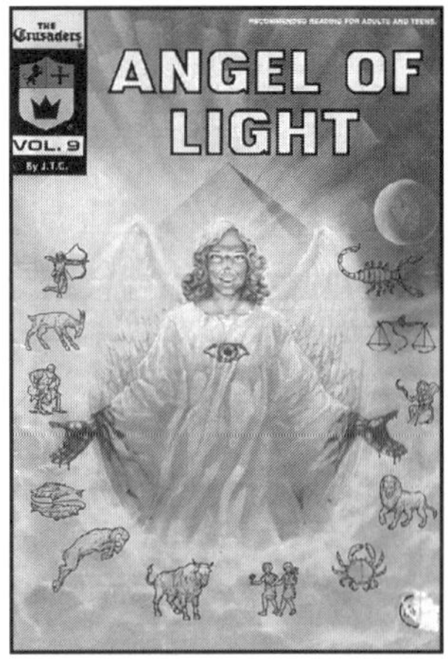

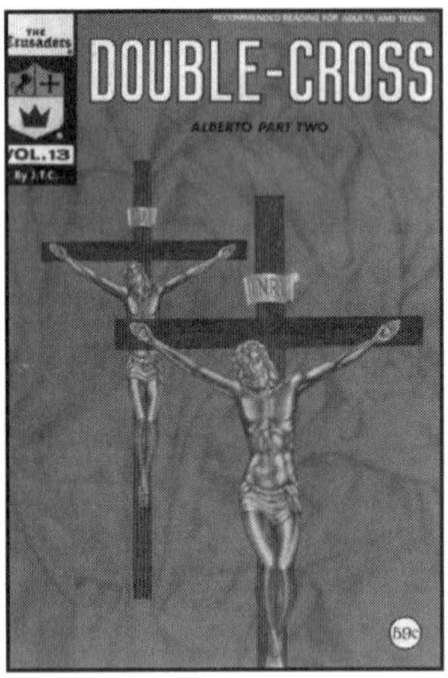

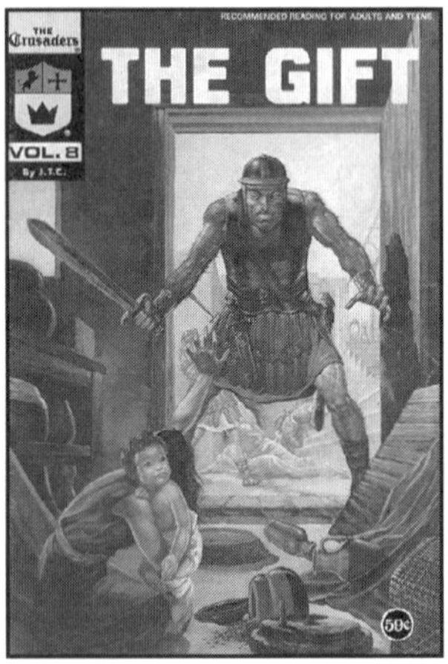

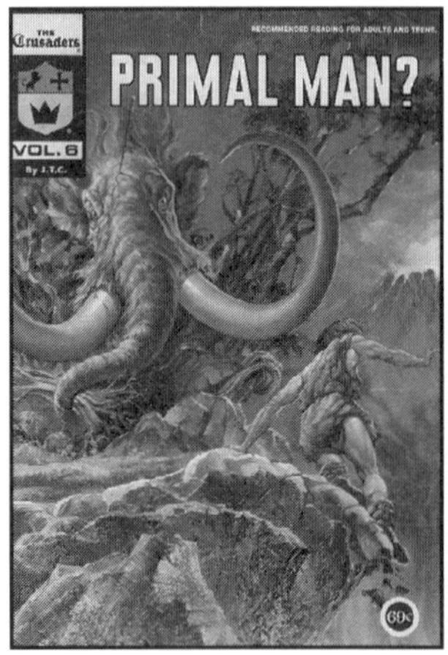

almost completely ignores the richer and riper art and ideology of the **Crusaders** series, and produces a somewhat distorted picture by doing so. Yes, the Jack Chick publishing empire is undoubtedly run by crazed bigots with very large axes to grind against Catholics, Muslims, Jehovah's Witnesses, Mormons, Hindus, pagans, Communists, gays, Freemasons, liberals and atheists, but it wouldn't quite be fair to suggest that they're racist too from the fact that "Blacks only turn up rarely"[4] in the comics. Because they don't. At least, they don't in the **Crusaders** series.

And who are the Crusaders? As Amok put it, they're two "butch Born-Again do-gooders" who "fight evil in the name of Jesus Christ!" And one of them is black. The more powerful and memorable one, in fact, and there are times when you wonder whether there's more than a wholesome Christian desire to promote inter-racial harmony behind the attention paid to him in the comics. One rather stunning bare-chested shot as he prepares for bed in **The Broken Cross** for example. But then the whole scene is rather odd. The dynamic Crusaders duo is sharing a hotel room and, although there are two beds, we only see Jim, the black half of the duo, preparing to occupy his and displaying upper body

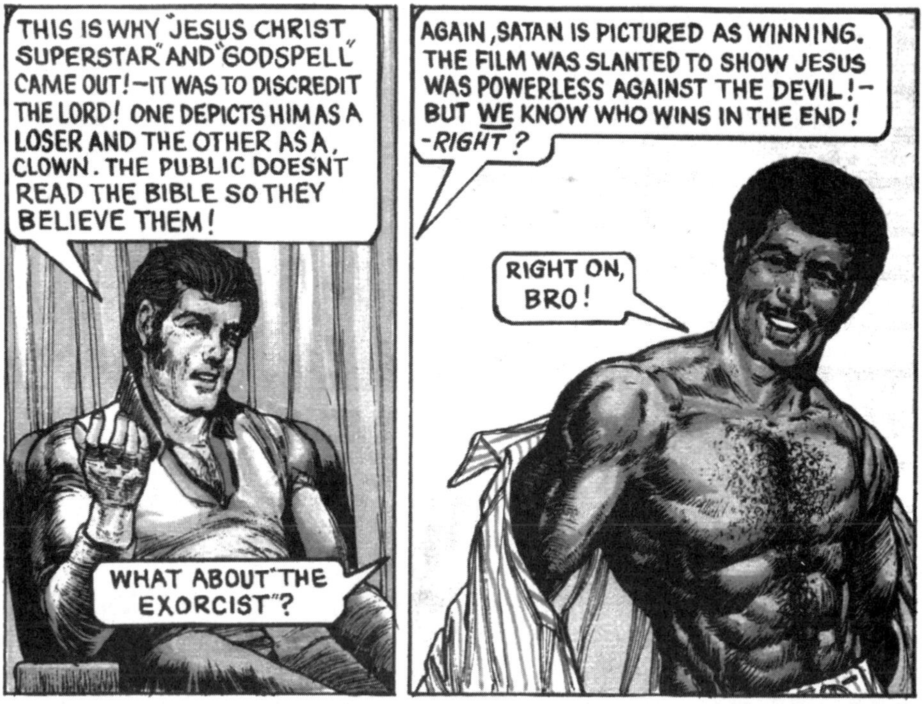

Tim and Jim, the Crusaders. *The Broken Cross* © 1974 Chick Publications

musculature and chest hair. Tim, the white half, spends most of the time in an armchair. He appears to have his legs crossed, and he also appears to stay there all night, greeting Jim fully dressed the following day with a cheerful:

"GOOD MORNING, BRIGHT EYES!"

To which Jim, sitting up in bed bare-chested once again, replies:

"HEY, MAN! WHEN DID YOU GET UP?... WITH THE CHICKENS?"

Upon which Tim delivers himself of the classic one-liner:

"I WANTED TO ARM MYSELF FOR WHAT WE HAVE TO FACE TODAY!"

This being a reference both to the coming battle with the gang of Satanists they have stumbled across and to the Bible he is holding. But is he holding a Bible purely for anti-Satanic research purposes, or to conceal his over-enthusiastic response when Jim gets out of bed and dresses for the strenuous day ahead...?

A disgusting little thought that seems to have occurred not just to prurient hell-bound infidels like me, because Jim and Tim are unequivocally fixed up with girlfriends in **The Gift**, a later issue of the series:

"GENTLEMEN, THE DINNER WAS DELICIOUS!"
"IT WAS OUR PLEASURE... *TREASURE*!"
"JIM AND I ARE LOADED TODAY SO WE WON'T GO DUTCH!"
"YOU HAVE ONLY ONE FAULT, TIM... YOU'RE *TOO* KIND!"

None of your equality-between-the-sexes nonsense with the Crusaders, you see, and, despite the positive anti-racist message elsewhere, none of your racial-intermixing nonsense either, because Tim's girlfriend, like Tim, is white, and Jim's, like Jim, is black. Both women are, of course, fundamentalist Christians, too.

And you can also probably forget part of the argument for Jack Chick's suspicious attitude to Jim and his hunky black bod given above, because Tanya, Jim's attractive Afro-haired sister-in-Christ, is given much the same prominence in **The Gift** as Jim himself receives elsewhere. She's the one who has all the inside info on why God told the Israelites to circumcize their boy-children on the eighth day — and not a day sooner or later:

"IN 1946/1947 MEDICAL SPECIALISTS MADE AN AMAZING DISCOVERY. HUMAN BLOOD NEEDS CERTAIN ELEMENTS TO CLOT... ONE IS CALLED PROTHROMBIN, WHICH NEEDS VITAMIN K TO FORM IT... ON THE 8TH DAY OF A NEW BORN MALE [sic] VITAMIN K REACHES ITS NORMAL AMOUNT. ON THE SAME DAY PROTHROMBIN SKYROCKETS TO 110 PER CENT EFFICIENCY, MAKING IT THE PERFECT TIME FOR CIRCUMCISION."

"SO *THAT'S* WHAT KEEPS THE BABY FROM HEAVY BLEEDING WHEN THE SURGERY IS PERFORMED?"

"THAT'S RIGHT, JIM! GOD DOESN'T MAKE ANY MISTAKES!"

In other words, the Crusader series is putting across the same over-played message about the staggering intelligence, beauty and decency of blacks as American television of the same period. In fact, seeing each issue of the series as an episode-on-paper from 1970s American TV is a very good way of understanding it. There's the same complete-story-in-each-instalment-with-no-loose-ends, the same adolescent morality, the same appeal to the lowest common intellectual denominator — hard words like "heretic" and "impious" are carefully explained in footnotes — and, often, the same clumsy attempt at feel-good humorous endings:

"IT HAPPENED!... I FEEL CLEAN AND BEAUTIFUL... MY LIFE *IS* CHANGED! TANYA... I *LOVE* YOU, I REALLY DO!"

"AM I *STILL* YOUR AUNT JEMIMA?"
"*NO!*... YOU'RE MY BEAUTIFUL SISTER IN CHRIST!"
"SHORE NUFF?"
"*YEAH!* IN FACT, *NOW* I EVEN LIKE YOUR HOG JOWLS AND TURNIP GREENS!"

[**The Gift**, pg. 32]

"TIM, GUESS WHO'S JOINING US AT THE MARRIAGE SUPPER OF THE LAMB?"
"A JEWISH TAXI DRIVER."
"RIGHT ON, BABY... RIGHT ON!"

[**Chaos**, pg. 32]

There's also the same admiration for physical strength and beauty and the same equation of ugliness with evil, and even something of the same belief in violence as a solution for difficult problems. Fortunately for the humour quotient of the comics, there's nothing of '70s American TV's blandness and refusal to take a strong stand against anything. If the Crusaders comics are crystal-clear what they stand for, they're also crystal-clear what they stand against. At its simplest — and these comics only deal in concepts at their simplest — if you aren't for Christ, you're against him, and that means the Crusaders are against you.

The list of the un-Godly is long and pretty much predictable, but the name in big, black, underlined-three-times capitals at the top is likely to be a surprising one for someone not familiar with this kind of fundamentalist Christian thinking. Public enemy number one in the Jack Chick Universe is the Roman Catholic Church, and nary an opportunity slips by to put the boot into one or another of her representatives from the Pope on down. Now, there's nobody likes a bit of Catholic-church-bashing more than me either as a spectator or as a participant, but although I could believe just about everything claimed in the comics about the church's more distant past, I'm more than a little doubtful about the picture they paint of the church's Machiavellian scheming since the Second World War. Oh sure, if a tenth of what's laid out in intelligent anti-Catholic polemics like David Yallop's **In God's Name** is true[5], the church is a hive of conspiracy and cover-up, but I don't think it's buzzing quite as busily as Jack Chick would have us believe:

"THIS IS FATHER DOMINIC FROM THE HOLY OFFICE. HE HAS SOME RECOMMENDATIONS TO SOLVE THE FATHER RIVERA PROBLEM."

"MY RECOMMENDATION, FATHERS, IS TO MAKE FATHER RIVERA'S DEATH LOOK LIKE AN ACCIDENT. WE HAVE A CATHOLIC ACTION MAN IN LONDON UNDER OATH, SWORN TO DESTROY FATHER RIVERA. THE HIT WILL BE MADE WITHIN A PROTESTANT DENOMINATION... WE HAVE VARIOUS ALTERNATIVES — FOOD POISONING, AUTOMOBILE OR TRAIN ACCIDENT, OR SCIENTIFIC DEATH IN A HOSPITAL. IT SHOULDN'T TAKE US LONG."

"THIS MUST HAPPEN BEFORE HE IS WELL KNOWN. IT COULD DAMAGE OUR GOALS FOR POLITICAL AND RELIGIOUS UNITY."

"NO PROBLEM."

[**Double-Cross: Alberto Part Two**, pg. 11]

This comic is the biography-in-pictures of a real person called Father Rivera, a Jesuit priest who has finally recognized the Scarlet Whore of Rome for what she is and broken free to join the ranks of Christ's true believers. And the church's

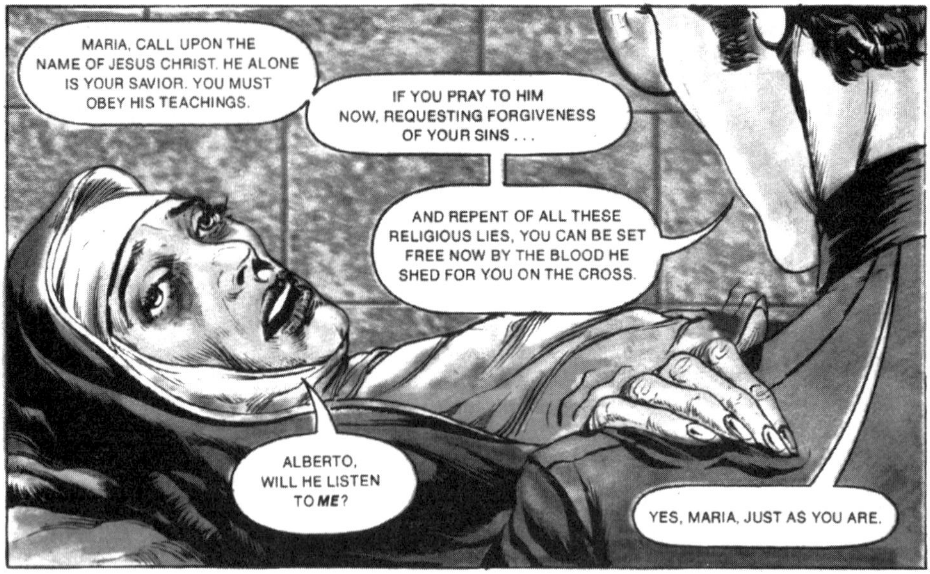

Father Rivera comforts Maria. *Double-Cross* © 1981 Chick Publications

vengeance was indeed swift in falling on him, if the comic is to be believed. How did she set about it? Well, it was a fiendishly cunning plot involving a pseudo-Christian dentist "very active in the 'Love Gospel' Movement" — always a danger sign in the Jack Chick scheme of things — and some orthodontic work. Eschewing unsubtle and easy-to-detect murder weapons like guns or knives, the dentist allowed a part of a dental tool to break off inside Dr Rivera's "upper left second bicuspid tooth", which he then capped with a porcelain crown to cover his devilish tracks. His hope was that the broken piece of tool would cause an infection that would "reach the brain, causing death", but for one reason or another the infection was slow to work and the dentist had the unsuspecting Dr Rivera back into his surgery on the pretext of having to clean his teeth. This time he intended there to be no mistakes. As Dr Rivera puts it:

"WHILE CLEANING MY TEETH, MY GUMS WERE SPRAYED WITH NERVE GAS..."

Alas for the success of the plot, a nurse let slip to Dr Rivera's wife in the waiting room that her husband was dying in the dentist's chair, and her swift intervention frightened the dentist sufficiently for him to give Dr Rivera a reviving injection. Even then Dr Rivera was still very weak and had it not been for the prayers of other true believers who had been alerted to his predicament, he would have succumbed to the after-effects of Rome's second ingenious assassination attempt:

"GOD ANSWERED THEIR PRAYERS, AND SAVED ME FROM CERTAIN DEATH."

On the other hand, this is one of those situations that never leave the Jack Chick school of theology at a loss. Dr Rivera didn't die at the Catholic church's hands, which meant God had saved him; another real person, Clark Butterfield, who seems to have been brought out of the church by reading Dr Rivera's story in the Crusaders series[6], did, which meant that he had gone "home to be with his Savior". Butterfield's story, however, which he tells himself in **Night Journey from Rome...to the New Jerusalem**, is at the heavily intellectual end of the anti-Catholic propaganda market, because it takes the form of a proper book that at one point uses the difference between the masculine and feminine forms of the Greek word for "rock" to attack the church's teaching.[7]

Nevertheless, it's linked to the Jack Chick series not only by its often hilarious logic but also by its paranoia. Just like Dr Rivera, Butterfield is sure the church is out to get him; unlike Dr Rivera, he is actually got. The book was published posthumously and its publishers remark of the dead author: "we deeply believe that he was killed by the forces of the Jesuits working through a Roman Catholic doctor in Detroit, Michigan".[8] Butterfield's death certificate is reproduced at the back of the book so that readers can see for themselves how he died of a brain haemorrhage at the age of 66, a highly suspicious 2·7 years short of the average life expectancy of an American man at the period.[9]

This kind of anti-Catholicism is a constant part of the Jack Chick message, but if the Roman Catholic church is the biggest and baddest of the true Christian's enemies, there are plenty of others, and the Crusaders series gets round to all of them sooner or later. There are the gays, for example, who are especially liable to illustrate the Jack Chick maxim that ill-favoured features and poor muscle definition are a sure sign of moral corruption and a hell-bound soul: the simpering, posturing, dwarvish gay producer at work on a pro-Evolution, anti-Creation TV series in the comic **Primal Man?** is straight from Julius Streicher's **Der Stürmer** school of caricature. He even looks Jewish, but isn't identified as such, Jews being probably the only extreme right-wing hate object absent from the Jack Chick rogues' gallery.

The same "ugly=evil" rule applies to everyone there besides the gays, all the same, and so, luckily enough no doubt for some of the target audience, you don't have to be able to read to work out who are the bad guys and who the good. Take a look at that sheriff in **The Broken Cross**, for example: fat, balding, and habitually wearing a snarl. He's just *bound* to be part of the network of young-women-and-puppy-sacrificing Satanists stumbled across by our heroes Jim'n'Tim, isn't he? And, of course, he is, although in this case you don't need the fat, baldness and snarling — or the racism towards Jim — to work out he's on the side of the Forces of Darkness, because he's also wearing a police badge that looks very much like a pentagram.

And yes, entertaining though the attacks on Catholics, gays, Freemasons, false Christians and others are, the real laughs are to be found when the Crusaders series turns its spotlight on the Satanists — who are, after all, the ones really behind all the rest. The anti-occult **Broken Cross** was the first comic

I read after snapping up the collection, and in a way I wish it hadn't been, because nothing that came afterwards was going to live up to it. It kicks off with a skimpily dressed young girl called Donna hitchhiking alone to Los Angeles. A camper van stops for her, she gets in — IT LOOKS SAFE!...THERE'S A GIRL WITH HIM! — and a few minutes later, after the driver and his female companion have skilfully tricked her into revealing that she's not meeting anyone in L.A. — ARE YOU MEETING ANYONE IN L.A.? *NO!* — she's been dragged over into the back of the van by two Charles Manson lookalikes and injected with a knock-out drug. Then it's off to a secret Satanic venue in good time for her to be sacrificed to the devil:

"WE DEDICATE THIS GIRL'S BLOOD TO LUCIFER! GIVE US THE POWER OF HER BLOOD!"

But what else can you expect when you behave as young Donna has done? When she was first picked up, the conversation went like this:

" WHATCHA DOIN' OUT HERE?"
"I'M SPLITTING FROM THE HOME SCENE!"
"HOW COME?"
"MY FOLKS ARE TRYING TO CRAM CHURCH DOWN ME!"

Jim and Tim enter the story when her body is discovered dumped by the side of the road with not a drop of blood in it. Instantly alerted to a probable black magic connexion, Jim tries to point the police in the right direction, but they refuse to listen:

"I'LL HAVE YOU KNOW, *BOY*... THAT THIS IS A GOD-FEARING COMMUNITY! WE'VE GOT CHURCHES, BOY SCOUTS, CAMP FIRE GIRLS, THE V.F.W., AND..."
"AND *WITCHES*!"
"@!!! LET ME GIVE YOU SOME GOOD ADVICE... *KEEP MOVING!*"

But the Crusaders' suspicions have been aroused, and more evidence of the secret horror lying behind the God-fearing façade of the community is soon coming thick and fast. A young boy's puppy disappears...and its lead has been cut. The two Crusaders call on the local pastor for help...a copy of the ecumenical **Common Bible** lies on his desk, and he's soon showing the pair of them the door after they ask him whether he's accepted Christ as his "personal savior". They visit the local library to do some research on the occult...and the shelves have been mysteriously cleared of all relevant material. Then comes the clincher:

"TIM, ISN'T THAT SOMETHING IN THE HEADLIGHTS? LOOK OUT! IT'S A MAN!"
[SCREECH]
"WE MISSED HIM!"
"(THANK YOU, LORD!) HEY! WHAT ARE YOU DOING OVER HERE? — DO YOU WANT TO GET

KILLED?"

"WHAT'S WRONG WITH HIM? – IS HE STONED?"

"COME ON OVER INTO THE LIGHT SO WE CAN SEE IF YOU'RE HURT!"

"JIM! LOOK WHAT'S HE EATING!"

"I CAN'T BELIEVE IT! IT'S HUMAN FINGERS!"

[CHOMP, CHOMP]

And guess what — the whole thing really happened. As a footnote informs the reader:

SUCH AN INCIDENT WAS REPORTED IN THE BIG SUR AREA IN CALIF., 1973.

Apart from the attack of vomiting that overtakes the Satanists when they're

***The Broken Cross* (inset and detail) © 1974 Chick Publications**

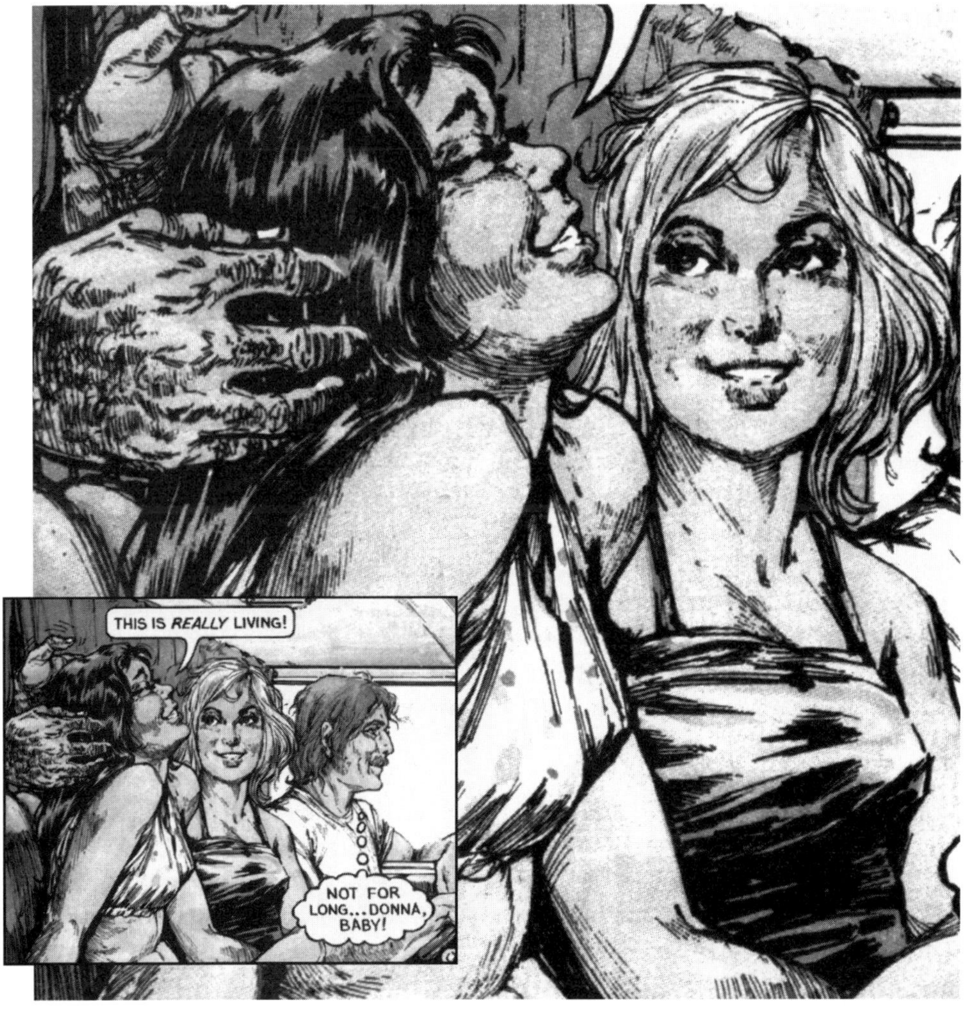

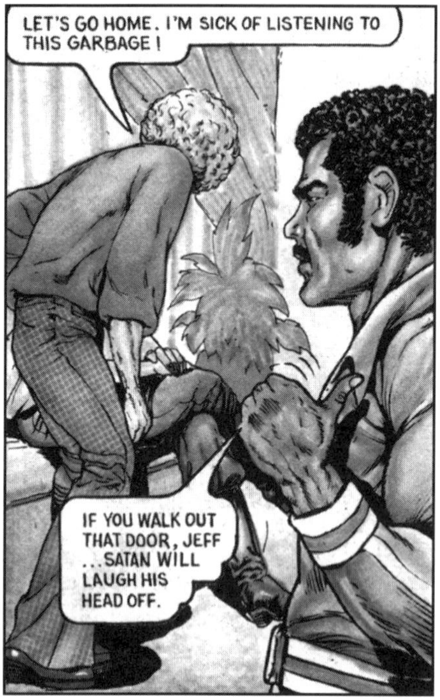

Angel of Light © 1978 Chick Publications

finally tracked down and informed by Jim that he has taken authority over them "in the name of Jesus", there are no more titbits for the prurient in **The Broken Cross**, but you can certainly find a lot of unpleasantness elsewhere in the series, if few of the laughs associated with it in its Satanic manifestations. The death'n'violence on offer ranges from a fairly mild field-of-corpses drawn from a photograph of the Jonestown mass suicide[10] to a Roman Catholic nun lying in the stinking blood and pus of wounds she's received from repeated flagellation sessions.[11] Jack is also anxious that his readers don't carry away the impression that Jesus was some kind of namby-pamby wimp, and all the bloody details of the Passion and preparations for it are lovingly rendered in close-up, from the blood-mixed sweat shed in the Garden of Gethsemane

> THIS IS KNOWN IN MEDICAL TERMS AS "HEMATIDROSIS" (BLEEDING SWEAT)... THIS STRANGE EFFECT SOMETIMES HAPPENS WHEN EMOTIONAL PRESSURES ARE SO GREAT THAT TINY BLOOD VESSELS BURST IN THE SWEAT GLANDS AND MIX THE BLOOD WITH THE SWEAT

to the crucifixion itself, after a crowning with thorns and a whipping that has left the big J.C. looking like something you might find in the fresh-meat freezer compartment at your local supermarket. And don't forget, as the Crusader running these details by a potential new convert puts it:

> "HE DID THIS FOR *YOU*, MARSHA!"
> "OH, MY GOD... I'M GETTING SICK!"
> "IT'S THE *ONLY* WAY HE COULD GET YOU INTO HEAVEN... THEY *ALSO* NAILED HIS FEET."

[**The Gift**, pg. 29]

This kind of shock-assault is the standard Crusaders tactic when they're faced with a brand they wish to save from the burning: an even commoner variant on it is a detailed description of the burning itself. Hell is a very big selling point in the Crusaders' soul-to-soul sales plan:

ONE MILLION SOULS POUR INTO HELL EVERY WEEK... (THESE ARE SATAN'S TREASURES)... ONLY THOSE COVERED IN THE BLOOD OF THE LAMB WILL MISS IT.

The picture accompanying this dire warning is something of a disappointment, though: a vague jumble of rocks, flames, Hallowe'en-masked demons and sinners who are naked but reveal little flesh. On the other hand, the dialogue between demons and sinners is pretty good:

"DIDN'T ACCEPT JESUS BECAUSE OF YOUR FRIENDS?... WHERE ARE THEY NOW?"
"I DON'T KNOW... ALL I'VE SEEN ARE YOU SLIMY, CREEPY, SMELLY @!#@! BITING DEMONS."

And if "slimy, creepy, smelly @!#@! biting demons" don't put the wind up you good and proper, just remember: they aren't ever going to lay off:

"I'VE BEEN HERE FOREVER!"
"OH, NO... IT'S ONLY BEEN A MILLION YEARS... THIS IS JUST THE BEGINNING! *HAW HAW HAW!*"

[**Angel of Light**. pg. 31]

And this comic has very likely been drawn by someone who's field-tested this hell-fire approach extensively, because the reaction of the two young people it's being used against by Crusader Tim in **Angel of Light** seems pretty realistic.

Angel of Light opens very effectively with what might be called a twist beginning. One man is reading to another out of a newspaper:

"LISTEN TO THIS... THE BODY OF ANOTHER YOUNG WOMAN FOUND IN GRIFFITH PARK EARLY THIS MORNING BRINGS THE TOTAL TO 17 MURDERS BY THE MASKED KILLERS."
"ISN'T THAT GROSS? WHAT'S THIS WORLD COMING TO? — ISN'T ANYONE SAFE?"
"THE KILLERS WORE BLACK SKI MASKS THAT HAD A YELLOW BAND AROUND THE MOUTH AND EYES."
"THEY'RE NOT HUMANS... THEY'RE ANIMALS!"
"THE GIRL WAS DRAGGED INTO A BLACK AND WHITE CAR – WITNESSES HEARD HER SCREAMS – MAN, THAT TURNS ME ON!"
"ME TOO — LET'S GO GET ANOTHER ONE!"

By which time man number two is wearing a black ski mask with a yellow band around the mouth and eyes and holding out an identical mask for man number one. Off into the night go the two serial killers — modelled apparently on the Hillside Stranglers — but their attempted kidnapping of victim number 18 at a bus-stop is foiled by the intervention of the Crusaders, who happen to be passing in their yellow Volkswagen. The Crusaders then drive the young woman, who's called Darlene, back to her boyfriend's apartment. Badly shaken by what's happened to her, she is musing aloud over how close she came to death and soon encounters the Crusaders' unique pro-active approach to post-traumatic stress disorder counselling:

> "MY GOD, I COULD BE DEAD RIGHT NOW."
> "THAT'S RIGHT."
> "IT'S A CRAZY THOUGHT, BUT... IF IT HAD HAPPENED... I MEAN IF THEY HAD KILLED ME... I WONDER WHAT I'D BE IN THE NEXT LIFE... I HOPE I'D BE A BETTER PERSON."
> "NO... YOU'D BE IN HELL RIGHT NOW!... I THINK THIS IS YOUR PLACE, DARLENE."

Later on the same night, Darlene and her boyfriend Jeff visit the Crusaders' apartment. Jeff wants to thank them for saving Darlene's life, and demand an apology for "scaring her about going to Hell!":

> "SORRY JEFF... BUT DARLENE IS ON HER WAY TO HELL... AND SO ARE YOU!"

Jeff and Darlene laugh, but they are persuaded to stay a while and listen as the Crusaders explain how Hell came into existence and how Jeff and Darlene are definitely on their way there — unless they accept Jesus as their personal saviour. The two young people pass through mocking incredulity, angry rejection,

Angel of Light © 1978 Chick Publications

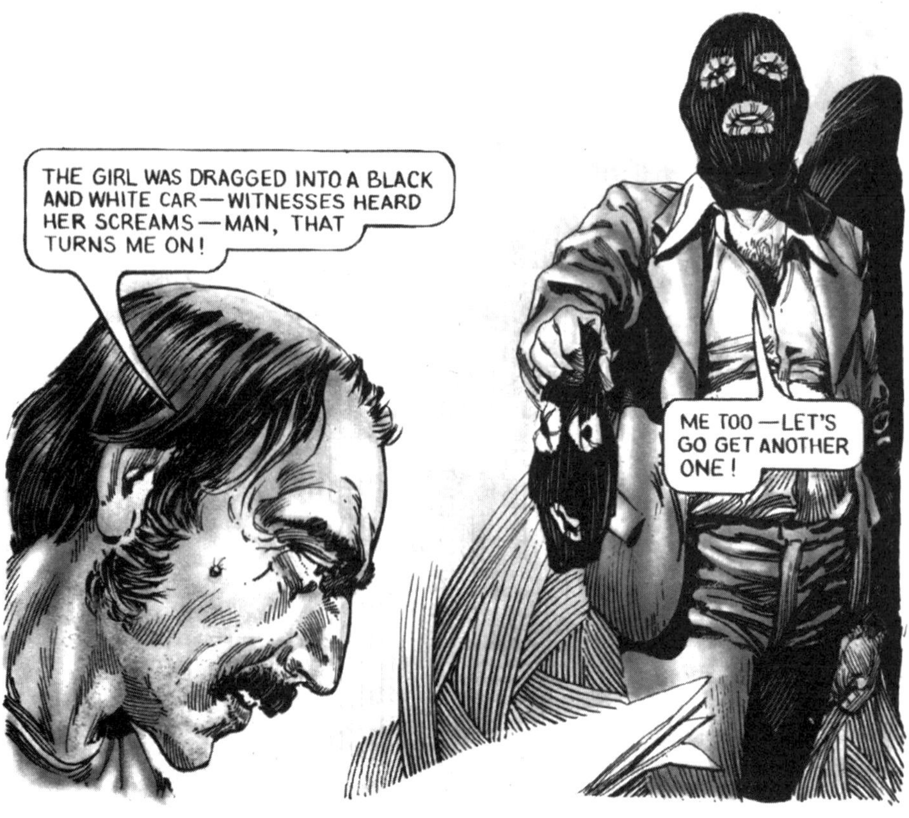

and, last-but-one, full acceptance of and horror at the fate that awaits then. Finally, they are weeping with joy and relief as they discover the escape clause in God's contract with sinners:

"LORD JESUS (CHOKE), BE MERCIFUL TO ME, A LOST SINNER (SOB) AND SAVE ME (SOB) FROM HELL SO I CAN GO TO HEAVEN (SNIFF)."

The following day Jeff, already shorn of the stupid-looking blond Afro he wore in his lost-sinner days, is attempting to sow the good seed for Jesus on his own account:

"DAD, UH... ER... DID YOU EVER THINK YOU MIGHT BE GOING TO HELL?"
"I'M WHAT? LISTEN, JEFF...DON'T YOU EVER TALK TO ME LIKE THAT AGAIN, YA HEAR! WHAT KIND OF @!!#! FANATIC ARE YOU?"

Apart from the sensational, get-the-reader-hooked opening, **Angel of Light** is simply a short manual in conversion techniques, intended to work both on the reader and for him when he accepts the message and sets out to make converts for himself. As always, the reader is supposed to think himself into the position of the lost souls who are shown on the inside back page of most issues beaming with relief and happiness at their acceptance into a new life with Jesus as their "personal savior": Jeff and Darlene in **Angel of Light**; Marty the Jewish taxi driver in **Chaos**; Sergei the Russian embassy official in **The Ark**; Marsha the would-be suicide in **The Gift**; and so on. Generally these people aren't particularly attractive, just ordinary-looking, unlike the fictional Crusaders who readers are supposed to imagine themselves being befriended and converted by.

Sooner or later in reading the comics, however, you are bound to start asking certain questions about them. Who actually is Jack Chick, and why is he the only name given on comics that are obviously drawn by more than one artist? The answer to the first question seems to be: not many people know. The article on the Jack Chick phenomenon in the **Comics Journal** points out that despite the enormous print-runs and widespread international influence of his comics and "tracts", no serious attention seems to have been paid to them:

While a great deal of research has been done into the demographics of the Christian right, nowhere in any of the sources I examined is there a single mention of what appears to be Chick's good-sized publishing empire in Chino, California.[12]

It seems likely that Jack Chick — note those initials — is some kind of pseudonym; what's certain is that Jack Chick, whoever he really is, cannot be responsible for all the work put out in his name: style and quality vary far too widely, and some of the comics are carefully tailored for non-American audiences by, presumably, non-American writers and artists. The Crusaders series, a thirteen-parter that began in the early '70s and ended in 1981, is also drawn by

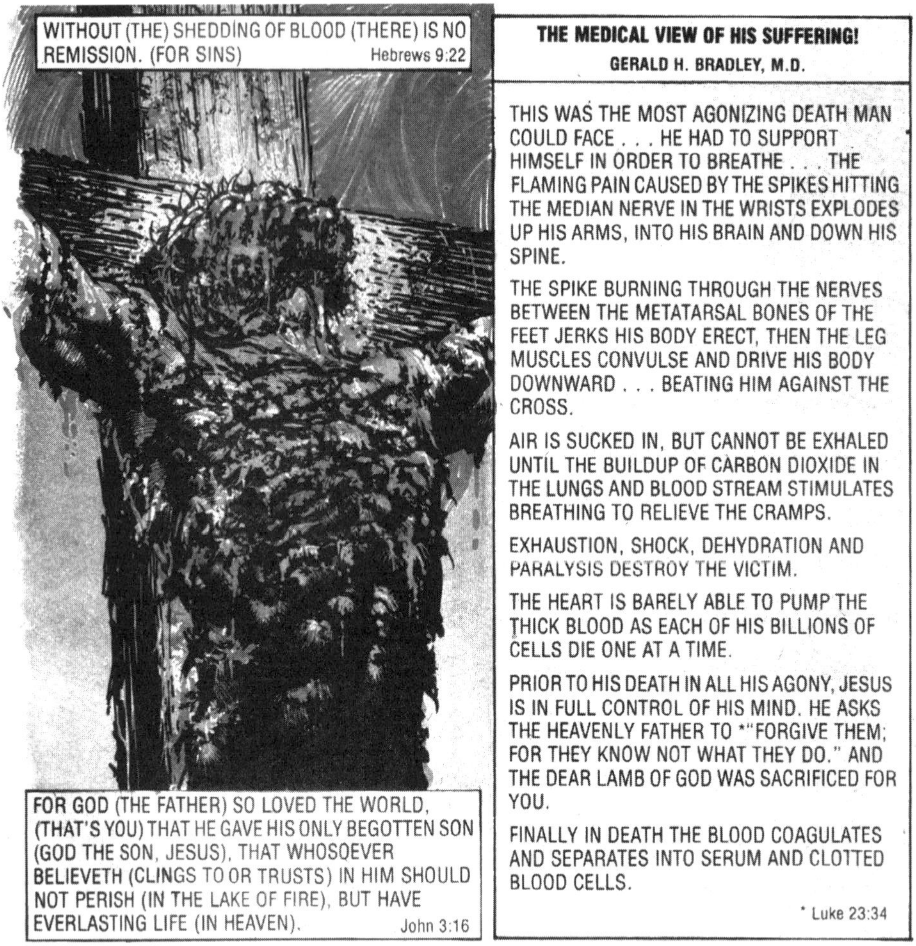

***The Gift* © 1977 Chick Publications**

more than one person[13], and the artistic talent on display ranges from the merely competent in the rather smudgy and cramped drawing of early issues like **The Broken Cross** to the genuinely gifted in the sweeping vistas and complex crowd scenes of late ones like **Double-Cross**. Only very, very rarely is there any downright bad work: the worst I came across was some faulty perspective in **Chaos** that made Jim's head appear to be brushing a hotel ceiling. Continuity errors also seem to be few and far between, and not very serious when they do occur — Jim calling Tim "Jim" during the "It's human fingers!" episode in **The Broken Cross**, for example — and I only spotted one real artistic howler: a drawing meant to be an aerial photograph of Noah's Ark that included the plane supposed to have taken the photograph.[14]

In general, though, you can't go far wrong with the Crusaders — if you're not looking for anything experimental or avant-garde, just unpretentious, mainstream comic art-work with strong lines and bright colours. Probably, of course, you won't be, but if you add the often hilarious, occasionally unpleasant, always interesting Christian message that goes with the pictures, you have a nigh-on irresistible package that is indeed, as the cover of each issue earnestly proclaims, "RECOMMENDED READING FOR ADULTS AND TEENS". Okay, I feel sorry for the pathetic and intellectually crippled people who these comics are really aimed at and who must have been converted by them in their thousands, but I've no doubt I'll be snapping up any further examples of Jack Chick's output to come my way. Just so long as I don't have to pay much more than 20p for them. Are you listening, Lord Jesus?

THE CRUSADERS

CAUTION: THIS SET OF BOOKS COULD CHANGE YOUR LIFE

1. Operation Bucharest
2. The Broken Cross
3. Scar Face
4. Exorcists
5. Chaos
6. Primal Man?
7. The Ark
8. The Gift
9. Angel of Light
10. Spellbound?
11. Sabotage?
12. Alberto
13. Double-Cross: Alberto Part Two

GOD LOVES YOU AND WANTS YOU TO EXPERIENCE PEACE AND ETERNITY IN HEAVEN.

WHAT YOU MUST DO:

1. **Admit your need (I am a sinner).**
2. **Be willing to turn from sin (repent).**
3. **Believe that Jesus Christ died for you (on the Cross) and rose from the dead.**
4. **Through prayer, invite Jesus Christ to come in and control your life. (Receive Him as Savior and Lord.)**

WHAT TO PRAY:

DEAR FATHER, I KNOW THAT I AM A SINNER AND NEED FORGIVENESS. I BELIEVE THAT CHRIST DIED FOR MY SIN. I AM WILLING TO TURN FROM SIN. I NOW INVITE JESUS CHRIST TO COME INTO MY HEART AND LIFE AS MY PERSONAL SAVIOR. I AM WILLING, BY GOD'S GRACE TO FOLLOW AND OBEY CHRIST AS THE LORD OF MY LIFE.

DID YOU ACCEPT JESUS CHRIST AS YOUR OWN PERSONAL SAVIOR? date________ YES ☐ NO ☐

IF YOUR ANSWER WAS YES, THEN THIS IS JUST THE BEGINNING OF A WONDERFUL NEW LIFE WITH CHRIST. NOW:

1. **Read your Bible every day to get to know Christ better.**
2. **Talk to God in prayer every day.**
3. **Tell others about Christ.**
4. **Be baptized, worship, fellowship, and serve with other Christians in a church where Christ is preached.**
5. **Read THE NEXT STEP. It contains vital information for your Christian growth.**

AVAILABLE AT CHRISTIAN BOOKSTORES OR FROM CHICK PUBLICATIONS.

COMPLETELY ILLUSTRATED 64 PAGES

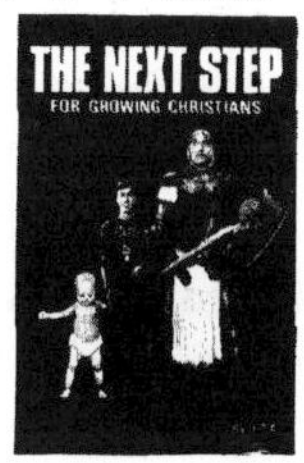

DONNER UND BLITZEN

THE STRANGE LAST DAYS OF THE LUFTWAFFE

I sometimes get the feeling that Hitler wouldn't have wanted it any other way. The end of the war, I mean. Periodically, men who believe they've been mistreated and rejected by society pick up weapons and set out to show everyone how pissed off they are about it all. You know the ones I mean. Michael Ryan. Thomas Hamilton. That guy down in Tasmania. Numerous wackos in the United States. And, I sometimes get the feeling, Adolf Hitler, because if you're a German and you want to get revenge on other Germans, you could hardly do it in a more spectacular way than he did.[1] The Third Reich was defeated well before May 1945, and everyone knew it, but those extra months of fighting helped the corpses and the rubble to pile up a lot higher before the Führer decided it was time to call it a day. I've read that if von Stauffenberg and his briefcase had been able to make that decision for him in July 1944, the casualty list for the Second World War would have been halved, because the war would have ended then and there with the Wehrmacht coup von Stauffenberg's assassination of Hitler was meant to set irresistibly under way.[2]

But, as we all know, although the briefcase blew up, the only things of Hitler's it took with it were his trousers and the last vestiges of control he had over a bad twitch in his left arm. The big consequence of von Stauffenberg's near miss was that the war carried on; there were lots of smaller consequences, amongst them this article, because those extra ten months of war were one of the most fascinating periods this century. Lots of people think that, and they have lots of different reasons for doing so: mine is what went on in the Luftwaffe. There were aircraft designed, built, tested and flown into combat in that period that were so strange they still don't seem dated, and perhaps never will. Like el Greco's paintings, large parts of the German jet and rocket aircraft programme in the Second World War can still strike us as utterly strange because no-one else at the time or since ever did anything remotely like them.

And I'm not, of course, talking about the Messerschmidt 262, the elegant twin-engined jet that entered the war in 1944. For its time — but as soon as I say that you know it's firmly inside aviation history, part of the linear evolution of aircraft from the wire and canvas of Kitty Hawk, N.C., to the carbon-fibre composites of the present. Some of the other German jet aircraft of the Second World War are still outside the straight line of that history. All of the rocket

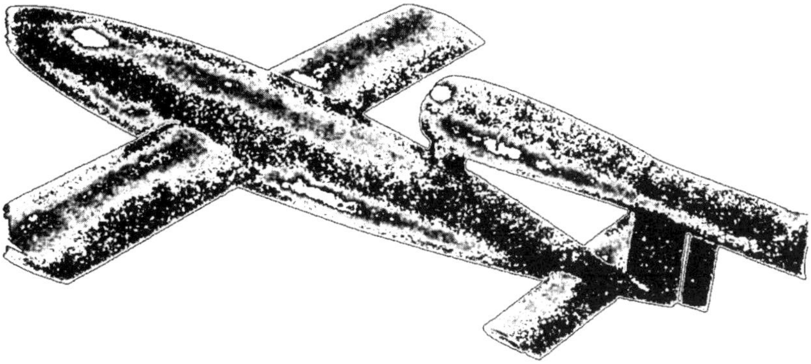

aircraft are. Some historians still believe that the Me 262 might have won the war for the Axis if it had been built early enough and in sufficient numbers, as it possibly could have been, and if Hitler hadn't insisted on its being flown in the unsuitable role of fighter-bomber — as he possibly didn't. The other new aircraft, all those other unfamiliar abbreviations and numbers — Ar 234, Ba 349, He 162, Hs 132, Ju 287, Me 163, Me 328 — never enter the historical algebra at all, because by the time they appeared there was no way different decisions on manufacturing and design were going to change the outcome of the war. Germany needed new aircraft in tens of thousands, and these aircraft only arrived in hundreds. Like powerful new drugs being tested in too-small quantities on a dying man, they did nothing to change the fact of his dying, but they did change the manner of it. The whole atmosphere of the war's end is different for their presence, and their futility — visible not just now, with hindsight, but also to those who were actually building and flying them — is a large part of their peculiar attractiveness.

Perhaps you could say "glamour", but it isn't really a suitable word. When I was a kid I never found war in general glamorous because I could picture what it meant too easily. War in the air was different: you didn't see who you killed, so I felt that military aircraft could have glamour — beauty even. Nowadays my imagination is strong enough for me to see readily through the falseness of that idea, and the only military aircraft I still find interesting are the ones I'm writing this article about — and if there's any glamour about these ones left, it's a very dark one, and the sense in which I use the word is very close to its original meaning of "black magic". Nazism was an occult movement, founded on human sacrifice, and the aircraft flown in the final defence of Nazism were built firmly on that foundation.

Here's one example of how. One of the strangest of these strange aircraft, despite the fact that it was a common-or-garden jet, was called the Heinkel 162. The jet engine sat in an large hump on its back, blasting between a curious twin-finned, H-shaped tail; apart from this hump the aircraft possessed a graceful if compact outline that is reminiscent of some present-day aircraft.[3] It was intended as a mass-manufactured, last-ditch defensive fighter to be flown against the Allied bomber onslaught not by experienced Luftwaffe pilots, of whom there were very few left, but by members of the Hitler Youth rapidly trained in gliders. One of its names, taken from this fact, was the *Volksjäger*, or People's-Fighter; another was the Salamander. Salamanders are important creatures in the occult tradition: they dwell in and rise triumphant from pure fire. The associations of the name were very probably carefully judged, and like the rest of the Nazi state the aircraft had lives sacrificed to it for its success. The He 162 Salamander was built by slave labourers, men subject both to murderous discipline and to a starvation diet. You would see a flower in a different way if you knew it had been fertilized with human blood; something similar happens when you look at the He 162. A very strange aircraft, and a very cruel one.

I don't know how much this applies to some of the other aircraft in this survey. All of them, simply by being designed and built when they were, are coloured by association with the Nazi state, but not all of them, I think, were directly associated with the darkest aspects of that state. The very, very strange Me 163 Komet was being built well before the final months of the war, before even the final years of it, and so slave labour was probably not involved in its production, and perhaps never could have been, because the technology of its engine was too advanced and complex. The Me 163 was a rocket aircraft. That still sounds strange, doesn't it? A rocket aircraft. Almost all of those ever flown did so on the German side during the latter half of the Second World War. Jet aircraft, because they take in outside air and mix it with their fuel, have one big advantage and one small disadvantage. The big advantage is that their fuel lasts a long time; the small disadvantage is that they aren't quite as fast as they might be, because the jet intake spoils their streamlining. Rocket aircraft, which don't take in outside air, have an advantage and a disadvantage too, only this time the advantage is small and the disadvantage is big. The small advantage is that they're as fast as their unspoiled streamlining can make them; the big disadvantage is that their fuel doesn't last very long.

And so the Me 163 was incredibly fast — it almost certainly broke the sound barrier well before the official "first" by an American pilot in 1947[4]— and incredibly profligate of its fuel. Pilots had about eight minutes of flying time in which to get aloft, find a target and attack it before their fuel ran out and they had to glide back to earth. Unlike most military aircraft, then and now, gliding wasn't a problem in the Me 163, or rather, it was so little of one that it became one: the aircraft, with its extremely wide wings and extremely short fuselage, had such good flying characteristics that losing air-speed during an unpowered landing was difficult, and Me 163's often landed too fast or too hard. And it was really not a good idea to do that in an Me 163. The rocket engine ran on a volatile mixture of concentrated hydrogen peroxide (*T-Stoff*) and hydrazine/methanol (*C-Stoff*). Technicians fuelling the aircraft before take-off wore special clothing and were very careful to avoid contact with either chemical, because they tended to dissolve human flesh rather rapidly. If traces of the fuel were left in the tanks on landing, and the landing wasn't smooth enough, they also tended to explode rather violently. More Me 163 pilots were killed by accidents of this kind with fuel than by Allied action, and the deadly way in which the aircraft punished mistakes, together with its squat appearance when viewed side-on, led to its being christened the *Teufels Eig*, or "Devil's egg".

The puzzling thing was that there was apparently an easy way to avoid such accidents, which was to fit permanent wheels to the aircraft. As it built up speed to take off, an Me 163 sat on a kind of wheeled trolley that detached as the aircraft actually took to the air — and sometimes, as it ran free, the trolley would encounter an unevenness in the run-way and bounce high enough into the air to hit and destroy the climbing Me 163 it had just detached itself from. Pilots who survived take-off and their eight minutes of powered flight had then to land without wheels on a kind of ski underneath the Me 163's belly: all this was difficult, dangerous, and also unnecessary, as the Me 263, a wheeled version of the Me 163, demonstrated when it finally appeared, too late to be manufactured in quantity or to see combat, in 1944.

So was the Me 163 another manifestation of the Nazi tradition of human sacrifice? Like the He 162, it had a name with occult associations: the Komet. Salamanders rise triumphant from fire; comets are nothing but fire, and they are not only portents of doom and dissolution, they are also doomed to dissolution themselves. Perhaps the Me 163 was never aimed solely at dealing death and destruction to Allied bombers and their crews, but was also an elaborate ritual — with an alchemical motif in the deadly corrosive fuel — in which the elite Luftwaffe pilots needed to fly the aircraft were sacrificed piecemeal for their failure to fly with the maximum possible skill.

And maximum possible luck. Even the best pilots needed luck to avoid accidents in the Me 163, particularly during the early stages of its development. It was then that Hanna Reitsch earned herself an Iron Cross, First Class, by severely injuring herself in a crash:

> at the place where my nose had been there was now nothing but an open cleft. [5]

Reitsch was a Luftwaffe test pilot and Nazi propaganda weapon who was perhaps the greatest aviatrix that the world has ever seen. Her vivid descriptions of flying the Me 163 in October, 1942, are in some ways as close as it is now possible to come to experiencing flight in this unique aircraft for oneself:

> To fly the rocket plane, Me 163, was to live through a fantasy of Münchhausen.[6] One took off with a roar and a sheet of flame, then shot steeply upwards to find oneself the next moment in the heart of the empyrean.
>
> To sit in the plane while it was anchored to the ground and be surrounded suddenly with that hellish, flame-spewing din, was an experience unreal enough. Through the window of the cabin, I could see the ground crew start back with wide-open mouths and hands over their ears, while, for my part, it was all I could do to hold on as the machine rocked under a ceaseless succession of explosions. I felt as if I were in the grip of some savage power ascended from the Nether Pit.[7]

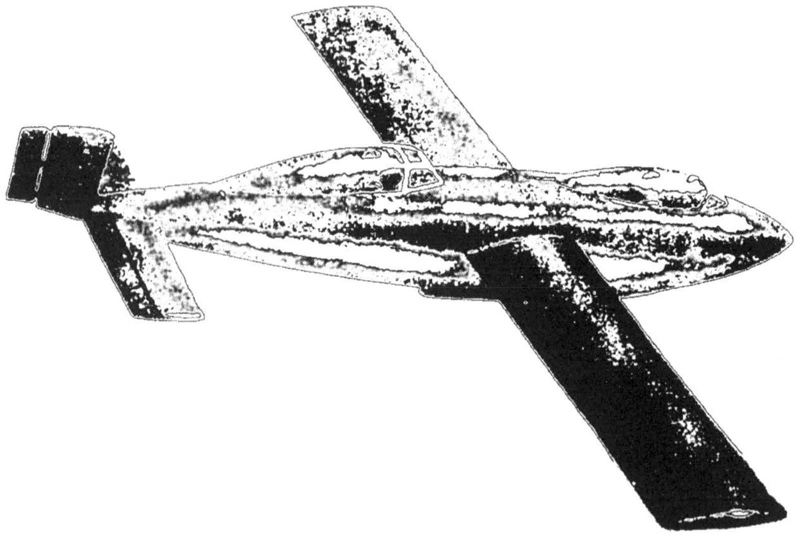

Later in the war, Reitsch was also involved in a test programme that added a curious footnote to the history of the famous V-1 "Doodlebug", the droning pulse-jet missile that made some English cities seem "infested with enormous, venomous insects" during the latter part of the war.[8] In 1943, with the war already more or less lost, Reitsch had proposed that a piloted version of the V-1 be considered for use against Allied shipping and similar large targets. The pilot would ride piggy-back on a bomber most of the way, parting company as the target came near and guiding the missile onto the target before bailing out at the last moment. The chances of doing so successfully were small, and the piloted V-1 would have been both a devastating and, for almost all of its pilots, a suicidal weapon. On the latter of these grounds, it was rejected in 1943; on the former it was resurrected in 1944. Reitsch was again test-pilot in the development programme, and again survived a serious crash, but in the end the weapon, which was named the Fieseler Fi 103, was never used in combat. Just as the Nazis made great efforts to conceal their extermination campaign against the Jews and Gypsies, believing that the mass of the people was not yet ready to fully accept the higher truths that motivated it, so they allowed no overtly suicidal weapon to be used by their armed forces. Even the aerial ramming attacks used against the Allied bomber fleets in the very last days of the war, when, with patriotic marching songs blaring encouragingly over their intercoms, pilots steered their aircraft directly at Allied bombers, were deemed to allow some reasonable chance of survival.

In Germany's partner Japan, where centuries of tradition not merely encouraged suicide but rendered it more or less obligatory under many circumstances, tacticians and designers had much wider scope, and German developments in jet and rocket technology were drawn on to aid the Kamikaze programme. Usually Kamikaze pilots flew ordinary aircraft adapted to their new role only to the extent of being packed with explosive and having enough fuel for a one-way flight; the Yokosuka MXY-7 — code-named *Ohka*, or "Cherry-Blossom" by the Japanese, *Baka*, or "Fool" by the Americans — was an attempt to design an aircraft specifically for kamikaze attack. One version used a rocket engine, another a jet, and both were almost certainly drawing on assistance from the Germans: Japanese aeronautics, which also produced a virtual clone of the Me 163 called the "Righteous Sword", did not have sufficient expertise in this kind of high technology. One of the last submarines sent from the Reich to Japan contained a complete example of the Me 163, but in Japan, as in Germany, extremely advanced technology was no match for the overwhelming numerical superiority achieved by Allied air-forces by that stage of the war.

The Catch-22 was that when resources were plentiful and manpower readily available during the early and middle periods of the war, the Luftwaffe High Command was not interested in the new technology offered to them by their designers, because the war seemed virtually won. Later, during the final period of the war, when resources were scarce and manpower more and more limited, they were very interested indeed, because the war seemed virtually lost. In that final period of the war, the Allies could more or less match the Luftwaffe's conventional aircraft one-on-one in technology and firepower, and because the ratio was far less in the Luftwaffe's favour than that, only unconventional aircraft offered the Germans any good hope of regaining control of the skies over Europe. Later still, when even hope had disappeared for all but the most faithful of the Führer's disciples, unconventional aircraft offered the best means of at least making the bomber fleets pay heavily for the destruction they were wreaking on the Fatherland. There was also the faint possibility that a prolongation of the war might see some disagreement emerge between the odd partnership of Western democracy and Soviet totalitarianism that made up the alliance against the Reich, and some of the Reich's most powerful men — Himmler amongst them — could even glimpse the prospect of engineering an alliance of the "civilized" Anglo-Teutonic nations of Germany, Britain and America against the barbarian menace of the Soviet Union. Every Allied bomber destroyed or crippled represented a tiny postponement of the war's end and a tiny lessening of the odds against this possibility, but only if the price paid in German lives and *matériel* was far less than that exacted from the Allies.

What was needed was an aircraft combining extreme ease and cheapness of manufacture, pilot-friendliness, uninterceptibility, and annihilating firepower. The Me 262 and 163 in their various ways met some of these criteria, and fell far short of others. Perhaps the strangest experimental aircraft to at least near service during the war, if not actually achieve it, would have met somewhat more of them. The Bachem Ba 349, or Natter ("Adder"), was a rocket aircraft of very simple and unusual design. Dwarvish in appearance, with stump-like wings and tail-fins and a fuselage only 6 metres long, it was designed for a vertical take-off from a ramp at such a fierce rate of acceleration that the pilot would probably lose consciousness and have to rely on automatic mechanisms to level his aircraft off at the right height for an attack with the Hs 217 Föhn air-to-air missiles that filled the Ba 349's nose-cone. The aircraft wasn't even intended to land again in its complete form: after the attack everything was to be discarded but the pilot and rocket motor, both descending by parachute for, it was hoped, a swift return into action. After unmanned test-flights, a pilot climbed into the Natter for the first time on February 28, 1945. He died about five seconds after take-off, another sacrifice to the dark Nazi Prince of the Air, and of 36 test-flights made before the Natter factory and launch site were overrun, only six more had been manned. Natter is the German for "adder" or "viper", but the only flesh this viper ever sank its fangs into had been German.

It also marks the end of this survey of highly advanced Second World War German aircraft that actually made it off the drawing-board and into flight — almost. One more phantasmagoric aircraft still awaits attention. Like the Natter, the Gotha Go 229 was built partly of wood, but there are few other similarities between the two aircraft. The Natter is, depending on your preference, either an ugly aircraft or a crudely functional one, or both. The Gotha 229 is beautiful: the entire aircraft is in fact a single giant wing, curved and streamlined like a shell or sea-smoothed stone. The Natter had no conceivable civilian use; the Gotha was not only beautiful to look at but also beautiful to fly, and might have existed solely to that end. Amongst the prop-driven aircraft that roar their clumsy way through the Second World War, it seems like an imperial courtesan amongst the ingenuous adolescent virgins of a provincial mayor's supper-dance, and had it ever achieved service it would have been so far in advance of anything the Allies could even hope to put up against it that the war might have been appreciably prolonged beyond what even the Me 262 and 163 might have achieved. Appreciably might have meant a month or two: by the time the Luftwaffe was eager to see its most potent weapons in service, the war was irretrievably lost by any natural standards of military judgment.

And a damn good thing too, of course. Although the hopeless odds against which German jet and rocket aircraft were developed and flown are part of what makes their story so fascinating and, yes, darkly glamorous, the only people who could support the underdog in this fight would be the sort of people who would rarely or never support an underdog anywhere else. Nazi Germany was rightly and fortunately defeated, but we can still marvel at the ingenuity and tenacity with which it tried to stave off its fate. All of the aircraft described here were touched with genius: that it was a genius employed in a very dark cause only, like the Nazi state itself, serves to increase their perverse appeal. Thunderstorms are wonderful things to admire from a distance. Being caught in one is quite another matter, of course.

WHAT IS TRUTH?

ANTI-DARWINISM AND DENIAL OF THE HOLOCAUST

The universe is six thousand years old.
The Holocaust never happened.
Compare and contrast.

I'm not sure when I first realized the epistemological links between the school of history that denies the reality of the holocaust and the school of theology that denies the reality of evolution. I'd like to think they occurred to me spontaneously; whether or not they did, they were demonstrated very clearly when I read a booklet published by the Dowager Lady Birdwood and called **The Longest Hatred**. This booklet, for whose dissemination Lady Birdwood has ludicrously (and shamefully) been prosecuted under race relations law, is subtitled "An Examination of Anti-Gentilism", and contains things that are interesting, things that I agree with (I'm sorry, as Dame Edna would say, but I do), and things that are, well, dotty.[1] Its theme is the "Jewish Conspiracy", two arms of which are, it claims, the '"Holocaust" hoax' and the '"Man from Monkey" myth — the Theory of Evolution'.[2]

Prima facie, they don't seem to have very much in common. After all, full-blooded conspiracy theorists tend to see everything as part of a grand design, from fluoridation of water to the ties worn by presenters of the nine o'clock news. That's true enough, but looked at more closely the two schools of thought start to reveal some interesting similarities. First of all, they are held almost without exception as corollaries of other beliefs. People who do believe in the holocaust or evolution can hold at the same time any of a huge range of sometimes mutually antagonistic religious and political beliefs. People who don't believe in the holocaust are always (I should say) anti-Semitic and almost always members or affiliates of extreme right-wing organizations. People who don't believe in evolution are almost always literalist religious believers, whether Christian, Jewish or Muslim (in the last case, anti-evolutionists comprise a far higher percentage of believers, because Islam has not yet entered its decadence and given rise to powerful liberal or reformed sects like Christianity and Judaism). It's unlikely that anyone has come to hold the wider belief by being convinced of the truth of the narrower: in both cases, you hate Jews or love the Lord Jesus before you start disbelieving in the holocaust or evolution.

Related to this belief-as-a-consequence-of-belief is a second important similarity, the fact that the two groups seek publicity in accordance with that most dreaded of political entities: a hidden agenda. In other words, they both have ulterior motives, though these are not necessarily conscious ones. The holocaust is denied by extreme right-wingers because the holocaust is the most obvious illustration of what can happen when the mechanisms of a modern industrialized state are controlled by extreme right-wingers. The message is: the holocaust didn't happen, so we deserve another chance. Evolution is denied by some Christians because it is in conflict with a literal interpretation of the Bible; in particular, with a literal interpretation of the first few chapters of Genesis. The message is: evolution is wrong, so the Bible is right and you should accept Jesus Christ as your personal saviour.

This is to express the causes of these beliefs very crudely, and also to employ a fallacious disproof of them that is sometimes called the *argumentum ad hominem*, or is at least related to it. To give a psychological or social or political explanation of a belief is not the same thing as disproving it. However, I have neither the space nor the historical and scientific expertise to refute holocaust revisionism and creationism here, and take for granted that it would be a somewhat pointless exercise anyway because the vast majority of my readers will not subscribe to either. This article should be seen as merely a brief guided tour to these two schools of thought that will concentrate on drawing out the little-recognized similarities between them.

Creationism is the name used by the religious anti-evolutionist movement, who take it from their belief in the literal truth of the "creation" story in Genesis. It is an important part, but only a part, of Christian fundamentalist beliefs, and any discussion of its origins ought, strictly speaking, to be subordinated to a discussion of the origins of Christian fundamentalism. This discussion would be a lengthy and complicated one, and for the purposes of this article it is probably best swallowed up in the observation that Christian fundamentalism is a modern movement, but not a modernist one. It is also perhaps interesting to observe that opposition to evolution is probably only seen as of great importance by fundamentalist Christians, and so there are as far as I know specifically anti-evolutionist groups only among Christians. Muslims, who are almost all in a sense fundamentalist, are not particularly concerned about arguing against evolution, because they would see belief in it as only a small part of the West-

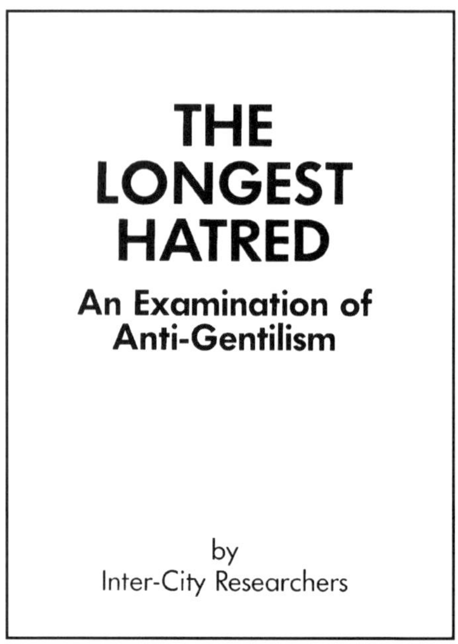
THE LONGEST HATRED

An Examination of Anti-Gentilism

by
Inter-City Researchers

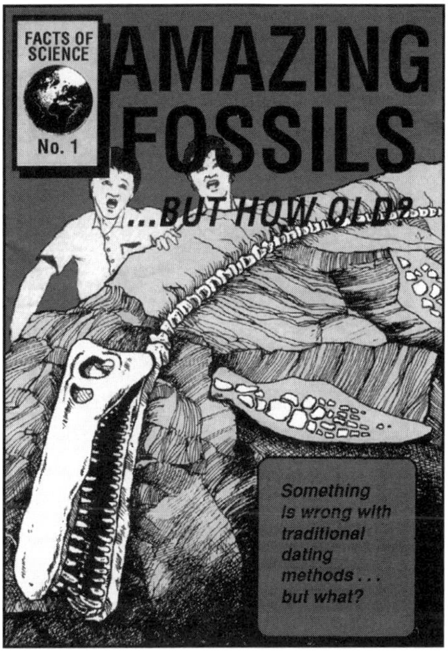

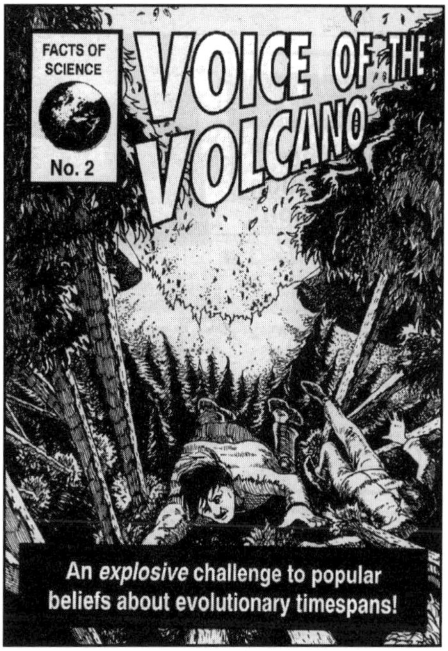

ern secularism to which, *en masse*, Islam is opposed. Opposing evolution is important to fundamentalist Christians because it is an important part of what distinguishes them from the liberal, "secularized" Christians whose equivalents are not yet found in Islam. Fundamentalist Judaism would resemble Islam in its attitude to Western secularism, I believe.

As might be expected from the relative youth of fundamentalist Christianity, the first big clash between creationism and evolutionary theory came fairly recently in the "Scopes" trial, in which a high school teacher called John Scopes was prosecuted in Dayton, Tennessee in the 1920s for teaching evolution "in defiance of a recently enacted state law".[3] The trial, in which the prosecution lawyer William Jennings Bryan, a prominent evangelical politician, was roundly humiliated, has been seen as a triumph for the forces of rationality and free enquiry over the forces of reaction and literalist superstition; it probably wasn't, as Stephen Jay Gould argues turgidly but convincingly in "A Visit to Dayton".[4] It produced, however, a very illuminating remark from Bryan:

> All the ills from which America suffers can be traced back to the teachings of evolution. It would be better to destroy every book ever written, and save just the first three verses of Genesis...[5]

The first three verses of Genesis are:

> 1. In the beginning God created the heaven and the Earth. 2. And the earth was without form, and void; and darkness was upon the face of the deep. And the Spirit of God moved upon the face of

the waters. 3. And God said, Let there light: and there was light.

This kind of absolutism is a very important part of fundamentalism and so a very important part of creationism, but because it is applied to science and scientific ideas, which have always been seen as abstract and remote by most people, it does not appear very frightening and so doesn't arouse very strong emotions. The absolutism of holocaust revisionism, on the other hand, certainly does.

According to its own introduction, the progenitor of present-day "Holocaust Revision" was a slim book called **Did Six Million Really Die?**,[6] which was written by a historian at the University of London under the pseudonym of Richard Harwood[7] and first published by the Historical Review Press in 1974. It is soberly and carefully written and not overtly right-wing in sympathy or tendency. According to the advertisement for it in the British National Party (B.N.P.) magazine **Spearhead**, it is also "fact-filled". This is accurate enough, though facts of course are not true simply because they are facts. Its central thesis is that six million Jews could not have been killed by the Nazis because, first, there were not six million Jews in Nazi-occupied Europe, as "proved" by census and emigration figures and, second, there was no Nazi policy of extermination of the Jews anyway, merely a policy of humanely enforced emigration to Madagascar, as "proved" by the historical record.[8] This reliance on statistics and documentation is one of the ways holocaust revisionism is distinct from creationism. Whether or not the holocaust happened, and if it did how many died during it, is a historical question, and the methods of those who seek to decide it one way or the other are identical, at least in principle. Taken to an extreme, an attempt to prove or disprove the holocaust would be archaeological or forensic: physical traces of it must still remain at death camp sites. This extreme has apparently been reached. Robert Harris, in an **Oldie** profile of the historian-controversialist David Irving, wrote of Irving's quondam denial of the holocaust:

> sooner or later people start turning away in disgust, and then you are really down there in the dirt, scrabbling around with the sad and the crazy, doing things like taking soil samples from Auschwitz to test them for traces of Zyklon-B [the cyanide preparation used in the gas-chambers there][9]

The reality of evolution, on the other hand, is not debated entirely within the same discipline by those for and against it. If Genesis is a literal account of the origins of the universe and life on Earth, it is an account that cannot be wholly proved or disproved by science, because it contains numerous miracles — direct interventions by God in nature that suspend or violate the regular and testable laws to which science addresses itself. Creationism is therefore not a scientific discipline, and another name under which it often goes, that of "Creation Science", is not truly defensible.

A good example of its non-scientific nature is found in what is sometimes called the "omphalos" argument, which is used to explain the universe's "superficial appearance of age". Omphalos is the Greek for "navel", and refers to the fact that Adam and Eve would be expected, as fully formed adult human beings, to have had navels: in other words, to have had, from the first moments of their existence, a *superficial* appearance of having passed through years of embryohood, birth and cutting of the umbilical cord, childhood, puberty and adolescence.[10] In the same way, the universe was created by God with a superficial appearance of age: for example, in the six thousand or so years since creation, only the light from the nearest stars would have had time to reach the earth, so the light apparently reaching us today from stars and galaxies millions of light years away was never emitted by those stars and galaxies, but was rather created by God en route to give the superficial appearance of having been so emitted.[11]

The "omphalos" argument is a fascinating one, not least in the questions about God's veracity it raises, but it's also a completely unanswerable one: there is no way of either proving or disproving it, and so it cannot be called scientific. It is a very neat way of resolving the difficulties posed for creationism by geology and cosmology, and finds echoes elsewhere in creationist epistemology. Other apparent difficulties in the creationist account of our origins are no more than that because:

> My friend, nothing can contradict God's word — if it seems to it may only be because we don't know enough yet.[12]

and because

> When all else fails, why not cut the Gordian knot of endless speculation and simply admit that God, and God alone, had the power to bring two of each of the basic kinds of air-breathing creature to the Ark?[13]

In holocaust revisionism the homologue of this creationist supernaturalism is the belief in the conspiracy by which holocaust "fictions" are maintained and to which all apparent difficulties in the revisionist account would ultimately be attributed. In **Did Six Million Really Die?**, it is remarked that "[b]y a curious coincidence, alleged 'death' camps were all in territory now controlled by the Communists"[14], and the book devotes an entire section to "fake atrocity photographs".[15] In **The Six Million Reconsidered**,[16] a later revisionist book that is openly and poisonously anti-Jewish, the theme is taken further. Of the exhibits in the Auschwitz museum and a "SHOWERS" sign over a gas-chamber door, this book remarks:

> Zyklon B, a cyanide liberating chemical similar to industrial fumigants still widely used in the America, was the German equivalent to U.S. DDT in the control of louse-borne typhus, an enormous danger in war-torn Europe. It was certainly used in "gas chambers" with sealable steel doors in delousing clothing. The Myth says "Brausebad" (showerbath) was used to trick Jews inside. But

this lettering is clearly too spiffy [smart] to be unretouched.[17]

Photographs showing piles of camp dead are in fact those of "dead German citizens ... slyly 'recycled' by our prolific Myth-mongers".[18] Other photographs are straight-forward fakes: barbed wire on cattle trucks is "too haphazard and 'arty' to have kept prisoners inside", and the true nature of a corpse hanging on the barbed wire fence of a camp is questioned: "Did the supposedly so-methodical Germans leave the unfortunate hanging in[sic] the fence — or was he a 'stuntman' from Hollywood?"[19]

The prominence of Jews in the film and publishing industries is seen as of great significance in this book: "The Myth's proprietors ... vend their wares in an astoundingly varied line of publications that are slanted, like championship billiard shots, to hit as many social strata and groupings as possible ... [one writer's] 'histories' are invariably riddled with pro-Soviet propaganda ... At this writing, the shekels are rolling in from the **Ilsa** series of sex-sadism films."[20]

Creationists do not accuse biologists and geologists of faking evidence for evolution in this way, but they too have a paranoid belief in a powerful propaganda machine devoted to spreading false and harmful ideas. **Jurassic Park** has been a bogey to creationists in the same way that **Schindler's List** has been to holocaust revisionists:[21] that both were made by Steven Spielberg, a Jew, is doubtless further proof of the conspiracy to many. Both creationists and holocaust revisionists link these propaganda machines to Communism. **The Six Million Reconsidered** devotes its penultimate chapter to "Jews and Communism":

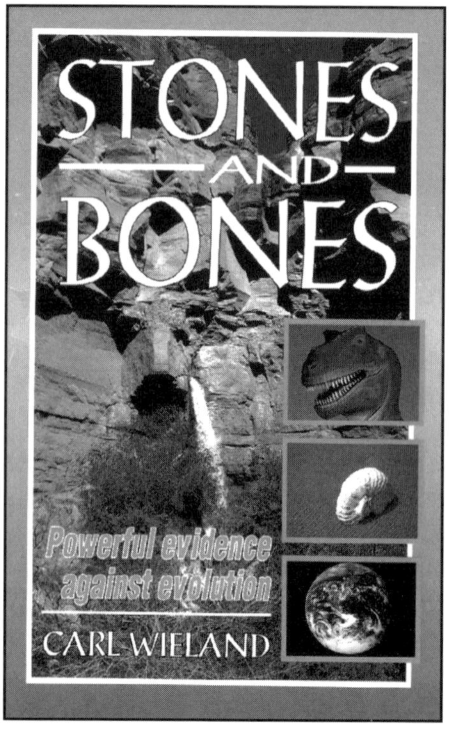

We still hear constantly about the Nazis' supposed "Six Million" victims. Meanwhile, world communism, murderer of millions, marches onwards. What is the Jewish role in Marxism?[22]

A passage from a Jehovah's Witness contribution to creationist literature makes a typical link between evolutionary theory and communism like this:

Yes, Karl Marx, the "father" of modern communism, was so delighted with Darwin's evolution work that he wanted to dedicate a book [the English edition of *Das Kapital*] to him! ... In fact the teaching of evolution in Western lands, in Christendom, often paves the

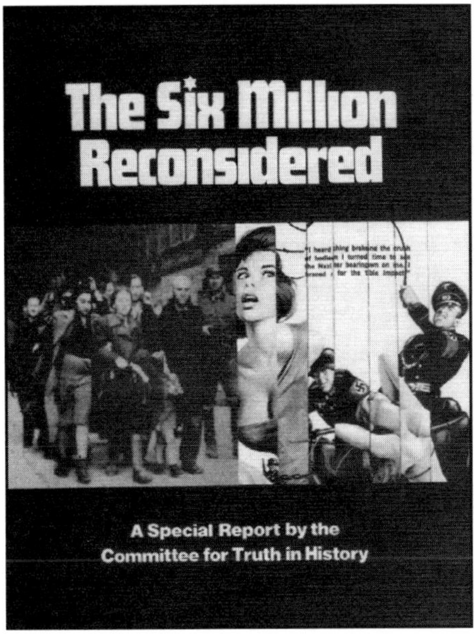

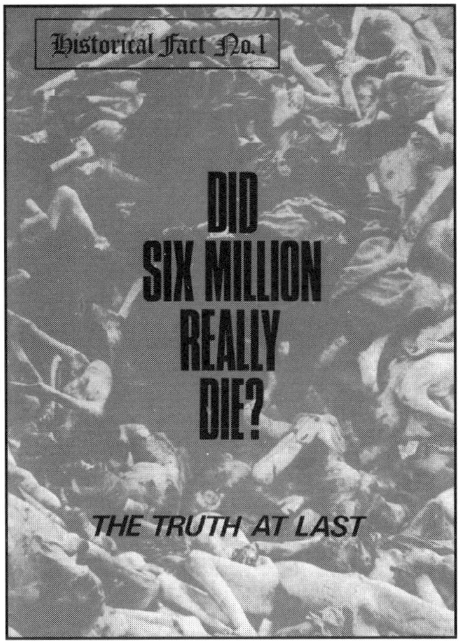

way for persons to accept communism and other godless ideologies.[23]

The further step, that of seeing evolution and communism as related parts of a world-wide Jewish conspiracy, is not taken in mainstream creationist circles, though it is doubtless available. In **The Longest Hatred**, for example, it is taken with gusto:

> Of all the many lies promoted and advanced by our lying news media and controlled State education system, none has more far-reaching consequences than the "Man from Monkey" myth — the Theory of Evolution. *The Protocols of the Learned Elders of Zion*, which numerous well-informed people claim spells out Jews' plans for the destruction of Christian Civilisation, state: "Think carefully of the successes *we arranged* for Darwinism [*Evolution*] ... To us Jews, at any rate, it should be plain to see what a disintegrating importance these directives have had on the minds of the Goyim [i.e. *human cattle*][24] [lacunae, editorial comments and emphases theirs]

Mirroring this mainstream creationist refusal to subscribe to the "Jewish conspiracy" is the fact that creationism is not generally subscribed to by extreme right-wing groups, which tend to be technophilic and heterodox in such religious affiliations as they have. Various forms of what might be called social Darwinism, in fact, are an important part of the ideology of these groups. A B.N.P. recruitment leaflet called "Where We Stand" speaks of the party's attaching

> the highest importance to sport and physical education in schools ... we intend to see much greater resources allocated to this vital part of young people's development.

In **The Eleventh Hour**, the B.N.P. leader John Tyndall's less intellectual but decidedly more readable emulation of **Mein Kampf**, much is made of the weak and flabby physical appearance of left-wingers, and at one point he uses an at least half-serious evolutionary metaphor:

> Undoubtedly, a number of left-wing activists do quite honestly believe the nonsense they spout. A look at some of them — which I and my associates regularly obtain at the frequent demonstrations they mount against us — is enough to explain why: quite clearly, a large portion of these 'comrades' are specimens of humanity some thousands of years behind normal people in the scheme of evolution — freaks and half-wits whom sane societies put in padded cells, or at least in occupations where they can be rendered harmless, but whom our own society of today has graciously honoured with positions of influence and power.[25]

Elsewhere he speaks of seeing a photograph of "a group of 'peace' campaigners in the 1920s" and being

> struck with how, in physical features and bearing, they so closely resembled their heirs of today ... distinguished by skinny bodies, sandals or plimsolls on the feet, a wetness of features and an indisposition to stand upright ... This *species* has changed little over 60 years ... Assemble any group of liberals on one side of any room and then assemble on the other side a group of equal number and sexual composition but of outlook fundamentally opposed to liberalism. Most of us ... would immediately be able to tell which group was which after the most cursory glance. Liberals, generally speaking, constitute the most unimpressive specimens of the white race. [emphasis mine][26]

This has definite overtones of the "muscular Christianity" of Victorian Britain, and of the right-wing imperialism both of Victorian Britain and of modern America, in whose politics fundamentalist Christianity plays a very important role. Creationist Christians and "scientific" holocaust revisionists could therefore both be seen as subscribing to Darwinism, the former in a disguised form, the latter openly. The open anti-Semitism of the holocaust revisionists is not found amongst the creationists, who would regard themselves as part of the central Christian tradition in which, since the end of the Second World War, it is no longer openly expressed. The compatibility of creationism and holocaust revisionism is nonetheless clearly demonstrated by the groups that link the extreme right and fundamentalist Christianity: groups like Lady Birdwood's Choice in the UK; groups like the Protestant Ku Klux Klan and its splinters and affiliates in America; and, in South Africa, groups like Eugene Terreblanche's AWB (Afrikaner Resistance Movement), whose swastika-like flag has been claimed as a symbol of militant Christianity. It seems likely, moreover, that anti-Semitism is latent or suppressed in mainstream creationism, because Jews play such prominent and obvious roles in the liberal media that promote evolution alongside abortion, feminism, homosexuality, lesbianism and other fundamentalist hate-objects. Neo-Nazis, for whom these things are similarly hateful, are not inhibited from pointing out and condemning this Jewish involvement; creationists are, anxious as they also are to avoid an association with the extreme right in the minds of the public they are seeking to influence and convert.

Nonetheless, as I hope I will have demonstrated by now, there are strong similarities between these two extremist schools of thought, and these are found not only in the gross details of their epistemology and systems of logic. They are also similar stylistically, that is, in the way they present and support their arguments. Propaganda for the extreme right-wing sets images of blond and beautiful Aryans against images of bestial and rebarbative Jews and left-wingers; propaganda for creationism sets images of blond and beautiful middle-class men and women against bestial and rebarbative caricatures of evolutionary theory. In their arguments, both employ *suggestio falsi* and *suppressio veri* : suggesting what is false and suppressing what is true. Although he has had the decency to place quotation marks around the operative word, the person who argued against the traditional ascription of vast age to fossils by talking of

> A 'fossilised' felt hat!!! It was discovered in a mine and found to be petrified in places — it was partly petrified![27]

is guilty of both. Petrification and fossilization are different processes, and the soft felt of a hat is anyway quite distinct from the bone and cartilage of an animal carcass.[28] Similarly, to argue that the camouflaging BRAUSEBAD ("Showerbath") of a gas-chamber doorway is fake because the writing is "clearly too spiffy to be unretouched" is disingenuous, at best, but it is typical of the kind of reasoning found in both holocaust revisionism and creationism.

My explanation for this would be two-fold. First of all, these arguments are aimed mostly, if not entirely, at the converted, and arguments for something one already believes never have to be as strong as arguments for something one does not already believe. Second, I think it is probably true to say that both creationists and deniers of the holocaust, of the rank and file at least, tend to be of low intelligence and little education: both ideologies flourish, after all, in America. Those at the top, actually producing or supervising the production of the literature that is consumed by the lower ranks, are either deceiving themselves in some more complicated and subtle way or quite knowingly and cynically setting out to lie in furtherance of their pursuit of power. David Irving, for example, the "free-thinking" historian mentioned previously who has at various points denied or minimized the holocaust, lacks neither intelligence nor ambition, and must realize with others of our would-be saviours on the extreme right that public awareness of the holocaust is one of the greatest obstacles to their being able to lay hand to the tiller of the ship of state. On the creationist side, the cynical and criminal motives of men like the televangelists, for example, are too familiar to need re-stating here.

But there are, of course, differences between holocaust revisionism and creationism, and one of them is very large. I would be able to publish literature

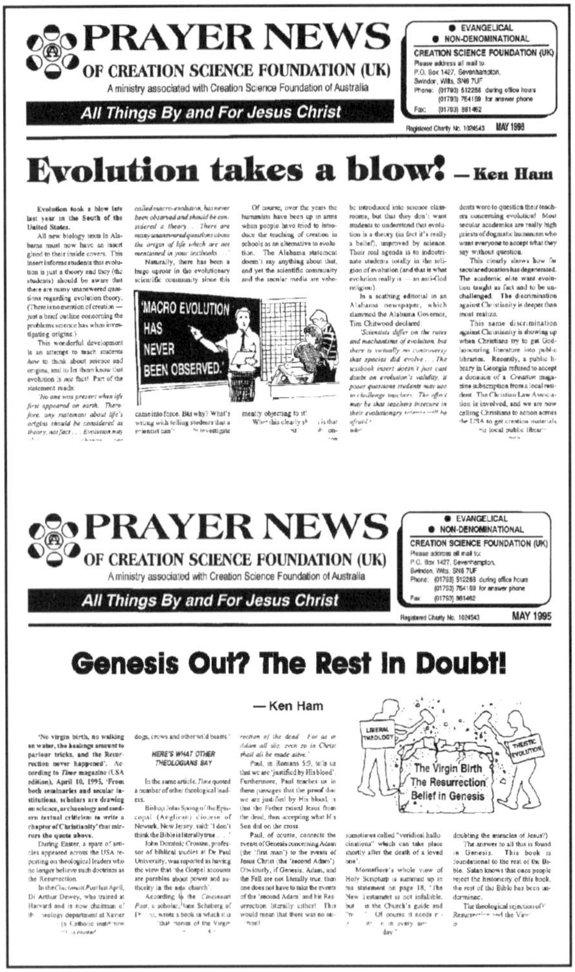

PRAYER NEWS
OF CREATION SCIENCE FOUNDATION (UK)
A ministry associated with Creation Science Foundation of Australia
All Things By and For Jesus Christ

● EVANGELICAL
● NON-DENOMINATIONAL
CREATION SCIENCE FOUNDATION (UK)
Please address all mail to:
P.O. Box 1427, Sevenhampton,
Swindon, Wilts, SN6 7UF
Phone: (01793) 512268 during office hours
(01793) 764189 for answer phone
Fax: (01793) 861462
Registered Charity No. 1024543 MAY 1996

Evolution takes a blow! — Ken Ham

PRAYER NEWS
OF CREATION SCIENCE FOUNDATION (UK)
A ministry associated with Creation Science Foundation of Australia
All Things By and For Jesus Christ

● EVANGELICAL
● NON-DENOMINATIONAL
CREATION SCIENCE FOUNDATION (UK)
Please address all mail to:
P.O. Box 1427, Sevenhampton,
Swindon, Wilts, SN6 7UF
Phone: (01793) 512268 during office hours
(01793) 764189 for answer phone
Fax: (01793) 861462
Registered Charity No. 1024543 MAY 1995

Genesis Out? The Rest In Doubt!

— Ken Ham

anywhere in the world saying that the universe is six thousand years old, and I would be breaking no laws. If I went on to add that six million Jews did not die during the Second World War, I would be arrested or prosecuted in many places, amongst them Germany, Austria, France and, I would imagine, Israel. Creationists do not get spat at in the street; holocaust revisionists are among the most despised and censored groups in the modern world. Bookshops selling the kind of revisionist literature I have described in this article are subject to regular violent attack from anti-fascist groups, and simple possession of it would be a criminal offence in some places; foreigners seeking to lecture on the topic are regularly barred from entry into the UK and the American radical Noam Chomsky was subjected to sustained and wildly distorted abuse for simply daring to support the right of a French academic to publish on the topic.[29]

This is of course perfectly understandable, and although anyone believing in freedom of speech would have to deplore it, he would also have to recognise that it takes its place beside much worse and more damaging examples of censorship and suppression. Nor would I want anyone to imagine that I would like to see some of the opprobrium that attaches to the holocaust revisionists being transferred to the creationists. However, I would like to point out that the creationists are in some ways far more dangerous than the holocaust revisionists, not least because they are far more likely to get their hands on and exercise power — in America at least, they are actually already in power in places like school boards and education committees. I don't think you have to be very mad to deny that the holocaust occurred. Perhaps you don't have to be mad at all. I do think that in some sense you have be very mad to believe that the world is six thousand years old and that the putative possession by Adam and Eve of navels is a good way of proving this. Neo-Nazis, who form the vast majority of holocaust revisionists, keep **Searchlight** in business, provide a lot of people with cheap thrills, and do not do very much else.[30] Fundamentalist Christians, who form the vast majority of creationists, already exercise a lot of power and are trying to exercise more.

And yet the words, if not the actions and ambitions, of both groups deserve respect and attention. Bernard Levin once remarked that the destruction of any book was a terrible thing because every book, whether by intention or not, casts some light on the human condition. Books arguing that the holocaust never happened are wrong, and may also be dishonest and even evil. Books arguing that the universe is six thousand years old are wrong, and may also be dishonest and even crazy. Nevertheless, to read such books, or even to know that they exist, is still a very valuable experience, and one that no reflective person could undergo without asking himself some important and disturbing questions. How do you know that the holocaust happened? How do you know that the universe is not six thousand years old? How can you be sure that you are right and they are wrong? In other words: what is truth?

RITUAL IN PRAGUE

THE BRUTAL LIFE — AND MAGICKAL DEATH? — OF HITLER'S MAN OF IRON

Sometime toward the middle of the 1990's, a cassette-only mini-album began to see limited circulation on the noise electronics underground. Entitled **MCMXLII**, the tape purported to be the work of a group called Heydrich, and contained five tracks: the two most interesting and original of these, "Open-Top Mercèdes and "Lidice Lullaby", had been due to appear on a compilation series put out by an electronic music label in Rochdale, but were pulled when the label boss became aware of the true nature of the material.

Heydrich, it transpired, had been the name of the deputy head of the S.S., and **MCMXLII** — 1942 — was the year he was assassinated by Czech partisans in the middle of a career remarkable chiefly for its brutality. The Lidice of the track "Lidice Lullaby" was a Czech village wiped out in reprisals after his death, all adult males being shot, all women and children deported to concentration camps: 15 or so were still alive at the end of the war. It seemed that the tracks and tape, like much else on the noise electronics scene, had distinctly unsavoury neo-Nazi overtones.

Or were the product of a much blacker sense of humour than most people are comfortable with. The curious lead-out track on the album, "Bella in the Nave with Phthisis", seems an obvious take on the Beatles' "Lucy in the Sky with Diamonds". "Lucy in the Sky with Diamonds" is LSD, so "Bella in the Nave with Phthisis" is... something that hardly needs spelling out. Track three, "Greater Palästina", is a an almost straight pirate — but only "almost" because it seems to be of deliberately poor sound quality — of a vocals-only mediæval Crusaders' song invoking God's help in a re-conquest of the Holy Land. The use of German in a title that is a direct inversion of the Zionist concept of a "Greater Israel" might seem to add weight to the suspicion that **MCMXLII** is a warped tribute to an evil man.

Maybe so. Heydrich the group haven't surfaced again, and one presumes they are now inactive or disbanded, but their quondam existence is certainly some kind of tribute to Heydrich the man, who, more than 50 years after his violent death, still retains his full complement of the dark Nazi glamour that was lost by the other *Reichsherren* in the squalid, airless tunnels of the Führerbunker and the drab, immediately post-war corridors and cells of Nuremberg. Heydrich died when the Second World War looked well set to be a

German walkover. Heydrich may have died to keep it looking that way. But we have some ground to cover before we can see quite what *that* implies.

Mention the name of Reinhard Heydrich, even to someone who's fairly well-up on the Second World War, and you're likely to get the response "Who?" This isn't entirely to do with the fact that Heydrich died in 1942, and so never had to scuttle for cover as the dust settled from the Third Reich's *Götterdämmerung*, and never had to end his life as a highly publicized and much regretted suicide-after-arrest, like Himmler, or receive weeks of world-wide publicity in the dock at Nuremberg, like Göring and Hess. Even at the height of his power within the Nazi state, Heydrich was a shadowy figure. He was dedicated, as the sub-title of one German biography has it, to the "pursuit of total power", yet he saw no way personal publicity could help him achieve that end. And, had things gone just a little differently, achieve it he almost certainly would: Robert Harris's flawed but interesting novel **Fatherland** (1990), set in an alternative history in which the Reich did win the Second World War, portrays Heydrich, with perfect plausibility, as the real power in the land by the 1980s, with Hitler increasingly reclusive and Himmler killed in a mysterious air-crash two decades before.

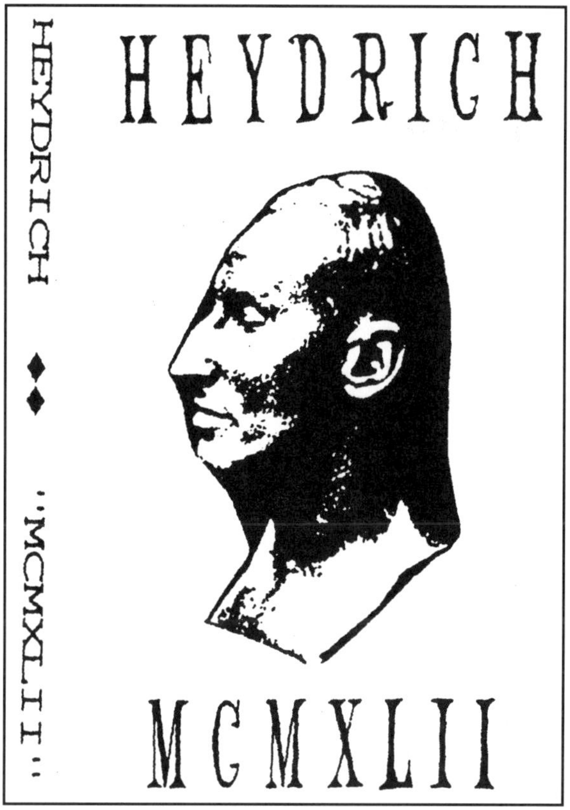

Heydrich — the band. Cassette sleeve

Perfect plausibility because Heydrich had been perhaps the fourth or third most powerful figure in the Reich having barely left his 'twenties, and died at only the age of thirty-eight. He had been born in 1904, the son of one Herr Bruno Heydrich, a composer, musician and singer who from both his appearance and his profession was believed, falsely, to be of Jewish extraction. Unfortunately for the Jews of the later Reich, any attempts to deny the rumours that circulated were undermined by the fact that Bruno Heydrich's father had died when he was 14, and his later stepfather's name was Süss, which, in Germany, is regarded as a typically Jewish name. And also one Bruno Heydrich found it hard to shake off: an entry for him in one musical encyclopaedia read "Bruno Heydrich (really

Süss)", and though the entry was changed, that very fact may have helped the rumours to survive, because it would have suggested that Bruno Heydrich had something to hide.

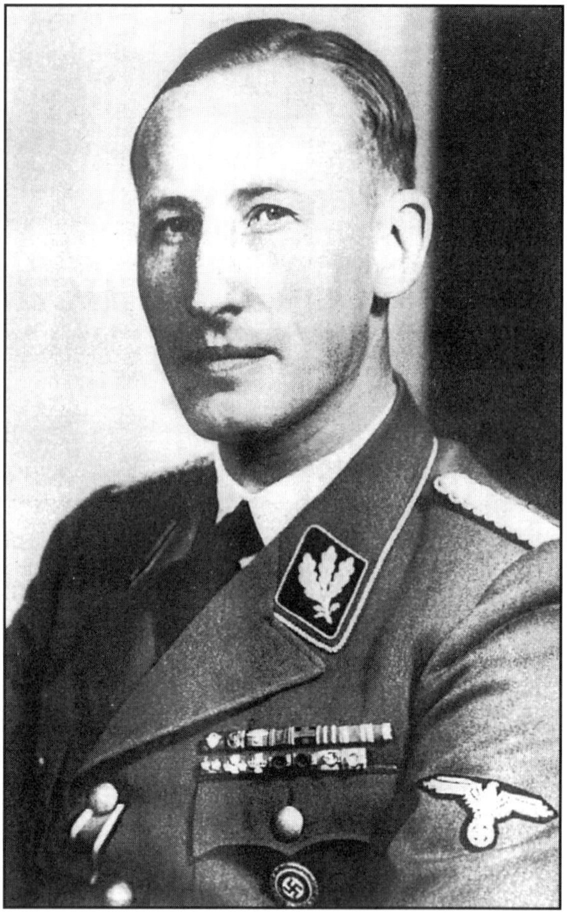

Reinhard Heydrich

But in fact Heydrich *père* did not take the whispers of his Jewish ancestry very seriously, and he even had a habit of playing on them by performing a skilful imitation of an "Isidor", as Jews were colloquially and contemptuously known. For his sons Reinhard and Heinz, growing up in increasingly anti-Semitic times, things were different. Both were taunted at school with chants of "Isi! Isi!", and most biographers of Heydrich have seen the later ruthlessness with which he devoted himself to the extirpation of Europe's Jews as driven by an overwhelming need to prove finally that he himself was not numbered amongst them. One story, probably apocryphal, is that he once came home drunk, caught sight of himself in a mirror, drew his pistol, and shot at his own reflection, crying "Take that, you damned Jew!"

But such irrational drives and hidden inadequacies are at work in very many politicians: in very many of those who seek public prominence in any way. Heydrich, however, was driven by personal demons in a demonic age, and the balm he used to soothe the smarting of his psychic wounds would be other people's blood. In 1936, after being expelled from Navy Training College, where he had again been bullied by his peers, this time for his interest in classical music and his high-pitched voice (he was nicknamed *Ziege*, or "Nanny-goat"), he travelled to Berlin for a job interview with a former chicken-farmer. The former chicken-farmer's name was Heinrich Himmler, and the job on offer was that of deputy in the *Schutz-staffel*, the organization that was fulfil the role of a praetorian guard for a former post-card painter called Adolf Hitler, and which is better known to history as the SS.

Heydrich, who had received some intelligence training whilst in the Navy and was a devoted reader of espionage novels, particularly British ones, impressed Himmler with his knowledge of political intrigue (which was in fact far less extensive than he succeeded in conveying), and was offered the job on the spot. The Nazi party of which Heydrich now formed an active part was at the time rather in the position of Christianity before the advent of Constantine: merely one, and not the biggest, of many competing parties and factions, some of the extreme left, some of the extreme right, with all shades of opinion represented in between. Whether Himmler was the true evil genius of the SS, however, or merely carried forward on the bow-wave of Heydrich's relentless will to power, by the time the Nazi party had found its own Constantine in the shape of the elderly and near senile President Hindenburg, Hitler's praetorian guard was more than equipped to exploit the vastly increased power that was suddenly provided to it. Göring, a dangerous rival for Hitler's political affections, had already been outmanoeuvred, and Hitler was increasingly reliant, and increasingly willing to be so, on an organization conceived as the purest possible expression of his own will.

Heydrich was at the heart of all these developments, and many in the higher echelons of the party, though not in the rank and file or the public at large, saw him as Hitler's anointed favourite, a clever young protégé being groomed for a distant but inevitable succession. Heydrich himself had no favourites, and no loyalties. Secret police forces are founded on and exist by the principle that information is power, and Heydrich sought information fearlessly and unceasingly, storing it in an infamous *Panzerschutz*, an armoured safe that was whispered to contain secrets capable of being turned against Hitler himself, should the occasion or the opportunity arise. No-one could believe himself absent from Heydrich's thumb-card indexes and files, Himmler least of all, and Himmler's fear of his deputy's machinations is said to have been behind Heydrich's removal from the centre of power at Berlin to the governship of Czechoslovakia and her sabotage-crippled armaments industry. The same fear is even whispered, when Heydrich's sojourn in Czechoslovakia proved so successful that he seemed an automatic choice for the governorship of France, to have played some role in Heydrich's assassination and death. Heydrich, some have said, was too dangerous to Himmler to be allowed to survive. Too dangerous? Or — and the question will later cease to be the paradox it now seems — too valuable?

For Heydrich was undoubtedly the jewel in the Nazi crown: the "Man of Iron", as Hitler eulogized him at his funeral, whom all the Third Reich's efforts in education and eugenics were bent at producing. He was a Nazi perversion of Renaissance man, wedding utter ruthlessness and administrational efficiency to intellectual and athletic abilities of the highest order. He was a gifted amateur musician, a skilled and ferociously competitive fencer, and found time and energy in the course of extremely demanding and important duties to train as a fighter pilot and fly combat missions, during one of which, over the Russian front, he was shot down and narrowly rescued from behind enemy lines. He seemed to thrive on a minimum of sleep and relaxation, a maximum of pressure and danger, and though he imposed no moral or humanitarian limits on the execution of policy, he was very clearly and readily able to distinguish when and where to employ the tactics of the iron fist, and when and where not. "Hangman Heydrich", the sobriquet given to him by the Allies to mark his Reichsprotektorship of Czechoslovakia, although it captures perfectly what Heydrich was capable of being, falls far wide of what Heydrich actually was in his attempts to reduce sabotage and win Czech armaments workers over to an acquiescence in, if not a wholehearted support of, the Nazi war effort.

Heydrich's success in Czechoslovakia, which may have increased Himmler's unease about the future, certainly did increase the Allies' unease about the present, and has been suggested as a chief motive for the assassination attempt set in train under the codename of ANTHROPOID. Leo Kessler suggests in **Betrayal at Venlo** that British intelligence also wished to avenge the capture and death of an agent in one of Heydrich's notoriously efficient and ruthless special operations. Add to these possibilities the strong desire of the Czech government-in-exile to demonstrate, in the certain knowledge that Heydrich's assassination would provoke unprecedented reprisals against the Czech civilian population, that they were still capable of sponsoring independent action against the occupiers of their country, and Heydrich's assassination seems a fairly straightforward matter.

And yet it needed a great deal of luck to come off: perhaps too much luck. Like his deputy, Himmler was a secretive and conspiratorial man, and there undoubtedly existed within the SS channels of information and chains of command owing loyalty only to him and out of the control, and perhaps even the knowledge, of his deputy. If news of the assassination attempt had reached Himmler by these means, he would have been presented suddenly with a means of removing the future threat Heydrich posed to him. Perhaps news reached both Heydrich and Himmler, but the former refused to take it seriously, as he is known to have taken the threat posed by the Czech resistance in general. In either case, the temptation for Himmler may have been great, and the more easily yielded to because complicity in the assassination would have been a sin of omission, not of commission. Heydrich flaunted his power over the people of Prague by riding daily through the city, to and from his headquarters at Hradcany castle, in an unescorted open-top Mercèdes. Himmler merely had to omit a direct order for more — in fact for *some* — security precautions, and then allow the Czech assassination team parachuted into the country by the Special Operations Executive to do the rest. And after that, ensure that the hunt for the assassins concluded in such a fashion as to allow no possibility of the truth's emerging.

And indeed, this hunt, conducted by the Gestapo, conforms in no way to that organization's reputation for ruthless efficiency. It was very badly bungled from start to finish, from the panic to erupt on first news that Heydrich was badly wounded in an assassination attempt to the eventual running to earth of the assassins in a crypt beneath an ancient church in Prague, from which the wanted men all emerged dead, useful to the Gestapo only to the extent of the terror their severed heads would later instil when exhibited to their families.

Alive, the assassins might have revealed that their task had been made easier by what almost seemed a complicity on part of the German occupiers: inexplicable to them, perhaps, but highly significant to the ears of certain in the SS who knew of Himmler's fear of Heydrich, and of the secret chains of command through which he might have facilitated the assassination. Had this been the case, Himmler would have been very anxious to prevent any whisper of the truth from coming to Hitler's attention, for even *treue Heinrich* — loyal Heinrich — would not have been proof against the Führer's wrath at any slightest hint of a complicity in the death of his favourite. Hitler himself delivered the eulogy at Heydrich's state funeral in Berlin on 9th June, 1942; Himmler stood close by with Heydrich's two young sons.

Himmler's grief, like that of Heydrich's former mentor Admiral Canaris, may have been entirely genuine, but if there was any trace of relief there, in what did it have its roots? In the realization that an extremely clever and cunning future rival no longer posed any possible threat? Or in the secret knowledge that the most important of all the Nazi enterprises, the unprovoked and wholly unexpected invasion of the Soviet Union, had been blessed by the sacrifice of the finest victim the Reich could provide? In other words, was Heydrich's death a ritual sacrifice, a "king-killing" of the type to which some say the English king William Rufus and the American president John F. Kennedy were subjected in 1100 and 1963, respectively?

Conventional history, and conventional historians, would say no, but neither has ever truly appreciated the nature of the Nazi regime. Nazism was not merely a political movement but also, and more importantly, a magickal one. Hitler was a black magician in not a metaphorical and derogatory sense, but in a literal: every aspect of the Nazi state, from its rituals and pageants to the insignia borne by its black-uniformed troops, had an occult significance and was calculated to an occult end: the ushering in of the new millennium of the Third Reich. Himmler was even more deeply versed in the occult than his Führer, and to recognize the worship of the death-principle to which he devoted his SS is to arrive at a true understanding of the apparatus of slave labour and industrialized mass-murder the SS constructed and ran in the concentration and extermination camps.

It is inconceivable, therefore, that careful occult preparations for the invasion of the USSR were not undertaken by both Hitler and Himmler alongside the more prosaic and more visible logistical and tactical ones. And yet both sets of preparations were upset by an impulsive campaign launched by Hitler to extirpate resistance to the Axis conquest of Yugoslavia. The delay that arose, although it lasted no more than six weeks, can with hindsight be seen to have been fatal: those lost six weeks saw the Nazi invasion of the USSR caught by winter with the campaign very nearly won. "Very nearly" would be as close as

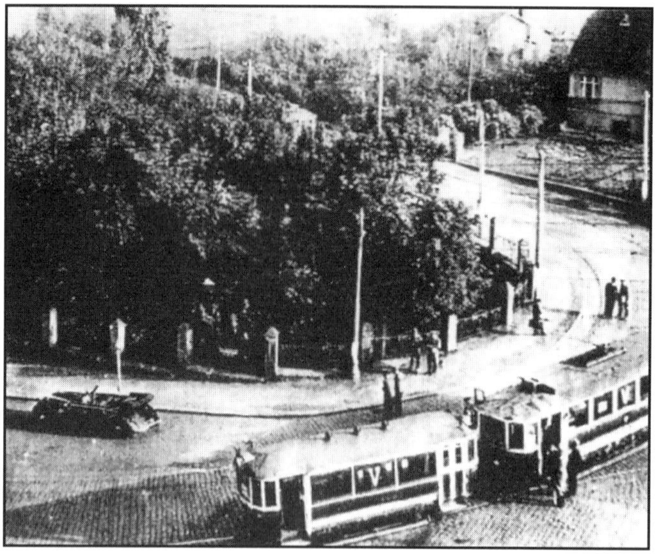
The Gestapo reconstruct the scene of Heydrich's assassination

final victory came in the USSR, and hence, in the war as a whole.

Hitler, more impulsive, more unstable, more inclined to trust blindly to his guiding *daimon*, would not have seen the true seriousness of the delay: it is said that he believed that the Russian Frost-Giants that defeated Napoleon would fight on behalf of the invader this time. Himmler, more self-controlled, more stable, more deeply versed in the occult, would have recognized the delay's seriousness, and may have turned, half in desperation, half in relief, to the crime he had long meditated: the killing of his threatening second-in-command. Who after all would be better suited as a sacrifice to success in the Soviet campaign than Heydrich, avatar of all the Aryan and Nazi virtues? Whose pain and humiliation could be better offered to the dark gods of Nazi destiny than Heydrich's?

And so, as Heydrich's contemptuously unarmoured, unescorted, roofless, dark green Mercèdes slowed to take a hair-pin bend and came within range of the three Czech partisans waiting in ambush, he may have been the focus not merely of political and military conspiracy, but also of magickal ritual. The bomb hurled at him, to explode under the rear-wheel and drive fragments of metal, leather seat-cover and SS uniform into his body, did not merely strengthen the hand of the Czech government-in-exile, nor merely avenge the British secret service for the loss of an agent three years before, nor merely remove a possible future threat from Himmler's path, but may have also been Heydrich's thunderous initiation into a hidden ceremony of Himmler's secret contrivance.

For the bomb did not kill him, and had itself been a back-up weapon brought into use when a sub-machine gun carried by another of the assassins had jammed. Heydrich was even able to draw his pistol, leap from the car, and pursue the three Czechs, loosing several shots at them before collapsing from the pain of his wounds. Taken to hospital, he would linger a further eight days. Of themselves, his wounds were not life-threatening, but they had destroyed his spleen, an essential part of the body's immune system, and once infection had set in, inevitable from the unsterilized pot-pourri of shrapnel that had been driven into his body, there was no hope for him. The recently discovered wonder-drug Penicillin might have saved his life, but all stocks were in Allied hands. Himmler visited him in hospital; he is said to have burst into tears when first told of the assassination, and to have mobilized all possible medical resources for his wounded deputy. Yet we cannot be certain that the grief was wholly unsimulated or unambivalent. Heydrich, wounded and in great pain, kept under constant anaesthesia, was in no position to defend himself from Himmler's machinations, and it is possible, at least, that even if Himmler had no part in the assassination attempt, he was ready to take advantage of it once it had occurred. Perhaps Heydrich's wounds were not so serious as was publicly stated; perhaps the SS doctors who worked sedulously to save his life were under secret orders to allow his death. All we know is that their efforts, sincere or not, were in vain.

A permanent SS honour guard was established at the spot Heydrich's Mercèdes came under attack. The Allies' response to the death of the "Butcher of Prague" was the commissioning of a movie-with-a-message, the propagandistic **Hangmen Also Die** (1942). Heydrich is seen only at the very beginning of the film. He snarls threats in German at gathering of Czech officials, then sets off in his Mercèdes to his appointment with destiny, accompanied by the snarling motorcycles of an armed escort that in reality never existed. The assassination itself is not shown: even hangmen can attract sympathy when they are violently attacked and badly wounded, and the truth in Heydrich's case, that he had behaved with great courage and endeavour, was impossible to relate. Better to leave the assassination veiled, and concentrate on the brutal measures taken to avenge it.

For brutal they undoubtedly were: many hundreds of Czech intellectuals and leaders of society were taken hostage, and, when Heydrich died, subject to mass execution. To the Nazi hierarchy, Heydrich's death had been murder most foul. To Allied High command, a justified assassination. To very few has it ever seemed a ritual sacrifice. The only man who may ever have truly known died himself less than three years later. *Treue Heinrich*, loyal Heinrich, after betraying a Führer who would choose 31st April, the occult day of days, for his suicide and petrol-drenched semi-cremation, was captured by British troops near Bremen. Meticulous in his organization and preparation to the last, he had carried with him a precaution against that very eventuality. As he was guarded closely in an interrogation cell preparatory to a complete body search, he was allowed a second to turn his head aside. That was all he needed. Lodged somewhere in his mouth was a glass capsule of cyanide; he flicked it out with his tongue, crunched down on it with his teeth, and swallowed his exit dose. Amongst the many secrets he carried out with him may have been the final truth about the death of a Führer-in-waiting. We will almost certainly never know.

NO NEWS IS GOOD NEWS

PSYCHIC VAMPIRISM IN THE MASS MEDIA

Human beings and their instincts evolved in small tribal groups where every individual could know and be known to every other individual. That's why we have an innate appetite for news about what other people are doing and having happen to them — particularly for bad news. The reasons are obvious. If Uncle Ugg-Raa was breakfast for a sabre-tooth tiger down at the water-hole this morning, it's good for us to know because it might help us to avoid being lunch. The trouble starts when the instincts that helped us survive in the world then start working in the world now, where there are getting on for six billion of us, all caught fast in the meshes of an electronic communications network that can whisk information from any point to any other point at the speed of light. Something bad is bound to be happening somewhere in the world right now. If it's bad enough, you'll be hearing about it very soon. Is that something to be grateful for? Steve Philips doesn't think so.

SIMON WHITECHAPEL *When did you first start to develop these ideas about the media and the role of news?*

STEVE PHILIPS About four or five years ago, when I came across a book called **Man of Lawlessness** by a guy called Tom Davies[1]. Before that I'd accepted more or less completely the idea that news is good for you — the right to know, the need to know, the intrinsic value of learning what's going on in the world. Even while I was reading the book, I was disagreeing with it, but its arguments stayed with me after I'd finished and I gradually began to agree with them.

Why?

Because they matched the way I could see the media operating.

Could you describe the book?

Yeah, sure. It's actually a "the-end-is-nigh" tract, because Davies thinks that the mass media are a kind of corporate Anti-Christ, ushering in the Last Days. Which will sound as though the book itself's not worth bothering with, but if you think that, you're wrong. I don't know how original Davies' ideas are, but I think it's perfectly possible to agree with them while disagreeing with the overall conclusion he draws.

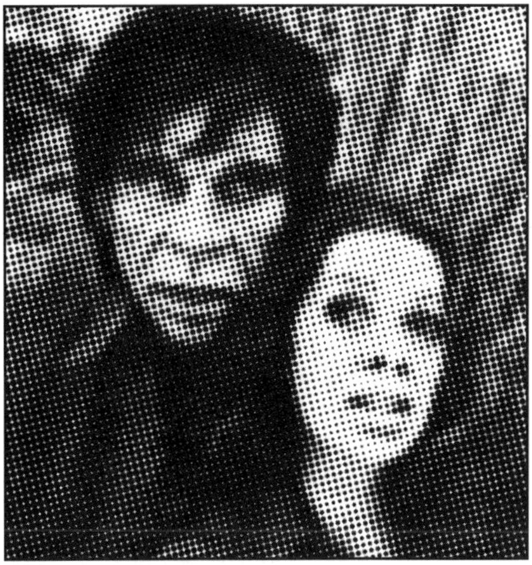

And the ideas are what?

That the media are obsessed with violence. That there's a kind of symbiotic relationship between real violence and the way the media feeds off it — bit more contentious, perhaps, but I think there's probably something in it. Also that the media are hugely self-important. Although Davies points this out in lots of places the thing I've particularly picked up on is the application of it all to "news", in inverted commas. You know, the whole News At Ten, Nine O'clock News, CNN, Sky News thing. And the radio. If you watch and listen with Davies' ideas in mind, it's truly a disgusting spectacle.

Could you give some examples?

There are examples on almost every single news programme you ever hear or see on TV or radio. What truly interests these programmes is death and suffering, and the wider the scale of it, the more they're interested. They ignore ninety per cent of the world unless something spectacularly violent or unpleasant happens there, like a ferry disaster or disco burning down, or something like that. But those are really just *hors d'oeuvres.* What they really like is something they can wring a lot of juice out of, which means something that happens closer to home. The Dunblane Massacre was the ultimate new-journalist's wank-fantasy. It had everything — violent death, suffering of the innocent, enormous amounts of emotional pain. Everything they love to linger over and rub our noses in while they wank themselves to orgasm after orgasm of fake sympathy and self-righteousness.

Are you literally suggesting this is a sexual thing?

Well, no, not really, not for most of the media, though I'm sure for a few journalists that does come into it. No, this sort of ghoulishness isn't directly sexual, though it may be a repressed or sublimated sort of sex. Maybe I could call it psychic vampirism — a thirst for other people's misery. It's in all of us, but it's getting worse and the people suffering from it worst are in the media — in news programmes.

William Burroughs would say that it's all part of a conspiracy of mental and spiritual assault — a kind of war waged against our senses and emotions by the mass media. Do you agree?

I don't know. I know very little about Burroughs and his ideas, but if that's what he says I can certainly see something in it. I'm not sure I like the word

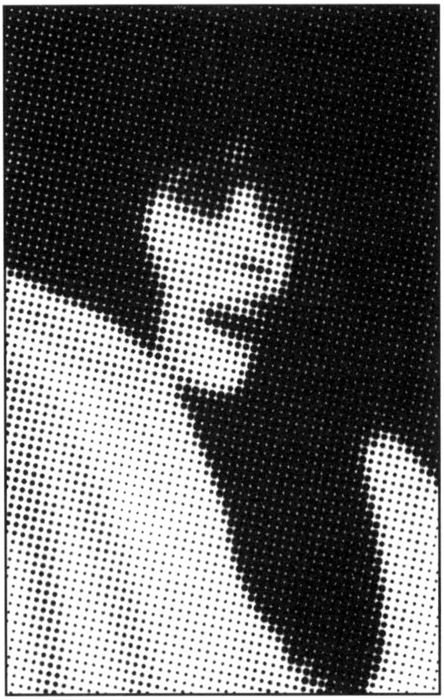

"conspiracy", though. I don't think it's a fully conscious process, not for most people involved. They just have a natural, unreasoning inclination towards this kind of behaviour. It's not something that's planned, at least not at the lower and middle levels of the organizations that put out the news.

How do you answer the claim that news programmes are intended to inform us, give us information about the world so we can make educated choices about it?

That's complete bullshit and a lot of people who claim that know it is. News programmes are about *entertainment*, not about information. Look at how many of them have theme music, usually minor key and portentous, just like a soap opera or Hollywood film. And look at what they're interested in — death, violence and suffering. Why is that necessarily more important than anything else? Does it matter to me that a department store has fallen to bits in South Korea and killed a hundred people?[2] I'm not being callous by saying that, I'm just asking, how does it matter? If deaths in South Korea matter, why am I not told about all the other deaths there? I'm sure far more than a hundred people are killed each year on South Korea's roads than in department stores, but that's not spectacular enough, it's not unusual enough, it's not interesting enough. In other words, it's not entertaining enough.

But what if buildings in the UK were being built in the same way, and there was a risk to people here?

Do you think that was the first thing to occur to the producers of news programmes when they heard that piece of news? Or the second, third or fourth thing? It's almost totally irrelevant: what they want is blood and suffering. Plane and train crashes always attract a lot of attention, but travelling by train or plane is very safe compared to travelling by car. If news programmes are so concerned about informing us and helping us to make educated choices, why don't they remind us of that when they report the latest plane disaster? They never try to set anything in a proper context, because that gets in the way of entertaining people and might actually do something to stop bad things happening, which is really the last thing they want.

Is entertainment the right word if death and suffering are what they're interested in?

Of course. We all have a taste for other people's suffering — it must be in our genes or something. Perhaps it helps us to feel better about our own sometimes less than happy situations, too. It goes back thousands of years — the gladiatorial games in ancient Rome and so on. News programmes cater to exactly the same taste, but they do it hypocritically, because they pretend that they're interested in informing us and educating us. I mean, Christ, what a sick individual you are if you want to watch gory deaths and mutilations in a *fictional* video nasty, but what an upright and active citizen you are if you want to keep yourself informed about every fucking *real* mass death there was in the world yesterday.

How would you explain the media attention given to the murder of Jamie Bulger then? That wasn't a mass death.

No, but it isn't just a case of mass death. That's what they prefer, all other things being equal, but they also like novelty. An unusual or spectacular single death is fine too, and the Bulger case was a particularly spectacular one. The media love all children's deaths by violence, but they particularly love ones they can extract a so-called moral message from. All that wailing and breast-beating about what a sick society we've become, about the evil influences at work amongst us. Again, bullshit, and again, designed to entertain us. Who doesn't like the warm, satisfying glow of a bit of righteous indignation? Who doesn't like to be able to shit on someone else from a great height the way we all could on Thompson and Venables [the two children found guilty of Bulger's murder]? The media did their very best to paint the worst possible picture of that death, and they sentimentalized it in the grossest possible way. Why exactly was it "Jamie" Bulger? Was that the name his parents and family usually used? Well, who cares, it's certainly the name that emphasizes how young and innocent the poor little kid was, isn't it? And the way he was so often referred to as "little Jamie Bulger" or the "toddler Jamie Bulger". I mean, Christ, he was three years old, thanks for keep pointing out that he was little as well. Is that part of the inform and educate news agenda? Again, the aim was entertainment and again, who cares if the emotions whipped up are synthetic and damaging ones — I mean, it's *news*, isn't it? Must be important.

So you don't think it was important that a three-year-old was killed by two nine-year-olds?

Honestly, no. That sort of thing is exceedingly rare and will remain exceedingly rare as far as I can see, but it's happened before and it'll happen again. Thompson and Venables were undoubtedly two twisted and evil little shits, but they were not the first signs of complete societal breakdown. I don't like the idea that Jamie Bulger suffered the way he did, but I'm not going to pretend that it matters much to me, because it doesn't. This country sells weapons of mass destruction that are responsible for the deaths of far more children overseas, in far more painful ways. Why is that not important?

Because it isn't as entertaining. There's nobody to *blame*, there's no moral frisson to be had from it. And they're only fucking wogs anyway. British jobs are at stake if we do anything about the arms trade. Another example: cars kill far more children in this country than die by murder. I could easily imagine some sort of modification to cars in this country — like those cretinous crash-bars — that would kill more children in a year than Thomas Hamilton managed, but they'd be killed in ones and twos in a run-of-the-mill way and it wouldn't be deliberate, so it wouldn't matter. Actually, it would matter to the kids and their parents. The only trouble is it wouldn't be as entertaining to us. I mean, Hamilton *meant* to do it, didn't he? He was *evil*. Some cretin who puts crash-bars on the front of his four-wheel drive and kills a kid because he fancies himself as some kind of urban warrior wouldn't mean to do it, so it would be OK. And if you start questioning cars, where would it end? No, news programmes are perfectly happy with the status quo and with people staying as ignorant as they've always been. As long as the deaths and the suffering keep flowing, everything's fine.

What solutions do you offer?

I'm not sure there are any. All I'm trying to do is spread these ideas — not original to me, as I'd like to emphasize again. We do need to know what's going on, but we've got to learn to take notice of what really matters. At the moment, that's decided for us and a lot of people agree with the decisions made on their behalf, because an awful lot of people are interested first and foremost in other people's suffering. Education is the answer. You might not agree with what I'm saying now, but think it over and bear it in mind when you're watching or listening to the news and I'm sure you'll see my point of view. I was an orthodox news-consumer before I read **Man of Lawlessness** and I disagreed with a lot of the things Tom Davies was saying at the time, but afterwards I changed my mind. I'm not saying my tastes are superior, but I am saying that maybe I've been helped to see things more clearly. The news is entertainment first and foremost, and what the news finds entertaining is death and violence and suffering.

Why do you not then condemn video nasties and similar things as well? Surely they're entertainment based on those things too?

Perhaps I should — I'm open-minded about it, but I have a feeling that as long as it's honestly and openly intended as entertainment, it's far less damaging. Fiction doesn't damage your optimism and your sense that there's good in the world or any point to living the way real-life stuff does. The news is entertainment, but it's not enjoyable. It's depressing — it corrodes something inside you. I suppose it's a kind of psychic masochism as well as a kind of sadism. Once you see that you're being entertained by real suffering, it changes your attitude towards it. You see it in a proper perspective and you can laugh at the way the media try to make bad things seem worse. Gilding the lily kind of thing, only in this case it's putting dung on the corpse or something. The best thing of all, though, is to stop watching altogether.

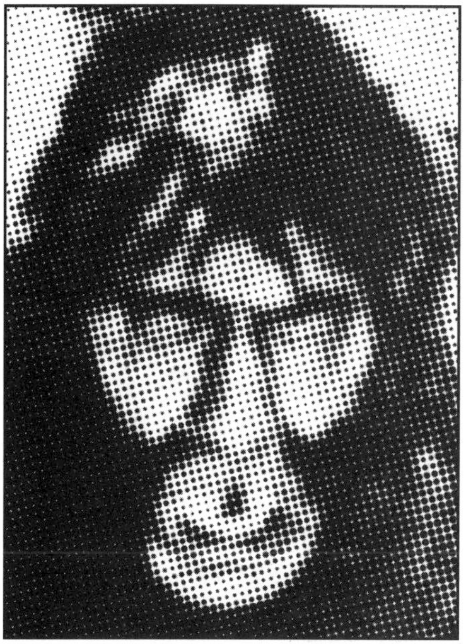

You don't need to know everything bad that's going on everywhere in the world right now, right this minute, every single day for the rest of your life. If something that really would affect your life happens, you'll hear about it without having to go to the news, but how often does that ever happen?

So you've stopped listening to the news?

I've tried. TV's easy, because I don't own a TV and hardly ever see any nowadays if I can avoid it. Everything I've said about the news applies to a lot of other things on TV, to a greater or lesser extent. I've also gone long stretches without listening to the radio news but it's difficult to avoid it sometimes and at least I am better able to cope with what I hear. Once you see what they're trying to do to you, it's easier not to let them do it. Newspapers are far better, because it's easier to avoid what you don't want to read, and I think they're more open-minded and more truthful too, in some ways. But they're about entertainment too, and death, violence and suffering are what interests them above all else. I've noticed a growing tendency for them to take spectacular photos from America too: no proper context, no real relevance, just an exciting picture of something like a hostage-taking after a bank raid or a flood victim being pulled from a flood, things like that. We're increasingly following the lead being set by America in deciding what's important in the news, and because what's important to America is American news, there's more and more American stuff in our papers that, when you think about it, has no relevance to us at all. The O.J. Simpson trial is a good example of that. The **Guardian**'s probably the paper most affected by this creeping Americanization, but it's happening everywhere, in the papers and on TV, on the radio. It's all part of what I've been talking about, because the American media are worst affected by the obsession with death, violence and suffering. It's going to get worse here, and the effects are going to get worse here too.

Depressing prospect.

Truly depressing, but there's no blood or violence in it, so don't expect news journalists to be interested.

WRITTEN IN BLOOD

STALIN'S BOYHOOD LESSONS IN TORTURE*

To many of my countrymen, Iosif Dzhugashvili is still a great hero. He made a mark in the world, achieved momentous things, and he was one of us. But, like Alexander the Great and Napoleon, the wider world does not see him as one of his true people. Perhaps you are guilty of these misperceptions yourself. For example, what nationality was Alexander the Great? A Greek? No, a Macedonian. And Napoleon Bonaparte? French? No, he was Corsican. And Iosif Dzhugashvili, whom you know better as Stalin? A Russian? No, he was Georgian.

And, as I have said, he is still a hero to many of us. Had he been in truth Russian, or Armenian, or Kirghiz, or Latvian — not Georgian, in other words — this group would be far smaller. But perhaps not so small as might be imagined. We are a small nation with a long history, and cruelty is nothing new to us. Stalin is our most famous son. Medea the witch is our most famous daughter. To save her lover Jason the Argonaut after his theft of the Golden Fleece, she dismembered her own younger brother and dropped his limbs one by one into the wake of the ship on which they sailed pursued by her father Æetes. When, later, Jason put her aside for a woman called Creusa, she gave the bride-to-be the gift of a beautiful garment, which proved to be poisoned, and caused Creusa to die in the greatest agony. Upon Jason himself she avenged herself by slaughtering two of the children they had had together, escaping from his anger in a chariot drawn by winged dragons. But she is said to have been reconciled with him in time, and to have dwelt with him in Colchis, where she had been born, until her death. Colchis is Georgia. A small nation, as I have said, with a long history, and one to which cruelty is nothing new.

And I think perhaps that this cruelty, as it was manifested in Joseph Stalin, needs explanation. Even by the standards of the Russians, even by the standards of us Georgians, Stalin was exceptional. His thirst for blood was unquenchable, and it is believed that he was planning a further debauch in this crimson beverage, fit to rival his gargantuan carousals of the 1930s, before the stroke that came upon him and kept him choking out his life for hours while his minions remained too terrified to enter his private apartments. Finally they did so, discovered him dying, and did what they could to see that he left the world in

* Adapted from an original article by Georgio Tskamorvili.

peace. But Stalin's death, like the lives of many millions of those over whom he had ruled, was filled with pain. In the end there was some small reckoning for what his cruelty had inflicted.

As I have said, I believe this cruelty needs explanation. Stalin's soul was surely very rich earth for a seed of cruelty to fall into, but whence came this seed? The anti-clerical point to his education by the Jesuits; many others, as I have already hinted, point to his nationality. But there is more to nationality than simply blood. We Georgians have a culture of our own, of which we are proud, and a unique language, of which we are especially proud. Unique in that, although it has affiliates in the region of Georgia, it is written in an alphabet used for no other language. Our pride in our Kartveli script is as great as, in the past, for almost all of us, and today, for many, our pride in that Joseph Stalin who, as Iosif Dzhugashvili, learnt that script and read and wrote in it for many years.

I too am proud of our unique Georgian alphabet, but I believe that it played some part in the forging of Stalin's will to power and blood and pain. It is a beautiful alphabet but, like many beautiful things, I believe it can be poisonous. Look at the letters set out on the page beside these words. Imagine each transformed into clean and cold steel. Imagine them of a size to be easily grasped and manipulated. Would not the Kartveli script, the Georgian alphabet, then represent a perfect set of instruments of torture?

Take the twenty-fifth letter, შ, the *šin* that begins the Georgian word *šlis*, meaning "to take apart, dissect". Is it not an instrument of crushing, designed for a hand to be set between those two thick knobs and that handle to be seized and cranked? Is not the twenty-ninth letter, წ, *tsil*, an instrument for sawing and tearing? And its neighbour, letter thirty, ჭ, *tshar*: do not that enclosed circle and twin handles suggest an instrument for the trimming, one by one, of the fingers? And letter nine, the vowel, ი, *i*: is it not an elegant set of pincers for the ripping out of the flesh? And its neighbour, letter eight, თ, *than*: is it not a hook with a comfortable, palm-filling handle? And letter nineteen, ტ, *tar*: is it not an ingenious device whose double-globed steel head is to be whirled, red-hot, in some vulnerable orifice of the body?

And so on, and so on. Go through our alphabet, letter by letter. To each you can easily assign some function in a syntax of agony. To learn the Kartveli script is to fill a chamber of your mind with a set of instruments of torture. To read a

აბგდევზთიკლმნოპჟრსტუფქღყშჩცძწჭხჯჰ

Georgian alphabet

АБВГДЕЖЗИЙКЛМНОПРСТУФХЦЧШЩЪЫЬЭЮЯ
абвгдежзийклмнопрстуфхцчшщъыьэюя

Russian alphabet

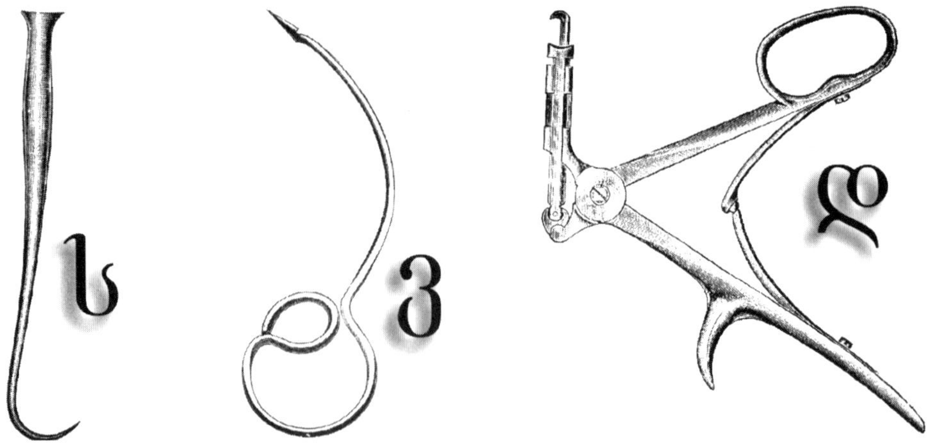

book, a newspaper, a magazine in Georgian, is to set those instruments whirring and slicing and gouging — but harmlessly, only on emptiness, only on unwoundable white paper. But we Georgians are trained nonetheless, from our first attendance of nursery school, in the theory of the infliction of suffering, in the potentialities possessed by the flesh of others for pain. That chamber of torture instruments in our minds is opened and used every day, but the instruments are put back as stainless at night as when they were taken out in the morning. For they are, of course, only black particles of ink on white paper, only ghostly tapestries on the enchanted looms of our minds. But they are always ready to be taken off the page, to be brought forth from our minds, and used as templates for the forging of real instruments of torture.

I believe they were so brought forth by Iosif Dzhugashvili. I believe that this is why he changed his name to Stalin. In Russian, Stalin means "steel". The name was symbolic of what he did to our alphabet. He took its potentiality for torture and made it an actuality. And yet he did this not only to our script, but also to the script of the people to whom the wider world believes he belonged. For the Russian alphabet too, I believe, trains its users in the theory of torture. Not only that, but in the theory of power. To torture is not necessarily to kill, but to achieve power one must be as ready to kill as to inflict pain. There, at the beginning of the Russian alphabet, stands the lesson of power: Гг, *ge*, which in both its majuscule and minuscule forms has the shape of a gallows. Stalin fed more gallows-crows than any man who ever lived, though he never neglected the lessons of torture given him by the first alphabet he learned. In the Russian alphabet, those lessons were reinforced. Many letters there are familiar, in shape at least, to those literate in Western European languages, but there are many strange ones. *Zhe* is very strange: Жж. It crouches on the page like a great black bird: head raised, tail straight, wings and talons planted wide; but I believe its secret significance is that of an instrument of torture. You use the word "travail" in English of a strong and drawn-out pain, but the word has only a faint echo of what must have been the horror to attach to its ancestral form.

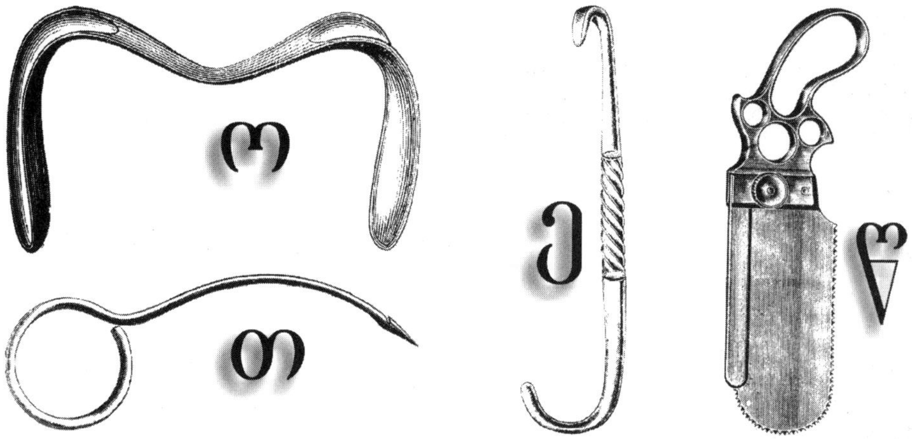

Travail is the Latin word *trepalium*, or "three-stakes", an instrument, or rather a ritual of torture in which the sufferer was tied to three stakes planted in the ground. *Zhe* to me is a trepalium, stained black with blood and waiting, unuprootable, for its next crimson feast.

Look elsewhere in the Russian alphabet and you will find, amongst familiar — but strangely pronounced — P and C and H and X, shapes that, like those of the Georgian alphabet, seem waiting only for a transformation into cold steel to be very fearsome engines of pain indeed. They are thickest at the end of the alphabet, stern shapes, with unyielding lines or hooked curves. Iosif Dzhugashvili absorbed their lessons here too, adding them to those of his childhood amongst the still stranger shapes of the Kartveli Georgian script. The Russian and the Georgian alphabets together have written a dreadful tale in black dried blood and white blood-drained flesh, but to me the Georgian remains the more beautiful, and by far the more poisonous. I am proud of it, but I am glad too that we are only a small nation, though with a long history, for to us cruelty is nothing new.

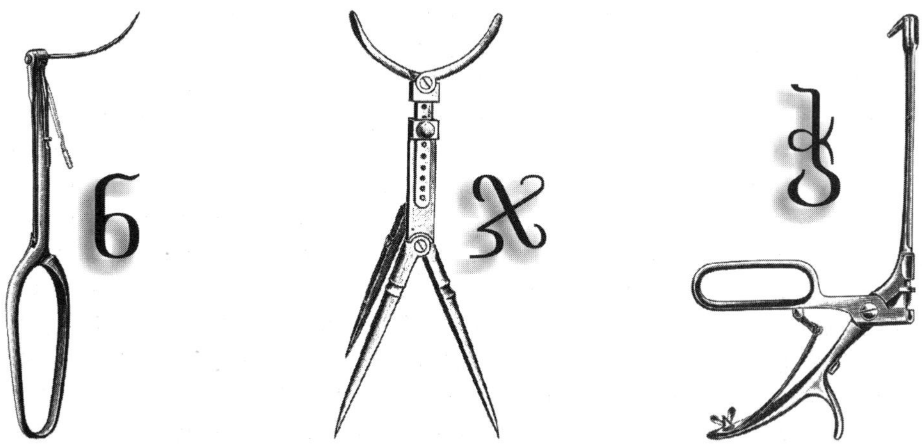

RUGGER-BUGGER

PSYCHO-SEXUAL SECRETS IN THE GREATEST SPORT ON EARTH

Cricket, so the old joke goes, is a game for gentlemen played by gentlemen. Ice-hockey is a game for hooligans played by hooligans. Football is a game for gentlemen played by hooligans. And rugby is a game for hooligans played by gentlemen.

Well, not quite. Rugby, it's much truer to say, is a game for homosexual sadomasochists played by homosexual sadomasochists. And watched by them. Which is not to say that there's anything wrong with a bit of honest-to-goodness homosexual sadomasochism. But honest is the operative word: rugby isn't honest about what it is. We're told it's simply a great sport. Nay, more than that: that it's the greatest sport on earth. And it's *character-building.*

So, I don't doubt, was the Hitler Youth. That isn't, by the way, such a ridiculous comparison. In fact, it's not ridiculous at all, because rugby is not only about sex and violence, it's also about the worship of strength, aggression and the will to power. It is, in other words, a pre-eminently fascist sport. Anyone who finds that statement a little strong might care to ask why rugby is the sport of preference for the two of the nastier communities on God's little green earth. One of them is the Ulster Protestant élite, responsible for some of the very least edifying episodes in the history of the Troubles, the other is the Afrikaners of South Africa, responsible for — well, we all know what they were responsible for, don't we? If those are the sort of characters rugby builds, perhaps we could manage very well without rugby's character-building.

And such links with political bestiality are by no means alone amongst the unsavoury artefacts to be dredged up from the psychopathological swamp of rugby's past and present. The sport began in 1823, for example, in the way it meant to go on, as a not very well-disguised means for a small élite to simultaneously work off homoerotic S&M energies and prepare itself for bloody but one-sided battle against poorly armed natives around the globe. The small élite was the middle- and upper-class pupils at British public schools, which were notorious at that time for two things: homosexuality and brutality. Rugby was a highly convenient means of combining the two, possessing moreover the enormous advantage of educating its participants in all the finest imperialist and fascist virtues: ruthlessness, aggression, physical force, and the

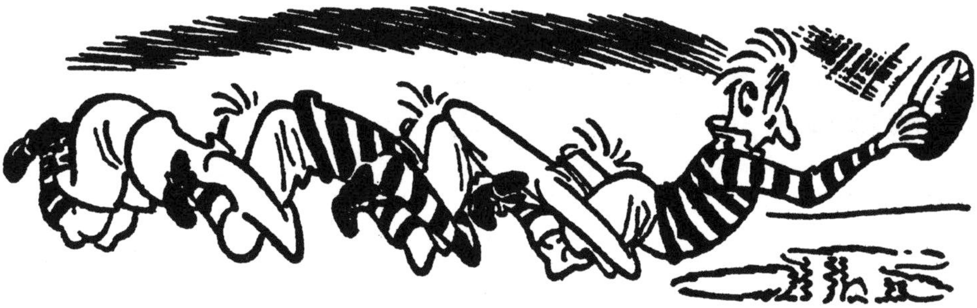

unquestioning worship of these things.

The simultaneous development of "muscular Christianity" — the stereotypical cold-showers-and-long-runs Victorian form of the religion — is by no means coincidental, for Christianity possesses a similar appeal to the homosexual sadomasochist. The pierced and bleeding, pale and near-naked ephebe has appeared not once in the religion but twice: the crucified Christ was joined during the first centuries of its development by the arrow-transfixed St Sebastian, whose image was a particular favourite of the homosexual and fascist Japanese novelist Yukio Mishima (Japan, indeed, with its long tradition of both imperialist fascism and homoerotic sadomasochism, is one of the very few countries in the world outside the Anglo-Saxon diaspora to have taken up rugby to any great extent). Rugby and muscular Christianity, furthermore, shared not merely a time of birth but also a place: both are inextricably linked to Rugby school and the regime of its most famous and influential headmaster, Thomas Arnold (1795-1842), who was widely acknowledged as the central figure in the development of public schools during the last century.

The young men moulded by the public-school system he devised and created went out first to build and then to maintain the British Empire, and the brutal morality inculcated of necessity in them was informed both by public-school Christianity, as has long been recognized, and by the public-school game *par excellence*, rugby — as has hardly been recognized at all. Indeed, Christianity and rugby share, besides the dark secret of being based on homoerotic S&M lust, even a ritualistic means of transforming and sublimating that lust into a publicly acceptable form. Just as at the heart of Christianity stands a codification of illogical and contradictory doctrine interpreted to the faithful by black-clad priests, so at the heart of rugby stands a codification of illogical and contradictory rules interpreted to the faithful by black-clad referees. The rules under which rugby is played are both fantastically complicated and, as many even amongst the sport's own aficionados are prepared to admit, unworkable except by the judicious and subjective assumption of myopia by the officials. Their primary purpose is, however, not to provide a setting within which a sport can take place but rather to provide a stage and an opportunity for the ritual enactment of intimate, violent, crypto-sexual bodily contact between members of the same sex.

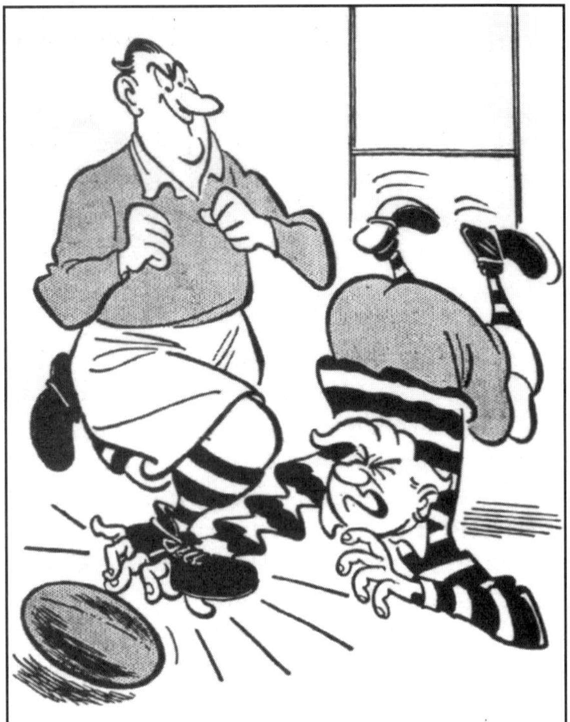

... knocking the ball from his hands and treading on his fingers when he goes to pick it up.

The Art of Coarse Rugby. **Michael Green, Hutchinson, London, 1960**

A comparison with rugby league, a development of rugby by heterosexual working-class men, renders this immediately apparent. One of the most obvious differences between rugby union and rugby league is that the latter does not employ the scrum (except in a severely reduced and little-used form). The scrum — a promiscuous mass of straining, perspiring, muscular male flesh — is, together with the even more often employed and promiscuous maul and ruck, at the heart of rugby's sadomasochism. One side's forwards, men carefully selected for their size, muscularity and aggression, bind themselves together into a single unit by seizing each other's members — and in some cases there is no *double entendre*, for the member seized through the cloth covering the crotch is unequivocally the genital — and lock heads and shoulders with an identical unit from the opposing side. The flesh-sculpture so created is of such a shape that the buttocks and thighs of all the participants are presented directly to their uninvolved team-mates and to the spectators, whilst their heads are hidden from view. The scrum is a ritualistic embodiment, to the accompaniment of bass grunts and steaming sweat, of one of the most common of homoerotic fantasies: that of brutally anonymous group sex.

In rugby league there is very little opportunity for similar displays, which, even when they do occur, are on a much more limited scale, just as there is very little opportunity in rugby league for the more loosely organized mass encounters known in rugby union as rucks and mauls, in which a pretended pursuit of the testicular oval of the ball affords ample opportunity for intimate and violent contact. It is from rucks and mauls that men emerge with blood-streaming wounds and bites, with gouged eyes and crushed testicles, and it is in rucks and mauls that the homoerotic energies powering the game achieve their most vicious and blissful release. Here have been forged some of the less-publicized dicta ("If you see a head kick it; if you see a cock pull it") and terminology ("bag-snatching" — the furtive and violent yanking of an opponent's scrotum) of this uniquely character-building sport, and here are worshipped with literal blood-offerings rugby's darkest and most puissant idols, hybrids of homoerotic pain- and power-worship and fascist will-to-power through ruthless and amoral violence.

And, just as the quasi-fascist imperialism of nineteenth-century Victorian Christianity was prepared for and modelled in miniature in the game, so wider currents in today's political and religious world create eddies there. Nowadays women too are arrogant and self-worshipping enough to demand a place amongst the parasitic ranks of the Christianity's priest-caste, where they may arrogate the power and prestige of a Creator-God and His ephebic son to themselves, and women as a political class have so far divested themselves of their traditional virtues of tenderness and compassion to have provided Britain with this century's most extreme right-wing prime minister. Women, in natural concomitance, have also taken up rugby, and it is now a ritual excuse for the release not only of homosexual S&M impulses and energies but also of lesbian.

And all the observations so far made on rugby's psycho-sexual and political origins apply in spades to the co-evolved form of the sport practised across the Atlantic and known in this country as American Football. British imperialism flowered in the early 1800's, bearing bloody fruit later in the same century in conquests in Africa and the Middle and Far East; for reasons already outlined, this is also the period of rugby's early development and growth. American imperialism flowered in the early 1900's, bearing bloody fruit later in the same century in Latin America and South-East Asia; for reasons easily adaptable from those given for rugby, this is also the period of American football's early development and growth. The sport was fostered in each case by Christianity, and just as American imperialism has been more vigorous and militaristic and American Christianity more fervent and credulous, so have the homoeroticism and sadomasochism of American football been richer and more fantastic in their manifestations. The sport has not been content with the most grotesque natural muscular development of the male body, but has re-created its players in new hyper-masculine forms by the imposition of thigh-, chest-, groin- and shoulder-padding, and of light-weight jackboots and glistening, glans-penile steel helmets. Where diffident British rugby clads the lusted-for buttocks and genito-anal region of its participants in baggy, thick-clothed shorts, self-confident American football packages the entire area for its participants' and spectators' delectation in a tightly clinging silk-like fabric, emphasizing the artificially enhanced bulge of the genitals and tautly muscled mounds of the male gluteal muscles. The comparative nakedness of the buttocks against the heavy padding worn elsewhere on the body is one of the most immediately obvious visual elements of the sport, and is an essential part of a carefully choreographed homoerotic ballet whose male participants are reduced to pairs of rapidly working buttocks dashing to and fro amidst the clash and crash of anonymous phallic helmets.

An additional ingredient is provided in the whole highly spiced homoerotic

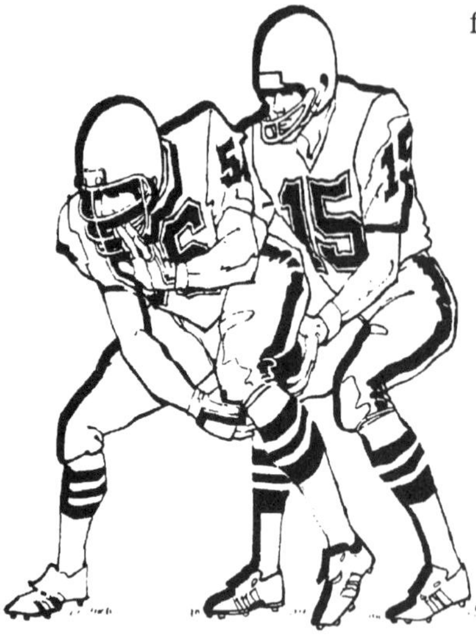

feast by the mingling there of different races. Black males are welcome in this violent enactment of white Christian homoerotic fantasy as they were welcome in the violent enactment of white Christian political fantasy in Vietnam, and in each case they have moved and suffered under the control of white masters: in Vietnam, the officers, overwhelmingly white in racial origin; in American football, the play-making quarterbacks, overwhelmingly white in racial origin. Black or white, however, all the young male participants in the homoerotic S&M ritual of American football must undergo pain for the delectation of the voyeuristic male coaches and spectators. Very few American-football players see out their career without at least one serious injury, and many are crippled for life by the attritional battering endured by their bodies, particularly by the knee joint, the most vulnerable part of the skeleton during the huge inertial and accelerational stresses of violent body-to-body contact. Brain damage too is common, just as it is in the similarly homoerotic and black-welcoming sport of boxing, and there is evidence to suggest a startlingly reduced life expectancy not merely amongst professional American footballers but even amongst college and high-school players of the sport.

It is in this suffering and sacrifice of life and limb that American footballers and rugby players are re-enacting the age-old homoerotic fantasy most famously and anciently embodied in the suffering figure of the crucified Christ, an image bloodily grafted onto the Christian religion when it fell under the control of the Atys-worshipping Visigoths of Rome, the homosexual sadomasochists *par excellence* of the ancient world. And, just as the ancient homoerotic cult contained secret ritual initiation and ceremonial, so does the modern. Rugby clubs are famous not only for their drinking, male bonding, and uncouthness, but also for their initiation ceremonies and practical jokes, which, just like the sport itself, but in a private and therefore even more feverish setting, afford opportunity for the enactment of homoerotic S&M fantasies. Almost all such ceremonies and practical jokes of which I am aware involve some kind of molestation of the genital or anal region or both,

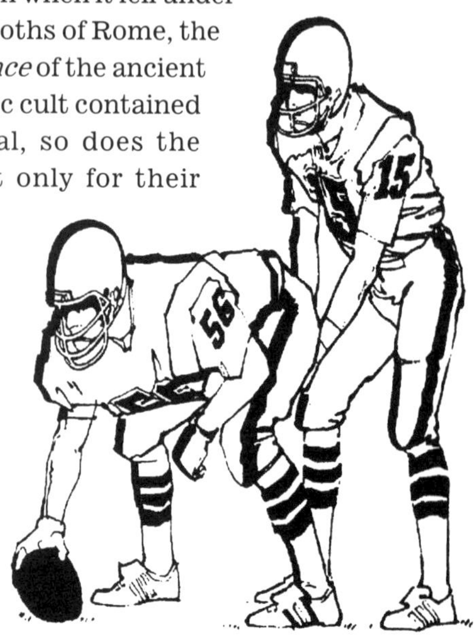

often with instruments or with the coarsely jocular use of such materials as shaving cream and aftershave. Just like the sport itself, many of the participants in these ceremonies and practical jokes are consciously aware of their true motives and of the sexual satisfaction they receive from subjecting members of their own sex to humiliation and pain, and, just like the sport itself, these motives are dishonestly concealed behind and subsumed within a too-hearty profession of rugby's unique "virtues": camaraderie, toughness and robust humour.

I would predict that something very similar holds true of the private and public behaviour of American footballers. Both sports are fascist in sentiment and effect, both involve the disguised ritual enactment of homoerotic S&M fantasies, and both are deeply unpleasant in so far as they pretend that none of this is true. One might perhaps adapt the words of an exemplar of the openly homosexual tradition so publicly despised by rugby's and American football's adherents and plead, "Don't put your son on the rugby field, Mrs Worthington".

Unless, that is, Ernst Röhm, the thuggish homosexual chief of Hitler's faecally coloured Brownshirts, possessed your idea of a character to be aspired to. In fact, just as George Orwell notes in "Raffles and Miss Blandish", his masterly essay on comparative sociology, that the Nazis were "at pains to discourage cricket, which had gained a certain footing in Germany" before and after the first World War, I should not be at all surprised to learn that the Nazis simultaneously were at pains to encourage rugby. Cricket, as absurd and boring a game as it may be to many people, demands skill and intelligence, not merely brute athleticism and hardly at all, at least in the past, physical strength and aggression. In complete contrast to rugby, whose strongholds are confined to the predominately white and Christian former British colonies, it has also flourished amongst the non-white and non-Christian races of the old empire. *Mutatis mutandis*, precisely the same observations are true of baseball and American football. Like Christianity, rugby and American football demand a soil drenched in male blood and semen for their growth. It is no coincidence that only the Irish rugby team preserves the old imperialist ideal of a united Ireland under the hegemony of a Protestant Anglo-Ulster élite, and no coincidence that Twickenham is accorded not merely the quasi-military appellation of rugby's "HQ" but also the quasi-religious appellation of rugby's "cathedral". Fascism and homosexuality are natural bedfellows, and rugby and Christianity are two of their most vigorous and obnoxious offspring. Balls are played with in one, balls are talked in the other, and balls of a different sort are of great interest to the pure-living and publicly homophobic followers of both. Rugger-bugger. Whoever invented that phrase knew what he was talking about.

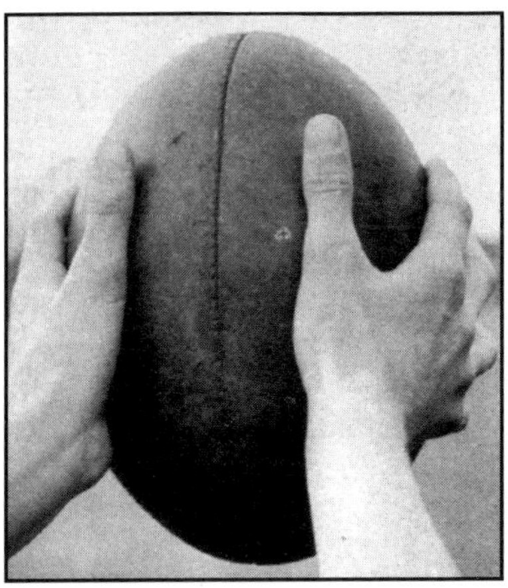

GILT BY ASSOCIATION

FROM H.P. LOVECRAFT TO ELECTRONIC DISTORTION BY WAY OF THE MALAYALAM ALPHABET

What's the link between a 1930's horror writer, an over-used font, and an industrial metal band from Yorkshire? No, it's not a trick question. And no, I don't think looking at the end of this article would help, though the answer is there. Try it if you like. No good? Okay, let's start here.

In my local library there used to be a number of fairly old books by H.P. Lovecraft. Hardback ones. The covers had no pictures, they were just yellow with the name of book and author in faintly ornate black lettering. The sort of lettering you might find on a tombstone, and on the covers it was even, by design I'm sure, faintly irregular and softened around the edges, as though by a century or two of sun and snow, wind and rain in a graveyard. Perfect for Lovecraft, and I think the font used inside was similarly well-chosen. Certainly I've never quite enjoyed reading him as much since, years ago, those books disappeared from the shelves.

I still don't know who the publisher was, although books by Robert E. Howard were included in the same series. In a more recent encounter I had with one of these Howard books, it wasn't quite so much the lettering on the covers as — I can be certain this time — the font used inside. Again it was faintly ornate, faintly worn, probably old-fashioned even at the time the stories were being written, yet alone several decades later when a British publisher collected them between hard covers. And again, it was perfect. I've always enjoyed the Conan story "The Phoenix on the Sword" — one of the few that combine blood-and-thunder with a bit of the unsettling perversity more often found in Clark Ashton Smith — and never more so than on my reading of it here. The font was the perfect background to the story because it, like the characters and settings and literary style Howard used, wasn't modern, and it helped them to carry your imagination away from the here and now to the there and then of Conan's world.

And again, as for the lettering on the H.P. Lovecraft covers, I'm sure it was by design. The font was deliberately chosen for the atmosphere it would evoke. It wasn't simply that it was faintly ornate and old-fashioned — lapidary, one might say — but that it was faintly worn-looking. And yet no-one sets out to create a worn-looking font until fonts become worn-looking by accident and it's discovered that they carry a certain atmosphere with them from that fact. Then some-one might decide to pursue the effect deliberately for the sake of the atmo-

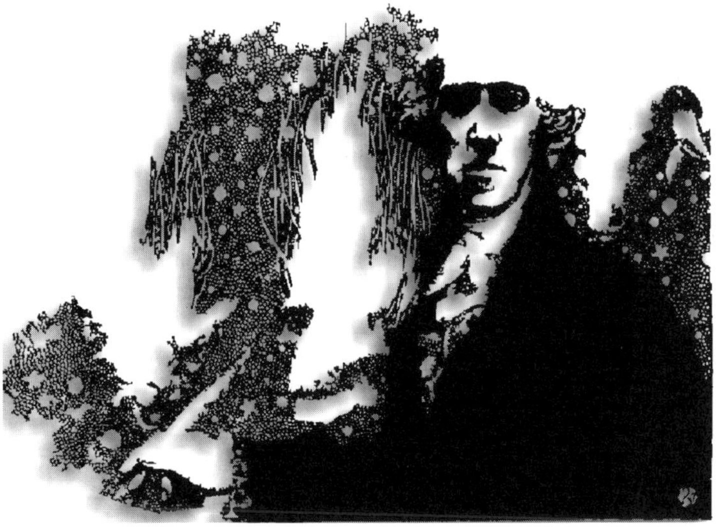

sphere it conveys. You might call this sort of thing serendipity: a happy artistic discovery made by accident. You might call it, as I have at the head of this article, "gilt by association": artistic value added to something by the associations it conveys. In either case, the effect can be explained by work done by a Russian physiologist nearly a century ago. This sort of thing is an example of Pavlovian conditioning, and it applies in the arts to far more than just fonts, as I will attempt to show, although fonts are offer some of the best and easiest-to-follow examples of it, and it's worth looking at some of these before we go any further.

Because, in fact, a font was the first thing to draw this phenomenon — let's add a silent "p" and call it "pserendipity" — to my attention. The font is usually called Old English, and part of this sentence is being printed in it to give you a good example of what it looks like. Though you will, of course, have seen it many times before. It's one of the workhorses of the printing world, often called on to evoke a particular genteel, antique atmosphere. You couldn't imagine it on the cover of a magazine devoted to the Internet; you'll almost certainly have seen it used somewhere like the sign on a tea-shop. Or Tea Shoppe, because although it's an attractive font, it's also become clichéd, and its basic associations are in danger of disappearing under less positive later ones. Still, it's a very good example of pserendipity, because the Old English script at one time had nothing old about it: it was the natural way some English was written, and its form was derived perfectly naturally from the way in which it was written by hand with thick-nibbed pens.

Then came printing. It was no longer necessary to create letters in that particular way, and the Old English script fell out of use — but not out of experience. People still encountered it in old documents, and gradually the form that the script took became associated with the period in which the script had been used. In Pavlovian terms, the form taken by the script, like the bell of Pavlov's classic experiments with dogs, was the conditional stimulus, and the period of its use, like the food in the experiments, the unconditional stimulus. Just as dogs began to show a conditioned reflex and salivated to the sound of the bell alone, so we think of the "Old English" period when we see the font.

Something similar happened with the old script used for writing German: here iſ part of a ſentence written in it. What associations does it have? To you and me it suggests Gothic castles, Frankenstein, and the Nazis; to pre-war Germans, it was just the alphabet they used to read their daily papers and write letters in. Again, it's an everyday font that became special once it ceased to be everyday, either by falling into disuse or by being seen by people who didn't habitually use it. To pre-war Britons and Americans, this font wasn't yet strongly associated with the Nazis, but had certainly acquired the first two associations I mentioned above.

I particularly enjoy the examples of these two fonts, because they are examples of an artistic effect that is first of all imposed by the medium and then, later, when the medium changes, becomes actively and gratuitously pursued. The old English and old German scripts took the forms they did because they were written by hand with a certain kind of pen, and these forms were more or less inevitable within fairly narrow limits. Then came printing, and the limits on the forms of letters widened enormously. There was no longer any need for letters to look like that, and in Germany there had to be a deliberate choice to retain the handwritten forms for use by printing machines. In England the handwritten script was discarded but later selectively re-introduced in printed form for its artistic effect.[1]

These relics of the medium in which a font was first developed are far commoner than might be supposed. A typical "Roman" font uses straight lines and simple arcs because those are the shapes easiest to carve in stone using a chisel, straight-edge and compass. The capital letters of the Greek alphabet are based on the same shapes for the same reason, but the lower-case letters are far more irregular and complex because they were taken from handwritten forms. The fonts used for South Indian languages like Tamil, Sinhalese and Malayalam are based almost entirely on arcs, because, it's said, these languages were originally written by hand on dried palm fronds, and using a pen to make a straight line would have split the frond. It's both strange and pleasing to think that the form taken by a South Indian font on a 1990's computer monitor was ultimately determined by the graphological characteristics of a dried palm frond.

Strictly speaking, though, that isn't an example of pserendipity, because these languages don't reserve these palm-frond-friendly written forms for special occasions in the way that modern English and German reserve the old English and old German fonts. I find that a pity, but there are plenty more fish in this sea, and, as I said earlier, fonts are only part of pserendipity. It also occurs in music. A fairly good example of it is the effect known as feed-back. Feedback

---

ABCDEFGHIJKLMNOPQRSTUVWXYZ
abcdefghijklmnopqrstuvwxyz

happens when sound produced by a loudspeaker is picked up by the microphone supplying that loudspeaker, reproduced by the loudspeaker, picked up by the microphone again, reproduced by the loudspeaker — and so on and so on. It all happens very quickly, and the sound can undergo all sorts of strange and unstable shifts in frequency: hence the piercing, undulating shriek that most people think of as feedback.

Originally, feedback was accidental and unwanted, but as popular music got louder and louder, it happened more frequently and became more familiar until one day someone actually set out to make it happen. In other words feedback, an unwanted, even dreaded sign of an abused or badly set-up sound system, actually became part of music. Who the first person to incorporate feedback into his music was I don't know, but certainly Pete Townshend of the Who and Jimi Hendrix, amongst others, were using it regularly in gigs and on records by the late 'sixties. Note, though, that the use of feedback isn't comparable to the use of archaic letter forms in a modern font, and it isn't an example of Pavlovian conditioning. The original association with feedback was an unpleasant one: something was wrong with the sound system. People who deliberately caused feedback did so not to evoke these associations, but for the sake of feedback's sound, which had qualities unobtainable in any other way. Using feedback was also a display of guitar virtuosity, because it was very difficult to control, and Jimi Hendrix's mastery of it, for example, was acknowledged as one of the ways in which he was supposedly the greatest guitar player on earth.

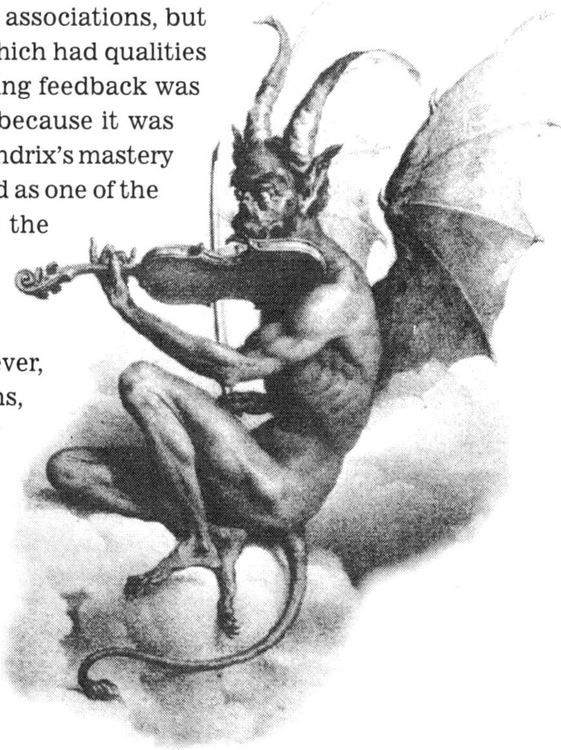

As soon as feedback was used by guitarists playing in a particular style and at a particular time, however, it started to pick up new associations, and these were probably responsible for its disappearance from popular music at a later stage. By the mid-'seventies it sounded old-fashioned, and was dropped for that reason; later, things began to work in the opposite direction, and bands set out deliberately to use "old-

ΑΒΓΔΕΖΗΘΙΚΛΜΝΞΟΠΡΣΤΥΦΧΨΩ

αβγδεζηθικλμνξοπρστυφχψω

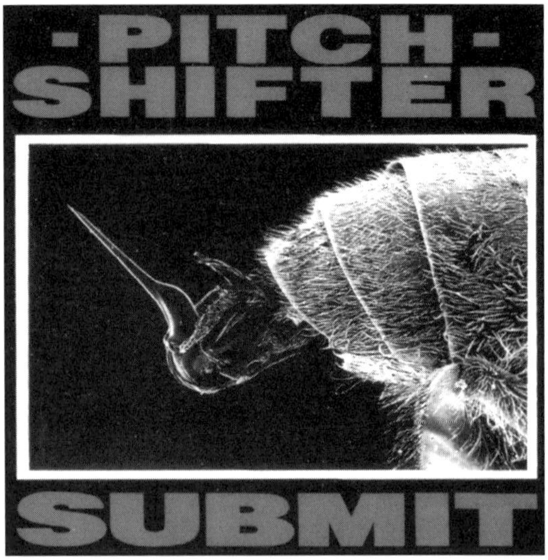

fashioned" sounds. If these sounds take the form they do because of the limitations of musical technology at the time, this might seem another, and better, example of musical pserendipity.

One possibility is the use by bands like Erasure of analogue synthesizers from the 'seventies, which have a particular tone no longer possessed by contemporary models. Or so it's claimed. I've never quite understood why, because surely modern synthesizers could be programmed to mimic their predecessors in such a way as to be indistinguishable from the original; if that is the case, the old synthesizers are being used simply for the sake of it. The use of a 'seventies synthesizer as a genuine piece of 'seventies technology by a modern musician would find its equivalent in a modern printer using a quill pen to write in the old English script. There seems a far greater charm in re-creating an archaic effect with modern technology than in creating that archaic effect with archaic technology. The choice is no longer so deliberate, so gratuitous. 'Seventies synthesizers sound like 'seventies synthesizers for a simple and blindingly obvious reason, and Erasure seem sadly unperverse in their use of them.

The same applies to the use of Mellotron organs and that strange, 'fifties-sci-fi-and-horror-film atmospherics instrument called the theremin (the one that makes that ethereal shimmering noise). If you want the particular sound they produce, it's musically unobjectionable to go direct to source, but aesthetically so unimaginative — as I've just said, so unperverse. The search for a genuine example of pserendipity in music has to carry on. It will begin, but not end, with the voices of punk and heavy-metal singers in the late 'seventies and early 'eighties. Singing is interesting in many ways to the aficionado of pserendipity. Vocalists rarely sing in the accent they use in everyday life, and sometimes it simply wouldn't sound right if they did: punk in a middle-class accent, for example. Then there's the so-called whiskey voice and its cousins: voices with the husky, strained quality associated with living life hard and fast, though it may be the way a singer would sound even if he or she drank nothing but soya-milk and never touched cigarettes, or it may be entirely put-on.

Then there's the over-used voice: too much of everything, especially singing. Punk and heavy-metal singers in the late 'seventies often had this sort of voice at gigs, because these styles of music encouraged shouting and a generally energetic delivery. Voices got strained, were used hard again, and got more strained. The result could be a singer producing unintelligible croaks and grunts. Like feedback, in the beginning this wasn't regarded as a good thing because it stopped the lyrics being understood and a lot of bands took their lyrics very seriously. Like feedback, I'm pretty sure that sooner or later someone set out deliberately to use this sound in their music: someone who hadn't strained his voice sang as though he had.

And like feedback, this isn't a perfect example of pserendipity. It was the quality of the sound that was musically interesting, not its associations. The croaks and grunts were *associated* with having a strained voice; they *sounded* unpleasant and animal-like. Their sound, not their associations, was why the genre known as death metal took them up, and you can actually hear the evolution of the "balls in the blender" vox by listening to death metal tracks from the early, middle, and late periods of its development. *Not* that you are necessarily recommended to.

The Swiss band Celtic Frost, for example, are generally recognized as pioneers of the genre. Their vocals are harsh and strained-sounding, but still more or less intelligible. In the next generation, the American band Obituary took things onto the next stage. Their vocals are harsher, more strained-sounding, and more or less unintelligible on first hearing. Lyrics are being sung, but you'd need to listen to them repeatedly to start to pick out anything from them. In the generation following Obituary, bands like Suffocation used vocals that are completely unintelligible, and that seem to consist primarily of a bass howling, bellowing and, well, vomiting.

In fact, Suffocation and their *confrères* seem to be approaching the limits to which the human voice can be tortured, and in fact it has been rumoured that their vocalist had the assistance of an electronic gadget or two. Which for traditional death-metallurgists is a no-no: death-metal vocalists should ideally be able to reproduce their vinyl style through a live, unadulterated sound system. Ergo the "balls in the blender" vox is only a small advance on Erasure's use of real 'seventies synthesizers to produce a real 'seventies synthesizer sound. This vocal style is artistically gratuitous, but not gratuitous enough. It took a band from Yorkshire called Pitch Shifter to make it so.

On their first couple of albums, Pitch Shifter used very deep and harsh-sounding vocals, similar to if not quite identical with those used by death metal bands, but whereas death metal bands produced their vocals by deliberately singing like that, Pitch Shifter produced theirs by deliberately putting their singer's voice through electronic distortion — using the device after which they actually named their band. I'll mention in passing that there are probably messages about technology and its effects on human beings to be picked up here, but my main point is that Pitch Shifter's vocals are aesthetically the next stage up. They can be directly compared to the use of advanced electronics to produce fonts that were shaped by the use of pen and ink many centuries ago. They are a good example of pserendipity. And that's the link between a 1930's horror writer, an over-used font, and an industrial metal band from Yorkshire.

A SHORT ARTICLE ABOUT FARTING

Pfffrrrummmp. So Enderby's end, prolepticly, at the beginning of Anthony Burgess's **Inside Mr Enderby**,[1] and so this article. Farting is a minor but fascinating topic: even the word itself is interesting. Well, I think so, anyway. It's one of what used, euphemistically, to be called Anglo-Saxon words...except that not all of them are Anglo-Saxon. Piss certainly isn't. Wank probably isn't. Fart, on the other hand, certainly is, being one of the most fundamental words in the common Indo-European vocabulary, up there with father, mother, sun, moon, water, and fish. Take your Grimm's shift from "p" to "f", a metathesis, a homorganic voicing and a few vowel-changes in hand and you can track "fart" up and down the branches of the language tree for millennia. Middle English *farten*. Old English *feortan*. Old Norse *freta*. Old Aryan *perd*. Sanskrit *prid*. Ancient Greek *perdein*. Lithuanian *pérdzu*.

And the Latin *peditum* and its descendants in the Romance languages — *pedo* in Spanish, for example — are suggestively similar, but apparently aren't related. There seems, in short, to be some kind of onomatopoeia going on here. One might even begin to construct a theory about the history of certain sexual practices amongst the Indo-European peoples...

But this is only meant to be a short article. The fascinating data of scatological philology aside, however, farting is certainly as old as the human race, probably as old as life on earth — on earth, that is, as opposed to in the water, where body gases are too important for the maintenance of buoyancy and balance to be discharged from the nearest available orifice in the careless manner of belching and farting land animals. The definitive text on the subject of farting has probably yet to be written. Salvador Dalí pointed the way to future scholarship when he supplemented his megalomaniac **Diary of a Genius** with an appendix on farting[2], but this is, after all, only an appendix. Various works appeared in the eighteenth century, including one by an anonymous author believed to have been the copromane Jonathan Swift, but these seem to have been too severely parochial and polemic in their scope. It is possible, however, that the definitive farting

> **FARTY FACT NO. 1:** There is a type of cake called a *pet de nonne* – "nun's fart" – made in France. It takes its name from the fact that it is so light and delicate.

text was written and then, in 1891, burnt by the widow of the man who had written it and whose name, nowadays, is associated principally with someone far less interesting.

Sir Richard Burton was surely better qualified for the task of chronicling the history and culture of the fart than any other man who has ever lived, for no other man has combined such a profound knowledge of languages with such extensive travels in so many parts of the world and such a passionate hunger for obscure and, to the conventionally minded, obscene knowledge. Burton was minutely informed in such fields as sexology, morbid anatomy, swordsmanship, Koranic criticism and, it cannot be doubted, farting. In 1872 he was given the post of British consul in Trieste:

> Although Burton felt himself to be in a genteel prison, Isabel [his wife] came to speak of Trieste as "my much loved home", and "my beloved Trieste". She entertained her women friends regularly on Fridays. Burton was often impatient with their chatter, and once interrupted their tea when he walked suddenly into the room, slapped a manuscript on the tea table and stalked out without a word. "Twittering with curiosity," as Seton Dearden [a Burton biographer] put it, several of the ladies "bent over the manuscript lying among the teacups. It was entitled *A History of Farting*."[3]

A joke? Almost certainly, but we shall never know whether Burton ever devoted any serious work to the topic, for any fruits of it would certainly have been included by Isabel in the holocaust she made of her husband's papers after his death: such of Burton's words on the topic as have survived did so because they had already been published. One of the funniest (although a purist would doubtless exclude it on the grounds that it is not strictly about farting) is found in the "Terminal Essay" Burton wrote to his translation of **The Arabian Nights**, and is a perfect example of the immense erudition of his "unembarrassed mind". He writes of a "Shaykh Nasr, Governor of Bushire", who would

> ask his guests if they had ever seen a man-cannon (*Ádami-top*); and, on their replying in the negative, a grey-beard slave was dragged

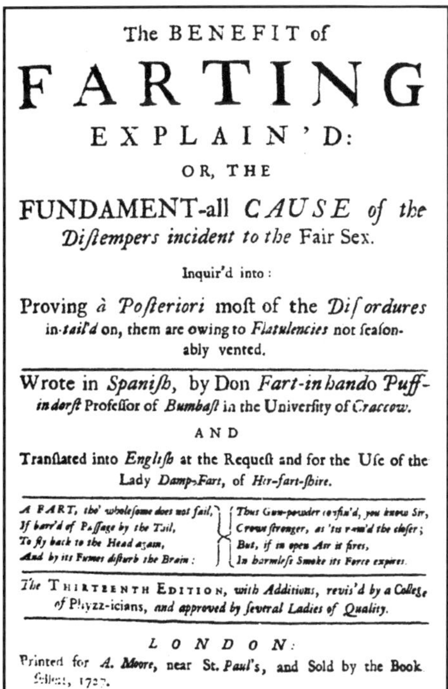
The BENEFIT of
FARTING
EXPLAIN'D:
OR, THE
FUNDAMENT-all *CAUSE of the*
Diſtempers incident to the Fair Sex.
Inquir'd into:
Proving *à Poſteriori* moſt of the *Diſordures* in-*tail'd* on, them are owing to *Flatulencies* not ſeaſonably vented.

Wrote in *Spaniſh*, by Don *Fart-inhando Puff-indorſt* Profeſſor of *Bumbaſt* in the Univerſity of *Craccow.*
AND
Tranſlated into *Engliſh* at the Requeſt and for the Uſe of the Lady *Damp-Fart*, of *Her-fart-ſhire.*

A FART, tho' wholeſome does not fail,
If barr'd of Paſſage by the Tail,
To fly back to the Head again,
And by its Fumes diſturb the Brain:
Thus Gun-powder confin'd, you know Sir,
Grows ſtronger, as 'tis ramm'd the cloſer;
But, if in open Air it fires,
In harmleſs Smoke its Force expires.

The THIRTEENTH EDITION, *with Additions, revis'd by a College of* Phyzz-icians, *and approved by ſeveral Ladies of Quality.*

LONDON:
Printed for *A. Moore*, near St. *Paul's*, and Sold by the Booksellers, 1727.

Title page for *The Benefit of Farting Explain'd*, published in 1727. Author is credited as Fart-inhando Puff-indorst... very likely a pseudonym (perhaps for Jonathan Swift?)

> in blaspheming and struggling with all his strength. He was presently placed on all fours and firmly held by the extremities; his bag-trousers were let down and a dozen peppercorns were inserted *ano suo* [in his anus]: the target was a sheet of paper held at a reasonable distance; the match was applied by a pinch of cayenne in the nostrils; the sneeze started the grapeshot and the number of hits on the butt decided the bets.[4]

Something more famous, and a pure fart-story, is found in Burton's **Arabian Nights** itself. A Badawi merchant called Abu Hasan is celebrating his marriage with an enormous feast, while his bride-to-be awaits his pleasure in a sumptuously decorated bridal chamber:

> At last the bridegroom was summoned to the chamber where she sat enthroned; and he rose slowly and with dignity from his divan; but in doing so, for that he was over-full of meat and drink, lo and behold! he let fly a fart, great and terrible.

Mortified by his gaffe — as Burton explains in one of his infamous footnotes, "The Badawi who eructates [belches] as a civility has a mortal hatred of a *crepitus ventris* "* — Abu Hasan slips away from the feast, saddles his horse, and rides off into self-imposed exile, "weeping bitterly". Ten years later, overcome by homesickness and hoping that his lapse will be long forgotten, he travels back to his home city and spends a week living there in disguise while he makes sure of it:

> He listened carefully for seven days and seven nights, till it so chanced that, as he was sitting at the door of a hut, he heard the voice of a young girl saying, "O my mother, tell me the day when I was born; for such an one [sic] of my companions is about to take an omen for me." And the mother answered, "Thou wast born, O my daughter, on the very night when Abu Hasan farted."

Whereupon Abu Hasan sadly departs once more, this time permanently, into "self-exile".[5]

It might seem as though any article on farting would consist of nothing more than a catalogue of such humorous anecdotes and stories; but that is not in fact the case. Farting, believe it or not, has also played a significant role in the history of religion: more specifically, in the religious theories promulgated by the ancient Greek philosopher-mystic Pythagoras, who was, in Bertrand Russell's words

> One of the most interesting and puzzling men in history. ... He founded a religion, of which the main tenets were the transmigration of souls and the sinfulness of eating beans.[7]

Which is to us, of course, an odd and

FARTY FACT NO. 2: In India, a Christian clergyman is known as a *paadrii*, from "padre". *Paad*, however, is the Hindi word for "fart".[6]

* "rattle of the belly", i.e. fart.

laughable combination; to the Pythagoreans it was as logical as the theorem of the square on the hypotenuse. Pythagoras taught that what bestowed life on an animal or human being was the soul, or psyche, and that the psyche consisted of breath, that is, consisted of air in motion. When a man dies, his soul leaves his body with his breath, after which it may wander in the form of a wind until it enters a bean. One can know that beans contain souls because beans give you wind, which is the breath of the souls contained in them. A woman who wishes to become pregnant may safely eat them, for the bean-wind will give life to the foetus, but all others should refrain, for what greater indignity or insult could one offer to the souls of one's ancestors than to discharge them through one's anus?

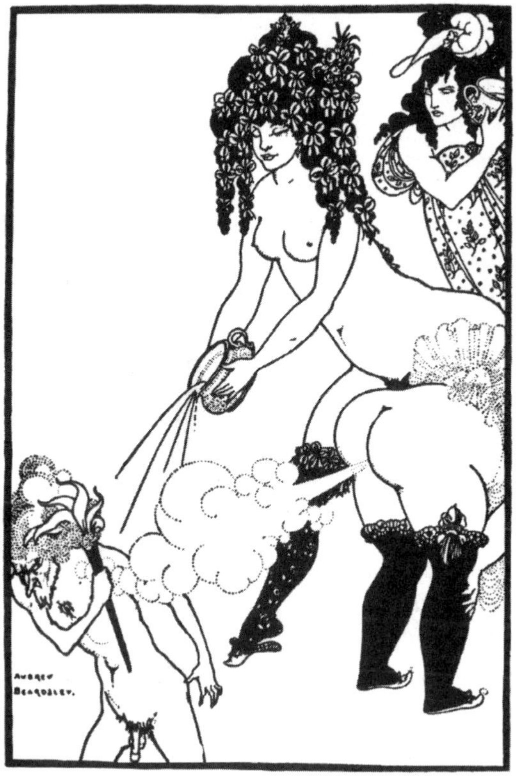

Lysistrata Defending the Acropolis. **Aubrey Beardsley**

This, at least, is a possible and reasonable interpretation of the Pythagorean bean prohibition, for I have never seen the connexion between the prohibition and the Pythagorean breath-theory of the soul analysed explicitly in this way. To us in the sophisticated twentieth century, the idea is ludicrous, but we needn't necessarily feel superior to the Pythagoreans if they did indeed hold to it. It is perfectly logical and they, lacking our morbid sensitivities about excretion and the lower orifices, would have felt no sense of incongruity in drawing links between the breath, the winds, and bean-induced farting. And think of the delicious revenge available if one could somehow discover which bean contained the soul of a departed enemy or hated relative!

FARTY FACT NO. 3: In the biblical book of Isaiah, strong emotion is twice described as causing the "bowels" to "sound", in the first case "like a harp". (Verses xvi, 11 and lxiii, 16).

If farting has been taken seriously by any other group or movement, religious or otherwise, I have yet to hear of it: farting, in every culture at every age, must very rarely have been regarded as anything other than funny. One thing it has certainly never been widely regarded as is sexually attractive, and

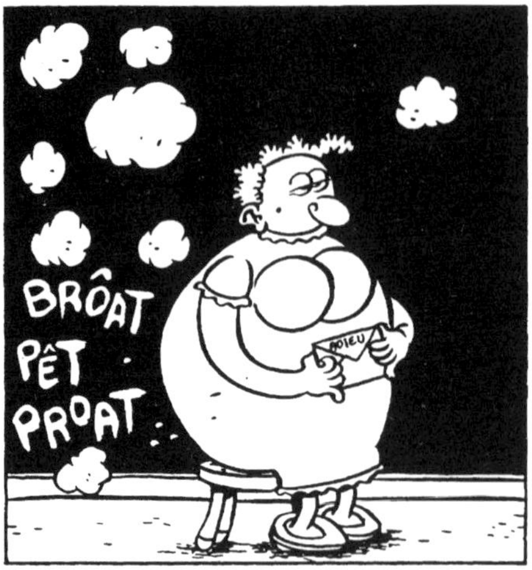

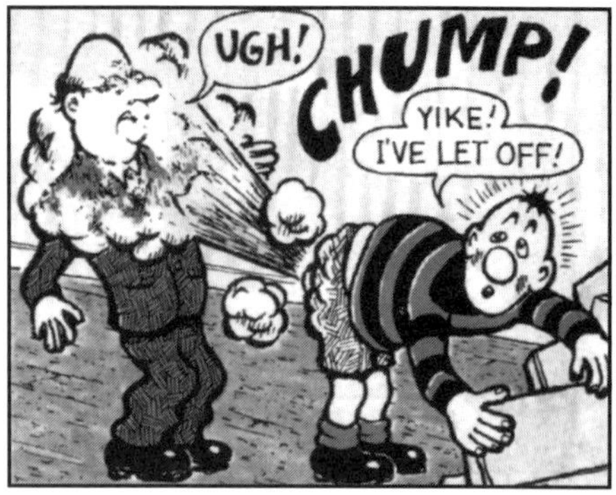

Farting comic strips. Left: Panel from 'Madame Prout' by Ivars, in *Suicides de Menage* © 1994, Éditions du Zébu. Right: Panel from 'Johnny Fartpants' in *Viz* © 1985/86 House of Viz/John Brown Publishing

the exceptions that prove the rule are mostly lost to us by the prudery and reticence of past ages. Be in need of sexual perversity, however, and you need go no further than the eighteenth century and the Marquis de Sade. Fart-fetishism is one of the very few Sadean pleasures that de Sade, for sure, both wrote about and practised — and practised, moreover, in the most direct and active fashion:

> After whipping both girls furiously with the heather broom, the marquis grabs Marianne, throws her down on the bed, and sticks his nose between the cheeks of her buttocks so as to inhale her wind ... The scene shifts to Marguerite's bedroom ... He has [Marguerite] lie down on her stomach, licks her anus, orders her to fart into his mouth, and finally proposes "to enjoy her from behind and in several other ways, still more horrible" ...[8]

Which, of course, with sodomy a capital offence for both parties, none of the prostitutes would allow — or rather, admit to having allowed during the subsequent investigation into the Marquis's "Cytherean" excesses, which had taken place in Marseilles in 1772 and in the course of which he had fed some of the prostitutes with "aphrodisiac" pastilles. The pastilles, which contained Spanish fly, made those who ate them very ill, and de Sade was soon back in prison railing against whores and the judicial system that protected them and prevented libertine aristocrats such as himself making use of them as they chose.

He was, of course, well aware that the welfare of prostitutes was merely an excuse for his removal from society as an embarrassment to his mother-in-law and her relatives, but the tirades were one means he had of relieving his feelings: another was the infamous books in which he occasionally describes similar scenes of fart-fetishism. Psychologically speaking, this of de Sade's many fetishes is not at all easy to marry with the naïve interpretation of him as an advocate (and probable practitioner) of a blood-crazed sexual bestialism aimed at sacrificing all women and children to its frothing patriarchal frenzy. Taking sexual pleasure from being farted at is masochistic; in everyday life, for example, it is a common means of degrading and insulting another person: ancient Greek even had a verb, καταπερδω (*kataperdo)*, which means "to express contempt with a fart". What de Sade was interested in, however, was not necessarily the exercising of power, but the experiencing of sensation. Farts are strongly flavoured in both the literal and the cultural senses, and their use as sexual fetish is rewarding for both reasons; it is also a form of masochism that does not injure or debilitate the masochist, and so does not affect his ability to enjoy further sensation.

But in his attitudes toward farts de Sade was, as in many other ways, a singular figure, and fart-fetishism is either very rarely indulged in or very rarely admitted to, or both. No, for the vast majority of people, farts are comic, not erotic. The inadvertent or otherwise inappropriate bottom-burp is a staple of low humour throughout the world, and those gifted with some exceptional talent in this area have always been able to earn fame and popularity by it — occasionally with tragi-comic results. Sometime around the eighteenth century, one Simon Tup, "the Farting Blacksmith" from Kirktable, Yorkshire, had

> the singular and ingenious talent of accompanying any instrument [with his farts] ... which he could perform so admirably in time, tone and tune, as to deceive the nicest judges ... The fate of this poor fellow was very melancholy; by an uncommon exertion which he made in the famous song "Blow high, blow low", he unfortunately broke a blood-vessel of which he instantly died.[9]

And he very probably never received the full monetary reward for his talents. In France, on the other hand, there has even been a class of fully professional farting performer called the *petomane*, who similarly entertained audiences by his skill at what might be called sphincteric mimicry. If **Le Petomane**, a film based on the life of the most famous of these performers and starring the late Leonard Rossiter, is anything to go by, the French fart-master had a considerably greater repertoire than his present-day British equivalent. The bemasked and becloaked Mr Methane, occasional guest *artiste* on the James Whale Show and star of his own videos, possesses considerable ability to fart at will, but, with little creative talent besides, will doubtless, if he has not already, suffer the fate of the farting schoolboy eponym of **Viz**'s "Johnny Fartpants" comic strip. Which is oblivion.[10] Fart-jokes, like farts, quickly grow stale. Fart-articles too. Pfffrrrummmp.

NOTES

AFTERLIFE

(pages 9 — 22)

1. Speaking of these companions, the houris or *hur*, one translator of the Koran (see note 16 below) remarks that they, like the rest of heaven described by Muhammad, "will be beautiful", but the prophet's "symbolic words need not be taken to mean that there will be eating and drinking, or dressing, or marriage, or any physical things of that kind. There will be life, but free from all earthly grossness." In other words, no nookie. Ordinary Muslims, on the other hand, have generally taken a different view.

2. *The Odyssey, translated into English, in the original metre*, Francis Caulfield, G. Bell and Sons, London, 1923.

3. *The Odyssey*, Frank Caulfield, Appendix B, under the note: "The following passage, being regarded as of doubtful authority, has been removed from its context."

4. Tityus, for example, is treated thus: "Likewise one might see Tityos, nursling of earth, the universal mother. Over nine full acres his body is stretched, and a monstrous vulture with crooked beak gnaws at his deathless liver and vitals fruitful for anguish; deep within the breast he lodges and gropes for his feast; nor is any respite given to the filaments that grow anew." *Aeneid*, Book VI, 597-600.

5. Ovid, *The Metamorphoses*, trans. Frank Justus Miller, Loeb Classical Library, William Heinemann Ltd., London, MCMLVI.

6. "Le Mythe de Sisyphe".

7. Lxvi, 24: And they shall go forth, and look upon the carcases of the men that have transgressed against me: for their worm shall not die, neither shall their fire be quenched; and they shall be an abhorring unto all flesh.

8. *The Spiritual Exercises of St. Ignatius*, with meditations and prayers, Father Liborio Siniscalchi, of the Society of Jesus. Translated from the Italian by a Catholic clergyman. James Duffy and Co., Dublin (not dated, but evidently from the nineteenth century).

9. *Exercitia Spiritualia Omnium Christianorum, ac Potissimum Ecclesiasticorum et Religiosorum, Usui Accomodata.* Acutore Joanne Baptista Pagani Presbytero. Dublini: Apud Jacobum Duffy, MDCCCLVI.

10. *The Spiritual Exercises of Saint Ignatius. A New Translation*, Father Corbishley, S.J., Burns and Oates, London, 1963.

11. I got the idea of Christianity or, more specifically, the Catholic church as a business from a remark to that effect made by the late Kenny Everett during his appearance on *Desert Island Discs*. Because of his Catholic upbringing Everett suffered hugely from guilt about his homosexuality, but he was reportedly reconciled to the church before his death from AIDS in 1995.

12. *The Catholic Encyclopedia: An International Work of Reference on the Constitution, Doctrine, Discipline, and History of the Catholic Church*, ed. Charles G. Herbermann *et al.*, The Encyclopedia Press, London, 1912.

13. "Hell", *The Catholic Encyclopedia.*

14. The *Gesta Romanorum* was a popular collection of stories during the Middle Ages. I haven't been able to track down the story in question there and don't remember the name of the feminist or where she made the claim, but it was probably Radio Four's W*oman's Hour* or some anilinguing feminist lek like that.

15. Introduction to William Sargant's *Battle for the Mind: a Physiology of Brainwashing and Conversion*, William Heinemann, London, 1957.

16. Translation in *The Holy Qur'an*, text, translation and commentary by Abdullah Yusuf Ali, Islamic Propagation Centre, Durban (not dated).

17. Chapter 16, "Heaven and Hell" in Mohammed Manzoor Nomani's *What Islam Is?* (sic), Haji Arfeen Academy, Karachi (not dated).

A GIRL'S SECOND-BEST FRIEND

(pages 23 — 31)

1. Sub-entry for "Earliest genus (Homo)" under heading "Earliest Man" in the "Human Being" section of the 1994 *Guinness Book of Records.*

2. *Stick It Up Your Punter: The Rise and Fall of the Sun*, Peter Chippindale and Chris Horrie, William Heinemann, London, 1990, pg. 244

3. Wrong, in fact. The New Zealand lesbian writer Jennifer Fulton's short story "Recipe for a Salad" describes a woman setting out an array of vegetables:

   a pretty strange assortment. Zucchini, cucumber, carrots, bananas.

   But not, it transpires, for a salad:

   "So you're giving up sex..." I prompted, making like my therapist.
   "I'm giving up lovers," Renee corrected. "And if I want sexual gratification, I'm going to look after myself..."
   "Uh huh," I said, ever the good listener.
   "That's how come I'm checking out the vegetables."
   I missed her point. "You what?"
   "I read about it," Renee told me. "Vegetables are a natural sex toy. I thought it might be better than using those electric things."
   I thought about my vibrator. "I doubt it, Renee." The voice of experience. I mean, vegetables???
   Renee pulled back slightly, sought my eyes. "You think I'm weird?"
   "No...no." I shook my head quickly. "I mean if you want a relationship with a vegetable, go ahead. Straight women do it all the time." I sniggered at my own joke, then fell silent.

   Taken from *Diving Deep: Erotic Lesbian Love Stories*, ed. Katherine V. Forrest and Barbara Grier, Naiad Press, USA, 1992/Silver Moon Books, London, 1993.

4. Hans Licht, *Sexual Life in Ancient Greece*, trans. J.H. Freese, ed. Lawrence H. Dawson, Panther, London, 1969, pt. 2, ch. 2, "Masturbation", pg. 284

5. Fred Chas. Forberg, *De Figuris Veneris: Manual of Classical Erotology*, chapter VI.

6. ibid., quoting Aloysia Sigaea (Dialogue II).

7. *Sexual Life in Ancient Greece*, Part Two, Chapter Three, "Tribadism".

8. Chapter 35 of Paul Gillette's translation and reconstruction, Sphere Books, London, 1970. This particular part of the *Satyricon* is in a very fragmentary state and the description of Encolpius's sex therapy is mostly a reconstruction, although the treated dildo and its anal insertion certainly survive in the original as:

   Profert Oenothea scorteum fascinum, quod ut oleo et minuto pipere atque urticae trito circumdedit semine, paulatim coepit inserere ano meo. 138 [Oenothea brought forth a leather dildo, which she dipped in oil, grains of pepper and crushed nettle seeds, and slowly began to insert in my anus.]

   Until well into the twentieth century, translations were leaving such passages hidden behind euphemistic paraphrases, or, as in the 1913 Loeb edition edited by one Michael Heseltine, refusing to remove them from the decent obscurity of Latin at all.

9. Chapter 94, Augustus, pg. 101 of *The Twelve Caesars*, translated by Robert Graves, Penguin, 1957.

10. ibid.

11. Thomas Nelson and Sons, Edinburgh, 1959. Quotation from the commentary on the Book of Exodus, pg. 174

12. Entry for "Fontaine, Françoise", pg. 206 of *The Encyclopedia of Witchcraft and Demonology: A historical and human compendium, culled from the World's great libraries, describing the witches' sabbat, incubi, succubi, werewolves, vampires, demoniacal possession, exorcism and tortures*, Rossell Hope Robbins, first published 1959, Crown Publishers Inc., New York (reprinted Newnes Books, Hamlyn, Feltham, Middlesex, 1984).

13. *Witchcraft and Demonology*, Francis X. King, Treasure Press, London, 1991, ch. 2, "The Devil's Faith", pg. 37

14. *The Encyclopedia of Witchcraft and Demonology*, entry for "Ointment, flying", pg. 367

15. As described in a poem that I have unfortunately been unable to track down again.

16. *Sexual Life in Ancient Greece*, Part Two, ch. 2, "Masturbation", pg. 284

17. pg. 402, *Index of Forbidden Books* [*Index Librorum Prohibitorum*], Henry Spencer Ashbee, Sphere Books, London, 1969. You might be interested to learn that "Pisanus Fraxi", the pseudonym under which this book was originally published, is an anagram of *fraxinus* and *apis*, the Latin for, respectively, "ash (tree)" and "bee" (*The Literary Companion to Sex*, Fiona Pitt-Kethley).

18. *The Oxford English Dictionary*, definition under "vibrator".

19. Warren Adler, *The War of the Roses*, Arrow Books, London, 1990, ch. 20, pp. 163-4.

20. Pat Califia, *Lesbian S&M Safety Manual*: "So You Wanna Be A Sadist? How to Make it Hurt So Good in One Easy Lesson", Alyson, Boston, Mass., 1988, pg. 54

21. Entry for "Auxonne Nuns", pg. 34 of *The Encyclopedia of Witchcraft and Demonology.*

22. *My Secret Life*, Book Four, Chapter XX, pp. 385-6 of the 1995 Wordsworth Classics Edition.

23. A policeman from Nottingham Junction,
Whose organ had long ceased to function,
Deceived his good wife
For the rest of her life
With the aid of his constable's truncheon.

24. *Rack, Rope and Red-Hot Pincers: A History of Torture and Its Instruments*, Geoffrey Abbot, Headline, London, 1993, pp. 124-5

25. Words of the dominant lesbian "Lavinia E." in Evelyn Theodor's *Lesbian Secrets*, Luxor Press, 1970, pg. 61

26. Maurice Lever, *Marquis de Sade: A Biography*, HarperCollins 1993, pp. 325-6.

27. ibid.

28. Police report quoted ibid., pg. 518

29. *The Guinness Book of Oddities*, Geoff Tibballs, Guinness Publishing, Enfield, Middlesex, 1995, pg. 166

THE REVENGE OF CELLULOSE

(pages 32 — 42)

1. No longer alone, no longer the sole glaring exception. Some of the *Planet of the Apes* novelizations have joined it.

2. ch. 11, pp. 132-3 of the 1971 Corgi paperback of James Mitchell's *Red File For Callan* (originally published as *A Magnum for Schneider* in 1969).

3. *Bullshot*, a novelization by Martin Noble based on a screenplay by Alan Shearman, Ron House and Diz White, Star, London, 1983, ch. 20, pg. 106

4. *The New Statesman*, Anna Morgan, Javelin, London, 1987, ch. 6, "Three Line Whipping", pg. 126

5. In the film and book *Dr Strangelove*, the character called President Merkin Muffley is another good example of this kind of subtle onomastic humour. The characters General Jack D. Ripper and Ambassador de Sadeski, on the other hand, are not.

6. ch. 8, "In which the battle is won by an oar and lost by a potted palm", pg. 43

7. ch. 1, "Happiness is a Warm Gun", pp. 25-6

ENDGAME

(pages 43 — 57)

1. *The Cosmic Winter*, Victor Clube and Bill Napier, Basil Blackwell, Oxford, 1990.
2. *Peake's Commentary On the Bible*, ed. Arthur S. Peake, Thomas Nelson and Son, Edinburgh, 1959.
3. "And [the strange beast] waxed great, even to the host of heaven; and it cast down some of the host and of the stars to the ground, and stamped upon them": Daniel viii, 10.

   "How thou art fallen from heaven, O Lucifer, son of the morning!": Isaiah xiv, 12. "Lucifer" is the day-star, or the planet Venus seen in the east in early morning.
4. pp. 269-272 and *passim*.
5. *The Great Extinction: What killed the Dinosaurs and devastated the Earth?*, Michael Allaby and James Lovelock, Secker and Warburg, London, 1983, pg. 63
6. *Peake's Commentary*, pg. 934
7. *Cosmic Winter*, pg. 162
8. *Cosmic Winter*, pg. 275
9. *Cosmic Winter*, pg. 276
10. *Rendezvous With Rama*, ch. 1, "Spaceguard".
11. Chapter 46, "Finale", pg. 242 of the 1995 Orbit paperback.
12. Moses, St. Paul, Marx, Freud.
13. Chapter 38, "Terminal Diagnosis", pg. 214 of the 1995 Orbit paperback.
14. *Meteor*, a novel by Edmund H. North and Franklin Coen from the screenplay by Stanley Mann and Edmund H. North, Hamlyn Paperbacks, Aylesbury, 1979.
15. Even more ludicrous is page 184's: "In the heavens, travelling at terrible velocity, the splinter made a frightening roar in its passage". *Meteor* cannot, however, even begin to approach the inanities of Robert Charles' *Nightworld*, which was published by Corgi in 1984 to exploit the soon-to-reappear Halley's comet. In the book, a probe is dispatched to take samples from the comet and accidentally inherits the mysterious dust-cloud following it. The probe then brings the samples, plus cloud, back to earth and everyone is plunged into darkness. Two other "meteor-strike" novels I came across too late to include in this discussion were Larry Niven and Jerry Pournelle's *Lucifer's Hammer* (Futura, London, 1978), which does seem to tackle the question of mass-psychological effects before the strike, and John Baxter's *The Hermes Fall* (Granada, London, 1978), which doesn't, although it does provide a great literary moment when it describes the hero being contacted by phone after a strenuous sex-session and an in-bed snack of "grilled cheese sandwiches":

   > Gary got up, naked, and went to the phone. Ten minutes later he was on the main road out of town, his fingers still slick from butter and cunt. Without taking his eyes off the road, he licked them clean. [ch. 6, pg. 61]
16. pg. 41
17. pg. 116
18. pg. 130. Compare Clarke's: "Human beings cannot remain for long in a state of perpetual crisis; the home planet had swiftly returned to something like normal. No one really doubted or dared to doubt that what the media had quickly named OPERATION DELIVERANCE could possibly fail." [Chapter 35, "Deliverance", pg. 201 of the Orbit paperback]
19. pg. 187
20. *The Guinness Book of Astronomy*, Guinness Publishing Ltd., Enfield, Middlesex, 1992.
21. "Perihelion" is the point in a planet's orbit closest to the sun; "opposition" is the lining-up of a planet, the earth and sun, with the earth in the middle. At perihelic opposition, therefore, planets tend to be at their brightest.
22. *Into that Darkness: From Mercy Killing to Mass Murder*, Gitta Sereny, André Deutsch, London, 1974 (Pimlico Edition 1995), pg. 157

23. pp. 365-6, Part Five, "The Battle", ch. 3, *The Last Battle*, Cornelius Ryan, New English Library Paperback, 1984.

24. *The Rape of Europa: The Fate of Europe's Treasures in the Third Reich and the Second World War*, Lynn H. Nicholas, Macmillan, 1994, pg. 233

25. *The Last Battle*, pg. 367

26. *China Wakes: The Struggle for the Soul of a Rising Power*, Nicholas D. Kristof and Sheryl WuDunn, Nicholas Brealey Publishing, London, 1994, pg. 73

27. pg. 74

28. All references taken from the 1947 Fontana paperback.

29. *Cosmic Winter*, pg. 6

30. *Cosmic Winter*, ibid.

31. *Nuclear Winter*, Owen Greene, Ian Percival and Irene Ridge, Polity Press/Basil Blackwell, Oxford, 1985.

32. *The Great Extinction*, pg. 89

GOLDEN LAUGHTER

(pages 58 — 84)

1. ... *praetextu verborum adhibito* ... ch. 34, *The Life of Heliogabalus*, Ælius Lampridius. The English translations of Lampridius are taken from *The Scriptores Historae Augustae*, translated by David Margie, vol. II, Loeb Classical Library, William Heinemann, London, 1924. The Latin text quoted in the notes was taken from a *Historia Augusta* downloaded from the InterNet at http:// tornade.ere.umontreal.ca/ brazeauj/histaugusta/.

2. *Do You Speak Venusian? A trip through the mysteries of the Cosmos*, ch. 6, "Dr Velikovsky's Comet", pg. 53 of the 1976 Wyndham paperback.

3. See, for example, *Halley's Comet in History*, ed. F.R. Stephenson and C.B.F. Walker, British Museum Publications, 1985.

4. ἡλιου τε γαρ ἐκλειψις περιφανεστατη ὑπο τας ἡμερας ἐκεινας ἐγενετο, και ὁ αστηρ ὁ κομητης ἐπι πλειουν ὠφθη, ἑτερον τε τι ἀστερον ἀπο δυσμων προς ἀνατολας το ἀκροφυσιον ἐπι πολλας νυκτας ἀνατεινον δεινως ἡμας ἐξεταραττεν ... Book LXXIX, ch. 30, in volume IX of *Dio's Roman History*, translated by Earnest Carey, Loeb Classical Library, William Heinemann, London, 1927.

5. *The Roman Emperors: A Biographical Guide to the Rulers of Imperial Rome, 31 BC-AD 476*, Weidenfeld, 1985, Herodian, Book V, ch. vi, "Macrinus and Elagabalus", sec. 7, trans. Michael Grant.

6. "Many of our current Christian practices come from Mithraism; the 25th of December was the birthday of Mithras; the first day of the week, dedicated to the Sun, was his holy day, as opposed to the Jewish Sabbath." Gilbert Murray, "Pagan Religion at the Coming of Christianity", pg. 632 of *Peake's Commentary Commentary on the Bible*, ed. Arthur S. Peake, Thomas Nelson and Sons, Edinburgh, 1959.

7. ...*libidinum eius* ..., ch. 16. The Latin text seems to be corrupt at this point; the English translation is that suggested in *Lives of the Later Caesars: The First Part of the Augustan History, with newly compiled Lives of Nerva and Trajan*, translated by Anthony Birley, Penguin, 1976.

8. Εν γαρ τοι ἱπποδρομιᾳ τινι ἐκπεσων του ἁρματος κατ' αὑτην την του Σαρδαναπαλλου ἑδραν το τε κρανος ἐν τῃ πτωσει ἀπερριψε, και ἐκφαεις αυτῳ (λειογενειος δ' ἐτι ἠν και κομῃ ξανθῃ ἐκεκοσμητο) ἀνηρπασθη τε εὐθυς ἐς το παλατιον, κἀν τοις νυκτερινοις ἐργοις ἐτι και μαλλον ἑλων αὑτον ὑπερηυξηθη. Book LXXX, ch. 15

9. See section 42, "Helius" etc. in *The Greek Myths*, 2 volumes, Penguin, revised edition, 1960.

10. *Tractum est cadaver eius etiam per circi spatia. Priusquam in Tiberim praecipitaretur*. Lampridius, ch. 15

11. αἱ τε κεφαλαι αὑτων [i.e. the heads of Heliogabalus and his mother] ἀπεκοπησαν, και τα σωματα γυμνωθεντα το μεν πρωτον δια πασης της πολεως ἐσυρη, ἐπειτα το μεν της γυναικος ἀλλως πως ἐρριφη, το δε ἐκεινου ἐς

τον ποταμον ἐνεβληθη. Book LXXX, ch. 20

12. In ch. 1 of the *Vita*, for example.

13. ... *adnexo pondere ne fluitaret, in Tiberim abiectum est, ne unquam sepeliri posset.* ch. 17

14. *Appellatus est post mortem Tiberinus et Tractatitius* ... ch. 16

15. *A New Dictionary of Biography, Mythology, and Geography, partly based on the "Dictionary of Greek and Roman Biography and Mythology"*, William Smith, LL.D., John Murray, London, 2nd edition, 1853.

16. γονεων ἀδοξοτατων ἠν, ὡστε και σφοδρα ἐικοτως αὐτον τῳ ὀνῳ τῳ ἐς το παλατιον ὑπο του δαιμονιου ἐσαχθεντι ἐικασθηναι [cf. ch. 7] ... και γαρ Μαυρος ὡν δεινως ἐδειμαινεν. Book LXXIX, ch. 11 and 27. Dio contradicts the latter dig when he describes the seige of Heliogabalus's camp, in which "the Moors who had been sent to Tarautas in fulfilment of the terms of the alliance fought most valiantly for Macrinus, as he was a fellow-countryman of theirs, and even broke through some of the gates" (ibid., ch. 32).

17. *et aiunt quidam Varii etiam nomen idcirco eidem inditum a condiscipulis, quod vario semine, de meretrice utpote, conceptus videretur.* ch. 2

18. *Fuit autem Heliogabali vel Iovis vel Solis sacerdos* ... Lampridius, ch. 1

19. *Et penetrale sacrum est auferre conatus cumque seriam quasi veram rapuisset, quamque virgo maxima falso monstraverat* ... ch. 7

20. In fact, this is precisely the excuse he did offer: see Herodian, ch. vi. The coin is reproduced in the section for Heliogabalus in Clive Foss's *Roman Historical Coins*, Seaby, London, 1990.

21. Dio, Book LXXIX, ch. 36.

22. Ibid.

23. Lampridius, ch. 20

24. *Nec erat ei ulla vita nisi exquirere novas voluptates.* ch. 20

25. Lemprière's *Classical Dictionary.* More recent research has shown Sardanapallus to have been a mostly mythical figure.

26. Cf. Lampridius, ch. 8, ... Varius et Heliogabalus et ludibrium publicium diceretur ... "He was called Varius and Heliogabalus and a public laughing-stock". For Hesychius see Liddell and Scott's *Greek-English Lexicon* and the entry for σαρδαναφαλλος.

27. Lemprière's *Dictionary*, entry for "Bacchus".

28. *Iunxit sibi et leones, Matrem magnam se appellans. Iunxit et tigres, Liberum sese vocans eodem habitu agens, quo dii pinguntur, quos imitabatur.*

29. Entry for CURRUS ("chariot") in Smith's *Dictionary.*

30. *Chambers Biographical Dictionary*, ed. Magnus Magnusson, W. and R. Chambers Ltd, Edinburgh, 1990.

31. Entry for "Chronology" in *The Catholic Encyclopedia: An International Work of Reference on the Constitution, Doctrine, Discipline, and History of the Catholic Church*, ed. Charles G. Herbermann *et al.*, London, The Encyclopedia Press, 1912.

32. ch. 4, "The Birthday Star", pg. 91 of the 1981 Corgi paperback of David Hughes' *The Star of Bethlehem Mystery: Fact? Legend? Or Miracle? The Astonishing Truth behind the World's Most Mysterious Celestial Event.* Despite the subtitle, a carefully argued and well-written book, and hardly astonishing in its conclusions.

33. "Dionysius, Exiguus" in *The Catholic Encyclopedia.*

34. *Vulgum ad bibendum invitavit et ipse cum populo tantum bibit, ut in piscina eum bibisse intellegeretur, viso quod unus bibisset.* Lampridius, ch. 21

35. For example, Liddell and Scott's *Greek-English Lexicon.*

36. και ὀς ἰδων αὐτον ἀνεθορε τε ἐρρυθμισμενως, και προσειποντα, οἰα εἰκος ἠν, "Κυριε αὐτοκρατορ χαιρε", θαυμαστως τον τε αὐχενα γυναικισας και τους ὀφθαλμους ἐπεγκλασας ἠμειψατο, και ἐφη οὐδεν διστασας, "Μη με

λεγε κυριον· ἐγω γαρ κυρια ἐιμι." Dio, Book LXXX, ch. 16

37. "Dionysius, Exiguus" in *The Catholic Encyclopedia.*

38. "Dionysius, Exiguus" in *The Catholic Encyclopedia,* and see entry for Homs/Emesa in *Monuments of Syria: An Historical Guide,* Ross Burns, Tauris, 1992.

39. Table reproduced from *Biblical Hebrew: The Original Language of the Old Testament, an expressive medium for conveying fundamental spiritual truths, full of simplicity and power,* R.K. Harrison, Teach Yourself Books, Hodder and Stoughton, London, 1995.

40. Subsequent discussion of Hebrew words will be based on Benjamin Davidson's *Analytic Hebrew and Chaldee Lexicon,* Samuel Bagster and Sons, London (not dated).

41. The Hebrew writing system doesn't recognize the signs it uses for vowels as part of its consonant-only alphabet, though it does use three of the alphabetic consonants, אוי ("y", "w" and the glottal stop), as quasi-vowels in some contexts.

42. *Saepe amicos suos cum Aethiopibus aniculis inclusit nocturnis mansionibus et usque ad lucem detinuit, cum pulcherrimas his diceret apparatas. Fecit hoc idem etiamde pueris et tunc, ante Philippum utpote, licebat.* "Philippum" is the emperor Philip the Arab (244-9), who passed laws against homosexuality.

43. This alternation between the consonants /k/ and /g/ may be very important in other names associated with Heliogabalus: see discussion later in the article.

44. *The New Bible Commentary Revised,* ed. D. Guthrie et al, Inter-Varsity Press, London, 1970.

45. *Peake's Commentary on the Bible,* ed. Arthur S. Peake, Thomas Nelson and Sons, Edinburgh, 1959.

46. As it may be elsewhere in Acts, where μεσημβρια/*mesémbria* appears for the second and final time in the story of Paul's conversion on the road to Damascus:

> And it came to pass, that, as I made my journey, and was come nigh unto Damascus about noon [περι μεσημβριαν/*peri mesémbrian*], suddenly there shone from heaven a great light round about me. And I fell unto the ground, and heard a voice crying unto me, Saul, Saul, why persecutest thou me? [xxii, 6-7]

47. *New Bible Dictionary,* ed. J.D. Douglas et al, Inter-Varsity Press, Leicester, 1962.

48. *Greek-English Lexicon to the New Testament,* W.J. Hickie, Baker Book House, Grand Rapids, Michigan, 1977.

49. The chronology is the *Chronicon Paschale,* but the date, like that given by Dionysus Exiguus for the birth of Christ, is almost certainly wrong, 130 AD being the one generally accepted today. See the discussion of Antinoüs's life and death in Royston Lambert's *Beloved and God: The Story of Hadrian and Antinoüs,* Weidenfeld and Nicolson, London, 1984.

50. It's also possible that there is a play on sound between the name of the queen, Κανδακη/Kandaké, and an ancient name of Gaza, Καδυτις/Kadytis, which is used in Herodotus 2.159. See the entry for "Gaza" in the *New Bible Dictionary.*

51. See Graves, *The Greek Myths,* 41, "Orion".

52. *Peake's Commentary on the Bible,* pg. 240, of Deuteronomy xiii, 24.

53. Commentary in *The Holy Bible, with the most approved marginal references, and explanatory notes, selected from the most esteemed Biblical writers,* ed. Rev. Ingram Cobbin, M.A., Ward, Lock and Tyler, London, (not dated).

54. *Peake's Commentary.*

55. *A New Classical Dictionary of Biography, Mythology, and Geography,* William Smith. "At a later time, however, he repudiated this literal understanding of our Lord's words".

56. *History Laid Bare: Love, Sex and Perversity from the Ancient Etruscans to Lawrence of Arabia,* Richard Zacks, Michael O'Mara Books, London, 1995 (taken from Sir James

Frazer's translation of Lucian in *The Golden Bough*, ch. xxxiv, "The Myth and Ritual of Attis").

57. *Iactavit autem caput inter praecisos fanaticos et genitalia sibi devinxit et omnia fecit, quae Galli facere solent* ... Lampridius, ch. 7

58. ἐβουλευσατο μεν γαρ πανταπασιν αὐτο ἀποκοψαι· αλλ' ἐκεινο μεν της μαλακιας ἑνεκα ποιησαι ἐπεθυμησε, τουτο δε ὡς και τῃ του Ελεγαβαλου ἱερατειᾳ προσηκον ἐπραξεν· ἐξ οὑ δη και ἑτεροις των συνοντων συχνοις ὁμοιως ἐλυμηνατο. Dio, Book LXXX, ch. 8

59. Smith's Dictionary, entry for "Meroë".

60. Note in ch. VI of Gibbon's *Decline and Fall of the Roman Empire*.

61. *The Caesars' Wives: Above Suspicion?*, Stuart Perowne, Hodder, 1974, pg. 147

62. Lemprière's *Dictionary*. There is probably some chicken and egg here, however. The mountain sacred to Cybele was also sometimes known as Ida, and was said to be the one from which Zeus snatched Ganymede to Olympus. Another link with Elah-Gabal and Heliogabalus is the fact that Cybele was worshipped in the form of a sacred, probably meteoric, stone.

63. *Dicebat praeterea Iudaeorum et Samaritanorum religiones et Christianam devotionem illuc transferendam, ut omnium culturarum secretum Heliogabali sacerdotium teneret*. ch. 2

64. και ὁτι χοιρεων κρεων, ὡς και καθαρωτερον ἐκ τουτων θρησκευσων, ἀπειχετο. Book LXXX, ch. 8

65. *Struthocamelos exhibuit in cenis aliquotiens, dicens praeceptum Iudaeis, ut ederent*. ch. 35

66. Birley, *Lives of the Later Caesars*, pg. 290

67. *Sed de nomine hactenus, quamvis sanctum illud Antoninorum nomen polluerit, quod tu, Constantine sacratissime, ita veneraris, ut Marcum et Pium inter Constantios Claudiosque, velut maiores tuos, aureos formaveris adoptans virtutes veterum tuis moribus congruentes et tibi amicas caras*. ch. 2

68. *elefantorum quattuor quadrigas in Vaticano agitasse dirutis sepulchris, quae obsistebant* ... ch. 22

69. *Idem numquam minus centum sestertiis cenavit, hoc est argenti libris triginta* (ch. 24). Compare the Vulgate's (Latin Bible's) "*At illi constituerant ei triginta argenteos*" ... "And they convenanted with him [Judas] for thirty pieces of silver" (Matthew xxvi, 15), and note the commentary in the Loeb text on this part of Lampridius:

> The evaluation of 100,000 *sestertii* = 30 lbs. silver, however, presents a difficult problem, for the biographer is not using the system in vogue under Elagabalus.

Nor, apparently, any other easily determined system, or perhaps any system at all.

70. *ursos decem et decem glires et decem lactucas et decem auri libras*

71. *Murenarum lactibus et luporum in locis mediterraneis rusticos pavit.*

72. *Iocabantur sane ita cum servis, ut eos iuberet millena pondo sibi aranearum deferre proposito praemio, collegisseque dicitur decem milia pondo aranearum, dicens et hinc intellegendum, quam magna esset Roma.*

73. *Habuit et hanc consuetudinem, ut octo calvos rogaret ad cenam et item octo luscos etitem octo podagrosos, octo surdos, octo nigros, octo longos et octo pingues, cum capi non possent uno sigmate, ut de his omnibus risus citaret.*

LORD OF THE RINGPIECE

(pages 85 — 97)

1. *Philosophy in the Boudoir*, "The Third Dialogue".

2. *Sexual Personae: Art and Decadence from Nefertiti to Emily Dickinson*, Yale University, 1990.

3. To be published by Savoy. Title, as of writing, undecided.

4. *The Marquis de Sade*, Weidenfeld, 1976.

5. *Swinburne: Portrait of a Poet*, Philip Henderson, Routledge and Kegan Paul, London, 1974, pg. 54.

6. From the prefatory note to the 1949 Pauvert edition of *Juliette*, reproduced in the introduction to Austryn Wainhouse's English translation in the Arrow series, 1991.

7. *De Sade: A Biography and a Note of Hope*, Messidor, 1994.

8. *Juliette*, Arrow, 1991, pg. 218

9. pg. 167; cf. pg. 358 and *passim*

10. pg. 861

11. pp. 161-2

12. pg. 825

13. pg. 196

14. pg. 1055

15. pg. 175

16. pg. 176

17. pg. 338

18. Bottle is supposed to be rhyming slang for "arse": bottle-Aristotle, Aristotle-arris, arris-arse, is one suggestion; another is "bottle and glass". "To lose your bottle" is, therefore, to lose control of the anal sphincter.

19. *Marquis de Sade: A Biography*, Maurice Lever, HarperCollins, pg. 525

20. pg. 1184

21. "Sade, Our Bedfellow", review of *De Sade: A Critical Biography*, Ronald Hayman, collected in *Homage to QWERT YUIOP: Selected Journalism 1978-1985*, pg. 278, Abacus, London, 1987.

22. pg. 147

23. Dave Mitchell's forthcoming study of Savoy.

24. pg. 791

25. pp. 791-4

26. pg. 642

27. pg. 642

28. For example, pg. 1019

IT'S HUMAN FINGERS!

(pages 98 — 113)

1. pg. 92, Amok *Fourth Dispatch*.

2. "The Other Side of the Tracts: Jack T. Chick's Pyramid Plan", Mark Barnette in *The Comics Journal* #145, October 1991.

3. Taken from the Jack Chick tract *Fat Cats*.

4. "The Other Side of the Tracts", pg. 94

5. The central claim of the book is that Pope John-Paul I was murdered to stop him cleaning up the church's finances and getting rid of the Catholic prohibition on contraception, but even if you don't accept the good evidence adduced in favour of it, the case made in general for the church's being revoltingly corrupt and money-grubbing seems pretty unanswerable.

6. "In common with so many other thousands of persons, I first learned of A.I.C. [Dr Rivera's organization] through the booklet [he probably means "the comic" but doesn't like to say so] ALBERTO. It was mailed to me by my closest Christian friend, with an accompanying note, 'Please read this booklet which was left by someone on one of the Teen Mission buses. Let me have your comments on it when we get together later his year.'

   "There are no accidents with God. That copy of ALBERTO was left on that bus in Florida, more than 1200 miles from me. The young man who retrieved it, Jim McKinnon, is the same man who, as a Detroit police officer, witnessed to me and led me to the Lord two years ago. This was God's design. It could not have been coincidence. The Spirit led my friend to pick up the copy of ALBERTO and mail it to me." *Night Journey from Rome...to the New Jerusalem*, Evangelical Biblical Christian Publications, 1985, pp. 10-11

7. "In the biblical text two different words are used for **Peter** and **rock** in the Greek. 'Peter' is **petros**, masculine, referring to a small pebble. 'Rock' is **petra**, feminine, referring to a huge cliff of stone or massive rock. So Pe-

ter was called a pebble. But the Church would be built on something more solid, rock. And aside from the aberrations of Rome, that rock has always been considered the confession of faith in Christ's divinity made by Peter. Moreover, the Greek word **kai** (and) may also be translated 'but'. So Christ said to Peter, 'You are a **pebble**, but on this rock I will build my church'". Discussion of Matthew xvi, 18 in *Night Journey...*, pg. 95

8. "Introduction", pg. 7

9. Estimate for American male life expectancy in 1975 given in the *Guinness Book of Answers*, Guinness Superlatives Ltd., Enfield, Middlesex, 1980.

10. *Double-Cross: Alberto Part Two*, pg. 31

11. *Double-Cross: Alberto Part Two*, pp. 5-8

12. "The Other Side of the Tracts", pg. 91

13. And also, I suspect, by more than one sex, which means Jim's body might have been interesting whoever was behind *The Broken Cross* after all.

14. *The Ark*, pg. 4

DONNER UND BLITZEN

(pages 114 — 120)

BIBLIOGRAPHY

Hanna Reitsch: Flying for the Fatherland, Judy Lomax, John Murray, London, 1988.

Hitler's Luftwaffe: a pictorial history and technical encyclopedia of Hitler's air power in World War II, Tony Wood/Bill Gunston, Salamander Books, London, 1977.

The Encyclopedia of the World's Combat Aircraft: a technical directory of major warplanes from World War 1 to the present day, Bill Gunston, Salamander Books, London, 1976.

The Sky My Kingdom (Fliegen, mein Leben), Hanna Reitsch, Greenhill Books, London, 1991.

1. Yes, Hitler was Austrian, but he regarded Austria as part of Germany, as did very large numbers of his fellow Austrians, at least until the war was over and they had to start pretending "It wasn't me, guv".

2. *Secret Germany: Claus von Stauffenberg and the Mystical Crusade Against Hitler*, Michael Baigent and Richard Leigh, Cape 1994; Penguin, 1995.

3. It's fairly similar to the Alpha jet, for example and very similar to the Fairchild Republic A-10: similar fuselage, almost identical tail, jet engines similarly set above the fuselage and so on.

4. Charles ("Chuck") Elwood Yeager in a Bell XS-1 at Mach 1.015/1078 kmph, 14th October, 1947 (*Guinness Book of Records*).The XS-1 was a rocket aircraft too, and almost certainly owed something to captured German technology.

5. *The Sky My Kingdom*, chapter 24, "I Crash in a Rocket Plane", pg. 177

6. The crest of one Me 163 combat unit showed a man in eighteenth-century costume flying through the air by hitching a ride on a cannonball. One of Münchhausen's stories was that he had escaped from a besieged town in this very fashion.

7. *The Sky My Kingdom*, chapter 24, pp. 173-4

8. Said of London in Evelyn Waugh's *Unconditional Surrender*, ch. 2, pg. 533 of the Penguin single volume edition of Waugh's *Sword of Honour* trilogy.

WHAT IS TRUTH?

(pages 121 — 133)

1. *The Longest Hatred: An Examination of Anti-Gentilism*, Inter-City Researchers, Inter-City Research Centre, London, 1991. An example of something I agree with: the claim that the international banking system has far too much power, and exercises this power in damaging and unjust ways. An example of something that is dotty: the claim that Jesus was not a Jew.

2. pp. 39 and 52 respectively.

3. pg. 133 of *Evolution, the Great Debate: the*

science, the discoveries, the story of the great debate, Vernon Blackmore and Andrew Page, Lion Publishing, Oxford, 1989.

4. pp. 263-79 of Gould's collection *Hen's Teeth and Horse's Toes*, W.W. Norton, New York/London, 1983.

5. *Evolution, the Great Debate*, pg. 133

6. *Did Six Million Really Die? The Truth At Last* (Historical Fact No. 1), "Richard Harwood", Historical Review Press, Brighton, Sussex, revised edition (not dated, but probably sometime after 1987).

7. These facts are taken from *The Six Million Reconsidered*, a revisionist book discussed later in the article, and how reliable they are I am unsure.

8. Mass emigration to Madagascar is known to have been considered by the Nazis as a means of solving the "Jewish problem". See any standard history of the Second World War.

9. *The Oldie* #2, 6th March 1992, pg. 13

10. I forget precisely where I came across this argument, but I think it's fairly commonly used in Creationist literature.

11. According to Genesis, light was in fact created before the bodies that emit it: see Gen. i, 3 and i, 16.

12. Taken from a Creationist comic called *Voice of the Volcano: Facts of Science No. 2* (no ISBN given).

13. J.C. Whitcomb in *Genesis Flood: The Biblical Record & Its Scientific Implications*, John C. Whitcomb, Presbyterian & Reformed Publishing Co., 1961, as quoted in *Evolution, the Great Debate*, pg. 162

14. pg. 15

15. pp. 23-4

16. *The Six Million Reconsidered: Is the "Nazi Holocaust" Story a Zionist Propaganda Ploy? Volume One in an Examination of the Jewish Genocide Claim Versus the Disaster of the Twentieth Century*, the Committee for Truth in History, Media Research Associates, U.S.A., 1977 (U.K. Edition by Historical Review Press, Ladbroke, Warks., 1979).

17. pg. 72

18. pg. 71

19. pg. 70

20. pp. 76-8

21. This film is referred to as "Swindler's List" in a curious series of supportive post-cards received by the Dowager Lady Birdwood during her Old Bailey trial for fomenting "racial hatred", and reproduced in Lady Birdwood's *Choice* newsletter. The post-cards came from York and were all of Clifford's Tower, which was the site of a massacre of Jews by Christians in the Middle Ages. This is not mentioned in *Choice*, and Lady Birdwood doesn't indicate her attitude to the post-cards, which also urged her to "Ask the Old Beak who makes the video nasties". See *Choice* #25.

22. pg. 81

23. *Did Man Get Here by Evolution or by Creation?* (author not given), Watch Tower Bible and Tract Society of Pennsylvania, 1967, pg. 170

24. pg. 52

25. pg. 148, *The Eleventh Hour*, Albion Press, London, 1988.

26. ibid, pg. 131

27. Taken from a Creationist comic called *Amazing Fossils... But How Old? Facts of Science No. 1* (ISBN 0 949906 11 5).

28. Thanks to BH for pointing this out to me.

29. For discussion of the vilification of Chomsky, see "The Chorus and Cassandra", in Christopher Hitchens' collection *Prepared for the Worst*, Chatto and Windus, London, 1988.

30. Yes, they burn down refugee hostels in Germany and kill people, but so do faulty wiring and carelessly discarded cigarettes. That's not being callous, merely trying to make the point that deaths and the things responsible for them do not become important simply because they get a lot of attention. Neo-Nazis generate a lot of media noise; so do air-

crashes. You're still far more likely to die in a car, and your freedoms are still far more in danger from mainstream political parties and fundamentalist Christians.

RITUAL IN PRAGUE

(pages 132 — 139)

BIBLIOGRAPHY

Betrayal at Venlo: The Secret Story of Appeasement & Treachery, Leo Kessler, Cooper, 1991.

The Killing of SS Obergruppenführer Reinhard Heydrich, 27th May 1942, Callum MacDonald, Macmillan, 1989.

Heydrich: Hitler's Most Evil Henchman, Charles Highton, Odhams, 1962.

Heydrich: The Pursuit of Total Power, Günther Deschner, Orbis, 1981.

NO NEWS IS GOOD NEWS

(pages 140 — 145)

1. Hodder and Stoughton, 1989.
2. A real event reported sometime in the past couple of years, according to Philips.

GILT BY ASSOCIATION

(pages 156 — 161)

1. I'm almost certain that in England too the first stage of printing used fonts based on handwritten letter forms, which were probably not those of the classical Old English font, but either way these handwritten forms seem to have fallen out of use much quicker than in Germany.

A SHORT ARTICLE ABOUT FARTING

(pages 162 — 167)

1. *Inside Mr Enderby* is a novel by Anthony Burgess, and in an Anthony Burgess novel even an onomatopoeia for a fart has deep significance. First come the musical instructions for the playing of the sound: p, f, ff, or *piano-forte-fortissimo*; and next the instrument on which it is to be played, the rump. And there's more — probably, but you get the idea.
2. "Appendix I", translated by Graham Snell in *Diary of A Genius*, Salvador Dalí, translated from the French by Richard Howard, Hutchinson, London, 1990.
3. Fawn Brodie, *The Devil Drives*, ch. XXXIII, pg. 265 of the 1986 Eland paperback; quotations from Seton Dearden's *Burton of Arabia*, New York, 1937.
4. The anecdote is preceded by another about the the Shaykh, who was "a man famed for facetious blackguardism, [and] used to invite European youngsters serving in the Bombay Marine and ply them with liquor till they were insensible. Next morning the middies mostly complained that the champagne had caused a curious irritation and soreness in *la parte-poste* [rear end]."
5. "How Abu Hasan Brake Wind", from *The Book of the Thousand and One Nights, the original unexpurgated translation by Sir Richard Burton*, ed. P.H. Newby, Panther, 1960.
6. It is also the Hindi word for "foot", an especially unclean part of the body to Hindus. It was from the god Brahma's feet that there sprang the *sudras*, the lowest of the four classes in traditional Hindu society.
7. *History of Western Philosophy*, chapter III, "Pythagoras".
8. Maurice Lever, *Marquis de Sade: A Biography*, HarperCollins 1993, pg. 61
9. From *An Essay on Wind; with Curious Anecdotes of Eminent Peteurs. Humbly Dedicated to the Lord Chancellor.* Anon (Charles James Fox?), "Printed and Sold by all the Booksellers in Town and Country", 1787.
10. In fact Johnny has recently made a return to the pages of *Viz*, but the old magic is entirely gone.

BIOGRAPHICAL NOTE

Simon Whitechapel was born in Madagascar, and has lived and worked in Singapore, India and Spain. As well as his non-fiction work for *Critical Vision* and *Headpress* magazine, he is author of the "superbly twisted" anti-novel *The Slaughter King*.

INDEX

Italics denote title of film, publication, or radio show

ALSO AVAILABLE FROM HEADPRESS / CRITICAL VISION

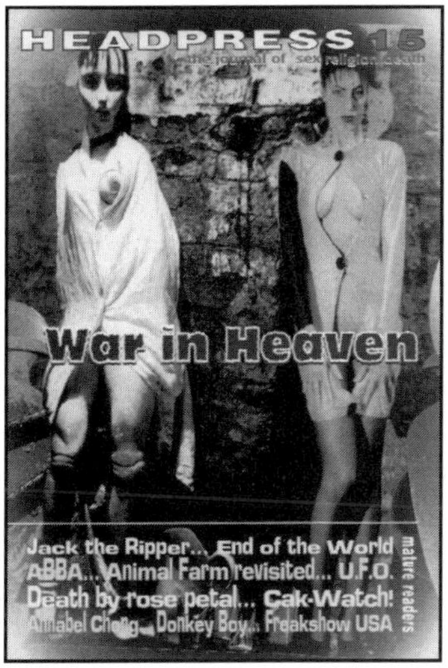

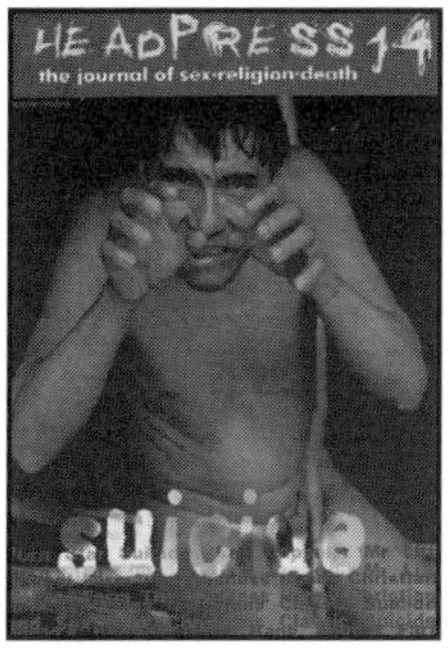

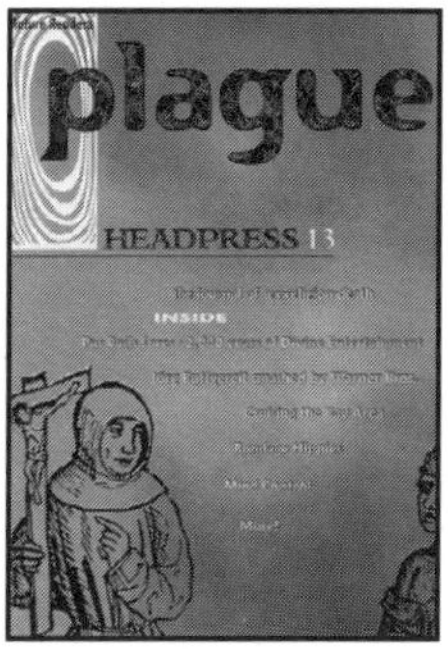

HEADPRESS

the journal of Sex Religion Death

For five years **HEADPRESS** magazine has enjoyed cult status at the forefront of "transgressive" writing. Incisive and cutting-edge essays on films and filmmakers, religious manias, fanaticism, weird crime cases, sex queens, curious music, fetishism, art, pornography, trash and sleaze. Now sees a radical new format — **HEADPRESS** goes book-size! 100 pages! Perfect-bound! Fully illustrated!

"An entirely healthy interest in violent death & deviant sex" — *i-D*

"Outrageous... our favourite grotesque magazine" — *Forum*

"Absolutely essential" — *Fortean Times*

Contents include

Bondage Hippies Or were they? An examination of a forgotten fetish relic from the Seventies. **Guts 'n' Roses** The coming apocalypse of the Ripper Millennium. **Dwarf Machines** How world leaders will soon dissipate consciousness with a glass of water. **Sex, Violence and Models** Gerry Anderson's U.F.O. **Sharing The Experience** Cruising the Bay Area. **She's Beautiful... Even though she's dead!** The strange phenomenon of porn stars who top themselves. **An interview with the Amazing Mr Lifto**... of the Jim Rose Sideshow Circus. **The Medical Art of Romain Slocombe** He photographs Japanese girls in bandages and orthopaedic collars. **Animal Farm** The rite-of-passage bestiality film that is known the world-over as Animal Farm. An in-depth critique. **Hollywood Death Styles of the Rich and Famous** A round trip on the Hollywood Graveline tour hearse. **Have you ever thought about the word ABBA...?** Agnetha Fältskog is pregnant...

HEADPRESS Nos 13, 14 & 15 are £4.95 each

(No p&p charge in the UK / Europe add £1.50)

Cheques/Post Giros (pounds sterling only) payable to: Headpress.

Headpress, 40 Rossall Avenue, Radcliffe, Manchester, M26 1JD, Great Britain

Send SAE / IRC for our full publishing catalogue